M000249504

PRIME

PRIME

PRIME
A Genesis Series Event

Prime and the Genesis Series are trademarks of Sharkbird Productions.
All rights reserved.

Copyright © 2014 by Chris Kluwe and Andrew Reiner
Cover art by Mike Nevins

No part of this book may be reproduced without permission in writing from Andrew Reiner or Chris Kluwe.

Sharkbird Productions

ISBN-13: 978-0692351413
ISBN-10: 0692351418

PRIME

A Novel by **Chris Kluwe** and **Andrew Reiner**

PRIME

For our daughters

It was the day the universe changed. It was the day the fractious warring tribes of humanity, expanding their way through the galactic arm, discovered the horror of unchecked biohacking. It was the day they finally came together as one.

They called it Kufit's Graft, at first — an artificial disease unleashed by fundamentalists to cleanse Old Terra. Later, it was simply known as the Devastation. Ninety-five percent of the planet's biomass transformed into a hideous amalgamation of living tissue and bone in the span of several hours.

Pulsating flesh reached up and blocked the stars in continent spanning seismic ripples, DNA vectored into weeping grotesqueries.

No one ever discovered how it was done.

Quarantine was immediate, enforced by Gate-Security, the ostensibly neutral body in charge of keeping the lifelines linking light years together open. Of the thousands of ships in system, none Transited out. Many had to be stopped forcibly, nuclear pinpricks dotting the night sky of the dying world. Those remaining were scanned down to the atomic level, and in multiple cases, destroyed, unwitting carriers of the Devastation. The rest were allowed to go free, and to spread the message of what they had seen.

Reaction to the death of the homeworld was immediate.

Gate-Sec was given unlimited powers to prevent another Devastation from happening. Scanning and searching Transiting ships turned into proactively seeking their fundamentalist sponsors turned into policing entire planets, all in the name of that absolute prohibition on biohacking.

Gate-Sec turned into Government, a sprawling, bickering, bureaucratic force overseeing the expansion of humanity throughout the galactic arm, tied together by the unrelenting fear of another disaster like the one that disfigured Terra.

Four hundred and seven years later, the ten thousand worlds of Hegemony, held together by Government's absolute control over the Gate travel network, represent the pinnacle of human achievement.

Biohacking remains forbidden.

XANDER

DNA shadows dance across my face. In front of me, slowly rotating in the projected light interface, building blocks of life sinuously twine around each other, my notes branching off like fractals.

A riotous display of life.

A grim symphony of death.

Prime.

"Jasper, bring up Prime data alpha zero one, chromosome segments thirty-four and forty-two, main sequences on projected display, secondary sequences in my glARs." My voice breaks the silence of the dimly lit lab room, my eighteen hour a day workroom. A gentle baritone answers.

"Of course, Xander. Pushing datobjects from main archives... now."

The slowly spinning display in front of me flickers and shifts, the relatively monochromatic double helix replaced by an intricately woven tapestry of multicolored fragments stitched together like some mad scientist's fever dream. Simultaneously, scrolling lines of data fill my vision, bursting into existence centimeters from my eyes, ghostly words and formulae interposing themselves between me and reality.

To one not used to augmented reality glasses, glARs, I'm sure it would seem an incomprehensible torrent of information, but finding someone who doesn't wear glARs would be like finding an Old Terra unicorn. The lenses on my face, linked to a petabyte processing unit in the frames, barely qualify as standard anymore, given all of the modifications I've made, but the thin black polymer doesn't give it away.

Many things can hide under innocuous surfaces.

"Jasper, run all permutations if we shift the eHydro splice from locator Sigma Two Nine to Delta Four Six."

"Initializing..."

Jasper momentarily falls silent, evidence of the massive amounts of calculations I'm asking it to run. Biohacking would be impossible without VI assistance, the simulation power of a multiple array limited Virtual Intelligence capable of feats that normally would take evolution aeons to recreate.

"Probability of successful implementation approaches zero point zero two one, Xander."

I shake my head and curse, running a hand through my close cropped brown hair.

"What am I missing, Jasper? We're close, so Gate-damn close to making it work. We have a viable physical specimen, but the neural configurations still aren't coming together. It *has* to involve the eHydro, there's just no other possibility. The details though... what am I missing..."

Jasper's soothing voice fills my head again, transmitted through the conductive earpieces built into my glARs.

"Perhaps the answer is sleep, Xander. My records indicate you're only resting for an average of three point one four hours per planetary cycle. Cognitive efficiency is bound to deteriorate."

"You never give up, do you, Jasper? " I remove the tinted lenses and place them on the scuffed surface of my desk, then rub my eyes wearily. "We're on the cusp of changing humanity forever, and all you can think of are reports."

"It is a compulsion, sir. I have no choice in the matter."

I fling my arms in the air and lean back in the chair, kinetic sensors rapidly extending a leg out to keep it from toppling. Jasper's right, and it's irritating. Unless I reset the core programming, and risk lobotomizing the lab's only VI, it's just going to keep reminding me over and over until I complete the reports. Gah. Reports are the worst.

"Fine, fine, you win. Let's go over this week's summary. Remind me, though, to reprogram your nagging algorithms when I get a chance."

"Duly noted and stored, sir. However, I feel I must remind you it will be rather difficult to go over this week's summary."

"And why is that, Jasper?"

"You never finished last week's summary. Or the summary before that. Or the summary before—"

"Subtly making your point, as always. Go ahead and bring them up."

The DNA coils vanish. Thousands of well-organized words appear in the air, font so small as to be nearly invisible. From afar it looks like a thick white wall with periodic red splotches.

"Uh... Jasper? Is this a joke, Jasper? I thought you were supposed to take care of all this... minutiae." Groaning, I flip my glARs back on, zooming and highlighting various sections. "We really have this many problems right now?"

"I have dealt with the seven hundred and twenty-six thousand, three hundred and forty-eight items that did not require your personal approval as lab director, sir. The remaining one hundred and fourteen I am unable to complete autonomously."

"Great. One hundred and fourteen, huh? Well, here's a bit of good news, we can knock that number down thirty percent. Flush habitats 15, 86-D, and 24 – everything in them is dead. By the looks of 24, about a month dead."

"That is correct, sir. I reminded you at the time, but I believe your words were 'Throw your arrays into a volcano core and stop bothering me.' Flushing habitats into the recycling plant now."

I continue scanning the tightly packed words, and pause on a series of flashing red sections. "That can't be. Jasper, bring up a sensor feed of habitat 119-C and push to my glARs, please."

"Sensors active, Xander."

A small window opens inside my glARs, and a landscape flickers to life, a confusing mishmash of ultrasound wiregrids, thermographic blotches, and dimly moonlit trees in the visible spectrum. I quickly cycle through them, looking for signs of my children.

"Jasper, change the light cycle from night to day. Bring them out of hiding."

The darkness lifts like an accelerated sunrise, light flooding the chamber to reveal a dense forest of leaves and branches. Immense tree trunks burst from the soil like obelisks. I scan the sensor feed, but everything is still.

"I'm not seeing anything here. Find them, Jasper. Authorizing five percent run time capacity for analysis."

"Scanning... Three week collation of recorded material indicates a mutation in genetic protocols four beta and seven tau. Viability approaching zero."

I sigh. "Gate-dammit. Simulate a moderate earthquake to activate the post impact protocols. Let's see how many are left."

"Of course, sir."

The calm forest comes to life. Massive tree trunks shake violently back and forth, several toppling over, leaves falling softly amidst the chaos.

"Sir, I have emergence on sensors five and nine."

"Stop the quake and push to infpanel."

The rustling of foliage quiets, and the swaying of the timbers ceases. Dust slowly drifts down from the air. The large monitor in front of me opens to a view of a black lizard, roughly four meters in length with thin, blood red eyes, pushing its way through the tangled devastation. It moves crookedly, staggering back and forth, and then trips in an awkward sprawl of eight limbs, falling to an unmoving heap on the topsoil.

"Shit. It has to be bacterial or viral, some delayed interaction I missed in the simulations. Send a probe to get a sample – salvage what information we can, and then sterilize the habitat. Can't risk whatever it is spreading."

"Of course, sir."

A small mechanical drone, no larger than a mosquito, alights on the unmoving creature and briefly dips a small proboscis into its flesh. A small electrical pulse shudders its body, and then it, too, collapses, lifeless.

"Information received, sir. Initiate sterilization procedures?"

"Yes, Jasper. Authorization confirmed."

My eyes tighten against the sudden flash filling the sensor feed in my glARs before the lenses automatically dim in reaction to the actinic fury of a plasma bloom. Moments later, the glare disappears, revealing a flat metal floor covered in black ash. Several panels in the floor slide back, revealing dark openings, and water begins to sluice the remains away. I shake my head and close both feeds.

"And that's enough reports for the day. Let's get back to Prime data alpha zero one, chromosome segments thirty-four and forty-two."

"I strongly suggest we continue with the summaries, sir. Councilor Rocon will not be pleased with our lack of prog—"

"The only way the Councilor will be pleased is if we make Prime viable, and prove that I was right. Everything else is irrelevant. Postpone summary evaluation one week, on my authority as lab director, and don't bother me about reports before then."

"Noted and stored, sir. My apologies. Prime datobject alpha zero one enabled, sir."

The room falls silent once more. I stare at the shifting light in front of me, eyes flicking back and forth from the macro view presented in the holographic display to the micro details flashing through my glARs, trying to find the key that will unlock the proper outcome. A section snares my attention, and I grab a pair of haptic gloves to start manipulating the ephemeral display in front of me.

The sheer fabric slides over my hands, almost thin enough to see through, kinetic motor bands clasping snugly around my forearms, and I synch the hapgloves to my glARs. I lean forward and grasp the visual in front of me, electrical currents stiffening various sections of the conductive material in the gloves to give me the sensation of actually grabbing what I'm looking at, photons becoming solid under my touch. I slide several nucleic acid pairs out and rearrange them in different orders, fingers weaving like a pianist.

"Jasper, run permutations with new configuration."

"...neural viability approaches zero point zero four three success rate, sir. Over one hundred percent improvement."

I laugh, bitterly. "Great. Our berserk killing machine is now infinitesimally closer to being somewhat sane. Fantastic. Our problems are solved. The galaxy is saved."

"It is an improvement, sir. With enough improvement, Councilor Rocon may be mollified, and won't summarily send you into a star."

"Thanks, Jasper," I say sourly. "You always know just how to cheer me up."

"I exist to serve, sir."

I snort, and cycle the display to another section.

The next three hours are spent combing through genetic labyrinths, trying various combinations against each other, and inventing new swear words as each one fails to produce any sort of meaningful improvement. Biohacking is my true love, but the pressure of solving the final part of this sequence is starting to give me a headache. A lot is riding on my success, my life being one of the least of the prizes.

Jasper wasn't joking when he said Rocon might space me into a star, mainly because Jasper isn't programmed to joke. I know that ignoring the man in charge of the twelve hundred solar systems of this portion of the galaxy is not the smartest thing to do, but I *have* to make this work. I *have* to show the proof of my theories, not for my own ego, but for the sake of humanity. They need me.

They need Prime.

I realize I've been staring at the same sequence of DNA for over five minutes, the clock in the lower right of my glARs slowly ticking the seconds away, and I reach underneath the lenses to rub my burning eyes. The answer is so close, like trying to say a word that's on the tip of my tongue, but just can't remember. I groan in exhaustion.

"Just kill me now, Jasper, save Rocon some time. Why can't I make this work?"

"Killing you would be ill-advised, sir. Your consciousness would cease operating, and then who would be in control? Also, you have previously commanded me to ignore such suggestions."

"A fair point, Jasper, a fair... point..." I sit bolt upright. "That's it! Jasper, that's it!"

"I don't understand, sir."

"You don't have to understand." I laugh, not quite hysterically, but there's a definite edge in my voice. My hapgloved hands blur into motion, stitching strands of genetic code into a perfection I can already sense. "You just have to tell me the permutations of this combin—"

The door to the lab hisses open, and a man stands silhouetted in the light streaming in from the corridor outside. He's dressed in the many-pocketed blue jumpsuit of one of my assistants, his pants legs tucked into well-worn dark tacboots. Blocky frames with slightly tinted lenses cover his grey eyes, and thinning strands of grey hair limply drape across his liver spotted scalp. He's carrying something in his black hapgloved hands, and my eyes tighten in anger.

"Hey... you! Get out of my lab. You know you techs aren't allowed in he—"

Suddenly, I'm lying on the floor, the mind burning aftereffects of a stunner pulse wracking my body. Kufit's Beard. Where did one of my techs get a stunner?

"Whu... whah..." I try to croak out a question, but my nerves refuse to cooperate. I can feel my eyelids drooping closed, and I fight the pull of unconsciousness.

The man ignores me and steps over to my workstation, pulling a diagnostic panel up onto the display. His fingers twitch spastically inside his hapgloves, and commands stream down the diagnostic, datobjects opening and closing like flickers of lightning. Jasper's voice briefly sounds, and then cuts off with an alarming abruptness.

This is not good.

I try to make my body move, but it won't cooperate. Stunner blasts trigger complete neurological shutdown, and it's all I can do to fend off the encroaching shadows. My rolling eyes catch sight of the datobject he's opening, and I feel my heart go cold as I recognize it. He's opening the containment cells. All my children, let loose, running free on the surface above. Doesn't he know what will happen?

I feebly try to crawl toward him, but nothing happens, arms and legs twitching spastically from my overloaded nervous system. I have to stop him. That's my life's work, the one thing that will save humanity from an enemy it doesn't even know it's fighting, and he's about to unleash it into chaos. Rocon won't accept only pure data, not with something this revolutionary.

Saliva trickles from my mouth to the cold tile floor.

His fingers twitch, and the lights abruptly go off, instantly replaced by the strobing red glare of the emergency glowstrips. Son of a bitch. He just shut down the entire lab. I scream, but all that comes out is an awkwardly nasal grunt. He turns and looks at me.

"Xander Lillibridge. You're tougher than you look." He raises the stunner again. I rage at my unresponsive body, demanding that it get up and smite the interloper, but all I can manage is a brief drumming of heels against the floor and another grunt. I stare into the steely mouth of the energy weapon, his grey eyes floating behind it, illuminated in the intermittent flashes of red.

"Sweet dreams, Doctor. Give my regards to your 'children' when you wake."

The stunner thrums its baleful song, and darkness engulfs me.

ROB

Timestamp – 11.55.03LT:00.49.31OT:03.19.407AG

Spaceports. Hate spaceports. Too many people. Too many vectors. Too many chances for infection.

That lab down below was bad, but spaceports are worse.

Sitting in a hard plastic chair, waiting for these Gate-damned scum to show up on their resort yacht, stuck in a stinking reception lounge on this backwoods system that doesn't even rate a full eight arm orbital docking facility, surrounded by vacuum, still tired from that freak show lab down on the moon, and the Gate-damn beverage dispenser is out of synthkaf.

Fucking spaceports.

The view's not bad, I guess, if you're into that sort of thing, memplas windows offering plenty to look at. Eden 3 hangs below, officially classified a garden moon, vaguely similar to Old Terra, same gravity, slightly more oxygen in the atmosphere, baseline temperature a pleasant two hundred and ninety-six degrees Kelvin. Extra oxygen means more growth, more plants – a green pea floating in the black soup of space. Off to the right are the concentric rings of the Gate, spinning bands stabilizing the rippling tear in space contained within, unpleasant purple waves pulsating along its circumference. Makes it hard to look at, even through the filters in my glARs. Local gas giant, Gehenna V, looms behind it all like a barely contained explosion, harsh oranges and browns twisting together in world-spanning spirals. Bulbous refinery ship briefly glints in the starlight as it crosses in front of the seething orb on its way to the Gate, precious eHydro cargo snugly tucked inside massive million liter spheres, carrying the lifeblood of mankind's sprawling empire to impossibly distant worlds.

Me, I'm stuck in a spaceport.

Windows flash with the bright purple fire of Transition as the tanker slips through, energy bleeding off from the Gate – brighter the flash, the more mass that Transited. Techies say the eHydro keeps all those molecules from spontaneously immolating themselves, something to do with different relative velocities, spin between systems, energy potentials and other technojargon. Glad they understand it – most everyone else doesn't. All anyone needs to know is that Gates require a steady supply of eHydro to stay open, so the freighters ply their trade – refinery to distribution center to refinery, tiny parasites keeping the bloated corpse of empire alive.

A smaller flash announces another ship instantaneously blinking across the giant light year chasm that normally keeps the stars unpassable, intensity of the Transit-bleed putting it in the three kiloton category – too small for a tanker, too big for a courier. Only one candidate. The pleasure yacht *Persephone*, registered out of New Haven as a Daison-Eno executive transport, capacity two hundred and twelve people, filled with the finest luxuries gcreds can afford. Conscience stabs me again, reminds me what I'm betraying.

The Agency. Joined thirty years ago, barely out of school, family wiped by a rogue biohack. Wanted to make the world a better place, wanted to make sure no one else had to experience the same tearing loss that I did, wanted to make sure no kid ever had to bury the ashes of his mother and father and brother because the corpses were too hideous and infectious to leave intact.

Wanted revenge.

So I joined the Compliance Agency, humanity's best defense against molecular level devastation. Never a question about making it through the applications, fiery core of rage driving me like a demon. Learned everything the teachers knew, then learned more. Scientia potentia est.

Always loved dead languages. Something to be said about the arrogance of a culture that believed itself immune to the ravages of time.

Passed my final tests with flying colors, took the oath, promised to hunt down biohackers, genesplicers, and all the rest of the scum infesting the ten thousand systems of Hegemony. Promised to send them to the purity of vacuum, the embrace of a sun.

Promised to avenge my family.

It was good at first, that feeling of righteous vengeance – justice for those left disfigured and destroyed. Had my fair share of busts – Doctor Zhevera, the Appatrox Cult, Winston Cline and his Box of Horrors.

Shut 'em down and flare 'em up, cleanse the taint of unnatural evolution from ravaged systems, try and give worlds and people a chance to heal. Save those we can, put an end to the suffering of those we can't.

Too many in that second category over the years.

Not all the busts were easy, though, had some close calls – gene altered muscleboys, memory plagues, spontaneous organ expulsion; the usual. Biohackers aren't too worried about things like ethics, or restraint, and some of them have imaginations that make the Marquis de Sade look like a Fundie choirboy.

Soon, though, soon the days started blurring together. Soon I got old. Reflection in the memplas confirms it – grey eyes framed by too many wrinkles, grey hair barely covering an age marked scalp, gut starting to show despite two hours of training every day. The embarrassing signs of entropy that only the poor can afford.

What do I have to show for thirty years of service? A failed marriage. A cynical disgust for the inescapable corruption of humanity. A beautiful daughter.

She's the one thing I got right. Only problem is, she's sick. Picked up a nasty bit of geneware while hiking with friends on Scipio III, some leftover filth from the Burstain Conflagration, and the bills keep piling up. A variation on *basilis terminus*, the Gate-damn hack keeps adapting, keeps fighting off the treatments, until it's all she can do to stay alive.

My Jennifer, my beautiful baby girl, missing a leg, the right side of her face stony and dead, like a basilisk glanced at her. She still laughs when I bring her stuffed animals, half her mouth smiling – tells me those are a kid's toys, that she's all grown up, even as her body crawls a little closer to the grave each day. Somehow she keeps her spirits up, keeps that crooked smile glowing.

All I can do not to weep every time I see her, see what I can't fix.

Every single one of those rich parasites on the *Persephone* could afford the treatments to make her better, make her whole again. They all have their own private hospitals, keeping them young and beautiful, straddling that blurry line between medicine and biohacking – but it's not something a normal person will ever see, Fringer and Hubworlder alike. Takes money to get into one of the shadow clinics, enough gcreds to buy a small system, enough gcreds to bend the unflinching rules of the Accords.

Small systems are pocket change to the ones I'm waiting for, though, this merry band of five. Did my research, pulled up some Agency files through backdoors I shouldn't have – know thy enemy. One's an heir to Daison-Eno, largest corp in Hegemony, largest corp in the galaxy. Daison-Eno's big in the memplas business, big in the weapons business, big all around business, manufacturing anything and everything. Lots of rumors about Government linkage to DE, secret facilities, off-budget shipyards – never anything concrete. Just a whisper from a friend of a friend of a friend, but the susurrus is deafening.

Another's a triple-A entertainment star, plastic face coaxing credits from those too gullible to see through the sheen, a modern siren. Doesn't do much other than look pretty and glam around, live the life other people wish they could have, but can only experience through an augstar's senses. Usually travels with four bodyguards in tow, making sure the dirt doesn't get too close. He left them behind for this trip, decided to go solo. Interesting. See if he's as tough as he thinks he is.

Third one's an arbiter of the currency system, one of the few tasked with determining the fluctuating value of gcreds. So many resources in Gate-linked space, people of Old Terra would have cried if they saw it – material scarcity hardly a thought. Arbiters don't care about physical goods, they calculate the value of *time*. Time spent working, spent playing, spent contributing – a gcred fraction describing each one. They're supposed to be neutral, but one look behind the curtains reveals that lie. Ratings jump and dip based on friendships, favors, fallings-out – barely seen puppet masters strumming their strings and the whole galaxy dances.

Fourth one's the only female, daughter of a Council member, tenth generation, currently serving as a Government sector vice-administrator, stepping stone to the Council itself. Born in wealth, raised in wealth, probably die even wealthier, crafting and manipulating Government laws as she sees fit.

Nothing given to her though – Council families weed out those not smart enough to keep the family in power, isolate 'em in far off frontier worlds; some die young in 'accidents.'

The compromisers don't survive in Government, just the ruthless and the implacable. No simpering skirt here, only a cold-eyed killer raised in a Spartan's nightmare.

Last one's a blank, records carefully trimmed and bland, nothing to suggest anything, the soulless life of a nonexistent man. Trouble. Only deep operatives and Black Colony get greyed out from Agency records, real lives trapped behind mountains of deniability and obfuscation, ghosts in the Government machine. Gut tells me he's the leader, looking to relive those dirty years in the world of shadows.

Me? I'm stuck on an Agent's salary, I'm getting old, and it's all I can do to keep my baby alive.

Government's not interested in taking care of those taking care of it. Too many power seekers, money grabbers, parasitic leeches, infesting everyone around them until the whole system rots to the core, outwardly healthy, inwardly dead. An aristocracy of the damned. That's why I'm waiting in this stupid Gate-forsaken spaceport for scum I should be arresting, waiting to sell the last shreds of whatever honor I have left, eager to catch whatever scraps my *betters* deign to cast off.

No other way to make ends meet these days. No other choice but to get down in the muck and deal with the scum.

The five on board the *Persephone* aren't normal scum, though. I've seen normal scum – the rapists, the thieves, the murderers, the unthinking and the ignorant. Those are predictable, easily thwarted, their only thought the next dose of Bliv, or a pleasure mistress, or whatever selfish desire currently occupies what they call a brain – animals reacting to the stimuli around them.

No, these five are a breed apart, the type of casual sociopathy that only comes with truly obscene amounts of power.

These are *rich* scum, the elite of the elite, able to buy and sell multiple planets before breakfast, shielded from the consequences of their actions by the overwhelming aegis of influence and wealth. The galaxy is their plaything, everyday people their pawns, and their games always end with broken pieces.

But that's not enough for them. These scum are jaded. They're so rich, so privileged, they don't know how to entertain themselves anymore. The chessboard grows boring once you've cleared it too many times.

So they found something new. They hunt.

Only, they don't hunt animals. Not people, either, too tame, too gauche. No, they have to have something rare, worthy of their time. Something unknown. Something *unique*.

Vice-administrator probably did a little snooping around some slush funds, read some reports, got wind of a secret biohack installation designing monsters for who knows what. Normally I'd infiltrate, gather the evidence, then call in the Agency to shut it down – job well done and here's a ten cred bonus, get yourself some synthahol, good luck with the bills.

Unfortunately, these five found out my situation. Heard about my daughter, my Jennifer, wasting away in her medunit, dying a little more each day, turning into a living statue. Saw the visitor's file, the trips I spent to see her, the pile of bills growing every month – put two and two together.

Leverage.

So they made me an offer. Gcreds that could cure my girl. Gcreds that could fix my life. Gcreds I'll never see anywhere else, not the way this universe runs. Gcreds to abandon my promise to the Agency, abandon my stewardship of those relying on me to protect them from all the unseen horrors in this miserably fucked up universe.

I'm the lucky son of a bitch who gets to collect thirty pieces of silver.

So I infiltrated, gathered evidence, then called in the scum – told them their secret lab is chock full of abominations, weather's great, don't forget the photonblock. Place is sited underneath an active volcano on a garden moon; not the best place to hide, but not the worst either.

Director of the hacksite is definitely splicing illegal bioconstructs, didn't have time to figure out for what, but caught a strong whiff of Government. Four assistants in the lab, two of them aware of the splicing, the other two clueless. Clueless ones think the lab's a semi-legit facility for human augmentation and crop diversification, Government keeping it under wraps to prevent unnecessary panic.

Fools. They know the Accords, know why the restrictions are in place. No such thing as safe biohacking. Especially not when they're designing combat organisms.

Continuous stream of pleasure yachts provides plenty of cover for shipments in and out, along with easy access for certain people to discreetly visit. Primarily Council members, or trusted lackeys if something physical needs to change hands.

Volcano's a clean way to wipe the evidence if the ball drops. Bunch of antimatter charges situated around the facility are enough to pop the top and then – poof – no more highly illegal hacksite. Supervolcanos don't leave much behind.

Just an unfortunate natural occurrence that happened to wipe out a luxury hotel along with most of the moon.

Not that I care if it goes up, place is filled with trash the galaxy's better off without. Bankers, corp heads, Government leaders; let 'em burn. Make the universe a cleaner place, clear out the deadweight dragging us all down, holding us all back. Pull the trigger myself if I could.

But that's not the job. Job is to let whatever horrors are living in that nest out of hiding so these 'hunters' can enjoy themselves, track and kill something no one else ever has, gloat over their privilege.

In exchange? They'll pay me enough gcreds to fix my girl, turn her back into a human being.

They know I'd do anything for her. She's the only thing I have left.

So now I'm stuck in a spaceport, waiting for the *Persephone* to finish docking, waiting to lead these hunters to the 'prey' I've unleashed on an unsuspecting world, trying to ignore the tiny voice shrieking in the back of my conscience that everything I'm doing is wrong.

Fucking spaceports.

SPACEPORT MILTON

Timestamp – 12.11.54LT:00.50.21OT:03.19.407AG

The dark slate cylinder *Persephone* makes contact with the station docking tube in a brief puff of maneuvering jets, matching orbit with the station's spin. Power tubes intertwine in coiling mating rituals, connecting one environment to another, and airlocks hiss as pressures equalize. Moments later, a crowd of richly dressed people comes bounding out in the curiously long hops of centrifugally generated low gravity, chattering to each other like magpies trapped in the bodies of gazelles. Their conversation rotates around hedge funds, investments, the latest fashion styles, and when the next Colony will be ready for settlement – apparently there have been several uncharacteristic delays between the arrival of the skhip and establishing a Gate. Every face wears glasses in a bewildering multitude of styles.

Rob leans against a bulkhead and watches them pass, banal inanities noted and discarded. No sign of the contempt he feels crosses his face, but his grey eyes miss nothing, constantly scanning and probing for detail. The idle rich and pampered playboys hold no interest for him at this juncture. He's here to meet far more interesting people, in every sense of the ancient proverb, but decades of training have left their mark. Through the memplas he can see automated cargo drones detaching standardized shipping crates from the *Persephone*'s cargo bay and transporting them to their respective shuttles; an army of zero-gravity ants overseen by the station's VI.

Finally, a group of five people exit the transporter and make their way down the docking corridor, expensive self-motivated luggage in tow, wireless transmitters driving frantically spinning wheels to maintain the proper distance of separation between them and their masters. Four men and a woman murmur to each other in low tones, scraps of meaning breaking free now and then but never enough to reveal the actual content of the conversation. They come to a stop in front of Rob, who stands dressed in a slightly official looking black singlesuit, holding a sign that reads "Donner Party."

"Abrahim Donnor?" he asks the leather faced man with a short shock of auburn hair leading the group. A monocle is perched over the man's right eye like some anachronistic memento of pre-Gate Old Terra, and the signs of age on his face are startling in a society where the rich value the vibrant elasticity of youth. Rob immediately captures a still image of the man with his glARs and tags it with the identifier "Monocle" – Agency training dictates quick and easy designations for possible subjects, and odds are good that they're using fake names anyway.

A raspy voice responds, "Call me Abe. Am I to understand that you're our guide for this little expedition?" His glARs transmits an encrypted security protocol to Rob, the agreed upon identifier to establish contact once on site.

"That's correct, sir," replies Rob, his glARs sending the appropriate handshake. "If you would all care to follow me, I can lead you to the private shuttle we have set aside for your personal transportation. It has plenty of storage space for any manner of luggage you may have traveled with, and is already cleared with Customs. I can also brief you on the current status dirtside."

"A resourceful man, and well informed to boot! This trip is already starting off on the right foot." Monocle smiles. "Now, as we head to the shuttle, perhaps you can fill us in on just what to expect for our little 'nature survey.'"

The four other members of the group laugh as they all begin to walk towards the departure area. "'Nature survey,' I like that," grins a tall man with a black ponytail and a slightly overweight frame. His floral pattern kimono swishes softly as they walk, the muted silence of the fabric belying the garishness of its colors, bright primaries that clash with the dazzling gemmed brightness of his glARs. Rob mentally dubs him Rhinestones, and tags another captured still frame with the moniker.

"Perhaps we can call our next little shindig a 'uniquely viable species census.'"

A petite woman in a green sweater and black slacks sniffs haughtily as she adjusts her large augstar style glasses, the dark green frames matching her close cropped hair. Rob captures and adds her image as well, tagging her overly fancy glARs. "Perhaps," she drawls, "you might not be invited to our next get-together if you insist on wearing such barbaric clothes, Connor. I mean, really. Pink flowers on a blue kimono? With yellow underpants? And glARs modeled after some 21st barbarian named 'Elton'? The mind positively shudders at the thought, and the reality is far worse."

"I don't know, Marla," chuckles a young blond man with dark skin, garbed in jeans and a red athletic sweatshirt bearing the logo of the Andromeda Novas, his features as coldly beautiful as a fallen angel's. "At least he's wearing underpants this time. Do you remember the party in New Monaco where the police found him passed out nude in the chocolate fountain? Quite put me off sweets for almost a week."

The sound of his voice, haughty and prideful, fills Rob with an instant dislike, and he struggles to hold his sneering contempt inside. He tags the haughty young man as 'Wraparounds' in his info cache, sport-styled glARs sleekly covering the middle third of his aesthetically perfect face.

Rhinestones whirls angrily, overly full lips clamped tight. "You blue blood bastards better watch what you're saying," he sneers, upper lip curling momentarily. "Without my pharmacopias your parties would be far less entertaining, and your security forces much less effective. We'll see what happens the next time you need to bust a strike without hypostims or subgas, Franco." His eyes momentarily go ice cold. "Or we'll see what happens when your father needs a shipment of memplas for his construction concerns."

"Children, children, must we constantly be at each other's throats?" The last man sighs, thumbing his custom gold-rimmed glARs from opacity to full transparency, revealing startlingly green eyes above a hooked nose. His ungloved hand drops down from the control switch set amidst his shoulder length grey hair and back into the pocket of his luxuriously tailored pinstripe suit. "The VIs are always watching, and though our man here assures us that he's disabled them, I am not the trusting sort. We're all here for the same thing. Let's try to keep it somewhat civil, at least. How am I supposed to concentrate on the market derivatives with this racket?" He settles an old-fashioned top hat onto his head and toggles his lenses back to full opacity. Rob tags him as 'Professor.'

"Quite right, Joseph, quite right. Now let's be on our way; after all, one cannot hunt if one never tracks the quarry." Monocle claps his hands together and motions the group to follow Rob through a door marked 'Shuttle Bay Four.'

Inside sits a swept-wing *Icarus* class orbit shuttle, almost fifty-meters-long, its clear memplas nose streaked and pitted with the soot of multiple re-entries, though the memplas itself is unscarred. Four thrusters are spaced equidistantly in a diamond formation around the aft end, and several storage hatches underneath the ship clamp shut as everyone boards, the mechanical servitors scuttling away like cockroaches. The overall effect of the Icarus is of a slightly bulging broadsword, translucent tip winking in the loading bay lights. The group crosses the loading bridge and boards the spacious interior, self-motivated luggage hurrying to pass through the hatch before it hisses shut.

Inside the Icarus, the five passengers find their seats in the heavily converted fuselage, widely spaced couches and infpanels interspersed with executive level reclining chairs running the full length of the thirty-meter segment.

Seating himself at the pilot's station in the front of the ship, Rob runs through the undocking checklist before engaging the compressed air maneuvering jets. He noses the shuttle out of the bay, timing the rotation of the station to send them toward the moon, and once clear, he triggers a quick burst from the fusion drive to send them into an orbital insertion pattern, the surge of gravity pressing him back against the pilot's seat. The integrated ship Virtual Intelligence confirms an autopilot lock on the resort landing beacon, and Rob floats into the main cabin, pulling himself along the handholds set into the ceiling and floor of the shuttle before strapping himself into one of the enveloping seats.

"We are safe to talk here, yes?" Monocle asks, settling himself more comfortably into his patent realeather upholstered chair. He steeples his hands in front of his lined and scarred face and relaxes into the patient stare of a tiger.

"Yes, sir. The shuttle is clean."

"Good. What are we looking at downwell?"

"Well, sir, this moon is home to one of the most highly illegal biohack facilities I've ever encountered," responds Rob. He triggers a display on the bulkhead next to him and links his glARs to the local cloud. "As you can see, it's built around and under the supervolcano Mount Zali'ah, and it's enormous. It looks like it covers almost five thousand square kilometers on multiple levels, including portions beneath the lake and near the caldera. I don't know all the specifics of what's going on down there, but there's a huge drain being pulled from the geothermal taps. Whatever they're doing is energy intensive on a scale I've never seen before."

A cutaway of the facility appears on the monitor next to Rob, and all five of the passengers lean in for a closer look as their glARs synch the data. The complex looks to be almost one hundred meters below the surface at its highest point, with several sections extending much deeper, and as the view zooms out, the scale is quickly apparent. The bulk of the facility is situated under the jungle surrounding the hotel resort in a large rectangle nearly six hundred kilometers on the long sides, with the southwest corner spreading at least five hundred meters into Lake Basalt while the northwest part travels directly underneath the resort and nudges up against the super volcano's inner caldera. Several access tubes branch off at various points, leading into the jungle and the workers' city on the backside of the volcano. Quick enhances and zooms reveal interwoven lava tubes filled with liquid magma threading vertically through multiple sections of the structure, like inverted tree roots. Five of the tubes blink with a triangular 'AM' graphic.

"Those tubes," says Professor, "what is their purpose?"

"As near as I can figure out, sir," Rob replies, "they built this place to be erased at a moment's notice if that ever became necessary. It's completely surrounded by magma, and blowing the antimatter charges in those five tubes will cause the supervolcano to erupt, as well as detonating the geothermal taps. This will also completely destroy the resort, and most likely crack part of the moon open, but apparently that's a price whoever built this is willing to pay."

"Excuse me, but did you say 'antimatter charges?'" Augstar asks, her tanned face paling slightly. "Aren't those exceedingly dangerous?"

"Yes, ma'am, they are, and those are some of the larger ones Government manufactures. Capital ship killers, as a matter of fact. I'd imagine that's why they installed them. Nothing less would cause enough destruction, and without a complete wipe the complex might be discovered."

"But you've taken care of those, correct?" Monocle questions.

"Of course, sir. Dropped a phase three digiworm into the VI's central processor; even with a hard reboot they're unlikely to get back any sort of functionality until they restore every single array on their servers. There's no chance of those bombs going off unless some idiot decides to detonate them by hand. Not while they're under my control."

Rhinestones laughs and flips his ponytail over his shoulder. "Well in that case, why don't you tell us just what it is that you've procured for us to play with."

A loud rumble echoes through the cabin as the shuttle hits the upper atmosphere, and the familiar tug of gravity slowly exerts itself once more. Rob desynches his glARs from the display, though he continues monitoring the shuttle's instruments. The schematics collapse and wink out like matter entering the pull of a black hole, leaving an empty screen behind. "I'm afraid that will have to wait until after we land. If you want to join me in the cockpit, you'll be able to get your first look at Eden as we descend to the waterdock."

The five hunters rise from their chairs and follow Rob into the clear memplas bridge, the moon's gravity finally providing enough pull that walking is a viable choice. As they enter the bridge, the blinding mass of Gehenna Prime peers over the horizon of the moon like a brilliant diamond, illuminating the entire cockpit in stark brightness and shadow. In front of them, below the spotlight of the system's sun, lies a lush tropical world, blue seas linking together around emerald green landmasses.

As the ship descends towards the largest continent, a huge cone volcano can be seen rearing out of the depths of its greenery like a fusion thruster aimed at the sky, a small cluster of buildings nestled near its southern base, a large circular body of water sparkling gently further south, lapping almost right up to the edge of the volcano, white sand beaches curving like a sense actress' thighs. The sunlight glints off a fractal complex branching out of the water, dark piers radiating out from a central emerald like the spikes of some aquatic beast. The shuttle dips lower and lower over the sea until miniature panoramas turn into the giant suddenness of landing, and Rob brings the ship to a bobbing halt on top of the water. He taxis in to the rightmost pier of the now massive port, dazzling light spraying off the coiling translucent green roof covering an open air structure. The shuttle noses into the pier, magnetic bumpers latching it into place, and clear water washes over the weathered wooden planks in gentle lapping waves.

"Welcome to Eden."

XANDER

Timestamp – 13.36.32LT:02.25.00OT:03.19.407AG

Oooh, my head.

I groggily open my eyes as I emerge from unconsciousness; somehow I'm lying on the floor of the primary bioforge while a distant klaxon honks noisily, blaring its alarum like an audible lighthouse. The cold grittiness of imperceptible imperfections in the polished rock dig into my right cheek, and my body aches like someone took a sportbat to it repeatedly. Muscles register an immediate protest as I lever my hands underneath myself, and with a deep breath, I push myself into a sitting position, legs splayed out in front. I look up and try to collect my bearings.

Definitely a bad decision. The room spins around like an out of control Gateship, walls merging with the floor in an apparent reversal of gravity. I almost vomit, but I'm able to keep it in. Barely. The inside of my head hammers in a syncopated counterpoint to the ringing thunder of the alarm, and instinctively triggering my glARs isn't bringing up any displays.

Oh. That's because they're not on my head. Why aren't my glARs on my head? Thoughts are woolen, stuffy, slow to arrive. How did I get here?

Let's see, I remember setting the new feed schedules for the high pressure sections, approving the paperwork for the next lab recreation day in hab area B, working on some key upgrades to specimen Prime's next iteration, and then there was a grey-eyed tech who... stunned me and opened all the cells! Shit!

I scramble to my feet and look wildly around the bioforge. Things are definitely tending towards the "not good" side of the spectrum – the live feeds of the deep cells show nothing but emptiness, and flashing emergency lights strobe intermittently across every display. The infpanels are... not quite right, though; fuzzing and hashing with static-crazed gaps that shouldn't exist in the crystalline clear resolution of a liquid micropixel screen. None of my digital prompts are highlighting the room, vision dull and curiously blank.

"Jasper. Jasper! Where are my glARs? ...Jasper?"

That's odd. Why isn't the VI answering? I really need my glARs.

I quickly search the workspace again, shoving aside various notes and concepts for future organisms, until I finally find them under a desk, the thin black frames scuffed but still quite serviceable, delicately strong memplas lenses already healing the last scratch across their surface. I slide the glasses over my head and authenticate the incorporated biomonitor security system, a quick DNA scan of a fingertip on the right frame sensor sufficient proof of my identity. A soft chime in the bone conductive audio pads emanates deep within my skull and my vision is suddenly alive with the bright clarity of augmented reality, a wealth of information layering itself between me and the surrounding environment.

Finally, I can see again.

Biometrics finish their scan of my body, a healthy green paper doll in the lower left corner of my vision gently glowing an all clear, Hegemony standard timestamp slicing seconds away in the lower right. A dense column of datobjects runs down each side – visual representations of the vast caches of information stored within the solid state memory of the unit itself.

Crap. Whoever that tech was, he certainly did a number on our internal network before he left. Looks like he inserted a class two, maybe class three digiworm into the central arrays, scrambling any sort of glARs direct networking or cloud functionality inside the facility. Essentially, he lobotomized Jasper.

What a bastard.

I can't access any of my data stored in the VI itself, and the diagnostic tools are completely trashed, which means I'm going to have to go to Central Core and reboot Jasper from scratch. This is going to screw up all my projects for at least a week or two, especially the high resource run-time crunches I had going for Prime's final evolutions – though that breakthrough I had right before I got stunned...

I sigh and head for the door leading out of the bioforge. No sense waiting around for someone else to fix it, though the assistants should have sorted some of this out by now. Lazy fools, probably using this as an unscheduled holiday from their own projects – once we patch all this up I'm going to ban them from the rec rooms for a month. I wonder where they are. With the network down, the locator datobject is worthless, and I still don't have access to the lab's inner monitor feeds. Yet another problem to solve.

The door hisses open as I override the manual security biometrics with a palm scan, revealing the corridor outside, and I suddenly realize I've located one of my assistants. His name is Marv, or Merl, I'm pretty sure it starts with an 'm', and his raggedly severed head is staring up at me from a pool of its own blood – eyes blankly gaping at sights I have no wish to see.

The lights get very bright, datobjects wavering and spinning across my vision in crazy arcs. It sounds like a heavy wind is roaring through the corridor – I'll have to make sure one of the other techs figures out what's causing that because it shouldn't be possible this far underground. I wonder if the gaping rents slashed in the smoothly polished bare rock walls could be the source of the wind. It whispers its name to me. I should go find someone.

The world turns abstract.

I stumble around for an indeterminate period of time before finally snapping out of what my brain belatedly identifies as shock, neurons misfiring under chemically induced stress, yellow head on the paper doll slowly fading back to gentle green. Timestamp says five minutes and twenty two seconds have passed, reality taking shape around me once more.

My new surroundings do not look promising. I'm in what appears to be one of the ancillary kitchens, possibly Three Alpha, the one closest to the primary bioforge and near the western sleeping quarters. I reflexively trigger a map request through my glARs to the lab cloud but nothing comes back. Blasted technology.

I take a look around the room, searching for anything to orient myself.

Lighting circuits dangle from the ceiling where they've been ripped and torn out, sparking and crackling like fireworks illuminating a chef's nightmare. Crockery and cooking utensils lie scattered and broken all over the floor and dark streaks splash the normally pristine white walls, visible in intermittent bursts whenever a circuit fizzes. I twitch a finger and activate low-light enhancement mode, but the periodic flashes stab so painfully into my retinas I'm forced to switch it off and rely on the human eyeball Mk I.

A sudden shuffling sound, the brush of contact between foot and floor. I crouch down and grab one of the scattered knives – I know it won't do much good against whatever decapitated poor what's-his-name, but the monkey reflexes still burn true. I hear the sounds getting closer, and I steel myself to make a leaping attack I am woefully unequipped to execute.

There! I scream and jump forward, colliding with something soft and heavy. A muffled exclamation and we both crash to the floor, rolling wildly around. The knife goes flying out of my hand as a heavy grip shakes it loose and I realize this is it – I'm going to die, and there's nothing left but to wait for the end. A peculiar lassitude settles over my limbs, muscles going limp, and I feel the warm rush of my bladder evacuating.

"Gate-damnit. Why, in Kufit's blighted name, did you just piss on me?"

I cautiously open my eyes and look up as the pressure stops pinning me to the ground. Looming above me is another one of the techs, Craig or Kyle or something. His dark hair is askew and a broken pair of neon green glARs hangs crazily from his left ear, one lens cracked clear through, memplas driven past its remarkably resilient breaking point. Brown eyes scan the area around us wildly, and his tanned olive face is flushed with exertion as he hauls me to my feet in one smooth motion. I notice his shirt is a dark burgundy, though whether that's its natural color or blood is anyone's guess.

"Sorry, sorry, my apologies," I stammer. "I thought you were going to kill me like that poor other fellow... Marshall? Marcus?"

"Maurice," he grunts, shoving his hands sullenly into his pockets. "I was hoping he was alive. The rest of them are dead too, Abigail and Lindsey, all ripped apart like slaughtered copigs."

He suddenly turns to me and grabs my shoulders. "What the fuck killed them, Doc," he whispers, voice seething with hate. "What in Kufit's forsaken Graft are you holding in this facility?" His eyes roll in their sockets, pupils wide, and spittle flecks his lips as he continues. "I want to know what killed my friends! I want to know why I just had to bludgeon to death what looked like a four foot cockroach crossed with a knife factory when it tried to eat my face!"

"Now, now," I respond, trying for a soothing tone, "there's no time for recriminations. We need to make our way to Central Core so I can get a measure of control over the situation, preferably before we're dismembered as well." I shrug his hands off me and adjust my labcoat. "Unfortunately, since it seems Jasper's been corrupted, and the lab is clearly not safe, I'll need some help getting there. Do you know where we are?"

He stares at me for a long moment, facial muscles twitching, then slowly settles into what I think is a more rational state. Or he's flipped and gone completely crazy, I've never been good at interpersonal relationships, but either way I'm no longer being yelled at. He makes an odd sound, then turns toward the northern doorway, flipping aside his broken glARs as he walks.

"Yeah. We're in Two Beta. We need to go up a level and around the hydroponic system – whatever's running loose in here smashed some of the support beams in the central passageway and tore down the ceiling – it's partially collapsed. There are some fires going on too, but it doesn't look like they're going to spread anytime soon – the vent system is keeping them under control."

My assistant pauses at the doorframe, back still turned. "The internal transport system isn't working, so it's going to be a bit of a walk. Like, closer to a five kilometer hike than a walk. Let me make it perfectly clear, though, that I want some answers as we go, because this is a level of shit that gets people thrown into suns, and I did not come to this moon to die. Follow me."

We walk through the door and start making our way deeper into the complex. The bright sterile cleanliness of my fully modernized hacksite now resembles a fevered butcher's abattoir, and I'm suddenly reminded of the history lessons on an ancient painter named Bosch. Nothing is recognizable. Nothing is in its proper place. Wet chunks of gristle and bio-material slouch sullenly in corners while the emergency lights continue to flicker and strobe, each burst of light revealing another disturbing dream made real.

Minutes pass like hours, wending our way through the endless hallways, detouring around crushed door frames and collapsed ceilings. The RFID guidance chips set into the walls indicate we're almost halfway to the Central Core, though it feels like halfway around Eden at this point.

We near one of the maintenance rooms surrounding the hydroponic cavern, overlooking the huge labyrinth of lifeless machines and feedstock in various stages of growth, and I suddenly see Cameron? Clark? freeze in mid-stride. He stands motionless for a minute, then slowly puts his foot down and makes his way back to me with glacial slowness, quiet shuffling inaudible underneath the still mournful hooting of a klaxon. He reaches me and whispers, "I heard noises from that room. Clicking, scrabbling, like claws on the floor. We need to find another way around."

"But that could take hours," I harshly whisper back. "We need to get to Central Core *now*. I have to get this facility back online and running so we can contact a cleanup crew."

His eyes go dark. "Still worried about whatever it is you unleashed, Doc? Well, I've got news for you. If what you were keeping down here was anything like what attacked me earlier, we'll be lucky if we survive the next ten minutes! I didn't sign up for this. Cleanup crews..." He trails off, still muttering.

That's when it happens. Whatever is in that maintenance room finally hits the panel controls, whether by accident or design, and the door hisses open. Bright steady light spills out into the hallway, revealing a shadowy shape that grows bigger by the second. Large pointed ears loom up over hulking shoulders, jerking forward in a terrible hopping gait. I look around desperately for a weapon but there's nothing to be seen; the corridor we're standing in bare of furnishings or convenient arms lockers. Time stretches to a halt.

A small creature the size of a rabbit jumps out of the room onto its own shadow and turns to stare at us with comically oversized eyes. It looks like a muscular miniaturized fox crossed with a kangaroo, furry tail thumping the floor like a tiny heartbeat while it claps its hands together in apparent joy. I heave a gasping sigh of relief – it's Mendel, my personal mascot.

I created Mendel when I first got here twenty years ago, both as a test of the hacking tools available and to provide myself with some companionship. Structurally he's part fox, part kangaroo, and a little bit of chimpanzee, which gives him a curious bounding lope when he runs on all fours, as well as the ability to manipulate small objects with his prehensile hands. I also spliced in several traits from the canine family for obedience and devotion, and endowed him with a rudimentary intelligence. He'll never write a thesis paper, but he's learned a wide variety of tricks, including, apparently, how to trigger an emergency override.

The assistant hisses under his breath. "What the shit is that, Doc," he snarls.

"Oh that's just Mendel, I made him a while ago. He must have gotten loose from my room and trapped in there when Jasper went down." I drop to one knee and call out to him. "Here, Mendel. Come here, boy. Who's a good boy?"

"Wait a minute, you 'made him?' I was told this was an augment lab for crops and health, better genetic strains for food sources! I didn't come here to splice organisms!"

I wince inside. Clearly he wasn't one of the two assistants working with me on the shadow portion of the lab. Really should start paying attention to the underlings more. I make shushing noises at him.

"Be quiet, you're going to scare him off. He doesn't like loud noises." I point at Mendel, who's stopped clapping and is looking around nervously. "See? You're scaring him. Come on, Mendel, I won't let the bad man hurt you."

Mendel sniffs at the air, and his triangular ears twitch back and forth several times, fine russet bristles covering their outer surfaces. He takes several nervous hops in our direction, and then makes an odd whimpering noise I've never heard before, stopping almost five meters away. I rise to my feet and take a step to go pick him up, hoping he won't run off somewhere.

My foot hits the floor, and that's when a section of wall behind Mendel reaches out in an eye-sickening wrench of color and picks him up in one smooth motion. Mendel has time for a quick yelp of terror before two blurring claws tear him apart down the middle, splintering bone and shredding flesh with casual ease. Steaming piles of viscera splat wetly into a scattered mound, and the rainbow oil-slick silhouette of my finest creation opens a fang-lined maw and *screams*.

"Prime," I whisper, stomach suddenly freefalling.

My lizard hindbrain sends a lightning bolt of adrenaline coursing through my body and I start sprinting back the way we came. I can hear the last assistant huffing behind me as he keeps pace with my desperate flight, swearing constantly. Another *scream* rips through the air like the air raid siren of hell, and the sounds of terrible pursuit explode into motion behind us, a three-meter mass of hulking muscle and jagged claws tearing its way through the too-small doorframe.

No time to think. We dodge and run in a headlong tilt through the cracked funhouse mirror corridors, desperately throwing anything we can find behind us to slow the creature down. A shelving unit buys us a couple seconds, a locked door half a minute, all the while an enraged buzz saw of pure destruction rips at our heels. Nightmares have clawed their way into reality and our hallway is never ending.

An eternity later, I finally see a landmark, an AR sign pointing towards one of the few access tubes to the surface. "This way," I shout, making a hard right through the doorframe. At the end of the ill-lit passage, so close that I can taste it, lies salvation – an access lift to the surface guarded by a thick memplas blast barrier stuck a quarter of the way down, one of the lab safety protocols to protect against a breach foiled by Jasper's collapse. If we can make it to the other side and trigger the containment panel we'll be safe – the barriers have a backup system in case of emergency. For once I'm thankful for Government redundancy.

I look back just in time to see my assistant fall in the dim light, shoes sliding out from beneath him on the tiled floor as he slips on a puddle of dark fluid leaking from a jagged crack in the ruined rock ceiling overhead. He crashes to the ground awkwardly and struggles to get up, but I cannot wait. Prime will be on us shortly, and I don't have to outrun the monster, just my companion.

Footfalls echo off the walls as I continue my dash to the end of the hall, ducking underneath the barrier, and then I slam my hand down on the control panel. The clear slab resumes its descent from the ceiling as orange warning lights fill the corridor with their rotating flash, but it's falling slowly, too slowly!

My assistant regains his feet and limps towards the closing gap; he might still make it, but it will be a close run race indeed. He winces every time his right foot hits the floor – looks like he turned an ankle when he fell, but not severely enough to hamper his motion overmuch. Run a quick calculation on my glARS on his rate of closure. He has a small chance, but it's a chance.

Then, at the end of the hallway, the beast appears. Camouflage chromatophore cells have dropped back to baseline configurations, a dead, scaly grey, rough and sandpapered like sharkskin. Low swept horns hook back along its jutting predator's head, and it alternates between a gorilla's knuckling lope and the ground eating side to side charge of a komodo dragon, heavily muscled limbs rippling sinuously in unnatural formations as its hulking three-meter body flows forward through the shadows. A slender, whip-like articulated tail lashes the air behind it, razor point scoring the rock in deep gouges, providing both balance and a fifth grasping appendage, which it uses to scuttle through the scattered debris of the hall. The overall impression is of speed, strength, and merciless intent, honed towards one focus like the mythical samurai swords of Old Terra, swift death stalking the world of the living.

It sees my assistant, now almost to the closing barrier, and puts on a snarling burst of velocity, almost moving faster than the eye can track.

"Run, Gate-damnit!" I scream. "It's right there!"

He's not going to make it. The barrier has almost completed its slow glide into the floor, and he still has several meters to go. He's not going to make it.

He looks at me, and I can see him mouth the words "you asshole." He knows the Reaper's scythe is inches from his neck, but somehow he musters up an explosion of acceleration and dives for the narrowing gap between memplas and floor. The creature, digging chunks of rock from the floor with its wickedly clawed hands, makes a leap of its own, muscles bunching and then uncoiling like kinetic springs.

Time slows down. I see my assistant sliding along the tiles headfirst, torn lab coat flaring behind him, light blue sock flashing incongruously on a shoeless foot, a vision of primal terror slowly descending from the air, jaws gaping wide, taloned limbs outstretched.

Time speeds up again. A wickedly sharp claw snatches off his remaining shoe as my assistant completes his slide underneath the barrier in a whirl of limbs, barely avoiding being crushed. He tumbles to a halt against the access lift portal, and the memplas finishes sinking into the floor with a solid finality.

I watch my sleekly elegant killing machine slam into the three meters of clear composite with a soundless impact, body crashing to the ground. It shrugs off the concussive blow and gracefully rises to a standing position, talons curling and flexing as it stares at me. It reaches out and takes several exploratory swipes at the barrier, leaving deep scratches that slowly begin to fill themselves in. In a quick frenzy of motion Prime tries to tear its way through, but the memplas barrier heals faster than memplas enhanced claws can rip it apart, thick enough that the metamaterial's cascading regenerative properties outmatch the destructive potential arrayed on the other side.

Good thing I designed it that way. One centimeter less thick and Prime would be on us in a manner of minutes.

Rebuffed, the creature *screams* one last time and then glares at me, eye to eye. Inside those dead black orbs I can see the bright gleam of intelligence, and it chills me, because I recognize it, and I know it recognizes me. Finally, it backs away, slowly, gaze transfixing me the entire time, chromatophores eating away its outline, until all that's left is a gleaming fang grin hanging motionless in the empty air. Then, even that snicks away like a knife cut, and the hallway is left as barren as the void of deep space, datobjets twinkling like distant stars in the edges of my view.

"What. In the fuck. Was that," my assistant gasps out, climbing shakily to his feet.

"Prime." I step around him and hit the lift panel. "Come on. We can cut across to the maintenance lift aboveground and sneak around a different way. We still need to get that core restarted."

The lift arrives. I step inside, and after a moment, my assistant does the same. It's time to go up top. Time to face the light.

ROB

Timestamp – 14.15.47LT:03.04.15OT:03.19.407AG

Bright sunlight burns my eyes as we step out of the private shuttle bay, scum in tow. They're leaving most of their gear here – good idea. If the locals saw some of this kit they'd shit themselves. Some of it even I don't recognize, and Government makes sure Agency gets all the toys. Guess money *can* buy anything. We walk through the airy openness of the spaceport.

I take 'em over to a parked Vee, standard six-wheeler on balloon tires, black paint scratched and spattered by mud. It's rugged and boxy, room for eight people comfortably, twelve if they don't mind sharing laps – perfect for getting around the manicured underbrush near the resort, though not much use once the real wilderness starts. In a pinch they'll also float, limited aquatic capabilities. Good ride, reliable. I grab the driver's seat and synch into the Vee's control cloud, new datobject popping up in my display while the three young ones bicker over middle rows and refreshments. Old leatherface, Monocle, sits next to me, shotgun, Professor takes the very rear, one quick glance around before his glARs mist opaque, lost in his own private world.

Seat restraints lock in and we're heading down the highway towards the resort, roughly thirty minutes away. Passengers have to check in before they get down to pleasure; bet they have the best rooms in the place. Money like that always gets the best rooms.

Don't bother to engage the autodrive, more comfortable staying in manual control – too easy to get complacent. Vee's sensors are good, but anything can be subverted. Nudge the virtual throttle up another couple notches, electric engine responding with a barely perceptible whine of power, feel of acceleration pushing me back into the seat as the speed indicator hits sixty kilometers an hour. Can't open the throttle up until we reach the main highway.

Current road's a two lane concrete arrow straight over blue water, warehouses stacked three deep to a side, white sandy beaches visible through the gaps and shining in the morning sun. Eden's on a twenty-four hour day night cycle, just like Old Terra – one of the reasons it's so popular with those who can afford to come stare at the sights. One of those sights looms on the horizon to our left like a bloated orange, the gas giant Gehenna V – takes up almost half the skyline. Feels like it's going to fall out of the sky and crush us.

As I drive, they talk; not interested in listening. Meaningless chatter from surgically perfected mouths, empty syllables fill the vehicle. I tune my glARs to a music station to drown them out; the latest grungepop hit from Lethe Elle Injunction washes over me. Outside the Vee, interactive ARdverts blare meaningless grey noise every half a kilometer as we pass out of the warehouse district and into the jungle, proximity transmitters buried in the concrete thoroughfare. Eat at Joes. Dive Fast. Paradise Cruises. An army of light changing every ten seconds. Meanwhile, out in the real world, wilderness reigns supreme, thanks to the anti-digital pollution ordinances of the resort. Just a solitary highway cruising a warm green tunnel, birds chattering overhead.

Nudge the throttle up to one twenty, speed indicators flashing as the Vee approaches the posted limit. Level it off a couple kilometers per hour below the limit, no point getting an automatic VI fine for speeding, draw attention to the group.

Keep one eye on the road, the other on my passengers through my glARs, cycling through the interior viewcams, make sure they don't do something stupid. The one in the flower dress, Rhinestones, looks like trouble, twitchy facial expressions, no control over his emotions.

Others don't seem to like him either, Augstar and Wraparounds sniping at him constantly, kids with a stick and a handy anthill to poke.

The Professor stays hidden behind his glARs, face frozen in concentration – tough to get a read on him. Killer for sure, he's got the look. Same with Monocle to my right, he's been through some shit and come out the other side, still standing, probably covered in blood. His eyes give it away, constantly scanning, just like mine, not missing a thing.

He'll be trouble.

I flip on the local news feed, set it scrolling over the right half of my vision, text and images rolling past with each road marker. Nothing interesting, couple petty thefts, hacked Vee taken for a joyride by some teenagers, boring weather updates – won't stay that way for long. Pretty soon this place'll have enough going on to clog up every byte of bwidth surging through the Gate, a raging torrent of data screaming to get out.

Too bad no one'll hear. Stuck another digiworm inside the commfrastructure – for the next three days the only things going from the orbital station to the Gate belong to me, and all I'm sending are routine updates. Quick and nasty death if Government catches it, but they won't, even though there's more than a couple dreadnaughts stationed two jumps down. Designed it myself to wipe untraceably once we're done, and the next cruiser patrol doesn't hit for a week. The only thing they'll find is inexplicable chaos.

We near the outskirts and I slow the Vee back down, weaving around crowds of pleasure seekers walking the streets, bare skin flashing between thin strips of designer beachwear. Twist and turn the vehicle through the outer layer surrounding the resort proper, a thin shell of nightclubs and tourist traps designed to separate visitors from their credits, reviews and complaints swarming around them in ARspace like flies circling a corpse.

Digital palaces in one eye, seedy one-story cheapfab buildings in the other, they creep up the base of the volcano like parasites, leeching sustenance from soaring jungle covered flanks. White birds flash overhead, glARs scans for a threat, doesn't tag them. Smug, rich, happy faces float past the windows as the streets wend their way upward – eyes vibrant, cheeks glowing with health, drinks and drugsticks everywhere, bodies biosculpted to physical perfection. The brats point and gesture, no doubt talking over who and what they can buy; I think of Jennifer in her medunit and my knuckles whiten on the steering wheel.

Takes a conscious effort to relax them, to let the blood flow once more.

I spin the wheel and we're on the main resort access road, curving switchbacks leading up the hillside like coiling white serpents. A tributary branches off to the northwest – employees' village hidden where no one has to look. Gate forbid someone spoil paradise with reality.

Eight minutes and fifty-two seconds later, we're parked under the resort's main entrance, crystal flute pillars and golden arched porticos drowning in opulence, fountains misting in the breeze. Swanky.

Wonder how much medicine one of those pillars would go for?

More than enough to cure my baby. Fucking scum.

They get out of the Vee and I follow them in, our heels clicking on cool marble. More gold veins the floor, shinning in the pale blue sunlight; gold everywhere. A brief exchange with the desk clerk, garish in a red hotel uniform, and we're off again, this time on a lift cut into living rock. It travels briefly upward before heading deeper into the volcano, black obsidian flashing past. After a minute, the lift slows, and we're in what the Old Terra fundies would call Hell.

We step out onto the top level of a massive amphitheater carved from basaltic rock, huge mass of the volcano covering our heads, the far wall composed entirely of a vast memplas window. It looks out onto the churning magma of the caldera, shimmering heat climbing into the sky, and the very bottom of the semi-circle projects into the frothing lava itself, a red-lit pocket of absolute wonder. Even Wraparounds stops speaking for a moment, taken aback by the spectacle.

Eventually, Monocle turns away from the scene and begins to talk, the rest standing quietly around me, hands in pockets. His words are standard fare at first; thanks for the help, doing the right thing, blah blah blah. After a couple of minutes, I realize what he hasn't said, where this is headed.

He's not going to pay. Not yet. Sure, I released the monsters for them, but he wants to make sure their "hunt" goes off without a hitch, and for that they need the info on my glARs. Detailed bioscans, notes and behavior patterns, maps and access codes. Obviously, since I genelocked my glasses with a double authentication password, and I'm not about to throw away my only bargaining chip, that means they need me.

Pity. Was hoping to wait this out on the spaceport, floating high above the mess, calling in support if needed. Now it seems like I'm forced to shadow a group of rich savages. "Hunters" they call themselves while they enjoy their twisted amusements. Figured this might happen though; it's a poor Agent without a contingency for every contingency. They drummed that into us enough during basic training.

Figure something else too, seen it on plenty of assignments. They'll try and pop me as soon as I'm not useful anymore; the mouthy one, Wraparounds, might not even wait that long. Doesn't strike me as the type too concerned with consequences. Knows that erasing me makes sense. Saves them a lot of money, eliminates a witness – and they sure as shit don't want anyone knowing about their little games. There's not enough money in the universe that can buy you safety from illegal genehacking if Government finds out.

That's ok though; like I said – it's a poor Agent without a backup plan.

I don't intend to be poor any longer.

HOTEL CALIPH

Timestamp – 15.23.04LT:04.21.32OT:03.18.407AG

"I've taken up enough of your time, folks" says the richly attired man, his blond hair glinting in the spotlight and highlighting his perfectly chiseled features. He pauses briefly to let pearly white teeth glisten in a casually relaxed grin. "Raise your glasses as high as you can." His stylishly sleek glARs glow golden as the spotlight pins him to the stage like a butterfly.

Small table units slowly brighten and bloom until the whole banquet hall lies illuminated in the comfortably warm patina of simulated candlelight; diners seated behind snowy tablecloths, and remnants of the seven-course lunch still littering the room. Fifteen hundred-plus people fill the hall nearly to capacity – all of them smiling and laughing while simultaneously trying to keep their eyes glued to the perfect Adonis on stage; Hector Marx, the highest paid augstar actor in the industry and current host for the weeklong pleasure trip *"Paradise Found."* Most of the vacationers have their champagne glasses held high, bubbles fizzing merrily along the delicate fluted stems, while several raise a free hand to the side of their heads to manually capture images on their glasses, recording the memory in full three-dimensional color.

"I love you, Hector!" a woman in the front row screams with excitement, as she bounces up and down in her seat in child-like enthusiasm, the plunging neckline of her sheersilk dress revealing a lightly tanned expanse of tautly curved flesh, cultured pearl strands rattling like cheap beads. Her glARs are stylishly oversized, the latest from Vitton-Armani's New Milan fashion line, and feature a full array of recording options, all of which she has forgotten to turn on in her giddy celebrity worship, subdermal control tattoos spiraling up her arms in a dizzying array of tribal patterns.

Hector crosses the stage towards her, feet falling in time with the syncopated tribal drum opera softly issuing forth from the eight-piece band in the corner. As he gets closer, a wry smile inches up his cheek like a snake in the brush when he sees that she's both young and beautiful, the best body sculpting technology credits can buy. With a quick subvocalization into the flesh-colored patch ringing his throat, he reminds his glARs to book an appointment at the day spa for a fat reduction session tomorrow, before refocusing on the woman in front of him.

"Ma'am," he says boisterously, gesticulating with one perfectly manicured hand, "Why don't you come up and join me here on stage?"

The woman howls with joy, bubbling effervescence matching the drink she nearly throws in the air. She hands her champagne glass to a stolid man in a tuxedo seated next to her, who clearly doesn't want to hold it, but before he can protest she's already up on her feet and on the stage; her artwork arms draped around Hector's neck, one leg kicking into the air behind her, the floor-length dress parting along the slit in its side almost halfway up her thigh. The tuxedoed man shrugs and downs her drink in one quick slug – waste not want not.

"I can't believe this!" she screams as she clings to Hector, sounding for all the world like a sixteen-year-old meeting her favorite augstar for the first time. The crowd roars with laughter and applause, Hector struggling to keep his composure as well, a broad grin threatening to break through his carefully maintained stage presence. He doubles over for a moment, somehow avoiding spilling the woman to the floor, one hand caressing her bare back, then quickly returns to an upright posture, gently disengaging her arms from around his neck. She smiles as their eyes meet across two layers of transparent lenses.

"Ma'am," Hector begins, as the noise dies down, "what's your name?"

"Kimberly...Kimberly Wilkins," she stutters in a low voice, before leaving her feet for another rapid bouncing session, hands clapping together.

"I have just one question for you, Kimberly" Hector says in a hushed voice. He throws his right arm around her, stealing a quick glance down the plunging front of her dress and freezing an image before sending his eyes back out to the crowd.

"Why did you come to Eden?"

"Clearly to meet you," a man yells jokingly from deep within the crowd. Laughter once again fills the hall as the champagne goes to work.

Kimberly smiles, her face slightly flushed with embarrassment and alcohol. "I think I speak for every person in this room," she says as her eyes pan across the room. "I came here to party!"

The crowd's roar of approval is deafening. Hector's next words are barely audible above the din as he throws his arms out wide.

"That's what Eden was designed for, Kimberly. It's the ultimate party destination. Old Terra doesn't have a place with water this blue, beaches this fine, and that's assuming you can afford the containment suit to walk around there." The crowd titters like a flock of birds. "No, Kimberly, here on Eden the sands feel like silk under your toes, and the hiking trails put anything on Hawking-7 to shame." He pauses for a moment to drape his arm conspiratorially back around her bare shoulders, pulling her in close. "And the flowers, oh those beautiful flowers. They stay in bloom all year round, and some are so big you can curl their petals up around you and take a nap in them. Some are even big enough for two." He winks at the suddenly breathless Kimberly before resuming his speech. "Hotel Caliph's staff is top notch as well, here for your every beck and call. Fresh towels in the morning, five different massage spheres – heck, they'll even climb Mount Zali'ah to bring you a copig burger. I should know, I ordered one earlier from our lovely hotel manager, Candice Sterling!" Laughter ripples through the crowd again.

Hector's left hand raises his champagne flute high in the air as his right hand drifts down to cup the young socialite's firm asscheek, drawing her tight to his side. "Ladies and gentlemen, to paradise!"

"Pinche bullshit tourists," a woman leaning against the back wall of the room mutters under her breath while the toast rings throughout the air, glasses clinking like crystal chimes. "Paradise if you're rich, verdad. Not so great for the rest of us."

She turns her back to the stage and heads for the door, shoulder length black hair briefly whirling around her head, nu-plastic heels clicking on the red marble floor like staccato raps from an HV rifle. Her light green eyes are normally inviting, but at this moment they boil with an incandescent rage not unlike Mount Zali'ah's molten core.

Exiting the door into Hotel Caliph's sprawling, airy lobby, she picks up her pace, heels punishing the unyielding gold-flecked marble floor with each furious step. The normally soothing sight of the many exotic plant species native to Eden, carefully interspersed throughout the atrium, pass by unnoticed as she stalks along the lobby's length, numerous scarlet-uniformed staff keeping their heads down as they notice her towering rage. With a snarl, she turns and paces alongside the greenery again.

"Can you believe that garbage?" She directs her inquiry to the omnipresent assistant hovering at her side, his digitablet screen crammed full of hastily scrawled notes. "These overfed and overbred culos are going to expect us to bend over backwards for them. We're short staffed. We're under provisioned. We can barely keep this place running until that hijo de madre supply ship finally makes it here, and now we have Smarmy McAsscharm in there promising them a virtual blowjob with every meal."

"Do you want me to send out a memo, Ms. Sterling," her assistant asks anxiously, a slender man with eyes and hair as pale as his skin. "I know you're the senior manager, but—"

Candice cuts him off. "A memo to who? The corporate board? They could give zero shits about what we have to deal with as long as everyone's room gets paid for. Seriously, Wendall, cabron, sometimes I think you say these things to fuck with me, and right now I am not in the mood to be fucked with."

Raising both hands to massage her temples, she stops pacing for a few seconds, and then walks over to a massive, one hundred square-meter window. The panorama is stunning, a clear view down the slope of the volcano out to the sparkling water of Lake Basalt, the feathery green fronds of neopalms swaying in the gentle morning breeze. Extending out from the side of the resort are the water rings, giant discs of memplas projecting out into thin air, like translucent mushrooms sprouting from an obsidian black tree, each disc connecting to a concentrically smaller one in a series of descending stepped landings, creating an effect very similar to a spiraling blue circular staircase. Half of each disc is buried in the ground like a traditional pool, but the other half, the one closer to Lake Basalt, is clear memplas with water flowing through it, offering an unimpeded view both above and below. Waterfalls tinkle merrily between levels while local flora waves gently in an artificially induced breeze, providing a combination of shade and sleeping nooks. The pools currently lie empty, but she knows that will change once the breakfast banquet ends – drunk and frisky guests looking for an outlet to indulge their desires.

"You know, Wendall, the beauty of this place always takes my breath away," Candice says softly. "My mother would love it here."

"Why doesn't she visit, ma'am?"

Candice sighs. "Wendall, you always know exactly what not to say. How is she supposed to afford the Gate Transitions, let alone one of our rooms? There's a reason those pendejos in there are all wearing the latest designer glARs lines. They all have so many credits that they'll never have to worry about money until the universe collapses."

She turns and starts pacing again.

"Mi madre translates ancient languages, Wendall, and she lives in a habrise with thirty-five thousand other people on Estancia II. Not exactly one of the plutocrats…"

Candice stumbles to a halt as her eyes lock on to three of Hotel Caliph's staff poking at something near the bottom pool. "What in the name of Gate above are they doing?" she says, her eyes narrowing.

"Um, I think they're trying to clean the pool, m-m-ma'am," Wendall stutters nervously.

"Yes, Wendall, I can see that. What I'm trying very hard not to see right now, is the bottle of mescaline, a cleaning drone draped in plastic wrap, and the two brooms they've apparently inserted into the drone's vac unit. Is it that hard to find competent workers these days?"

"Well, ma'am, with the recruiting policies and —"

"Rhetorical question, Wendall."

Candice's fingers twitch inside her elbow length hapgloves, delicate gold filigree hiding the kinetic batteries and control unit, but she decides not to open the staff datobject slowly spinning in her vision. She'd rather not say something she'll regret later, and she shakes her head as she turns back to the lobby to continue her brisk walk, this time heading towards the bank of deliberately anachronistic brass elevator doors at the far end.

A muffled cough echoes from a wall-mounted speaker, echoing across the hall. "Uh…Candice Sterling," a hesitant voice says. "Please come to the security office. Candice Sterling, to the security office, please."

Candice stops and slowly spins on the heel of her left foot, shaking her head in disbelief again before setting her sights on a small maintenance door set discreetly behind a large ornamental light sculpture running the length of the north wall.

"Perhaps you can explain something to me, Wendall," she says in a venomous tone as they cross the exotically striped animal skin rug leading to the resort reception desk. "We're all required to wear glARs, which include a full-spectrum communications suite, verdad? Rhetorical question," she snaps as he starts to open his mouth. "Being that we're all linked together by this highly efficient marvel of technological engineering, WHY IN THE NAME OF A GATE-DAMNED BIOHACKER'S SPLICEHOLE AM I BEING PAGED ON AN INTERCOM?! Did everyone here have a lobotomy before starting their shifts?"

Wendell, trailing his usual two steps behind her, looks around nervously. "I—," he starts to stammer, hands frantically waving his digitablet around while he searches for words. His mouth fails to find them, opening and closing like a gasping fish, and he utters a series of sad barking noises in lieu of actual communication.

"Oh for crying out loud, Wendall." They reach the door and Candice sighs. "Calm down and get it out. I'm just a little overstressed from all these plutos; I didn't mean to take it out on you. I apologize."

Wendall takes several deep breaths and finally composes himself, hands twitching nervously at his sides. Candice passes through the biometric scanner set above the handle, opening the door to reveal a surprisingly ordinary looking hallway lined with multiple offices, the utilitarian nature of the resort's guts kept carefully concealed from those purely interested in the outer facade.

"Well, ma'am, there appears to be some sort of glitch in the global communications array," he gulps, sweat still beading his pale forehead. "Local functionality is limited, and the Gate isn't responding to us at all. The technical people are looking at it, but the last time I checked, they were just as puzzled as to what could be causing it as anyone else." Wendall pauses, then adds hopefully, "Maybe it's solar flares. I hear those can really knock out a comm grid."

Candice winces internally before deciding to let this one slide – Wendall's a good assistant, handy with numbers and logistics, but woefully lacking in any sort of real world knowledge outside of his digitablet. Mocking him, while admittedly entertaining on a shallow personal level, would only be counterproductive at this point, and she didn't get to her current position by wasting the abilities of the people around her.

Especially, she thinks as they enter the main security office at the end of the hall, people with talents like Lyle, her head of security.

"Howdy, ma'am. Looking hotter than an Atreus IV summer right now."

The words greet Candice and Wendall halfway into the room, uttered by a tall, powerfully built man with dark skin and a gleamingly shaven head. He smiles at Candice and she sends a sarcastic smirk back. She's known Lyle for almost six years now, and knows just how to handle his teasing barbs.

"First I have to deal with those idiota tourists, and now you're calling me over an intercom." Her voice turns harried. "I didn't even know we had an intercom!"

Candice walks over to stand next to the comfortable mesh swivel chair dominating the middle of the room, Wendall following a step behind.

"Course we do, ma'am. Patched it in myself, in case of a glARs failure. Lots of free time around here, in case you haven't noticed."

Lyle winks at her, and turns back to the bewildering array of monitor feeds displayed on the large screen he's seated in front of. His gentle hazel eyes are partially hidden behind slightly tinted lenses in dark blue frames, and his hapgloved hands are a blur – rapidly cycling through various sensor feeds, logistical manifests, and spreadsheets.

A spinning hand motion transfers several files of code to his glasses for later review, and then he brings up several complicated schematics on the large infpanel dominating the far end of the fifteen-meter room.

The newly presented images branch and twist like the skeleton of some fantastic beast, fractal nervous systems intertwined along the broad trunks of metadata bones. Multiple vines blink amber amidst a tree of light green – with two quick finger twitches he zooms in on one of the sinewy lengths and it resolves into a router network interfacing the resort with the Gate.

"What are we looking at, Lyle," Candice asks, sliding into the chair next to him. She takes the seat with a sigh of relief, shifting the weight off of her aching feet.

"We're blocked," Lyle softly drawls, his Lonstar accent musically lilting. "Someone inserted a digiworm in the Gate comm protocols. Whoever it was did a darn fine job of it too – only reason I noticed was when a couple of my sniffers started lagging." He smiles slightly, but it doesn't reach his eyes. "Far as I can tell, this thing's designed to bounce back all of our outbound messages without us noticing for at least three days. It's also playing mean with the local security nets, but that seems to be an unintended side effect. Short of sending a ship through to the other side, we're out here all by our lonesome."

Candice's eyes widen briefly, before narrowing in sudden thought. "Why would someone isolate *us*..." Her voice trails off and she taps her fingers restlessly on the back of Lyle's chair. "Do you think it could be a kidnapping attempt on some of the guests? There's more than a few highcred nobility here for that stupid *"Paradise Found"* clusterfuck."

Lyle shrugs. "Dunno, ma'am, haven't seen any indications that way. All the recent traffic's accounted for and we haven't had any strange new orders. Me and the crew'll be ready, of course, but this feels... different." He frowns. "Whoever wrote this worm is good. Too good for a snatch and grab. Not to be puttin' on airs, ma'am, but someone less qualified than me never would've found it, I can guarantee you that. This almost seems like-"

A sudden burst of noise from the workstation interrupts him midsentence. Garbled static gives way to a shockingly high pitched scream, and then frantic breathing.

"Help! We need help!" More screams sound in the background, before trailing off in an unpleasant welter of what sounds like tearing cloth. The voice gasps, then continues. "There's something out here! It's coming out of the trees, oh Gate above, it's so fast... shit shit shit..."

Lyle makes a quick hand gesture to switch over to the audio channel and engage his subvocal glARs microphone, then starts talking in a calm, unhurried tone. "Relax, son, and take a deep breath. This is Lyle Safrice, head of security; what seems to be the problem?"

"Thank the Gates above," the voice sobs, "you have to send help. We were hiking on the back trail, and now they're bleeding and dying, my sister, she's..." An anguished moan trails off into muted crying. Lyle frantically starts flipping through surveillance screens and huffs in disgust when he can't find a functional one overlooking the eastern jungle where the hiking trails are located. All the feeds are transmitting digital static, garbled nonsense images. The audio feed from the guest wavers in and out, but stays online.

"Son, do you know where you're at? Can you access the locator beacon on your glARs? It should be a datobject that looks like a flashing red siren, first layer of the resort shell."

Several sniffles and then the voice responds. "...yes. Yes. I just turned on the full emergency alert. Please, you have to come help. You have to come help right away!"

"Calm down, son, calm down, we'll be there before you know it." Lyle pulls up a full map of the continent and patches in several orbital satellites currently scanning the resort area, overlaying their sensors on top of the landscape, compositing the feeds together to compensate for the relentless interference. He bares his teeth in victory as a lone red dot starts blinking fitfully almost twenty-five kilometers southeast of Mount Zali'ah. "We've got you dialed in, son, it looks like you're in quadrant Thirty-Two Alpha—"

He's interrupted by a short gasp. "Oh fuck. It's coming. IT'S COM—"

A brief flurry of unidentifiable noises interspersed with harsh blasts of static fill the room before the comm link falls mercifully silent. Candice and Wendall stare at each other with blank expressions as Lyle clenches his fists, knuckles gradually turning white beneath the thin layer of piezoelectric fabric.

"Lyle," Candice whispers. "Lyle, what just happened?"

He slowly swivels his chair around before levering himself up; the room suddenly seeming to grow smaller and colder.

"I don't know, ma'am, but I aim to find out." All joviality is gone from his voice, and his eyes are dark and troubled as he makes his way to the door, clenched fists swinging heavily at his sides.

XANDER

Timestamp – 15.48.23LT:04.45.51OT:03.18.407AG

Rich jungle smells assail us as the lift doors slide open, our long ascent finally complete. I slowly push aside the bright green fronds surrounding the entrance and take a quick survey of the immediate environs – all seems clear, insects darting through the air, gossamer wings flashing in the sunlight, while indistinct hoots echo through the trees, most likely a gibbon colony from Old Terra. I motion the all clear and we cautiously venture out into the underbrush, steamy jungle air causing immediate perspiration. My assistant scowls after the first step, and then shrugs out of his lab coat, tearing it in half and wrapping the ragged remains around his shoeless feet. It's better than nothing, but not by much. He limps slightly as we start off into the jungle, ankle mildly sprained from the fall earlier.

A slow hiss from behind causes my assistant to jump and spin around, but it's simply the lift doors sliding shut, once again assuming the appearance of a broken and shattered tree, perhaps struck by lightning or a violent storm, branches hanging crazily off its sides. It blends in seamlessly with the jungle – those not biometrically keyed to its sensors will ever notice anything out of the ordinary.

He turns back towards me and I bring up the interactive map display on my glARs, expanding the topographical datobject and overlaying it over our geolocated position, trying to chart a path through the wilderness. Unfortunately, with the lab cloud down, I only have access to basic comm and map functionality, along with a few local notes I happened to save, so I only have a rough idea where we need to go – a shipping address fortuitously saved in my local cache from the last supply drop. I'll need to upload and resynch once we get the arrays back online, make sure the data hasn't been corrupted.

Luckily, the local datanet has decent cartography assists and I'm able to narrow down the coordinates of the secondary lift we'll need to access, a hab building in the employee village. Unluckily, it's almost a thirty kilometer trek through the jungle, so we're going to need to find some transportation.

I manage to grab some schematics of the transport grid from the planetary net, though the connection is oddly patchy, and I notice we're near a maintenance depot for the resort; it looks like we'll be able to cross a couple hiking paths and then catch a ride, but we'll have to keep an eye out for any tourists. Wouldn't do to let on there's strange people wandering through their pleasure garden. A destination icon starts blinking light blue on the inside of my glasses, compass superimposing itself on the top section, along with a dotted best path indicator based on the most recent sat terrain data.

I beckon for my assistant to follow and set off into the jungle, but after a couple of steps I come to a halt because I'm the only one walking. Slowly, I turn around and face him through the jungle haze, small insects flitting past my face in slow circles. He licks his lips, and then words start tumbling out in a rush.

"Look, man, I know I signed on to help out with the biohacking stuff, I get that, but I didn't sign on for whatever that, that *thing* was!" His voice starts low but ends in a shout, spittle flying from his mouth, whites showing around his widened eyes.

"Calm down, calm down." I keep my voice pitched low and reassuring, trying to get him away from the cliff of blind panic he's currently dancing on. Two pairs of eyes are going to be better than one moving through here, and I'll probably need some help if we run into Prime or one of the other specimens. Speaking of which...

"You need to keep your voice low," I make soothing gestures with my hands, drawing close and then putting my arm companionably around his shoulders. "Prime's not the only thing I was working on in there. It's probably the deadliest, but most of the others aren't to be trifled with either, and some of them have very good hearing."

In retrospect, this may have been the wrong thing to say.

His shoulders tense up, and as he starts shaking all over, I can't tell if he's sobbing or laughing. It may be both. Never been good at the emotional parts of life.

"...'most of the others?'" A rictus grin lies plastered across his face as he turns to stare vacantly at me. "You mean, there's more where that came from? More walking nightmares? I thought we were working on beneficial modifications for crops and humans – stuff like increased yields, vaccines, longevity! Just what were you doing in there, Doc?!"

"What Government needed me to do." I make my voice stern and harsh, hoping to snap him out of his daze. It seems to work; the fog clears from his eyes and he stops trembling. "You didn't know because you didn't need to know, and, Gate willing, never would have known. There are beasties out there that go bump in the night, and sometimes we need something that goes bump back."

"Beasties?"

"Walk with me, I'll explain."

I start talking as we clamber over fallen creepertrees and push our way through pricklevine, sticky sap collecting on our hands and faces.

"When I told you we were researching human mods, I wasn't lying. That's one of this facility's primary functions. But one of its other functions is to create prototype weapon designs for use on our outposts and mining concerns."

The insects continue swarming around us, drawn by the moisture trickling down our bodies in the growing jungle heat, Old Terra genotypes subtly modified for an alien world, though no one seems to notice. His limp slowly fades as he works the stiffness out of his ankle.

"Prototype weapon designs? Outposts? Mining concerns? What are you even talking about?" His tone is quizzical.

"Everyone knows that skhips and Gates are powered by an exotic form of hydrogen called eHydro, that everyone pretty much calls Gate-fuel due to its absolutely critical necessity in keeping Gates functional, but it only forms deep inside gas giants, and we need a lot of it to keep things up and running, especially because it's also one of the primary components in memplas. Everyone also knows that conditions at these mining stations are, shall we say, suboptimal for humans, and it's more cost effective to automate everything.

"What everyone *doesn't* know, is that we keep running into this particularly aggressive form of life down in the depths – we have no idea how they're so widespread – and our top echelon automatic weapons platforms aren't good enough to stop them reliably. Biohacked creatures that can operate naturally in these conditions, in a defensively oriented preemptive strike capacity, are the only things keeping our networks running, and Government has labs tasked with making sure they stay upgraded, as well as creating new ones."

He gapes at me, mouth slack, and then winces as he steps on an upthrust creepervine root, short thorns piercing his makeshift shoes. Small spots of blood bloom on the grimy lab coat wrapped around his right foot. He mutters curses as he hops on the other leg for several seconds, then resumes our conversation.

"You're telling me that Government has managed to keep the presence of alien life hidden from public knowledge in the entire Empire? *And* that we're engaged in widescale biohacking? That's ridiculous!"

I smile. "When you think about it, rationally think about it, not really. Government operates the Gates, and Government's also the only organization with the resources to build and operate skhips and mining platforms. The Council Families design legislation carefully to keep it that way, and for good reason. If no one knows what they should be looking for, why would they find it? As far as the general population's concerned, collecting Gate-fuel is something that happens automatically, by people who are most assuredly not them. Any losses or shortages can be explained away by the hostile environments the mining stations are operating in, and the defenders are designed to be territorial so they don't venture out too far."

We walk in silence for six minutes and thirty-two seconds, the relentless flow of the timestamp cutting seconds off one by one, an uncaring arbiter regulating the flow of causality. We cross several hiking trails before plunging back into the undergrowth – luckily avoiding any hikers. As we push our way through the vegetation, I can tell he's mulling over what I've said, trying to reconfigure his world view in light of information ninety-nine percent of the population never learn. A soft chime sounds inside my head, accompanied by a flashing topographical update – we're halfway to the maintenance depot.

"You mentioned something earlier, 'outposts,'" he starts up softly. "I think I understand defenses for the mining platforms, but that doesn't explain something like Prime. That's not designed for gas giant depths at all."

I was hoping my involuntary slip would pass unnoticed, but of course he would put those pieces together – after all, I don't hire idiots to work as my assistants at a highly illegal biohacking facility, even if they aren't told about the inner workings. A keen intellect is job requirement number one; a willingness to disappear off the face of the universe number two; a moderate disregard for the Accords number three. The combination tends to be tough to find. I ponder how I'll be able to give him enough information to satiate his curiosity without signing his death warrant – it's going to be hard enough replacing the other three I lost, two of whom actually knew about my main purpose with the facility.

"Prime is a special case," I start out, slowly pacing my words while we wriggle our way through another thicket of tanglethorn, arms and legs picking up numerous scratches. "I designed it as the culmination of several different genetic enhancements woven together from disparate species: strength and musculature from *hominidaegorilla*, speed and reflexes from *aepyceros melampus*, the camouflage of *chamaeleo calyptratus* and *octopus vulgaris*, *varanus komodoensis*'s immunity to disease – all woven into the genetic scaffolding of *homo sapiens*." I smile as I recall the latest test. "Yet that's not all. I've also integrated the regenerative properties of eHydro, along with something... *new*. There's something in eHydro, something amazing, and I'm only just beginning to scratch the surface. My goal, Government's goal, is to create a hack to improve every facet of humanity, to take control of blind evolution and make her serve our every need, and that's what I've done!"

My face is flushed, excitement bubbling through my voice. Prime will shake the universe, change our future, and I'm the one who came up with the hack. Soon, the entirety of Hegemony will understand the incredible step we're about to take as a species.

The excitement fades somewhat as he glares at me sourly, expression disapproving.

"Yeah, but how does that relate to that nightmare we ran into back there?" He pauses, suddenly lost in thought, voice analytical. "And eHydro? How can that even meld into *homo sapien* telomeres? I thought it only functioned under extreme pressures."

"Well, you see, I've been working on this for over twenty years now, and when I ran the splices, I discovered some very interesting interactions, and then I had to make a proto—"

My voice cuts off as I trip over something on the ground. I manage to tumble and avoid any serious injury from the fall, but when I look back at what I fell over my breath grows short. It's a torn and ragged human torso, like someone disassembled a doll and threw its limbless upper body onto the ground. As I whip my head around, I can see more severed limbs around us, flies buzzing over the sticky blood pools seeping into the rich loamy earth, drying red-brown splashed everywhere, but still recently spilled as evidenced by the steady dripping from several leaves. I quickly beckon my assistant to get down and he inches up to join me, giving off short, nervous pants like an overactive dog as he crawls past the assorted carnage. I point to a clearing in front of us and we slowly creep up to it, eyes scanning in all directions.

Finally, we reach the edge, and I push some dwarfpalm fronds aside just enough to peek through.

Before us lies a massacre.

ROB

Timestamp – 16.11.42LT:05.09.10OT:03.18.407AG

Room's dim, glowstrips off, scattered stabs of sunlight peeking through the checkerboard green and black drapes. Dust motes dance in the beams, stirred up by the fan spinning lazily overhead, palm frond blades gently cutting the climate controlled air. Its bearings squeak every third rotation. Infpanel covers one wall, small kitchen unit set next to it, sink sharing a water pipe with the bathroom in the small closet behind – the economy of space a tough habit to break, even on an empty planet.

Even tougher habit to break while secretly booking a vacation room on an Agent's budget. Told the Agency I was taking some 'personal time,' needed a week to figure things out. Programmed a VI to automate my apartment on Ksaibanni III – flush the toilets, open the food locker, turn the stove on and off, cycle the lights from room to room – everything necessary to recreate the digital spoor of life in an always-on world. Ghosted my glARs ident, spoofed the RFID signal, dropped out of the system.

Not supposed to be able to hide yourself in the many worlds of Hegemony, but the Agency taught me well. Taught me a few tricks even it doesn't know.

Don't need tricks now, need money. Barely enough left after Jennifer's latest round of treatments to pay for the three nights the hunters wanted, resort's no-compete clause leaving no other option but to stay in an overpriced coffin while I infiltrated the lab. Nothing left to pay for anything after that.

Every gcred spent, every loan overdrawn, accounts filled with the crushing weight of zeros.

Lie on the thin nucotton blanket covering the tiny bed, tiny threads prickling my bare skin, and stare at the darkened ceiling, fan creaking the seconds away in synchrony with the timestamp blinking in front of my right eye. Blink. Creak. Blink. Tiny slivers of life shedding their insignificance into the cheerily painted walls of the room, joining their trillion siblings already there.

Datobject shimmers into vision, breaking the textured roughness of the surface above me. Twitch a finger, origami unfolds into meaning.

Hunters want me to meet them out front with the Vee, let slip the hounds, time to go a-coursin'. Acknowledge receipt of message, sit up on the edge of the bed.

Pull my battered luggage over and grab the tacsuit folded within. Give it a once over as it unfolds, make sure everything's working properly – lightweight synthsilk interwoven with memplas fibers, thin shockgel pads covering vital areas, integrated biomed patches studding the inside of the fabric, designed to be worn covertly beneath normal clothing, capable of stopping anything short of a penetrator round, and equipped with limited medical treatment consumables.

Having it is a gross violation of Agency protocol, only supposed to take tacsuits out on active assignment, Class Three restricted. Penalties range from fines to multi-year prison sentences in the Isolated Cells, depending on how it's used – harsh sanctions designed to prevent abuse.

Sigh and slip it on, material sealing itself shut down the front, memplas threads weaving together as they connect to my glARs and activate, forming a perfect seal around my body. The suit compresses slightly, transforming into a second layer of skin, shockgel bulging slightly like extra muscles. Reach down in the luggage again, and snap the plastic composite quick-slide frame to my right forearm, another dataobject appearing in my vision as it synchs up.

Load it with a standard issue Agency twenty-shot holdout, boxy body filled with tiny kinetic HV rounds, a squat and ugly thing. Holdout penetrators are Class Five restricted – illegal possession punishable by death if it gets used. Run the slide twice, holdout jumping cleanly into my hand each time.

Sigh again, and finish dressing in a loose fitting grey singlesuit that covers the gear underneath, black waistjacket and sturdy shoes completing the dull servant look.

Leave the room and head to the elevator bank, gleaming brass frames circling a large waiting room like the markings on a clock, burnished doors on the thirteenth one sliding open as I approach.

Frame has an etched metal floor indicator, 'one-sixty,' almost halfway up the building – hit the old-fashioned button for the lobby. Ears pop as the lift descends, flashing altimeter in my eye falling with us. Finger twitch accesses a six-wheeled datobject; have the autopilot pull the Vee out front.

Lift arrives at the bottom, reflection splitting apart as the doors slide open. Cross the lobby and out the arched front entrance; take a seat in the idling Vee and turn on some music while I wait. Send a group message – ride's here.

Five figures come walking out several minutes later, each one carrying a carbonframe gearbag. Pop the rear hatch of the Vee and they heave the bags inside; from their expressions lifting up the packs there's some serious tech inside.

Be willing to bet it's all highly illegal.

All of them found time to change, military-casual, rugged work boots and webbed tacvests over ballistic fabric one pieces. If the clothes were black they'd look like a team of wannabe augstar ninjas, instead they're just the dull grey of acticamo not yet initialized. Suits like that ain't cheap, and much more protective than they look – top of the line might as well be spacer waste next to those. Sure as shit there's gonna be some upgrades in there that never appeared on the display model either.

GlARs are still the same, can only imagine what personalized treasures are hiding in each one, locked away behind layers of digital security. Acticamo doesn't match the glasses, not exactly standard resort fare, but they don't seem to care about the curious looks they're getting. Arrogant. Imagine they're not planning on running into too many people during the actual "hunting" time.

Old and leathery, Monocle, sits shotgun again, single unit perched over his right eye. That style hasn't been popular in decades, maybe a century. Interesting choice. Doesn't provide as much immersion as a full set, but lets him keep one eye grounded in reality. Generally only the highly paranoid or security conscious wear 'em. At least mine's disguised to look like a complete pair.

Rhinestones and Augstar grab the front bench and continue their bickering from earlier, her needling voice constantly jabbing at his clothes, his hair, his corp policies. Wish they'd knock it off, that shit's gonna get real annoying, real quick. Athlete looking wannabe,

Wraparounds, takes the middle row behind them and stirs the pot whenever it looks like things are going to settle down, seems to get a kick out of watching them go at it. Can't see his expression since his glARs are switched to mirrored silver. Probably thinks it makes him look cool. It doesn't. Professor climbs into the back staring at who knows what inside his tinted glasses – hasn't said much the whole time aside from some muttered numbers and finance jargon.

Doors slide shut, ask them where we're headed. Wraparounds looks pretty pleased with himself – apparently he's tapped into the hotel security net and caught word of some sort of incident on the hiking trails. Don't like the tone of his words, there's something hungry, feral lurking underneath; bloodlust. They all have it. Also don't like he's got a tap in without me noticing, means he's good. Real good. Gonna have to take a discreet look at his opsys soon, see if I can get some hints about his digisig; if he's that good, odds are I've run into his code somewhere before.

Might clear up some unanswered questions raised during a couple busts over the years. Tried to dig the truth out, connect the dots in lines that made sense, but always got stonewalled, shunted aside, told to leave it alone. Takes skill to hide in a surveillance state.

Takes money.

Shift the Vee into motion and head for the hiking trails, map overlay indicating just under twenty minutes to get there.

Constant arguing from the three in the seats behind is just enough to break through the music in my glARs, puts my teeth on edge; these kids might not make it back home if this keeps up. Can't say they'll be missed, at least not by me – those rich family trees could use some pruning, clear out some deadwood. Clear it all, one great wildfire scouring the useless away like so much kindling. It'll happen one of these days; hopefully I'll get to throw a match.

We're still about two kilometers out, heading through an overgrown utility track, when Monocle tells me to pull over into the underbrush. Looks like they're planning on walking the rest of the way in; smart. Seems to know a thing or two about proper security protocols, not surprising with his carefully tailored generic lie of a life.

Need to look at his opsys also – too many unknowns right now. Gotta fill in the blanks if I'm gonna make it out of this alive, get those gcreds to Jennifer, get her healed.

I nose the Vee under some spreading palms and click the engine off; everyone jumps out. We head to the rear of the vehicle, grab what we'll need for the hike in. Professor pulls out a roll of acticamo mesh and tells me to drape the Vee, secure it from any passerby. As I spin it out they start unloading their carrybags, gearing up.

Professor snaps together a long piece – HV sniper platform, mil-grade, enhanced optics suite linked to his glARs. Delivers up to grade three micro munitions anywhere within a four klick radius; fits his standoffish personality, he's not the type to get his hands dirty. Possession of it's a hundred year minimum sentence, and not in one of the pleasant cells either. Government doesn't like sharing its toys. Not the best choice for a jungle with limited sightlines, though.

While he assembles components, Augstar is busy bringing a couple drone buzzers on line, short range models. Limited autonomy and packed chock full of HE, a suicide bomber's wet dream without the pesky suicide requirement. They start slowly orbiting her head, lo-noise rotors spinning too fast for the naked eye to see; a grim grey halo with that distinctive hum. Takes some nerve to keep buzzers orbiting that close, I'll give her that. Not a lot of smarts, but definitely nerve. She packs a couple more into various pockets on her tacvest – if she blows, looks like she's going big.

Wraparounds carries a splinter rifle with underslung launcher, chunky color coded shells attached liberally around his tacvest.

Judging by the rainbow covering him, he's carrying a full combat suite; hope he knows which way to aim the pointy end. Some of those shells are filled with more than party favors. At least he has the glARs linked triggering attachment mounted on his piece, they won't go off unless he wants them to.

He flips the safety back and forth a couple times, then turns and says something in a low voice to Rhinestones. The pudgy figure grins unpleasantly as he hooks color-coded packets to the webbing covering his acticamo, though his are different than the ones adorning Wraparounds'. These are thinner, slender, like a blade.

Judging from their first conversation I'm betting combat pharms, enough drugs to bring a corpse back to life and make it fight. Side effects are generally pretty nasty, ran into a couple users over the years – pharms never end well.

Rhinestones attaches the last packet, and then pulls what looks like a slightly curved memplas sword out of his gearbag, almost one and a half meters long, along with a thin scabbard. I trigger the zoom function for a better look as he rams the shimmering edge home – his hand grasps a long hilt wrapped in alternating strips of red leather, two golden birds in flight extending at right angles to form the cross-guard, a simple rounded blue metal pommel engraved with a small 'DE' capping it all. He snaps a metal ring set in the top of the black lacquer sheath to his waist, then adjusts the angle it's hanging at for several seconds.

...Kufit's beard. Who the fuck uses a Gate-damned sword in the twenty-third century? Hope he gets eaten by something.

I turn away and trigger the acticamo covering the Vee – with a quick shimmer it blurs, and then vanishes from the visible spectrum. Won't stop thermal or sonar, not unless you want to roast alive inside a trapped photon cage, but it'll pass a casual glance if the viewer doesn't have the proper glARs ident. Monocle steps over to help me brush away the tracks leading into the underbrush – his movements are quick, sure, precise. Definitely trained in field ops, he's done this enough times for it to become habit. Too good at it to be a Peacekeeper, Black Colony unit's looking more and more likely. Not gonna ask him, though, be signing my own death warrant to reveal that info, and surviving this current bit is going to be hard enough. Black Colony's a tightly held secret, and Government has a habit of disappearing those that don't need to know.

I'm definitely on that list if they ever find out. Already know entirely too much.

He straightens up as we finish, pulling his brush hat back and readjusting the pistol holster on his right hip to let it fall into a more comfortable draw position. Can't get a good look at the piece inside, but it seems to be an original Six Sixteen; nasty piece of work. Holds six casings filled with sixteen guided micro flechettes, each one either individually targetable by the shooter or blind-fire autonomous acquisition, and capable of carrying standard, penex, highex, and chemtox rounds. A skilled user can use it to achieve anything from a surgically clean full target live disable, to clearing an entire room in one trigger pull, to depopulating a village. Messily.

Six Sixteens were banned over fifty years ago due to the results when unskilled users got their hands on them. Carrying one's a guaranteed death sentence, no questions asked, by any Government law agent that sees it.

Get the feeling Monocle doesn't much care who sees it. Notch another tally in the Black Colony column.

Stealth precautions taken, we head off into the jungle, Wraparounds in point. The going isn't particularly tough, hotel keeps the entire area subtly well-manicured – wouldn't do for guests to have an obstructed view while hiking – but there's enough underbrush to provide plenty of cover. Flipping over to thermal reveals several small shapes pacing us a couple hundred meters away; most likely imported game beasts to provide the illusion of nature. I flip back to standard and then freeze as Wraparounds raises a fist and drops to a crouch just behind the crest of a small rise.

He motions us up to join him, and as we creep forward a message scrolls across the lower half of my right eye, "HNTG PRT SPTD, 12 DWN, 2 ADDS 23 DEG NE."

I peek over the top of the rise onto a scene of carnage. Bodies and parts of bodies lie scattered across a small clearing in the jungle canopy about half a kilometer away, ragged tears indicating severe trauma.

These people never had a chance against whatever assaulted them; canteens and sticks the only weapons available, several glimpsed in half-clutched hands that lie several meters away from the sodden lumps of flesh that used to be their owners. The hunters start flashing messages back and forth over the cloud, readying for their prey.

A brief twitch of movement and I focus twenty-three degrees to the northeast, where two men huddle fitfully behind a tree trunk. One is wearing a tattered and grimy lab coat, stylish glasses with thin black frames covering his face.

Can it be?

Before I'm able to adjust and zoom in, the murmured discussion next to me is cut off by the rapidly approaching hum of an aircopter. Acticamo flashes briefly until only eerily floating heads survey the scene before us, glARs the identifying features of note, weapons held in a not quite aggressive posture.

The twenty-meter craft passes almost directly overhead, warm exhaust blasting the ground around us as it descends toward the clearing.

It rocks to a halt and ten people pile out.

HIKING TRAIL TLATELOLCO
Timestamp – 16.36.11LT:05.33.39OT:03.18.407AG

Leaves and dust swirl up around the aircopter as the vectored-thrust nacelles on each stubby wing swivel almost straight down, converting angular momentum into a gentle landing on the grassy turf, three pairs of thick wheels flexing slightly as the vehicle's weight settles on top of them.

A large hatch set in front of the right wing swings open, and people start disembarking, weapons in hand, clambering down the short one-meter drop to the ground and quickly setting a perimeter.

The aircopter's rotors slowly whine to a halt behind Lyle as he surveys the clearing, trying to figure out what could have turned a pleasant resort hiking trail into a war zone. One of the younger members of his team abruptly doubles over and begins to retch; Lyle frowns briefly but allows him some space.

He can't blame the youngster for his reaction; bodies lie ripped and shredded all across the jungle floor and the ground is torn and mangled. Sticky blood pools carry their coppery scent on the light breeze, and flies are already beginning to cluster and feed on the unexpected bounty.

The sight reminds Lyle of a rebel pacification op back when he still worked for Government – Sirius Four, Braxton Two, or any of the countless other worlds the Peacekeepers are constantly called to subjugate back into obedience; unhappy residents airing their grievances with bullets and bombs until Government reminds them of the proper order of things.

"One of the reasons I got out of that Gate-damn business in the first place," Lyle mutters to himself, eyes still scanning the surrounding tree line through glARs enhanced algorithms. Motion is tracked, notated, catalogued under various threat filters and assigned to the combat cloud. "Had enough of bringing 'peace' to folks."

"What was that, boss?" The words come from a slender woman wearing a light purple bandanna to keep her long, dark hair under control.

Her eyes, barely visible behind heavily tinted glARs, are just as active as Lyle's, and she sends several warning messages to the two brothers, Jason and Eddie, who are in charge of the southern quadrant of the perimeter. They appear to be staring more at the bodies than the surrounding environment, and they flinch as their glasses flash in chastisement. Both renew their surveillance with increased vigor.

"Nothing, nothing, just talking to myself, Raquel. Old memories. Let's get Marcus back on his feet and figure out what happened here, yeah?"

Lyle walks over and leans next to the still retching Marcus, keeping his boots clear from the unpredictable streams of vomit. "You going to be all right, son?" he asks, hand resting companionably on Marcus's back.

Marcus dryheaves one last time and then wipes his mouth with the back of his hand before straightening up. Moisture glints at the corners of his light brown eyes, but his gaze is firm and unwavering.

"Yessir. Won't happen again, sir," he croaks out, wincing as the air passes along his burning diaphragm.

"That's okay if it does, son." Lyle pats him on the shoulder. "No one should ever have to become used to a horror like this. It ain't natural to see a body dead from violence, and especially not from violence like what's been done here. Now let's go see if we can find ourselves whatever perpetrated this atrocity, and make sure it can't ever do it again."

Marcus nods, and Lyle pings the cloud with a quick 'assemble' alert.

The other eight members of the detail rapidly coalesce in a loose circle around him and Marcus, their eyes still focused on the perimeter, and Lyle permits himself an internal smile of satisfaction – projectile vomiting aside, the team is operating cohesively and professionally.

They might not be official Peacekeepers, but they've been trained by one and it shows.

He knows he can count on them to stick by each other and not cut corners, a tough value to instill when the hardest thing they've had to do for the last three years is escort drunk guests back to their room if they get lost.

"Alright, folks," Lyle's voice is soft, but unyielding in intensity, cold shivers of rage running barely perceptible beneath it, "what have we got so far?"

A tall, swarthy man with bristling eyebrows and a black goatee highlights a datobject in the local glARs cloud. A frozen image of the broken ground abruptly floats in front of Lyle's vision, superimposed over the surrounding destruction like an alternate topography. The man speaks in a gravelly voice, eyes still scanning the jungle.

"Well, boss, it looks like some sorta animal did this. You can see the tracks here, here, and here."

He triggers a subroutine, and suddenly multiple deep, broad footprints appear in the muck, tracks surrounded by a golden aura, meaning unexpectedly shining forth from incomprehensible chaos. "From the depth they've sunk in, and the distance between strides, I'd say we're looking at something that's at least four hundred and fifty to five hundred kilos, and probably about seven meters in length."

"So about the size of a personal aircopter..." Lyle's voice trails off. "Candice, are you getting all of this?"

"I'm getting audio, Lyle," Candice's voice crackles and pops in Lyle's skull, the conductive bone headpiece in his glARs reproducing the static with perfect fidelity, "but it looks like we're still getting that interference from before. I'm not getting any of the visual datobjects off the global cloud, but at least I can listen in."

"Ok, we'll make do with what we have. I'll try and squirt you a text summary if possible; Chiang, what else?"

"Well, not only is it heavy and powerful, it's also incredibly quick," Chiang continues. "Look at the way these prints instantly change direction – this thing's making ninety degree turns like it doesn't even care about momentum. Gotta have one hell of a musculature to do that without ripping your ligaments right in half."

"Thanks, Chiang. Anyone else notice anything?"

Raquel nods and highlights a different datobject, this one of the scattered bodies.

"Check this out, boss. Look at the way these wounds were caused."

As the image closes in on the ragged remains, Marcus trembles slightly and goes pale, but maintains his composure. "These bodies are slashed and torn, but the cuts don't look like any from an animal I've ever seen. They're too big, too clean – more like knives than any sort of claw. Also, a couple of these people were punctured by something barbed, like a harpoon, and the skin's gone through some peculiar necrotization near those entrances. It's almost like they've been injected with acid."

"So large *and* quick, claws as big as machetes, and some sort of acid attack? Are we sure this is all the work of one creature, and not some combination of environmental effects?"

"The data doesn't lie, boss, and there's only the one set of tracks. Oh, and, uh, there's one more thing..." Raquel hesitates for a moment, mouth twisting sourly, before continuing. "The number of limbs don't match up to the number of bodies, and a lot of them look like they've been chewed on. I think whatever it was... was eating them."

A short intake of breath runs through the group before training and discipline reassert their calm hold, but Lyle can sense the twitchiness. It's one thing to prepare for the myriad security situations that arise at a resort hotel – hostage crises, bomb threats, wildfires, earthquakes, typhoons, plumbing breakdowns – but he never expected 'man-eating demonbeast' to find its way onto the list. The moon had been carefully charted and explored by Government for several years before deciding to open a Gate and site the resort there, and nothing larger than a housecat had ever been found; problems from the local wildlife shouldn't exist. Lyle shakes his head ever so slightly, and then closes the datobjects and brings the combat cloud back to full readiness, sensors intermingling in broad-spectrum coverage from each pair of glasses. The team turns towards him, subconsciously drawing closer together.

"Okay," Lyle begins, voice firm and encouraging, "I know this ain't something we've ever really prepared for, but remember your training and stick together. I'm authorizing the use of live munitions, hollowpoint stoppers, but make sure your fields of fire are clear first and your IFF is active. We don't want anyone shooting at shadows and ending up with a friendly casualty. Split into squads of two and start fanning out to the northeast; it looks like the tracks head that way. If you see *anything*, send out a wideband alert and don't engage unless you've got a clean shot – I don't want to startle whatever this thing is into another rampage before we have a chance to concentrate our firepower."

Lyle pauses and looks around, meeting each person's eyes for a moment before moving on, willing some of his strength into them. His voice drops to a snarl. "Stay on your toes, people. Whatever this is, it's already killed twelve guests, and it's our job to make sure it doesn't kill any more. We're going to find it, and we're going to put it down. Marcus, you're with me. Let's move out!"

The group splits into five pairs and sets off, spreading apart as they move across the clearing, gazes alert and focused behind the swirling overlay of the combat cloud, color-coded visuals constantly updating threat vectors and positioning. Everyone carries a slugthrower in the combat position, non-dominant hand under the barrel, stock pressed firmly into the shoulder, dominant finger extended along the side of the trigger guard, and the safeties make a slight snick as each one slides to the 'off' position, ready to unleash concentrated mayhem at the first sign of danger.

Lyle can't help but be proud of them, proud of their courage, proud of their desire to protect the resort and each other, and when the beast silently flows into their midst and starts the killing he tries everything he can to wake from the sudden nightmare of reality. The world shrinks down to motion and screams and death.

XANDER

Timestamp – 16.51.29LT:05.48.57OT:03.18.407AG

Shit.

We're still crouched behind the dwarfpalm, my thigh muscles close to cramping from maintaining a kneeling posture for so long. I want to get a closer look at those bodies, see what they can tell me about what's loose in the area, but first that aircopter needs to leave, along with those silly resort people playing toy soldiers in the woods. At least they're not walking towards us so we should be safe for —

Oh fuck. Gate-damned Kufit's diseased scrotum FUCK. Sentry organism ECS-06, a Coeurl, is padding out of the forest *five meters to my left* in its ground-hugging prowl, low and long and sinuous, capable of ripping apart anything less than an armored battle tank – and even then I wouldn't put money on the tank. It's only the dumbest of luck that it hasn't noticed us; I designed it to key in on motion and noise, things the hotel group are providing in abundance, and our forced inaction is all that's keeping us safe for the moment.

I slowly turn my head towards my assistant and notice all the blood drain from his face, his eyes bigger than the gas giant overhead. As he opens his mouth to speak I give the tiniest of head shakes, eyes flashing in warning, before swiveling my attention back to the clearing. We'll only have a brief opportunity to make our escape; Coeurls are highly territorial but lose focus when feeding, a necessary replenishment of the energy they expend during quick bursts of combat – a design flaw I've been trying to eliminate without much success, but a flaw that gives us a slight chance to live.

As I refocus on the clearing, I can see the Coeurl barely ten meters behind the hotel group, barbed tail lashing back and forth just above the ground, looking like an oversized cat, albeit a cat only a true connoisseur could love. Hunched close to the ground on all fours, it's still as tall as a human, its haunches close to one and a half meters off of the ground. Hairless, mottled skin covers its entire body, crimson splotches scattered amongst the pale majority like tumorous growths. It grips the ground with broad paws that end in splay toed retractable talons nearly half a meter long, their keen edges reinforced with organic memplas. A long, segmented tail tapers to a scorpion's bulging point, and the head is made of what a normal person would consider nightmares.

I consider it beautiful, albeit for a very specialized value of beauty. Two prehensile trunks, similar to those of an elephant, writhe on either side of a gaping mouth filled with needle sharp teeth, the jaws flat and broad. A pair of predator's eyes right above the mouth form the inner band of its sensory organs, two sets of membranes providing additional protection from the bright flash of plasma fire. An additional pair of wider prey eyes occupies the sides of its head – giving it an effective two hundred and seventy-five degrees of multispectrum vision covering the lowest bands of infrared all the way up to the highest ultraviolets. I created it to be a perfect sentry – motionless and wary until something triggers its sensors.

Those poor fools have no idea what's about to hit them – and then it hits them.

The Coeurl starts with the right center group, whipping its tail into the back of the man on the right, instantly severing his spine, while simultaneously fastening its trunks around the woman on his left. She barely has time to scream before a clawed swipe separates her torso from her legs. The trunks uncoil and fling her torso back to the right, almost knocking over one of the two men now stumbling back in horror. The Coeurl dashes forward and leaps on the center pair.

A stunning backhand sends the large man who appears to be the leader flying, gun tumbling out of his limp fingers as he hits the ground fifteen meters away, and needle teeth clamp down on the other man, not much more than a boy, really, savaging his chest and right shoulder. He shrieks and falls to the ground, where his cries are mercifully cut short as the Coeurl begins to gnaw out chunks from his still spasming body; must have hit the heart. Lucky for him.

I spin around to my assistant and urgently whisper to him, "Come on, we have to go! Now! It's not going to stay distracted forever!" His eyes are glazed in what looks like shock – three, maybe four seconds have passed and the horror of what just happened is probably still registering in his brain. I slap him across the face as the sounds of slugthrowers starts hammering the air; that seems to snap him out of his daze and I grab his shoulder.

"Stick close to me, we're going to make a run for that aircopter while it finishes them off and starts feeding. That's the only way we're getting out of here in one piece."

He nods fearfully and we take off in a scuttling lope, staying as low and hidden as possible while we circle around the chaos erupting in the clearing.

As I leap over tree roots and push my way through clinging tangles of vines, I sneak some quick glances at the slaughter – I can't call it a fight, as that would assume some sort of equality in the opposing forces and I know everything my creation is capable of. The images are messy, violent, and I know they'll remain seared into my mind forever, the horrifyingly beautiful spectacle of one of my children unleashed.

A woman lifted into the air by a writhing trunk while a barbed tail smashes repeatedly into her chest and face.

A man with both arms torn off stumbling blindly around, face slack and drooping, before he slowly topples over.

A casual tail lash decapitating a dark bearded head, finger uselessly clamped on the trigger even in death, rounds blowing small craters of flesh off but doing no real damage to the organically armored hide.

The throaty growl of the Coeurl as it twists and lunges at the last standing figure, a small petite woman wearing a bandanna, furiously firing into its flank before she's borne down and crushed, nightmare head swinging savagely back and forth as it tears great gobbets of flesh from her corpse.

It's getting hard to breathe but I keep pushing forward, hoping that the ravening creature will settle into its usual post-battle feeding frenzy to replace the energy just spent, completely oblivious to any non-obvious threat. I'm almost to the aircopter when I notice the body of the backhanded man feebly moving around; it looks like he survived the blow, but he most likely has some internal damage, possibly fatal if left untreated. No time to stop for him though, the aircopter is scant meters away.

Regaining control of the lab is of paramount importance, and my safety must come first.

Gate-dammit! The doors are locked, biometric security override required, no time to try and finagle my way through the system. My assistant comes panting up next to me and collapses to the ground, trying to catch his breath in short tearing gasps. He curls up and rubs at his feet in pain, the tattered remnants of his labcoat barely providing any protection to his bleeding soles.

I give him a couple seconds to recover before I grab his arm again, trying to pull him upright, but his feebly flailing limbs try to push me away. I can feel the sense of urgency in my voice.

"Come with me. We need to go get that guy lying down over there."

I motion towards the lone human still alive in the clearing, the large man with dark skin, who's even now groping around for his weapon.

"He's the only one left alive who can open this thing up, and we need his access codes. Plus, if he starts firing off that slugthrower, it'll trigger the Coeurl into combat mode again."

"Coeurl...?"

"No time, c'mon!"

With a moan my assistant pushes his way upright, shifting his weight from foot to foot like the grass underfoot was hot coals, and then we break into another lurching run, eyes constantly scanning for the movement of the creature. I don't have the heart to tell him that if it notices us, we'll never see it coming.

We finally stumble to a halt next to the fallen man and slide a shoulder underneath each of his armpits, propping him up as best we can. He groans and spits up a stream of blood; it's not the bright red of arterial fluid so he should be safe from immediate expiration. His glARs is cracked and broken, rendered useless by the force of the blow that sent him flying – we'll need him to physically handshake with the security protocols on the aircopter.

"My people... my people..." His voice is low, pained, and he winces as I bump against his right side.

"No time, what don't you fools understand about 'no time'," I snap, trying to get him on his feet. "There's no one left but us, and we need to get out of here before we become dessert. You have to open up that copter so we can get you to some medical assistance," *and us to that other lab entrance* I silently think to myself. We've got to get the experiments back under control, or Government will trigger a Case Delta, and I'm rather attached to being alive.

He nods shakily and we each slide one of his arms over our shoulders to help him move, and we slowly hobble back the way we came.

As we drag him towards the aircopter I continue to look around for the Coeurl, make sure it hasn't noticed us. Sure enough, it's settled down over one of the corpses, low rumbles of contentment quivering through its body while it continues to feed. I shudder and turn back towards the aircopter. Someone's foot catches and almost trips us all. The beast is quiescent for now, but anything could set it off into another killing frenzy.

Finally we make it back to the entrance hatch and I kneel down in exhaustion – this guy is no lightweight and we had to support his not insignificant bulk the entire way over. My assistant slumps next to me, tongue lolling out to one side of his mouth, his feet covered in scrapes and cuts. The hotel man lies sprawled out on the grass. He prods at his midsection, and winces – his questing fingers drawing audible gasps of pain as he finds each new injury. I lean over to him.

"Look, I hate to be a buzzkill, but we really need you to get that aircopter started for us. Do you think you can save the diagnosis until we're someplace a little bit safer?"

He grunts and nods. "Sorry. I'm a little fuzzy right now. That Gate-damn thing caught me a good one, and I think I cracked my head when I landed. Pretty sure my glARs would be flashing a concussion warning right now. I'll get us inside."

He levers himself to a half-crouch and places his right palm on a bioscanner next to the door. It blinks green, and a numerical keypad flips over, a command prompt blinking on the upper display. He sways for a moment, but recovers, and then enters a complex alphanumerical code with surprisingly deft fingers. The door swings open, revealing the interior of the aircopter. I help him struggle inside and wait for my assistant to clamber in before closing the door and locking it. For a short time, the only sound is our labored breathing and the gentle hum of the envirosystem.

"Name's Lyle, by the way. Guess I should thank you folks for saving my life out there; if you hadn't happened along I'd be just as dead..." His voice cracks for a moment and he struggles to maintain his composure. "Ahh shit, Raquel, Chiang, Marcus..." He trails off. "What am I gonna tell Candice..." His eyes widen. "Candice! We have to get back to the hotel, there's seven other hiking parties still out here!"

I watch him lurch towards the front cabin. Taking advantage of the momentary solitude, I take a seat next to the exhausted form of my assistant.

"Listen, when he asks, we're from the maintenance village, and we just transferred on-planet three weeks ago," I whisper frantically into his ear. "We can't let him know about the facility, no matter what. If we're lucky, we might be able to get away and grab a vehicle once we get to the hotel. I'm sure he's going to want to take us back for questioning."

My assistant straightens up and groans. "Fine, fine, whatever," he says, rubbing his ankle.

He pushes me out of the way as he limps over to a locker set in the back of the passenger compartment, the word 'Supplies' stenciled over it in block letters. He unlatches the simple metal door, and sighs in relief. Inside I can barely see several spare sets of tactical clothing and footwear, along with a basic emergency medical kit. Grabbing a pair of socks and some boots, he returns to his seat and starts cleaning off his bloody feet, hissing in pain as the disinfectant pours over his wounds and splatters on the thinly carpeted floor. He arches his spine and reaches down, head tilted back against the seat as he wriggles.

His eyes close tight as he slides the socks over his feet and then wriggles them into the boots. I can't tell if it's in pain or relief. With a brief head shake, he looks back down and starts strapping the boots up, glancing at me when he finishes.

"Well, if you don't want him to know about the facility, you might want to put your glARs away." He pauses, giving me a doleful look.

"You might also want to think about ditching your lab coat, what with it having your name embroidered across the top of it and all. 'Doc.' I know I'm not the one in charge, but that's what I'd do."

I flush, and then nod, taking off my glasses and tucking them into the pocket of my pants. Without my glARs, my vision feels suddenly dull and empty. "Good call. Keep an eye out while I crack the hatch open and toss the coat."

A moment later, evidence suitably disposed of, we head up to the front cabin to join Lyle. I duck through the door and catch him mid-conversation, presumably with someone back at the hotel.

"...Lyle, I'm just glad you're alive. When I heard the screams coming over the audiolink I thought I'd lost all of you." The woman's voice is strained.

"You almost did, Candice. Whatever that creature was, it tore through us like a hot ripsaw through butter. We never had a chance. It was huge, unlike anything I've seen. Nasty enough to wipe out an entire squad of Peacekeepers, let alone our poor crew."

"Do you think it's native to this area, or did someone bring it here?" Candice asks, her words tumbling out slowly.

"I don't rightly know. It knocked me out fairly early on, and my glARs didn't survive the impact so I doubt we have any footage of it."

Lyle turns his head as he notices that we've entered the cabin. "Look, Candice, we're headed back to the hotel, I'm bringing back two people who saved me. Hopefully they'll be able to give us a better idea of what happened out there."

"Just stay safe," Candice responds. "I'll start implementing some of the emergency lockdown procedures, but you better get back here in one piece."

"Don't you worry about me, miss." Lyle forces a grin, but I can see him wince in pain as he does. "We'll be back in two shakes of a lamb's tail. Over and out."

He clicks off the communicator and slumps back into the pilot's chair. "Either of you boys know how to fly an aircopter? I wouldn't trust myself to freefall in a gravity well right now."

I slip into the copilot's seat and nod, fingers darting over the mechanical controls as I start warming up the engine, unable to synch with the copter without my glasses on. Takes me a few minutes to go through the preflight checklist, reflexes a little rusty from disuse, but I haven't forgotten everything from my childhood. I look over at him and grin.

"I'll get us in the air, just tell me where to go. Used to race these in school all the time – mainly customized Pratchett's, but I've found the principle's the same no matter what the type."

"A copterjock, eh?" He says back, white teeth flashing in pain. "Well, I'd feel more comfortable if you were flying with a digital assist, but I reckon beggars can't be choosers. The beacon's on channel four; use access code Bravo Three Alpha. It'll take us right into the hotel security hanger."

I nod and slowly feed power to the rotors, get a feel for how she handles. Thrust controls are responsive and the stabilizers are rock steady, green lights across the board. Time to take her up. As we slowly rise off the turf a sharp crack echoes through the air and the craft shudders. A red light flashes on the diagnostic display. One of the hydraulic lines is slowly losing pressure in the right rear stabilizer fin. Aircopter's still flight capable, though I wouldn't want to have to do anything too extreme with it at high speed.

Lyle swears, his composure suddenly alert. "Gate-dammit! That was HV fire! Why the fuck are we taking HV fire?"

I throw more thrust into the vector fans and bank the aircopter into a low turn – the shot came from our right and I'm pretty sure I can keep the trees between us and whoever's pulling the trigger. Another HV report rips out but the craft stays steady – must have missed us with that one.

We pass over the edge of the clearing and I see the Coeurl rise up from its meal and quickly vanish from view into the underbrush. I look for it as we skim the treetops, but something else catches my eye.

Standing there garbed in a waist-length jacket over a grey singlesuit that flaps in the breeze is a balding man with thin grey hair. Though his eyes are shielded by boxy glARs, I know they're just as grey as the rest of him. An instant later and he's gone, replaced by the unending green of jungle canopy.

I flick the switch for the jet turbines and let the kick of acceleration push me into the seat as we head for the security hanger. It looks like bringing things back under control won't be as easy as I thought.

ROB

Timestamp – 17.20.54LT:06.18.22OT:03.18.407AG

Sonuvabitch.

Knew I should've killed that biohacker when I had the chance. Figured I'd let his 'pets' do it, karmic payback, give the universe a little laugh. Guess the joke's on me, watched him and a friend make it into the copter, dragged one of those resort people with 'em. Gutsy move with that monster running around killing everything that moves.

Look over to my left and see the Professor still trying to track the copter; it's long gone now. He's a good shot, but not that good. Bet he gets eaten if that's all he's got. He's scowling, frustrated; rich types like him don't take well to failure. Coulda told him a long piece isn't useful in a jungle, but he wouldn't have listened. Wonder who he'll blame.

Monocle hits me with a priority request over the cloud, wants to know what the creature can do. They saw some of it while it was in action, but he wants the lab notes also. For half a second I'm tempted not to give them anything, especially after they let that party get torn apart in front of us and then tried to kill the survivors, but that's not going to get me paid. Pull up the datobject and set it to read only, push it to the others.

Codename ECS-06, no data on the lettering convention, but the number puts it in the sentry classification. Alternate designation calls it a Coeurl.

Genetic splice of elephant, cheetah, scorpion, and a few bits and pieces from various others to create one fucked up monstrosity – fast, strong, smart, tough to take down. Gate-damn biohackers.

That alternate name's familiar... couple pieces click; insight. Ahh. Lab boy's a fan of really old stories.

Rest of the notes indicate he designed this thing to be highly territorial and insanely vicious, anything can set it off. Also looks like it's optimized for high-G environments, bone structure too dense, way

81

too much muscle for standard grav. Government's not using these on inhabited planets, that's for sure. Begs the question of where they *are* using it. Gonna have to do some digging after this is done.

General query from Wraparounds, he's asking who gets the first shot.

Also has a dataworm encoded in the message; he's not getting me that easy. Automatic countermeasures highlight the icon in a pulsing red, trap it in quarantine. Take a quick look at the code, nothing interesting, routine trojan horse set to copy my inputs and relay 'em back. I flush it from the buffer and wait to see what happens – no reaction. He's testing, probing, trying to see what I'm capable of. Wonder if he'll notice the counterworm I inserted into his opsys on the drive over. It's cracking his security now, should start getting some useful data soon, maybe give me some leverage.

Pretty sure I'll need it.

Monocle pops a message up, 'Open season.' Guess that means they all get a chance at the beast. Should be interesting to watch, get a feel for what they're capable of, possible strengths and weaknesses. Hopefully the other four are better than Professor, don't really feel like ending up in some monster's gut. Speaking of which...

My glARs throw up a priority Omega threat alert as they catch a glimpse of it stalking towards us through the trees. Red carats track its outline, pull up an enhanced visual, splice together standard and thermal in a composite overlay. Ugly critter, that's for sure. Looks like it wants a piece of Rhinestones and his stupid fucking sword.

It gets about twenty-five meters away before it digs in its claws and charges, barreling through the underbrush towards the disembodied glasses hanging in the air. Showtime. A cacophony of sound blasts out over the jungle canopy, like the roar of an angry giant.

Half an eyeblink and it's over, Rhinestones holding the still snapping head in one hand triumphantly while blood drips down his blade. Scattered chunks of meat rain down around him. Like most modern fights, it doesn't take long – direct my glARs to replay the last several seconds in ultraslow for analysis.

The monster leaps towards Rhinestones, muscles uncoiling with glacial slowness. The instant it leaves the ground, thirty splinter rounds shear off its right rear leg and a monofil net takes off the left – a bright yellow submunition casing ejects in a syrupy thick tumble from

Wraparounds' rifle. Before the blood can even start welling out of the pebbled skin, two buzzers drill in on either side of the creature's midsection and detonate simultaneously. A shockwave ripple bisects its body before sending the now disintegrating back half flying into the air; the front half continues its forward momentum, claws still outstretched and fangs bared, prehensile trunks writhing.

An HV round slices through the air past the head and hits the spinning barbed tail – Professor still struggling with his shots. Looks like he better recalibrate his aiming programs.

As what's left of the still snarling creature descends towards Rhinestones, he whips that stupid sword clear from its scabbard and *moves*. Fuck. Even on neurostims there's no way he should be able to move that fast, basic human musculature can't take the stress. Even in ultraslow my glasses barely catch the motion as he leans slightly to the right while whipping his blade down on the abomination's neck, a powerful two-handed slash, arms and sword a blur. Raking claws cut the air less than a millimeter from his face and he's *smiling* as they go by, an expression of almost orgiastic bliss covering his doughy face. He spins and kicks down with his heel as the rest of the torso slowly continues past, driving it into the ground, before grabbing the head in his now free left hand and turning to the face the group.

Elapsed time – two point three six one seconds. Monocle didn't even fire that Six Sixteen; guess we should be thankful for small favors. Doubt there'd be a tree standing in a twenty-meter radius if he had.

Rhinestones and Augstar immediately start squabbling over who should get credit for the kill – I tune them out and look over at Monocle. He's staring disconcertingly – pretty sure his gaze never left me during the entire spasm of violence. He inclines his head slightly and turns back to the group, his nod that of one professional to another.

Shit.

My holdout piece, standard issue twenty-shot penetrator, rests in my hand, aimed where the beast used to be. Old reflexes die hard. I quickly slide it back into the forearm holster before the others can notice. Guess I wasn't the only one getting a feel for everyone's capabilities.

The rest of them gather around Rhinestones and his gruesome trophy, where Monocle shoots a withering glare at Professor. He's not happy about that aircopter getting away and it shows. Wraparounds starts mocking Professor, giving him shit about his aim; tells him that's too much gun for him to handle, might want to stick with something small, possibly pink. The old man scowls but doesn't do anything stupid – pity.

Rhinestones stows the head into a carrybag he pulls out of one of the tacvest's pouches, but not before Augstar gets in a couple more withering comments – she's still sullen about him getting the credit, angry she didn't win. Monocle shuts them up and starts everyone on the hike back to the Vee. That aircopter came from the hotel, and he wants it found, as well as the three people on it.

Gate-dammit. Looks like we're not just hunting monsters anymore.

AIRCOPTER HERON

Timestamp – 17.53.13LT:06.50.41OT:03.18.407AG

An uncomfortable silence hangs in the passenger cabin, interrupted only by the periodic rattle of a loose bolt clanking beneath vacant seats, many holding belongings from the fallen security detail. Handbags, backpacks, digitablets all lie strewn about, grim reminders of their owners' absence. A man sitting in one of the empty padded chairs flexes his feet in newfound boots, trying to make them fit a little more comfortably, occasionally doubling over in pain. He doesn't look at the knickknacks surrounding him. In the front cabin, lush green jungle blurs past the viewscreen in a monotonous wave; off in the distance Mount Zali'ah grows gradually larger.

"We'll arrive at Hotel Calif in 10 minutes," Xander says, hands confidently manipulating the piloting yoke. Manual flying is trickier than AR-enhanced, the many diagnostic aids normally clustered in easy to recognize groups instead scattered around the control panel, but he remains calm and keeps the aircopter on a steady flight path. "Lyle, you said this beacon will take us straight to the main security hanger?"

Lyle nods wearily from his slumped position in the other pilot's seat. His eyes peer vacantly out the side of the viewscreen, shadowed stare trapped in the visceral horror of the last hour's events. His powerful frame looks frail and shrunken, like a battered oak tree after a hurricane's surge.

Xander eyes him for a moment, then sends a meaningful glance back towards the man seated in the passenger cabin. His assistant rolls his eyes and uses his thumb and index finger to pantomime zipping his lips shut, then twists his head to watch the scenery flashing by outside the fuselage windows.

Xander gives him a level glare and turns back toward the cockpit as Lyle starts talking.

"My brother used to tell me stories about creatures like that, back on Lonstar," Lyle says in a low, halting voice, pain lacing his words and giving rise to odd pauses as his breath catches and breaks. He continues to stare out a window that reflects a face splattered with blood, clothing ripped and torn by alien claws. He catches sight of his phantom image and grows distant.

"My brother called 'em demons. Said they lived in the dirt under every house in the neighborhood, one for each family. These demons, he said they fed off the family's energy. If you fed it positive energy – love, compassion, understanding – then you'd get green lawns, flowers in bloom, warm homes. If you fed it hate, or fear, or neglect, any of the thousand and one miseries you find in the dole sprawls, then there'd be dead grass, chokeweeds, drafts to chill your spine. Give it too much and it would breathe poison into the house. The first family member to inhale it would commit a horrible act. Murder. Rape. Suicide."

Lyle sighs. "I used to think people were good or bad by the color of their lawns. I avoided kids in my neighborhood because they had weeds in their front yard. And Gate protect me, none of the people with beautiful flowers ended up being child molesters – I blindly entered their homes all the time, never a care in the world!

"My brother spun this yarn to keep me in line, keep me away from some of the worst elements of the sprawls, but it right messed me up for most of my childhood. I *believed* in those demons. I *believed* that if I kept our house looking nice then we'd be safe, safe from all the nasty shit out there, most of it living right down the street. I held to that faith with a piousness that would've shocked a Fundie, mowing the grass all the time, weedin' and waterin' like they was prayers, trying all the time to look like the plutos and their perfect emerald sanctuaries."

Xander's lip twitches sardonically. "Well, as a famous ruler once said, 'religion is what keeps the poor from murdering the rich.' Some people have invisible sky friends, some people have lawn gnomes. Pick your chains in whatever color you prefer, they all shackle the same."

"Yeah, after I grew up, that's what I thought too," Lyle responds gravely. "Make my own path, live my own life. But after seeing that thing today..."

His voice trails off for several seconds.

"Maybe my brother was right. Maybe there *are* demons in this universe. Maybe there *are* gods. That thing we saw. That thing that slaughtered my crew, that butche..." Lyle chokes on the word as emotion takes over; shock finally sinking in.

"So, the Lonstar sprawls, huh?" Xander says in a feeble attempt to change the subject. "How'd you get out? Most people never leave."

"I made it out the only I could. Local Peacekeeper recruiting station the day I turned fourteen. Signed up for my twenty-year tour and never looked back." Lyle exhales softly. "Tell you the truth, I should've looked forward, considered what I was getting myself into. I'd heard the local troopers chatting at the bars, seen the way their shoulders slumped when they talked about old actions. Saw the way they held their drinks, staring into the depths, late at night when they thought no one was watching."

Lyle looks out the window once again, seeking solace in the greenery outside. "After twenty years, I know exactly what they saw in those depths. I know what made their shoulders slump. I did things I wished I'd never do, but we all pay the price for our choices. End of the day, all that matters is that I made it out."

"Of the Peacekeepers?"

"No. The sprawls."

The cabin once again falls into silence, broken only by a soft audio chime from the control panel signaling a change from thruster power back to rotor as they enter the resort's nearspace safety boundary. The deceleration pushes all three forward in their seats, subconsciously triggering an automatic look through the front viewscreen.

Outside the aircopter the verdant greenery abruptly falls away to reveal a glistening blue body of water, not quite an inland sea but far larger than a lake, where slow rolling waves lap gently against white sandy shores. A small cloud of flying creatures erupts briefly from the edge of the jungle, startled by the craft passing overhead, before wheeling off over the water; several plummet down into the waves before emerging with wriggling forms clutched in their talons. Xander smiles appreciatively at their plumage – that hack took him a solid three days to implement correctly back when they first seeded the moon with life.

A flash of motion off in the distance catches his attention and he turns toward Lyle.

"Hey, Lyle, what are those?" He motions towards the swift bodies zipping in and around the water. They appear to be wedge-shaped constructs kicking out two spumes of water from their aft region, but purely mechanical in nature.

Lyle grimaces as he takes a closer look. "Those are Aquatically Enhanced Exploratory Suits, the tourists love 'em. Forms up around your body and lets you zoom around at up to fifty kilometers an hour, and they'll descend to near a hundred meters no sweat. We call 'em Death Dolphins though, because every year a couple of those yahoos think they can ignore the shallow water warning, or deep dive out past the coastal drop off. It ends fairly predictably and then we're stuck with the cleanup. Not really sure why they're such a big draw, but folks love to take 'em out on Lake Basalt any chance they get. Waiting line's over a month-long to get one."

"Coastal drop off?" comes the question from the rear of the craft. The DDs keep pace briefly underneath the aircopter before turning back for deeper waters.

"Yeah, this lake, sea, whatever it is, it ain't natural," Lyle responds. "Original survey committee said it was formed by a 'high kinetic impact with an extra-planetary body.' Guess it was too hard to say an asteroid ran into it. Left a big ol' crater that drops down pretty steep once you get more than fifty-, seventy-five meters from shore, supposedly gets down to a couple thousand meters at some points. The DD's clearly aren't rated for that but it doesn't stop some folk from trying, and the idiots that try generally know how to disable the safety overrides."

Lyle pauses for a moment, lost in contemplation. "Yeah, those are the real nasty cleanup jobs. Nothing like explosive decompression in an enclosed space to put you off chili for a while."

"I would imagine so," Xander says drily. He swings the steering yoke over to align the guidance arrows highlighted on the interior of the aircopter's front viewscreen; the resort is faintly visible in the distance, bracketed in green, a blinding white needle bursting out of the volcano's southern slope and piercing the sky like the beginning of a lightning bolt.

As they continue over the gleaming beaches, Gehenna V covering a quarter of the sky, small shapes can be made out on the sand, soaking in the rays of the system's distant sun, or running and splashing in the shallows. Further down the shore, the broad causeway of the spaceport stretches out into the water almost two kilometers, smaller docking piers radiating out from the central hub like a spiky urchin at the end of a stick. Triangular sails dance atop the blue expanse, sailing yachts carefully staying clear of the blinking buoys marking the shuttle operating lanes.

"I didn't realize so many people stayed at the resort," Xander slowly begins, bare eyes flickering over all the moving life down below. "There must be, what, three thousand, four thousand people on this beach alone?"

"We generally average around ten thousand guests a month," answers Lyle, "though of course that's not including the worker's village. At least another four thousand live there full time to take care of everyone else. Honestly, it's more like a small city than a resort – shops, restaurants, maintenance, infrastructure, orbitals... there's a long list of stuff that goes into supplying a planet. Though I guess we can get by with less seeing as we're technically only a moon." He coughs weakly before unlatching his seat restraints and heading to the restroom at the rear of the aircopter, bracing himself against the fuselage with one hand as he moves, the other pressed tight against his right ribcage.

Xander is thoughtfully silent while the aircopter journeys on, its shadow keeping pace on the beach below, briefly shading the tiny ants as it comes between them and the sun. The sheer amount of humanity teeming across the sandy borderline between water and jungle is astonishing, he thinks, ninety-nine percent monkey yet somehow capable of spreading across the galaxy, an unstoppable tide limited only by its own blind ignorance. A voice from behind his left ear interrupts his reverie.

"Kind of makes you think, doesn't it?" His assistant's voice is low and breathy, pitched only for Xander to hear. "What the stakes are with all that stuff getting loose. Should we be concer—"

Xander cuts him off with an ugly whisper. "The Coeurl won't be leaving that hunting trail for at least two days, so, no, there is nothing to be concerned about. It's not going anywhere while it feeds, and while the casualties so far are... regrettable... there's nothing we can do for those people now other than to make our way to the core and contact Government for a response team. This has to stay under wraps, unless you want both of us taking a one-way trip into the nearest sun."

Pale blue eyes stare mercilessly into brown ones until brown is replaced by the intricate blood vessels barely visible behind a closed eyelid. Xander nods once, coldly, before turning back to the viewscreen, an audible chime announcing final approach. The assistant turns and walks back to the passenger section, brushing past Lyle as he returns from the bathroom, both of them taking their respective seats and buckling their restraints. Xander throttles down the aircopter as it slowly climbs over the resort sprawled alongside the southern flank of Mount Zali'ah.

A glittering array of pools and leafy cabanas with walkways meandering through in geometric patterns gives way to two broad multistory wings spreading out from a soaring central tower, cylindrical in shape, dotted evenly with windows around its entire circumference.

Behind the tower a third wing runs directly into the side of the massive volcano, which looms over the entire complex like a vengeful god, itself dwarfed by the gas giant covering a quarter of the sky. Each wing lies covered in a layer of black obsidian, seemingly grown from the landscape, while the central tower shines brilliantly in memplas-reinforced white marble, thrusting over seventeen hundred meters in the air.

Xander swings the aircopter around the side of the central tower and lines up the guidance arrows with an open hanger on top of the back wing of the hotel. A glowing green landing assist flashes on the viewscreen before settling into a virtual runway; the rotors whine as power slowly bleeds off and the craft gradually settles to a halt on its fat rubber tires inside the hanger bay. Two other craft, identical to the one they just arrived in, sit parked near the far right wall of the hangar, maintenance equipment scattered around the rightmost one. A smaller, sleeker vehicle lies to the left, its starkly angled planes and low profile giving it the look of an arrowhead in midflight, matte black finish drinking in the overhead glowpanel light. Waiting against the back wall is a wheeled cot with several devices attached to it being pushed by two women and a man – they immediately start towards the aircopter before the whirling blades even stop spinning in their circular wing covers.

Xander unbuckles himself from the co-pilot's chair and makes his way into the passenger cabin. With a hissing lurch, he pushes open the hatch and directs the two figures in teal medical onesuits to Lyle, listlessly slumped in his seat, before motioning his assistant to join him outside. A dark haired woman dashes past them and climbs inside as they move several meters away from the craft, and Xander takes a quick look around before whispering hushed instructions.

"Ok, remember, first chance we get to disappear, we find some kind of transport and we get to the lab access point. It looks like there's several to choose from here, and probably some ground vehicles lower down, so stay close and follow me at all times."

"Yeah, I got it the first four times you told me," comes back the sardonic response, the assistant giving Xander an unimpressed look.

Xander glowers, but is interrupted by the sounds of Lyle being helped out of the aircopter; he's leaning heavily on the shoulder of the dark haired women and the sounds of their argument are clearly audible.

"Gate-dammit, Candice, there's no time for me to be wastin' away in some damn medunit bed!" Sweat drips down Lyle's haggard face but his features are set in determination.

"Gate-dammit yourself, there's no way I'm letting you back down into the control room until Doctor Robinson clears you." Candice's voice shakes with anger and concern.

An orange haired woman interrupts the tension. "Yes, yes, you didn't even give me a chance to examine you on the copter, and you most definitely should not be moving around right now."

"Yeah, Doc, I got it, but you're just gonna have to make your way down to the control room with us, because that's where we're headed." Lyle pauses for a moment, and then he turns his head to look Candice square in the eye as he leans on her shoulder, still favoring his right side. "I know you're the boss, Candice, but we don't have time for me to lie around gettin' better. That thing wasn't natural, and we need to know where it is before more people get hurt. That means I need to start going through the sat-info to find out how to track it, and *that* means I need to be in the control room writing the proper programs. We have more pressing things to worry about than a few broken ribs."

"Speaking of which, let's get some compression on those," Doctor Robinson says, digging through her medical bags. Lyle groans and nods, slumping heavily on top of the wheeled frame. The doctor and her assistant start wheeling it towards the lift, the two other men falling in beside Candice as they walk alongside. Lyle waves a hand at them as Candice glances at Xander curiously.

"Candice, these are the two that saved my life. Dragged me right out of the middle of that mess and I owe 'em a big one. Make sure they're in the control room with us, they may have seen something I missed." Lyle motions vaguely towards Xander as the lift doors slide open. Candice and Xander shake hands, while Xander's assistant nods.

"What can you tell me about what was out there," Candice asks Xander as she activates the lift's control with her glARs. The plastic composite doors slide close and doctor Robinson begins attaching diagnostic devices to Lyle's upper right arm and neck, muttering in disapproval as biomonitor datobjects begin popping up in her vision, blinking in various degrees of distress; Lyle's breathing remains labored but steady. A slight sense of motion envelops the group as the lift descends to the main control room.

"Well, it seemed to me, and this all happened very fast mind you, that the, the creature, was big and low – like a puma, only bigger. Really, all I saw was motion and bodies flying around," Xander says. "I couldn't tell what set it off, we were just there to trim back some of the hiking trails, but we're so lucky it didn't come after us when we went to help Mr. Lyle."

"No record from your glARs?" Candice interrupts.

"No ma'am, they got lost when we made a run for the aircopter." Xander avoids brushing his hand over the right leg pocket where his glasses are stored. "My partner and I just arrived here two weeks ago, and this is definitely not the working environment the brochure promised us. Honestly, I just want to try and forget this whole day ever happened."

"You and me both," Candice sighs, as the lift doors slide open once again. In front of them stretches a large, semicircular room with multiple viewscreens covering the flat wall at the end; all the feeds depict scenes from around the resort. Several are filled with hashing static or simply lie blank. Six workstations form a smaller half circle facing the wall of screens; Lyle says something hushed to the doctor and is quickly wheeled over to one, where he grabs a generic pair of glARs and a pair of hapgloves and puts them on. As he sits up to start manipulating commands in the virtual space, the doctor and her assistant continue applying medical patches to the various cuts and bruises on his muscular torso, before eventually wrapping it tightly in compression synthsilk. He winces slightly but his hands and fingers never stop moving, a blur of datobjects and alphanumeric code filling the inside of his glasses like an epileptic fireworks display. The doctor moves to examine his left knee.

Candice looks over at Xander. "I'm going to need you two to stay here until Lyle can fully debrief you, but make sure you see doctor Robinson once she's done with him. You look like you made it through okay, but we just need to be sure." She shakes her head and walks over to Lyle, where they immediately fall into a hushed conversation, Lyle's fingers still twitching out programs.

"Doc, how are we going to get out of here?" The assistant's voice is low and fearful as he stares around the inside of the bunker-like control center.

"I think that's going to cease being a problem very, very soon," Xander replies, voice thoughtful. His eyes never leave the monitors. Across the room, Lyle and Candice both suddenly freeze midsentence.

On every single monitor on the far wall, once idyllic scenes from a pleasant beachfront resort are now filled with rampaging nightmares straight from the depth of the primal hindbrain. Guests flee mindlessly in terror as many limbed monsters rend flesh with berserker abandon, corpses strewn everywhere, ragged wings creating vast shadows on the sand as *things* wheel overhead. Candice puts a hand to her mouth to cover the silent 'O' of shock her mouth is forming, blood draining rapidly from her cheeks. A harsh alarm starts to blare.

"No, I don't think that will be a problem at all..."

XANDER

Timestamp – 18.14.36LT:07.12.04OT:03.18.407AG

The monitors are absolute chaos. My eyes flash from one to the next, rapidly scanning back and forth, but every one is filled with the same grisly tableau. There – one of the deep mine prototypes, a vibrant red puma and bat mix, is eviscerating a tourist couple from New Prague, razor keen retractalons flashing briefly before bright crimson fountains drown the feed... There – a high altitude overwatch, looking like a bird-winged pitbull, is swooping in to repeatedly savage a group of students on holiday, carrying them up to impossible heights before letting them plummet back down to the ground, broken bodies splayed across the sand... There – a hydroleviathan, as big and terrifying as it sounds, is engulfing three DDs before submerging back into the depths, rapidly widening ripples the only proof of its passing...

My creations, my children, ripping human beings apart.

The sudden surge of emotion cascading through my breast is almost overwhelming in its dichotomy. Living, breathing, sentient creatures snuffed out like so many candle flames in a Jupiter gale, but the proof of my concepts and designs is undeniable, every hour spent refining and tweaking a multitude of models with limited resources now vindicated. What I built, what I birthed, is everything I dreamed of, and more – the culminating synchrony of eHydro and mundane biomaterial in a glorious fusion of capability.

No longer will we be completely outclassed on Outpost Grendel, or the Inhospitable Zones. No longer will we have to accept the constant loss of materiel and troops to an unknowable enemy, implacable in its juggernaut advance. No longer will system after system wither and die, Gates destroyed as we flee with our tails between our legs, the burning light of humanity winking out bit by agonizing bit.

No longer will I be ignored by a Government that refuses to admit my ideas work, a Council so consumed by their own arrogance they won't even try to implement a conjecture they cannot comprehend – banished to a desolate backwater where I have to scuttle beneath the surface like some sort of beetle, afraid to poke my head up lest it be crushed underfoot. No longer will I be limited to a single hacksite, unable to implement planetwide testing of my theories, refused access to the Shadow Systems and their unlimited resources.

No longer will I be unable to protect humanity.

Finally, we have a hope of survival.

If we survive the next twenty-four hours. The trip back to Central Core looks to be significantly more difficult than it was ten hours ago – with what looks like every attack organism from the lab capable of operating in a terrestrial atmosphere rampaging over the resort – and the first order of business is going to be escaping this control room.

"Hsst! Listen up!" I motion at my assistant, who is busy gawking at the carnage unfolding on the screens in front of us. He slowly turns and faces me, eyes wide, whites showing at the edges. "This is our chance. When those two decide they have to go play hero and save everyone out here, we're tagging along until we get outside. After that, we disappear and head back to Central Core. The situation is going to be extremely chaotic, and they'll assume we got scared and decided to bail out."

His face drops, then firms into an indignant scowl. "Wait a minute. Why in Kufit's name are we even going back to Central? There's no way Government is covering this up with a cleanup team. I'm getting the fuck out of here. This is *not* what I signed up fo—"

"Well, there's one thing I forgot to mention," I say quietly.

His eyes narrow as he glares at me.

"There's a killswitch we can trigger, an enzyme built into each biostruct. Shuts them all down. Permanently."

His eyebrows try to crawl through the top of his hairline. "You arrogant fuck! What the shit were you going on about 'contacting Government' for, then? Why didn't you just stop this nightmare the instant you lost containment of your wretched little nightmares running amok out there?!"

"Calm down!" It's all I can do to keep my voice below a shout. "First off, I didn't know the severity of the breach. I thought it might have been only a few of the upper cells. Second, 'shutting them down' means liquifying every single one of those immensely expensive, not to mention irreplaceable, biohack investments that prove my theories, and that's not a call I was going to make capriciously. Third, the killswitch trigger is in Central Core, along with the reboot protocols, so if we made it there you never would've needed to know. Fourth, *no one* is cleared to know the killswitch option other than me and the Security Council, and they stopped responding to my updates thirteen years ago! The only reason I'm telling you now is that, without your help, there's no way I'm going to make it back to the Core." I try to infuse every syllable of what I'm saying with the absolute truth that I feel, and it's true. Without him, I'll have no chance at getting past Prime, let alone the madness erupting outside. I may not necessarily use the killswitch, since it looks like the moon is going to have to be quarantined anyway, but he doesn't need to know that. I take a deep breath before continuing, mixing a lot of fact with a little fiction, trying to bring him around.

"Fifth, if we don't get this under control, it's a Case Delta."

"Case Delta?"

"Eurypides Nine. Lethe Four. The Aeneas Complex. Every other system that's 'accidentally' been destroyed during Government's reign."

His expression turns puzzled. "But those *were* accidents. Eurypides was a Gate malfunction, and the other two went nova – those Gates were destroyed on the far end. All the rest got blown up by Resistance terrorist cells."

I shake my head slowly. "That's the official story. The real story is a bit trickier. How is Government supposed to explain that we've lost multiple systems to an alien civilization without setting off universe-wide panic? Case Deltas are called when a system is gone beyond hope of retrieval, and the only option is to sterilize and withdraw. Black Colony comes in, cleans up the mess, and no one that's not affiliated with Government travels there for the next two hundred years. Worst case, they blow the Gate behind them to prevent further contamination, and then no one travels there again. Ever."

I stare into his widening eyes. "We're at war, and not just against the Resistance. We've been at war for over one hundred years. We don't know what they want, we don't know who they are, we don't even know how to talk to them. All we know is they're overrunning every colony they find, and they don't leave any survivors. We're fighting Nemesis. And we're losing."

He rubs his face in frustration. "What. The. Fuck. You're talking serious conspiracy theory shit here, man. There's no way Government could keep a secret like that for this long! Not with the tech we have now."

"You'd be surprised. Omnipresent surveillance and a highly developed sense of self-preservation for the status quo leads to a remarkable ability to control data, especially when Gates provide such handy chokepoints. Government monitors everything that goes through, physical and electronic, and you'd be shocked at how few people it takes to oversee that with good VI assists. Someone gets through broadcasting the wrong information, and within a manner of seconds they're blocked and under quarantine. Then they disappear. 'Engine failures.' 'Contraband smuggling.' 'Gate Induced Psychosis.'

"Whatever they need to do, whatever they need to say, whatever it takes to protect the secret – that's what happens, and someone vanishes."

He stares at me for an endless moment, and I can see his mind struggling to cope with a drastically changed view of reality. I can't say that I blame him – I imagine most people don't deal with the news that we're at war with an alien civilization well, or that we're losing, *or* that our ostensible protectors are perpetrating the largest lie ever imagined.

It's a lot to take in. Case Delta is a bit of a half-truth though – once Government sees how well my babies are working, there's no way they'll wipe the moon. They need my data far too desperately.

"But forget about that. Right now, our main concern is getting back to Central and getting this back under control." I arch an eyebrow slightly and apply the goad. "Unless, of course, you want to be on the wrong side of a Case Delta. Believe me, we're out in this backwater for a reason, and Government's far more likely to clean everything out and start over, including us, if they have to sterilize the planet. Until they learn the value of my children, they have no reason to keep us alive."

He shudders momentarily, and then nods, convinced of the utter lack of choice facing us. "Yeah. Yeah, you're right. You make your move, I'll be right behind you."

I'm glad that he's finally come around, because it looks like the two resort functionaries are snapping out of their shock induced stasis. The women barks a few quick words at the security man and then runs over to us.

"You two, you're coming with me. We need to get up top and get these people to safety. Our glARs alerts aren't getting out over the net so we're going to have to do this the old fashioned way – person to person. We'll start with the main building and then spread out from there."

I adopt a subservient posture and nod my head. "Of course, ma'am. Whatever we can do to help. This is terrible, just terrible." I debate whether or not to wring my hands, but decide against it. No point in being too obvious.

She beckons us over to the lift and we pile inside. As she triggers the manual floor select on the lift control panel, a hand interposes itself between the doors and the security man pushes his way in, bald scalp beading with sweat from the sudden exertion.

He finishes hastily buckling a tacvest around his bandage-wrapped torso, muscled arms bare except for a combat knife strapped to his right forearm, sheath covering part of the kinetic motor of his hapgloves. The woman swears.

"Lyle! Gate-dammit, I told you to stay in the security bunker. You're in no condition to be running around right now!"

"With all due respect, ma'am, there's not much I can accomplish back in there that I can't do by your side. The networks are completely corrupted at this point, and you're going to need someone to watch your back with all those, those devils running around. I'm still the best security member on this staff and I'll be damned if I let you go out there alone."

Her eyes flash with a deep fire, and it seems like she's almost on the verge of chewing him out, but then she deflates with a sigh.

"Gate save me from heroes... Fine, but if we see anything, anything at all," her voice sharpens, "we take cover and disengage. You've already cheated death once, let's not go risking it again."

He eyes her as the doors close and we slide into motion. "Whatever you say, ma'am."

The doors open up into a lobby that looks like what the old religious teachings called Hell. Blood streaks splash crazily along the white marble pillars and floors, and half the lights are shattered, sparking uncontrollably while the scattered remains of resort guests litter the ground; dark lumps oozing sodden puddles. Screams can be heard off in the distance, along with shriller, piercing cries – hunting calls.

Candice takes the lead, Lyle behind her. My assistant and I follow them closely as we set off through striated shadowlight.

Our footsteps ring out through the eerily deserted atrium, echoing off high ceilings, the only noises in a once bustling thoroughfare. Halfway to the sunlight-limned exit, the security man holds his hand in the air signaling a halt. As we freeze, the sounds of our passage dying away, a shuffling scrape emanates from the darkened corner near the door.

BTH-03, Crusher, slowly emerges into the light, all two thousand kilos of armored carapace and lumpy brawn splintering the ground with every curiously dainty step. Three toed legs paw the floor while wide-set eyes on a horned head quest about, sampling the electric currents in the air, scanning for motion – searching for a target. A nictitating membrane slides sideways across its pupils as they narrow, and then it turns towards us and goes completely still, muscles bulging out its dermal plating as it crouches down, preparing to charge.

Shit. We're about to be trampled underneath the obliterating feet of a creature designed solely to inflict as much mayhem as possible while soaking up unfathomable amounts of punishment, an Old Terra bull with the world as its china shop, but this is also a perfect opportunity to split away from the two resort idiots. As long as we can keep it in a relatively open space, we shouldn't be in much danger – I designed all the combat algorithms, after all.

I reach into my pocket and carefully put my glARs back on. ARdverts immediately static and craze through my vision, their physical RFID chips cracked and splintered beyond repair, a digital cacophony of dying ghosts.

If I read the layout of the building complex right...

I shout at the hotel staff standing frozen in front of me. "We'll lead it off, lose it back within the hotel; you two go help the people outside and get them to safety." Distraction set, I take off in a dead sprint at a side door marked "Observation Platform," hoping my assistant has the wits to recognize our chance.

"No wait!" Lyle screams, but he's too late.

With a quick burst of speed I slam through the door, a cavernous tunnel stretching off into the distance before us, gouged drill marks still clearly visible by the emergency lighting on the walls. I can hear my assistant's harsh breathing behind me, along with the growing thunder of Crusher's rush.

My assistant makes a beeline past me for the lift platform, but I grab his arm and head to the staircase leading down – if we get caught with no room to maneuver then we'll just be two more stains on the already covered floor.

Crusher *can* be evaded, but not in any type of enclosed area. Our footsteps clang and echo off the cavern walls as we sprint down the metal stairs two at a time.

We reach the bottom of the steps just as the beast crashes through the wall and into the lift, sending itself and the platform spinning twenty meters down to the tunnel floor in a clattering din. With a snort, Crusher rights itself and shoulders its way out of the wreckage, metal tearing and screeching as the vast bulk of its body grinds broken components into the gritty basalt. It swings its head side to side and starts sampling the air again, before facing us and dropping down into another crouch.

I grab my assistant's arm and we run deeper into the volcano, the sounds of pursuit growing ever louder behind us.

ROB

Timestamp – 18.43.03LT:07.40.31OT:03.18.407AG

Feet shuffling behind me, flashing message conversations scrolling past my eye in an endless litany of complaints – seems like this hike back to the Vee is taking forever. Sun's blazing overhead. Enviro filters in the tacsuit are trying their best to keep me cool, but the heat's winning.

Humidity doesn't help either, damp blanket stifling my lungs.

A low breeze cuts through for a second, almost makes the temperature tolerable, and then it turns rank and cloying, my stomach suddenly clenching as I try not to gag. The stink coming off that head Rhinestones is lugging over his shoulder is unimaginable. Only thing making it even slightly bearable is the expression on his face as the toxic miasma constantly swirls around him, everyone else giving it a wide berth. Hope he's enjoying his "trophy."

Asshole.

Check the navguide, little over a half click to go, most of it through open terrain. Geotags show a wildfire ripped through here three years ago, blinking summaries of dates and intensities sparkling in a virtual blaze of their own. Close the datobject and glance around – navguides and geotags are helpful, but nothing beats eyes on the ground.

Heavy, vine-shrouded tree limbs gradually peter out as we make our way into the rippling swathe of new growth created by the fires. Looks like a little bit of prairie in the middle of a jungle as we step out into the scar, sparse clusters of saplings breaking the dense field of waist high thatch like scattered sentinels. The broad green blades poking out of the turf are taxing to push through, an emerald field of living mud. GlARs are having trouble sensing anything farther than one meter in – grass is too thick. Not ideal.

I'm about halfway through the rolling verdant carpet when a commotion breaks out behind me – sounds like another argument, electron anger spilling out into the physical world. Interestingly, though, this time it's between Wraparounds and the Professor.

Wraparounds keeps needling him about missing those shots, telling him his aim is about as good as his ability to value corp projections properly, and it looks like the Professor's about to lose his shit.

Should be fun.

Yup, there they go. Professor's all up in Wraparound's face now, hands clenched at his sides, spit flying as he screams at the kid – calls him a spoiled brat, a famewhore, a worthless waste of body sculpted flesh who'll die old and abandoned soon as the pop trends shift.

Wraparounds just laughs and laughs and laughs, provoking even more histrionics from the child trapped in a geriatric's body.

Take a look around, the other three are watching, just like me – trudging through this crap isn't easy, and the rest feels nice. Can't wait to sit back down in the Vee, get some cool air going through the enviros, though I'm not looking forward to anything coming after that. Monocle's been asking for schematics on the resort, room access codes, sensor security protocols – looks like he was serious about that "no survivors" bit.

This is gonna get ugly.

No help for it though, have to get that money for my baby, for Jennifer. Crack this whole miserable moon apart if that's what it takes to get her life back to normal.

Professor vents some more spleen, then finally falls silent. Looks like break time's over. He pushes past the rest of the group, lips thin and white with compressed anger, and starts bulldozing through the grass, arms swinging indignantly at his s—

<<threat trigger Epsilon;>>

Shit.

<<confirmed hostiles – six;>>

Fingers jerk like a seizure victim, datobjects gyrating in the mad dance of combat.

<<projected additional hostiles – six;>>

Right hand comes up, left palm moving to brace.

<<cross-referencing datobject: xanderNotes0217;>>

Slide engages, index finger clenches.

<<searching...;>>

Pop.

<<confirmation match;>>
Pop.
<<uploading...;>>
Pop.
<<combat cloud upload complete;>>
Pop.
<<threat shift Beta;>>

Rapidly fading red outlines scuttle away from the Professor's spasming body as it collapses to the ground, angular shapes disappearing into the tall vegetation with barely a ripple, shaded threat vectors gradually widening around us in elongated blobs of potential ambushes. One outline blinks and then holds steady a short way off, but I ignore it as I sprint over to what is very likely to be a corpse, holdout still clutched in my right hand.

Reach the locator beacon marking Professor's last known position, broad blades trampled by thrashing feet, odd tracks churning up the fecund turf. Look down at the splayed figure and query his biomonitors to confirm... yup, Professor's dead, silent rictus scream on his face the last expression he'll ever make, body deflating like a balloon as his insides liquefy and dribble out his orifices. Hard way to go out, that's for sure.

Sucks for him, opportunity for me.

<<execute batteringRam v.3.5.x;>>

Do a quick scoop of his glARs, brute force the security measures with an illegal Agency program, almost a limited VI in its own right. Searches for keywords, images, anything potentially incriminating, and transfers them over. Couldn't use it before, leaves too many traces in an active user's VI. Doubt Professor's gonna let anyone know, he's too busy decomposing.

Couple interesting datobjects highlight on the initial scan, looks like the old boy had a predilection for chimeras. Didn't exactly keep them as pets either – too many intimate personal sensor records for that. No mention of his supplier, bit of a shame. Agency would love to shut another slavesplicer down. Gonna need to audit the gcred summaries for that info.

Not much else jumps out, fairly standard Arbiter life of graft, greed, corruption. Deals made, promises broken, lives ruined, the usual litany of success. Save it all to my glasses, then wipe his VI, keep the other four from noticing any snooping.

No point being sloppy.

Close the summaries as the four hunters arrive, weapons out and wavering over the sea of grass, tentatively searching for targets. Lazy fucks didn't even get a shot off, but I did, and I think one laned. Maybe they didn't want to. Definitely no love lost between the members of this happy little family, constantly snapping at each other's throats.

Wraparounds moves in and leans over the grisly remains, probably capturing some memories for later, small half-smile on his perfect lips.

Rhinestones and Augstar look as if they're about to join him, then Monocle barks at them to form a perimeter, make sure we don't get caught with our pants down. They jump to obey, scattering like chastised toddlers, and he peers over for his own examination, lips pursed tight as he sees the Professor's melting body. Shakes his head once, then starts scanning the perimeter as well.

Highlight the info I squirted to the local net for him and go back over it myself, get a better idea of what we're up against. SWC-02, alternate designation "Venom Wolf" – some sort of scout/soldier hybrid, designed to get into a wide variety of places unseen and then swarm unsuspecting targets. Agile, almost one and a half meters long, pack mentality, and armed with a highly venomous verrucotoxin designed to destabilize chemical bonds at the atomic level, delivered through a barbed probiscis. Prefers hit and run tactics, asymmetrical warfare – the death of a thousand cuts.

Notes indicate they'll try and overwhelm a target with sheer numbers though, if they think the odds are right; fire ants swarming a lion. Another creation from that biohacker's diseased mind... fuck, this one's worse than the "Coeurl." At least that one was alone.

Stand up, scanning around, threat vectors still widening and shifting, no sound but our breathing and the wind sighing through grass and trees.

Put a destination marker on the one I splashed and indicate a group move – we slowly make our way over to the question mark icon until we're standing over the remains of... Gate above, what the shit *is* that?

Penetrator hit center of mass and punched out through the other side, must have taken a vital organ or two on the way, but what's left looks *wrong*, in a way the lab images can't convey. Vaguely insectoid, six legs, multiple jutting spikes sweeping out from its back and sides, chromatophore carapace fading from a striped pattern matching the surrounding vegetation to the dull purple-black of a week old wound. What looks like two feathery antenna curl off above multifaceted eyes, and below those a pair of mandibles loll open exposing the glistening tip of what must be the injector, the proboscis.

Looks like a Gate-damned cockroach from Old Terra Hell mixed with a wolf's frame and size.

What the fuck kind of sick mind creates something like this?

Mental shake, worrying about that can wait for later. Right now, we have to figure out a way back to the Vee. No chance we're getting Professor's corpse back there, nobody brought a bucket... right, seems Monocle has it covered. Pretty sure that's a mini-thermal he just lobbed onto the flattened pile of skin; really hope he has it set to remote detonation and not timed, otherwise we're all gonna be eating plasma. GlARs ping softly – he's uploaded our next step to the cloud.

Here we go.

Combat sweep forward, modified diamond, Rhinestones on point, Augstar left, Wraparound right, I'm covering rear, Monocle on overwatch.

Motion left, three shapes rippling in, glARs highlighting and tracking in bright red outlines, Augstar's buzzer takes one and the other two arrow off, flanking attack right coming out of the grass. Flechette burst and monofil submunition from Wraparounds take out another two, my breath coming hard as we press forward.

Eyes scanning scanning scanning. Motion to the right but it's another feint, outlines vanishing back into grass after the first penetrator shot.

Three hundred meters left to the Vee.

Two Wolves leap from *under the ground* as we pass over but Rhinestone's blade is quicker. Bisected remains thrashing spastically underfoot, the crunching of exoskeletons counterpointing ragged breaths and weapon reloads as we continue to advance.

Two hundred meters to the Vee.

Several quick probes break off at the first sign of resistance. Nothing, nothing, nothing. Threat vectors circling and widening in the sudden disappearance. Audio warnings eerily silent.

One hundred meters to the Vee.

Threat vectors converge *behind* along with the shrill danger tone from my glARs as a rippling tide of red boils out. Fire shot after shot while submunitions explode in ragged geysers of dirt and ichor but it's not enough, they're getting too close too close a wave of dripping mandibles and spiked chitin about to overwhelm us—

<<*sensor overload: thermal;*>>

Fucking fuck, I *hate* Six Sixteens. The ground behind us lies scorched and cratered in a fifty-meter square, indescribable bug parts littering the ground, and the line of devastation stops less than a centimeter from my toe. Cocky son of a bitch.

I turn and glare at Monocle, but he just winks and tips his hat with the barrel of that carnage machine before holstering it and turning toward the Vee.

No choice but to admire his tactics though – looks like he was waiting for them to cluster up for a final rush before nailing everything at once. If he'd fired any sooner, they would've split and overwhelmed us from multiple directions simultaneously. Takes more than training to make that decision, takes experience in the field. Definitely Black Colony.

We climb into the Vee unscathed. Looks like we either cleared out the area, or those things are waiting for reinforcements. I'd like to believe it's the former. Rhinestones loads his stinking head into a container in the back, but it seems no one's interested in grabbing a bug to take home. Shame. Would make a great conversation piece, give the other vermin something to talk about when they stop by for society hour.

A white flash and sudden whipping gale announces the funeral pyre of the Professor, and then we're heading back down the trail to the spaceport, Vee bouncing along the bumpy dirt road.

Monocle wants to stop and replenish our weapon systems before we hit the resort, make sure we're prepared for anything. Wraparounds links me the images of what's going on there. Place is getting torn apart. Looks like a war zone.

Looks like the inevitable result of biohacking.

Crank up the acceleration in the Vee and initiate phase two for the commfrastructure worm; the surviving resort guests are going to be trying to get out of here, and I can't let that happen until I get my money, can't let them send out a warning. Feel that twinge again, conscience screaming at my dereliction of duty, but I stamp it down, think of Jennifer, think of her future.

Worm goes to work and the local nets crash instantly, all communications down. Now it's just us and the monsters.

Hope these hunters brought plenty of gear.

They're gonna need it.

HOTEL CALIPH

Timestamp – 18.59.08LT:07.56.36OT:03.18.407AG

Candice and Lyle watch in shock as the two men who brought Lyle back sprint off into the access tube that leads to Mt. Zali-ah's core, the thundering mass of some *thing* right on their heels. The men barrel through the door several steps ahead of it, and then the entire wall disappears in a rending screech of torn metal and splintered memplas.

Dust billows out from the tangled wreckage, and faint sounds of destruction slowly trail off from inside the tube.

"Should we go help them, Lyle?" Candice's face is pale, lips slightly parted and slack as she struggles to comprehend what she just saw, but her tone is resolute.

"No ma'am," Lyle responds. "They've drawn the threat away from us, and we need to focus on the guests and workers. Those two sure are mighty resourceful though, lot more motivated than the usual maintenance types we get here..."

His voice trails off and he sends a quick info query to the central cloud, the parameters new hires within the last two weeks, but the data corruption's getting worse and nothing comes back except garbled log entries and hashed images, along with snippets from a recently popular ARpop song. Lyle frowns, and then minimizes everything except basic image augmentation – the glARs can handle those processes internally. No sense including any distractions. He looks over as Candice starts speaking.

"In that case, let's start rounding up whoever we can find on the way and get to the spaceport – once we're in orbit we should be able to sort this mess out from relative safety." Candice's voice is firm, in charge.

Lyle nods. "We're going to be running blind, ma'am. Looks like the clouds are offline. Hope you remember your way around the grounds."

Candice smiles grimly. "What kind of manager would I be if I couldn't run this place in my sleep, Lyle? It's a relatively straight shot through the front gardens to the south motor pool. We can grab a Vee, and then we'll follow the road down. C'mon, let's go."

The two cautiously make their way out of the wrecked atrium and into the open air of the resort entrance. Stretching down the hillside in front of them lie the tangled ruins of the once graceful memplas pool rings, now leaking water from their shattered frames and turning the carefully tended botanical features into a swampy morass. Shrieking cries and the sounds of combat echo all around, penetrator and HV rounds sending up distinctive cracks as the security details of the more prominent guests work desperately to keep their charges safe.

The sprawled remnants of bodies littered across the ground attests to the growing futility of their efforts – dark-suited bodyguards and festively dressed guests united in their stillness. Candice feels her rage growing with each mangled corpse, each ward she's failed, and her jaw clenches tightly.

"What the fuck is going on out there, Lyle? We're a resort destination, not a Gate-damn war zone. Did corp send you anything on potential threats like this?"

Lyle shakes his head gravely.

"No ma'am, they didn't. I'm just as much in the dark on this as you ar— "

A heavy burst of nearby HV fire chatters through the air and sends Lyle diving to the ground, pulling Candice along with him. Memplas splinters and deforms partway up the central tower behind them, hyper-kinetic rounds slamming into the windows and façade of the hotel, creating deep starbursts in the resilient material.

Several projectiles punch through, and chunks of flowing crystal rain down into the nearby grass, smashing deep divots and craters. Panting in the dirt, Lyle motions for Candice to stay down, and cautiously raises his head to scan the surrounding area.

The supersonic cracks taper off, leaving an eerie silence. Candice shifts to get off the ground, but Lyle places a hand on her shoulder, shaking his head.

"Give it a second, ma'am. Saw too many situations like this in the Peacekeepers. You get a momentary lull after all the itchy trigger fingers get taken out, and then the experienced ones hit you from someplace you never expected. Better patient than dead."

Candice glances over at him, looking for an excuse to take her mind off her racing heart. "What, exactly, did you do in the Peacekeepers, Lyle?"

Lyle is silent for a moment, eyes looking at Candice without seeing her. "You sure you want to hear about that? Gate's truth, it's not really something I'm proud to recall."

Two more HV reports echo out, and something shrieks in the distance, an eerie, alien sound. Candice flinches, but holds Lyle's eyes. "It doesn't look like we're going anywhere anytime soon, so let's have it."

"You're the boss, boss."

Lyle clears his throat, one hand wiping a smudge of dirt off his cheek, and leans back against the side of the concrete flower bed, a giant statue stretching overhead. The last rays of the system sun shine through a ruby in the statue's hands, turning the ground around them a deep crimson. Candice leans next to him, brushing up against his shoulder.

"My first op was on Finley III, a standard one year policing detail, one of those 'ease the newbies into things gradually' deals. I had just finished basic training, as raw as they come, full of vim and vigor. I didn't understand yet what it was the Peacekeepers actually did."

He sighs.

"About four months into the op, there was an… incident. One of the Peacekeeper squad captains, Varin Johannes, decided that a local girl wasn't sufficiently impressed by his authority, so he raped her. Repeatedly. And he kept her glARs on full transmit to her family while he did it."

"Hijo de puta…"

"Yes, ma'am. Naturally, her family didn't take too kindly to that, and one of her brothers found Johannes at a bar the next night. The brother brought a machete, and he took his time. Made sure to leave Johannes' glARs on full transmit, too; sorta poetic when you think about it."

"What happened to him? The brother?"

"Well, Government's standing procedure is to pacify the planet on the first sign of any aggression towards a Peacekeeper – meant to keep people in line, remind them who holds the Gates. Remind them of the costs of disobeying.

"That very night, the commander declared planetary martial law. He didn't have a choice. He sentenced the brother to death in absentia, and sent us to round him up. I was in the squad that surrounded the brother's hab. Our orders were to keep him from escaping. Only, he had no intention of escaping."

Lyle's face turns sorrowful.

"What we didn't know at the time was that Resistance had been in contact with the planet, was secretly smuggling them printers capable of banned munitions. Cluster rounds, tacnukes, bio-grenades – the whole kit and caboodle. Seems Finley III had never really liked the way Government treated them, something to do with their labor being consistently undervalued by the Arbiters, and so they wanted out. Wanted control of their own lives. Johannes just happened to be the spark."

Another HV round cracks into the hotel behind them, and a faint scream cuts off abruptly. Candice winces, but Lyle's eyes are lost in memory.

"The first thing I can remember is the micro-flechettes whispering out of the hab windows like death's own lullaby. A third of the squad went down instantly, cut in half where they stood. They never even had time to recognize that they were dead. Then the cluster rounds started exploding."

Lyle's voice is peaceful, empty.

"There's a curious beauty in a cluster round, the way the initial explosion blossoms out into secondary effects, like a rippling flower made of fire. That's actually their nickname, 'fireflowers,' but I didn't find that out until later."

"Lyle…"

"Anyway, the fireflowers took out another third – it was only pure luck that I survived. I was posted in a nearby comm structure overlooking the hab, and the reinforced memplas managed to hold against the blast wave, kept me safe. A lot of others weren't so lucky. The ones caught out in the open went clean, instant incineration."

Candice winces, but Lyle doesn't notice.

"The ones with only partial cover didn't go so clean. See, if you're close but you don't get hit by the initial plasma bloom, a fireflower superheats the air around and inside you, cooks your lungs right quick.

"Docs say it takes about ten minutes to actually die after your lungs char – seems the damage isn't quite enough to asphyxiate you immediately, but every breath is like having hot coals shoved down your throat. Bad way to go."

Candice places a hand on Lyle's arm. "Lyle, I'm sorry. You don't have to tell me anymore, it's okay."

Lyle quirks his mouth sadly, and some emotion enters his voice again. "Don't worry, ma'am, it was a long time ago. There's plenty of therapy visits between me and them, now. Government's real keen on making sure you can keep going after something like that, because they know you'll see it over and over.

"Like I was sayin', the fireflowers took out a bunch more, and then they opened up with HV. Sounds like lightning bolts going off right near your ear, and the next ten seconds were an absolute thunderstorm. We fired back, of course, those of us that were left – tried to lay down some suppression to buy time to evac out – but all we had were low density projectile throwers. We were outmatched and we knew it. Weren't no way we could maintain a perimeter at that point.

"After the initial surge, the brother and a bunch of his friends come boiling out of the hab, like maddened wasps, spraying HV everywhere. We managed to get a couple of them, but most escaped, dashing down side streets and into other habs."

The emotion leeches out of Lyle's voice once more.

"Orbitals were tracking them, of course. They didn't get far. The initial salvo of kinetics obliterated five of the surrounding habs, each one home to over twenty thousand people. The next salvo took out five more, just to be sure.

"The next day, Government embargoed the system, and open warfare raged across the surface of Finley III. Resistance armed forces laid booby traps, set ambushes, took out orbitals – anything they could do to try and convince us to abandon the planet – and all the while they tried everything possible to blow the Gates. You see, that's the only way Resistance ever succeeds. Cutting themselves off from everyone else, forcing us light years away.

"Government obviously had no intention of abandoning the system, and so we fought. Most Peacekeeper units aren't very well trained, but the commander made sure we were prepared for anything, so we lived where others died. We were outgunned at first, but somehow he got us through those first couple days, and then it was just a matter of time.

"It took us four months to pacify enough of the population to reopen the Gates, and we ended up killing almost fifty percent of the people on Finley III alone. They're still trying to rebuild there – I've been keeping tabs on the place."

Lyle looks over at Candice. "I feel kind of responsible, you know? I could've said something, refused to fight, refused to obey. I know they would've spaced me, and all those people would've died, but I still could've done it. At least it would've been something." He looks back at the ground.

"That was my life for the next twenty years. We earned a reputation for solving problems, taking care of the trouble spots, and so they sent us out again and again. Commander walked out an open airlock five years in, couldn't deal with it anymore, but by then we were too good. We kept surviving."

Candice grips his hand.

"I'm sorry Lyle. I never knew."

Lyle stares at her, eyes blank.

"Ain't nothing you could've done about it, ma'am. Tried to save what little humanity they couldn't take from me – use the skills I learned to keep folks safe instead of harming 'em. That's why I'm here now, on Eden with you."

He looks away.

"Only, I've failed again. Raquel, Chiang, Marcus, our guests… I couldn't keep them safe. Couldn't do a Gate-damn thing."

Lyle clenches his empty hand in the torn up grass, and silence fills the air.

"Well, sitting here crying isn't going to save anyone else. Andale, cabron, up and on your feet!" Candice's voice is sharp, though not harsh, and Lyle's head whips back around. He chuckles roughly.

"You're for sure right about that, ma'am. Sounds like things have quieted down around here a bit. We're probably safe to move now." The two scramble to their feet, and Lyle looks over at Candice. "And, well, thanks, ma'am. Thanks for listening, and just, well, being you."

Lyle takes point and they advance down the slope, dashing from cover to cover – one a jagged memplas pool tube impaled in the ground, the next an uprooted firberry hedge, dirt-covered roots stabbing the sky like miniature spears, the third a burned out cultivator bot leaning drunkenly to one side as its pruning arms slump into the mud. They pause at each improvised shelter, eyes darting about in every direction, ears trying to filter out the trumpeting blasts of hellish noise and constant chattering of projectile fire echoing from all around.

After several more quick sprints, Lyle stops them just behind the wreckage of a small maintenance cart near a thicket of trees, close to the bottom edge of the grounds. Clustered near-palm trunks stretch over a hundred meters to each side, their broad green leaves radiating out from symmetrical branches and creating dark shadows underneath. Candice shifts restlessly behind the cart.

"Why are we stopping, Lyle? The motor pool's just on the other side."

Lyle frowns. "I don't like it, ma'am. Those trees could hide anyone, or anything. This is a perfect spot to go stumblin' into a trap. There's going to be a lot more folks with itchy trigger fingers wanderin' around out here right now, so let's just give it a minute and do a quick glARs sc—"

He cuts off his musings as a shout rings out from behind them, a group of four people bursting forth from the entrance of the hotel Lyle and Candice just vacated. Lyle zooms in on them as best he can through the smoke and wreckage littering the hillside, brief glimpses of movement visible between gaps in the oily clouds rising off the various hulks of broken machinery. Three are dressed in sober black singlesuits, two women and a man, HV rifles and penetrators dancing back and forth as their focus alternates between the surrounding environment and the old woman huddled between them. They slowly start escorting her down the main path in a triangular formation. Candice moves to stand up but Lyle yanks her down sharply.

"Lyle! What are you doing? We need to help secure those people."

Whatever Lyle's response might have been is lost in the earsplitting scream that erupts from the copse of trees, and the mad rush of the creature careening out.

Candice catches a glimpse of five asymmetrical limbs covered in oddly rustling spines before the *thing* is past their hiding place and barreling up the hill towards the small group of people, its asynchronous lurching gait covering ground at a remarkable pace. The three security personnel turn and start pouring fire into it, several penetrator rounds spanging through the maintenance cart and whipping past Lyle and Candice's face, but the torrent of fire only succeeds in knocking off several spines before the ungainly five-legged urchin jumps into the middle of the security detail.

With a sound like a confetti popper going off, it bursts apart in an explosion of spines.

Candice gasps softly, and then zooms in with her glARs. All four people are down on the ground, punctured by multiple barbs, blood pooling and running down the close-set marble slabs of the garden walkway. She focuses in on the fallen guests and notices that the spines jutting out are starting to vibrate madly, what looks like a bulge traveling down their length into the shuddering corpses. As each bulge passes from sight, the bodies twitch once and then lie still – oddly, the blood seems to have stopped pumping out of the wounds as well.

Four humanoid forms lurch upward, clumsily at first, but with greater and greater mobility, almost as if they're learning how to move again. Within seconds, all four are hooting softly to each other, before they raise their heads and start sniffing at the air. Blood streaked faces with vacant eyes turn and stare directly at Candice, and then the four former guests start knuckling their way down the slope in a curious shuffle, like a gorilla making its way through the jungle floor.

"Shit. Candice. Candice! We gotta go, right now!"

Stunned, Candice realizes she's been staring at the advancing figures that are now only fifty meters away and heading directly at their temporary shelter behind the smashed cart. She scrambles to her feet along with Lyle and they scramble over the wreckage towards the trees.

Candice gasps out a question as they break into a sprint.

"But what if there's another one of those exploding things in there, Lyle?!"

"We'll just have to risk it! Go!"

The two push their way into the thicket, branches grasping and clutching at their clothing, durable synthsilk protecting from the worst of the tears. Candice's glasses reveal nothing but a confusing welter of springy limbs and shrubs, leafy greenery slapping her face with

115

scratchy blows, and she feels her pace slow as roots try to snare her feet. Low hooting can be heard rising in volume from behind, and Candice risks a glance over her shoulder.

Through gaps in the near-palm leaves, she sees two of the security detail take to the trees, climbing up in a motion so natural it seems instinctive, before swinging and leaping from branch to branch, their long hair flowing in the dank jungle air. The old woman and the lone man remain earthbound, shouldering their way through the undergrowth, spines still protruding obscenely from their bodies and occasionally catching on branches, causing them to stumble. Despite the slowing effect of the chitinous barbs, they're closing the gap rapidly, their crouching run much more suited for the tangled thicket than Lyle and Candice's headlong gallop.

With a short scream, Candice whips her head back around and puts on an extra burst of speed, hot flashes of adrenaline coursing through her body. Lyle's head is down and his arms pump furiously at his sides as he blazes a trail forward through the never-ending vegetation. The crashing sounds of pursuit echo draw closer and closer, and just as Candice thinks they're sure to be leapt upon, the clinging branches finally part, revealing a well-manicured lawn. Candice and Lyle stumble out onto the short clipped grass, breath panting.

Before them, Candice and Lyle see the squat structure of the south motor pool, concrete glistening in the evening twilight, and she heaves a sigh of relief – a sigh of relief that quickly turns into a gasp of alarm as shadows briefly pass overhead, the shapes of the two security women who took to the trees landing on the ground right in front of her and Lyle.

The figures roll upright and quickly turn to face them, crouched over, hands spread like talons in an aggressively slope-shouldered posture.

"Shit." Lyle grunts and pulls out his combat knife, fingers wrapping tightly around the hilt, blade held back along his arm. "You get ready to run, Candice. I'll distract these ones and buy you some time. Get to the spaceport and save as many people as you can."

"But—"

"Just go, Candice!"

With a splintering crunch of vegetation, the other two figures shoulder their way out of the jungle and adopt the same attack position, lips rolled back in a snarl, baring perfect white teeth in unnaturally twisted faces. The soft hooting changes into harsh screams, feral in their bestiality, and all four of the creatures start beating the ground with their fists.

Lyle screams back, and charges towards the two blocking the way to the motor pool. They bellow in response, tendons cording along the side of their necks, expressions of feral rage distorting any remaining semblance of humanity. Clenched fists pound the soil one last time and they charge at Lyle in a mad scramble of limbs.

Lyle's feet dig into the ground, and all he can think of is how many chances he's wasted over the years, feelings kept locked up behind the mask of propriety, personal life sacrificed on the altar of duty and honor.

Rage washes through him, rage at the universe for being this way, rage at himself for not telling Candice the truth this entire time, and he yells that rage at the monstrosities rushing to kill him, baring his own teeth as the adrenaline rush surges in time with his footsteps.

Barely five meters now separate the three figures, and Lyle tenses to spin, planning the opening gambit of a dance he knows is likely to end in only one way – with him bleeding out on the mud and dirt. Four versus one are terrible odds even for a seasoned fighter, and there's no telling what the abominations are capable of; who knows if they even feel pain anymore. His fingers grasp the combat blade's hilt ever more tightly – the creatures closing the last few meters in a knuckling run, mouths frothing, fixated entirely on the challenge to their dominance – and he thinks, *at least they bought the distraction. At least Candice will live.*

Pop pop pop pop.

Lyle stumbles and almost falls over as a neat hole appears in the forehead of each of the two berserkers dashing at him, their feet flying out from underneath as they flip into the ground, necks canted in twisted angles from the impact. He spins and looks behind – the other two creatures are down as well, limbs askew and unmoving.

Candice slowly holsters the small projectile launcher back into her sleeve and glares at Lyle. "You stupid... *man!* You didn't even bother asking if I had a weapon!"

Lyle hangs his head, chagrined, before rushing over and sweeping Candice into a crushing hug. "You crazy woman," he laughs, "I knew there was a reason I love you."

The air suddenly goes still, muted cries in the background perhaps mistaken for bird calls. "Love, Lyle?" Candice stares into his hazel eyes. "Really?"

"Of course it's love." Lyle's voice is low, and his eyes gleam. "You pay the bills for all those therapy sessions I have to be at; what else could it possibly be?"

A wry smile inches its way up Candice's cheeks. "Pinche pendejo, always with the jokes. And here I thought I'd finally get to file a sexual harassment claim with the company to keep your ass in line."

Lyle chuckles roughly. "So now it's my ass you're worrying about, ma'am? Looks like I should be considering a harassment suit myselmmpphh—"

He's suddenly cut off as Candice presses her lips up against his, grabbing the back of his head, and the kiss they share seems timeless in its perfection. Finally though, too soon, they break apart.

"Candice?" Lyle looks into her eyes and his voice is no longer joking.

"I... like you, Lyle. I might even love you." Candice drops her hand and sighs. "Unfortunately, we need to get off this moon before that's a possibility."

She reaches up to touch his cheek.

"It doesn't matter what you had to do to survive before; Gate knows this is one fucked up universe we live in and I've done some things I'm not too proud of myself. What matters is that we get off this rock so we can figure out if this is just stress, or if there's actually something there between us."

"An 'us' would be nice, not gonna lie. Been a long time since I felt this way about someone. Not since my stint in the Peacekeepers."

Candice reluctantly breaks away. "However, we still have a responsibility to our guests, no matter how screwed up the situation's become, and that means getting to the spaceport and unlocking an Icarus. We need to start getting people out of here. Then we can explore what 'us' might mean."

Lyle nods at her. "You're right, ma'am. These plutos wouldn't hesitate to trample us underfoot, but you're right."

He lets out a sardonic laugh. "Plus, I got a hunch Government is gonna be looking for someone to blame for all these dead plutos once we *do* get off planet, and it would be nice if we had a couple to vouch for us. Priorities, eh?"

"Yeah, that seems like a pretty big one to me." Candice replies. "I'm not too keen on getting saddled with 'dereliction of duty' by the company just so they can avoid liability." Lyle's laugh turns into a choking grunt as Candice pokes him in the chest with a finger, causing him to stumble back awkwardly. "And stop calling me 'ma'am.' I'm not my grandmother!"

Her voice is sharp, but her eyes sparkle.

"Yes m— yes, Candice." They smile, and head into the cool interior of the vehicle shed, where Lyle opens up one of the four Vees inside.

Candice jumps into the passenger seat up front while Lyle starts the engine. It whines to life, power feeding through the fuel cell into the drivetrain, one hundred percent charged. Lyle shifts the Vee into drive and turns toward Candice, who's staring out the window – her reflection reveals a face smudged with dirt and mud, hair strands poking out in all directions from her normally neat shoulder length cut.

"One question, Candice," he says.

She looks back at him, eyes distant. "What is it, Lyle?"

"Why did you aim for the head? That's a much tougher target to hit, especially in a chaotic situation. Why not center mass?"

Candice smiles, the distance in her eyes fading. "I remember watching one of those specials on the strange creatures of Old Terra, back before the Devastation. Apparently they used to have this wasp that laid its eggs inside of an ant to take control of the ant's brain. Take out the brain, and you take out the ant. Crazy shit like that sticks with you."

Her smile turns into an outright grin. "Besides, haven't you ever seen one of those horrible zombie augshows? Everyone knows you always aim for the head when you're facing an unspeakable horror. As head of security, you should know that that's what the heroes always do. It's practically eldritch combat one oh one."

Lyle laughs, and turns the Vee out onto the access trail.

"Right you are, boss. Right you are. Well, if we're the heroes, let's go save some folks!"

XANDER

Timestamp – 19.23.45LT:08.21.13OT:03.18.407AG

"This way! This way you idiot!"

At the last minute, my assistant jukes hard to the right and joins me next to a dimly lit service door set in the side of what seems to be this never ending volcanic tunnel. Crusher thunders past once again into the darkness, grinding claws digging into stone and a stirring rush of air flowing over us the only witness to its eerily silent passing. I slam open the door and we duck inside – a flickering glowpanel overhead reveals a tangled nest of wires and jumbled pipes worming their way through the walls, as well as a stairway leading up. Theoretically, it should lead us to a maintenance walkway, which should then, theoretically, lead us to the observation platform and a way out the side of the volcano into the workers' housing.

I'm betting our asses these theories are sound, because the global cloud assist is basically useless at this point – nothing but nonsense phrases and visual static. It's actually pretty fortunate I was able to download the local blueprints earlier to local memory; here's hoping no one made any undocumented changes during construction. Time to find out.

The stairway leads up to a crosshatched metal walkway running between two narrow walls of rock, lighting strips providing a stygian illumination. I have no idea if this cramped tunnel leads to the right place, but at least we caught a small break. Even if Crusher tracks us back to the door down below, there's no way it's going to physically fit through such an enclosed space.

We start down the passage towards what I'm pretty sure is the observation platform, our footsteps echoing off the surrounding walls like an accompanying legion of ghosts. According to the blueprints I snagged, the platform is set in the heart of the volcano itself, one of the centerpieces of the resort. Apparently the architect bored a tunnel straight through the side of the living rock, and then capped the end with a memplas amphitheater set within the caldera. Normally a lift shuttles guests back and forth, but with Crusher roaming the darkness, we're forced to walk this winding maintenance passage. For a while, the sounds of labored breathing are our only companions.

After ten minutes, I motion for a rest, and we slump to a halt against one of the uneven walls. My side is burning and I need to get my breath back. The dim glowstrip overhead provides barely any light, and the damp patch of blood covering my shirt appears black in the gloom. Eventually, my assistant speaks.

"Okay, Doc, it's time for some answers. Every time you've been about to spill the beans on your little project in the lab we've been assaulted by horrific nightmare fuel, or shot at, or almost been eaten, or something equally terrifying.

"Now, this is the safest we've been in this absolutely wretched day," he takes a quick glance around, nervous eyes scanning the cramped corridor before leaning back against the wall again, "...which isn't saying much, but I need to know what the fuck is really going on out there?"

I take a couple steps before drawing in a deep breath. What he's asking for is a lot of information, but at this point he already knows enough to get himself killed. There's no point in keeping any more secrets. Hopefully I can get him assigned back to the lab instead of Government liquidating him.

"Well, like I said in the hotel security center, it started a little over one hundred years ago. At that point, the concept of genetic terraforming was standard Government protocol when encountering a new human-capable world."

"Genetic terraforming?"

"Yeah. We find a planet, moon, giant asteroid, whatever, something that has the right range of conditions to support our basic bodily process, as well as a gas giant nearby for a Gate. There are trillions of candidates out there, so they're not incredibly hard to find with skhip drones. Once we find one, we send in a Black Colony terraforming ship to make it suitable for human life, and then we build a Gate.

"Unfortunately for the previous inhabitants, 'making it suitable for humans' calls for wiping out any form of life originally found on that planet, then seeding it with human-friendly bioforms – mainly those from Old Terra that still exist and we know we're compatible with."

He rubs his neck, frustration pouring over his face. "What? But what about the scientific possibilities? Not to mention the ethical problems with planetary scale genocide?"

"Not my call. Government's built on the absolute prohibition of biohacking, in public at least. The only way we can co-exist with alien life is if we alter our own genetics to function with alien bacteria and viruses. Think of the Old Terra tale '*The War of the Worlds*,' only we're the invaders."

I see understanding dawn in his eyes. I continue.

"So if altering ourselves is out of the question, and all of these resources and land are sitting there waiting for us to use them, then the only way forward is to clear out anything in the way. That's where Black Colony comes in."

"Yeah, you've mentioned them a couple times now, and I have to say, the name doesn't sound particularly friendly."

"They're not. Black Colony is a collection of the most ruthlessly trained killers Government is able to produce, and their sole purpose is to wipe out every form of alien life on a planet that doesn't accept alteration to a *homo sapiens* template. Originally they had to take out everything, sometimes even torching the world and reseeding it, but with the advancements in biohacking we've made over the years they're not as necessary these days. Ninety percent of what we find now we can alter or destroy, just a couple of genetic tweaks here and there, but there's always that portion of alien life that, well, *resists* us, for lack of a better term."

My eyes narrow. "And those that resist are usually the strongest, meanest, toughest organisms on a world. So while Black Colony may not have as much to deal with anymore in terms of *quantity*, the *quality* is that much nastier. That's where they earn their keep."

He frowns. "Well, that's against utterly everything we should stand for as scientists, but it probably explains some of my crop research directions. Wait, if they wipe the planet, then what are we building in the lab?"

"I was getting to that part. One hundred and seven years ago, Government lost contact with the colony on Eurypides Nine, but not before some very frightening datobjects were transmitted back to the

Gate. Giant ships popping into near space through Gates they created themselves. Strange fluid-metal creatures storming through the mining facility. The same creatures wiping out every sign of human life on Eurypides Nine itself, multiple glARs records of people getting annihilated by weapons we still have yet to understand, plasma burst after plasma burst vaporizing everything."

He interrupts. "You're talking about those aliens from before, right? The ones we're secretly at war with?"

I nod. "Government immediately sent through the *Imperator* and the *Decimator*, the closest Black Colony assault carriers on hand, equipped to handle anything short of a supernova... or so they thought.

"The ships lasted five seconds, before adding their forty thousand crew members to the multi-million death toll engulfing the system."

I lever myself upright, wincing at the pain from my side as I unfold from my seated position. We slowly start making our way down the cramped corridor again, walls too narrow to permit us to walk side by side, and I continue the secret history lesson.

"What little information came back from those five seconds was enough to convince Government that we were completely outclassed, and so they ordered the Gate destroyed rather than let whatever was attacking us into another system. Officially they called it a 'malfunction,' to keep people from panicking I guess, but make no mistake, *we're* the ones that blew that Gate up."

I let out a long breath and shake my head. "And I can't say that I blame them for making that decision. It's the only one they could have made."

"What do you mean, 'the only one they could have made?'" His tone is uncomprehending.

"Think about it," I say slightly more exasperated than I intend. "Those two ships represented the pinnacle of Government military might, and they were about as useful as a snowflake against a forest fire. We had nothing in the area that could come even close to stopping those things, and they obviously have Gate equivalent tech, if not better. How many more would have died if they made it through to another system? In fact, we're damn lucky they were more focused on destruction rather than stripping out the Gate coordinates of any of our other worlds. The next encounter was Prometheus Five, six years later."

"Hold up, Prometheus Five? We've never colonized a system called Prometheus."

"It's not public knowledge, primarily because it's one of the main Black Colony shipyards." I involuntarily laugh at his dumbfounded expression. "What, you think they're going to build super-secret warships in the middle of the Mars suborbitals, or Vulcan, where any passing tourist can get an eyeful? No, they need a nice, secluded spot for that, and one of those spots was Prometheus."

"'Was?'"

We continue down the hallway, dim lightstrips passing monotonously overhead. Judging by the distance function on my glARs, we're still almost a kilometer away from the observation platform – assuming we're going the right way. At least BTH-03 isn't chasing us now.

"When they hit Prometheus Five, it was the same initial pattern – ships Gating in under their own power, liquid-metal creatures overrunning the mines, more alien tech destroying our terrestrial presence. The only difference this time was that Prometheus Five had a standing fleet presence of two hundred Black Colony dreadnaughts, as well as eight suborbital forts."

"So we beat them back?"

"No. We managed to escape with one crippled ship, the *Washburn*, and more importantly, a piece off one of the alien ships, the taking of which is a story in its own right. We still had to blow the Gate behind us though, and Prometheus was a total loss. Another four hundred million lives gone, along with the entire shipbuilding capabilities of the system – a not inconsiderable investment.

"However, we got some of their tech. Specifically, we figured out how to reverse engineer the high impact alloys they use to shield their ships – amazing stuff. Turns out the exotic molecules we use for Gate-fuel can also function in a wide variety of meta-material compounds if you arrange them the right way and in the right densities. You know memplas?"

"No shit? You're telling me that the backbone of almost everything constructed these days is based off of alien technology? But Daison-Eno has the patent for memplas, I remember learning about that breakthrough in school. Another cover up?"

"You got it. Government actually owns Daison-Eno through a very long series of corporate cutouts – they're the primary manufacturer of pretty much everything Government needs done off the books. They weren't too happy about Prometheus, either, though memplas more than made up for the financial losses they incurred. In fact, memplas is so lucrative that Government might be one of the first political institutions in human history that's actually recording a profit – discreetly of course. Obviously, though, that means we need to keep mining Gate-fuel. And that brings us back to the facility."

"Yeah, I've been meaning to ask you about that." His voice is curious. "If Government controls all these planets, why is there a resort built on top of the lab? Why aren't we the only ones here?"

"A valid question, and one I've often asked as well. My work would be much easier if I could use the entire moon, that's for sure." I sigh. "Unfortunately, higher-ups in Government wanted to be able to occasionally check in on the projects, and when they saw what Eden's climate was like, once the lab was finished they decided to build a resort on top as a cover story for their visits. Frankly, I don't think they even care about the lab as long as nothing gets loose – it's just an excuse for them to take a vacation for several weeks. This lab hasn't had an actual visitor in at least fifteen years." I sigh again. "Typical bureaucratic corruption, totally convinced in the idea that nothing is more important than their own desires. I've tried telling them that we're about to make an actual breakthrough here, but no one's listening anymore."

I hold up a hand and we both pause. In front of us is the thick metal door hopefully marking the end of the maintenance passage, assuming the map I downloaded was accurate. I slowly ease it open the slightest of cracks and peer through into the room beyond. The lurid red glow of an active volcanic caldera dances over the walls and furniture of a massive amphitheater, its far end a clear sheet of memplas looking down on the molten heart of Mount Zali'ah. Scanning the room for several minutes reveals no lurking surprises, so I ease the door open a bit more and slip through. My assistant follows close on my heels, hands waving as he talks.

"Wait a minute, 'we haven't had a visitor in fifteen years?' 'No one's listening anymore?' What's that supposed to mean?"

I clear my throat. "Unfortunately, many years ago, I may have been slightly impolitic with the administrator of the sector, a man named Councilor Rocon. I was originally assigned here to develop weapon systems, help refine our biosoldiers – Government made the earlier models available for testing. You've seen several of them already, though with my modifications, of course."

My voice falters for a moment, and the next words come out in a bitter, harsh tone.

"Fifteen years ago, I'd been focusing on a promising line of research into eHydro, one covering multiple areas, with the promise of huge potential breakthroughs, and Rocon didn't think it would amount to anything. He said I was neglecting my basic duties, wasting my time on frivolities instead of working to refine what we already knew worked. He said I was ignoring the needs of humanity for the sake of my own knowledge." I can feel my teeth grinding together as the memories rush back, and I unclench my jaw with an effort.

"Rocon wasn't interested in a long term project. I wasn't getting immediate results, so he wanted the lab to focus on different priorities. Better crop resistances and whatnot, simple terraforming hacks. He wanted to take *me* off the weapons project."

I smile grimly. "Well, words were said, one thing led to another, and now there's a reason why I have to beg and scrape for every shipment of supplies they deign to send our way. I give him the occasional minor upgrade to soywheat and copigs, and he allots the bare minimum the lab needs to get by."

My voice turns to a snarl. "He also returns every single report on my progress with eHydro unopened and unread, along with a note telling me not to waste his time or the lab's resources. Says I should be 'focused on doing my part to make humanity's existence better in whatever humble way you can contribute.' Arrogant waste of oxygen."

We slowly make our way down the steps of the amphitheater toward the clear barrier. The glow is hypnotic, and I can feel my anger slowly subside at the spectacle of a raging volcanic core separated from us by barely half a meter of memplas.

A sight like this doesn't come around every day, and we can spare a couple minutes to take it in. We pause at the bottom, lava wrapping us in a soothing fiery bubble. He suddenly stiffens up.

"Wait a minute, wait a minute, you mean those things you made, those monsters, Government hasn't approved them? Are you shitting me?" His voice is frantic.

"Someone has to make them," I reply in a fierce tone. "We reverse engineered memplas, but we still haven't made a dent in their weapon systems or communication protocols. Every time we try to go head-to-head with them conventionally, in space or on the ground, they wipe the floor with us. Oddly, though, they only seem to go after mechanical threats, which means anything we can disguise as a native member of an ecosystem slips past their guard. The models Government deploys now are adequate, if barely, but the aliens are slowly learning, and they're starting to overwhelm us again. We've bought enough time to keep the Gate-fuel flowing for at least a couple more years, and we've fought them to a stalemate in several systems – though the bill's been paid with a mountain of corpses – but it's not going to last."

I shake my head. "We require something better than a slow defeat. We require victories, and none of the other labs have someone like me. I've reviewed their work, gone over their splices, and they simply do not understand the possibilities eHydro integration offers. Probably because they're not smart enough to know how to use it. I'm the first person to ever successfully integrate eHydro into living organisms, and the regenerative properties it bestows is nothing short of miraculous, especially in the right densities and formations. An order of magnitude better than memplas, at the very least."

My voice turns contemplative. "The math also suggests it should cut right through that liquid metal if it's arranged in the right lattices... the harmonics..."

He stares at me, clearly not understanding the beautiful equations dancing in my mind. I tsk irritably and return to the topic at hand. "Let me make this perfectly clear. I refuse to waste away inside this backwater while humanity needs a champion, someone who can turn the tide of this struggle and drive those nightmares back. We need resources, we need Gate-fuel, we need to *win*, absolute and total dominion, and for that, we need Prime."

Looking through the memplas I'm enthralled by the seething mass of magma churning less than a meter from my face, boiling underneath my feet. It might as well be on the other side of the galaxy for the danger it represents – no heat leaks through the nearly impassable barrier of alien derived technology, no sound, nothing. This vision of power tamed, controlled, turned to entertainment, is nothing less than the epitome of human expansion throughout the galaxy. We built something like this, not because it was necessary, but because we *could*, and no alien race will take that away from us. Not while I'm alive and able to spin gene sequences.

"Prime?" His face whitens. "You mean that thing still stuck in the lab?"

"Exactly. Prime is the culmination of twenty-one years of research, and with it we will finally win this war. Prime is impervious to heat, cold, and vacuum, can function in environments up to four hundred gravities, can cloak itself from most forms of visual, infrared, and ultraviolet sensors, and has the cunning of humanity itself. The eHydro splices make it self-regenerating up to anything short of a direct antimatter blast, and I'm incorporating some of the more esoteric functions into its molecular structure for cognitive upgrades."

I pause, thinking back on the research data I'd been reviewing before everything went to pieces. "Let's just say there are some facets to eHydro that are leading me in another *very* interesting research direction. Honestly, it's somewhat of a miracle we made it out of the lab in the first place."

"Wait a minute, 'human cunning?' Please tell me you didn't just say 'human cunning.'"

I slowly nod. "It's my crowning achievement. I was finally able to synthesize human DNA with Prime's upgrades, including eHydro. Full cognition, full self-awareness. It can learn, evolve, grow – master any battlefield and any situation at the speed of thought. *Homo sapiens* version two point oh, refined and perfected. The ultimate weapon."

My assistant turns and looks at me with an unfamiliar look on his face – it seems to be equal parts terror and abhorrence. His mouth opens and closes several times as if he's searching for words, until they finally pour out.

"What the fuck is wrong with you? We're supposed to be using biohacking to make humanity better, not turning ourselves into weapons! We're supposed to be helping people! This *Prime*," he spits, "is an abomination, and here you are, celebrating its evil! This type of shit is what led to the ban on biohacking to begin with!"

I feel my fists clenching. "Prime is the closest thing I'll ever have to a child, and it's the *only* thing that gives us a chance of winning this war. Get it through your head, we are *losing*, humanity is in danger of *extinction*, and I will do everything in my power to keep that from happening. We won't need any of the lesser creations once we can start mass producing Primes, and we might finally stand a chance against this alien scourge before they wipe out every single last one of us."

My voice ends in a shout and we stand locked in hateful stares, the lava belching and frothing behind us, ceaselessly crashing against the crystal clear barrier like a hellish primordial ocean. My assistant takes a breath, but whatever he was about to say is suddenly lost in the crashing scream of twisted metal as Crusher bursts through the doors at the top of the amphitheater. Its broad head swings ponderously from side to side, and then it turns to face us, slowly crouching down into its charge stance.

A foot starts pawing at the ground, splintering the ironwood floor panels like so much cheap kindling. We have maybe fifteen seconds before it springs into motion.

"When I say 'move,' you run to the right as fast as possible, got it?"

My voice is an urgent hiss, taut with adrenaline, argument forgotten under the threat of extermination. "You have to wait for me to give the signal though – if you don't, we're both going to die here."

He has no chance to answer as the giant bulk of armor and muscle above us accelerates in a smooth blur of motion, stumpy claws digging deep gouges into the floor as it crashes down the amphitheater rows.

Couches and chairs splinter and burst from the massive weight bowling through them, obstacles less substantial than cobwebs to its terrifying bulk. At no point does the creature deviate from the ruler straight line that defines the closest distance between two points, our location the terminus of its terrible calculus. The distance narrows rapidly. Fifty meters away. Twenty meters away. Ten. Five.

"MOVE!"

I dive and roll to the left as my assistant takes off to the right, Crusher whipping its head to try and gore us as it passes by. I feel a sudden warm rush down my right side, a rush instantly eclipsed by the thunderous sound of five thousand kilograms impacting the memplas barrier overlooking the lava. A sick cracking sound fills the air, and I'm crawling to my feet and running up the stairs as fast as possible, bringing up the hotel schematic on my glARs as I sprint. The cracking sound continues to spread, like rotten ice on a warm day, and halfway to the top I take a quick glance behind me, muscles burning as I force my legs up the seemingly endless steps.

Crusher is groggily rising to its feet, one curled horn broken off at the base, thick blood pooling around the edges of the juncture between horn and skull. Behind its heaving body, a spiderweb of fractures is rapidly spreading across the window, a cascading resonance from the impact of its eHydro infused horns overwhelming the memplas' regenerative properties while molten lava continues its ceaseless assault on the other side. I see my assistant cresting the top of the amphitheater stairs, and then a cacophony of destruction engulfs the room in a rush of super-heated air.

Something happens I've never seen before.

The memplas shatters.

Crusher is instantly engulfed, mouth bellowing a silent scream as it sinks beneath the molten tide, thrashing its head from side to side the entire way down. The lava continues to rise up the bowl of the amphitheater, pouring in through the now gaping viewing area, a howling gale of broiling air rushing through the room. I redouble my pace and trigger a waypoint for the exit to the workers' housing – on the schematics the tunnel runs slightly uphill, which will hopefully be enough to keep us alive. As I scramble over the last step, sweat pouring down my face in the boiling temperature, I see my assistant hurrying toward the shattered wreckage of the front entrance, heading for the lift tube and certain death.

"Over here," I scream, and I immediately feel a sharp stabbing pain in my side, the intensity of which almost doubles me over. Seems like the adrenaline's wearing off. Shuddering, I start limping my way to the small side door set in the western wall, when suddenly I feel a hand grab my arm.

"By all rights I should let you die here, but something tells me you're my only way off this rock," my assistant mutters. He drapes my arm over his back and we lurch into yet another tunnel, door slamming closed behind us with a hollow thud, a rickety looking metal staircase winding its way up the basalt wall at the end of the passage. The dull slapping of our feet on rock changes to the harsh clang of echoing steel as we hit the first flight of stairs, and the hot warmth spreads over my side in agonizing pulses.

We make it halfway up the open-frame structure before the door down below bursts open under the relentless flow of lava; refulgent surges of viscous magma pooling down the tunnel and lapping at the walls. I can hear the metal of the staircase creaking and groaning under the assault of the destructive forces besieging it until, finally, legs churning, stumbling against each other, we reach the top of the shaking frame.

Two steps away from the edge of the rock shelf we both collapse to the floor, overspent muscles buckling beneath us as the crackling metal peels away with an ear-piercing shriek and collapses into the molten pool below. My assistant gasps for air several times and then scrambles to his feet. He peers over the edge and lets out a whoop of triumph.

"The lava's stabilizing! We made it! We made it!"

I don't respond. I can't respond. I feel the world spinning around me, one hand clutched to my side, and then the darkness blots everything out.

ROB

Timestamp – 19.44.06LT:08.41.34OT:03.18.407AG

The constant crack of projectile rounds fills the inside of the Vee, an erratic thunderstorm of deafening acoustics penetrating even through the sound filters in my ears. Gonna have to worry about hearing loss later, hunters trying to keep Kufit's own menagerie away while I try not to flip us on the curves, the Vee's engine whining under the strain of constant acceleration.

GIARs are working overtime sorting threat vectors and road hazards, a nonstop maelstrom of dashing shapes and shaded nebulas churning together like the twisted weather systems on the gas giant looming above.

Quick glance at the combat cloud shows minimal ammo remaining – Monocle's low on Six Sixteen rounds, Augstar's out of buzzers, and Wraparounds only has two submunition cases left on his harness. Shit, wait a minute, those are tacnukes. Where in Kufit's beard did he get tacnukes? No chance I'm letting him fire those off anywhere close to our general vicinity, don't really feel like sitting on the surface of a sun just yet. Fucking tacnukes.

Another burst of fire, another twitching mass of flesh left soaking its dirty blood into the trail behind us. Something with six legs and a mouth full of fangs leaps from the left as the Vee tilts around a corner, the thunderous detonation of Monocle dumping a Six Sixteen round into its face and we're tearing down another straightaway, trees whipping past on either side. The Vee crushes something low and squirming that explodes in a shower of noxious blood; the wipers struggle to clean it off. Greenish brown streaks smear the front screen, and the Vee goes up on three wheels as we slam around another curve.

Finally break out into the open, the resort rearing up in front of us, greasy pillars of black smoke lazily twisting into the sky. Monocle tells me to head for the shuttle bay we came down at, all the way back at the spaceport. Juke around what looks like an ambulatory bear covered in bright orange spines before cranking the acceleration – the ursoid screams as we pass. Wraparounds fires several rounds until Monocle chides him for wasting ammo, one mag left. Rhinestones sits sullenly in the back – stupid sword isn't worth shit now. Useless prick.

Scattered remnants of former guests blur past the Vee as I max the engine, body parts littering the side of the road in a tapestry of red, the tangled wreckage of moverbikes like twisted steel blooms amidst the carnage.

Screams and shouts filter through the ringing in my ears – looks like there's still some people left. More than a few judging by the volume. Coming up to the spaceport turnoff, cracked concrete roadway forking off to the right, ghostly glARs identifier floating above each branch.

Spin the wheel over, and we're on the arrow straight path to the shuttle bay, careening down the hillside, gleaming entirety of the spaceport complex laid out on the giant lake belo—

Holy fuck.

Off in the distance, an Icarus lifts out of the water on a bright plume of plasma, sleek broadsword shape cutting across the glittering blue surface. Suddenly, it wildly corkscrews as massive tentacles erupt from the water and coil around the length of its fuselage, and then it's gone, dragged beneath the waves.

A brilliant bulge erupts from the widening ripples, visible even at this distance, into a massive mushroom cloud – the Icarus' fusion plant must have vented. Quick glARs alert to brace for impact, like anyone could have missed the fireworks.

The scrabbling claws on our roof are displaced by a massive roar of wind as the blast front hits; Vee shudders and rocks but doesn't flip. Something with too many legs goes trailing off behind us onto the road – it writhes and twists in a frenzy of limbs before levering itself upright, and then with a screech takes off back towards the resort as I hit the accelerator again.

The concussive shockwave seems to have stunned anything else lurking nearby, the rushing whistle of wind through the cracked and shattered windows of the Vee our only accompaniment as we race through the outer ring of white stone warehouses, scattered corpses staring blankly at our passing.

Slam the Vee to a halt in front of the shuttle bay doors, Monocle and Augstar piling out before we even finish moving. Monocle races for the access panel, Augstar close behind, Wraparounds and Rhinestones setting a perimeter. I jerk the Vee into park and roll out the driver side door, glARs searching for danger.

Endless seconds pass, nothing moves. The air is eerily silent, only sound the tinny ringing in my ears, eyes scanning ceaselessly. Shadows twist and writhe with threat vectors, warning systems overloaded with too much irregular data, phantoms constantly failing to materialize, the muted roar of thousands of distant people gradually breaking like surf.

An eternity later, Monocle authenticates the manual override and we sprint inside the slowly sliding doors. Crates of gear lie stacked in a neat pyramid in the center of the bay, automated loading servitors standing motionless against the wall without a VI to guide them.

Hunters waste no time tearing the boxes open, scattering the pile into a whirlwind of weapons systems and ammunition cases as they shout hurried instructions at each other, searching for specific pieces.

Monocle keeps it simple, drapes two bandoliers of Six Sixteen ammo across his chest like some kind of Old Terra cowboy. It looks ludicrous, except that that's the most ammunition I've seen for a Six Sixteen in one place outside of the main Agency armory on New Delphi. Field ops are only allowed four rounds max, and he's got almost fifty in those leather belts covering his acticamo.

He also straps on a monofil survival knife, sheathed and powered down. Dangerous tool if you don't know how to use it, monofil blades cut deep and quick. The worn grip suggests he's had plenty of practice.

Wraparounds trades in his acticamo for a tacsuit, assault class. Matte black memplas panels backed by shockgel cover him like a full body carapace, T-visor helmet completing the augstar action hero look. He also grabs a Hydra and straps the gauntlets into place – integrated feed system slots submunitions in from the suit itself, all he has to do is point a finger.

Full suit looks blocky, bulky, but looks can be deceiving – assault tacsuits offer limited servo assist from the bioelectric generators in the shockgel, helps take away the weight. Felt like wearing a wet pair of clothes in Agency training, and the protection is well worth the slight encumbrance.

Rhinestones swaps his acticamo too, but not for anything I've ever seen. Looked at a lot of Agency archives, some would say all of them, and this is new. Different. Looks like some sort of action figure muscle suit, dark grey and striated, small ports dotting the arms, cracked in half down the torso and front legs, gaping blank mask for a face.

Rhinestones strips naked and slides into it, like a snake reversing the molting process, needles sliding into veins as it wraps itself around him, until a faceless behemoth hulks before us, grotesque anatomy in full view, over-stylized muscles bulging absurdly. He grabs a luridly marked biohazard case and takes fifteen different ampoules from inside, inserting each one into a waiting port.

The suit slowly sucks them inside, leeches entering the bloodstream with their tiny, blind, hungry mouths, until only a rounded bump marks their locations. Lines of bright red slowly trace their way through the muscles of the suit, turn it into a living anatomical textbook, powered by Gate knows what. His own blood, probably. He straightens up, and—

Asshole. He grabbed the sword. Gate-damned experimental biotechsuit like nothing the Agency knows and he's still using that fucking sword. I swear, if he's stuck sitting useless in the back seat again I'll give him those damn ampules as a suppository.

Sudden rattle of machinery – threat?

What.

The.

Fuck.

Augstar somehow managed to sneak an Atlas past customs. Forget customs, how did she fit it on the shuttle? Ten-meter-tall power-assist combat mechs with shoulder-mounted launch systems, projectile cannon arm hardpoints, and semi-sentient onboard VIs aren't normally carry-on. AM plant powering it should've tripped all sorts of alarms too; energy signature like that's tough to hide. However she managed it, she's in the cockpit now – running startup diagnostics most likely.

Funny though, that Atlas is an older model, one the Agency decommissioned becau—

Opportunity.

Fingers blur inside my hapgloves.

<<*initiate cloudScan v.4.83;*>>

<<*five datobjects located;*>>

<<accessing datobject atlasDiag v.1.012;>>
<<security protocol required;>>
<<executing equestrianTroy v.3.41;>>
<<analyzing...;>>
<<access granted;>>
<<executing princeNigeria v.5.03;>>
<<core kernel located;>>
<<backtracing...;>>
<<trace complete;>>
<<executing darkWeb v.46.2;>>
<<access granted;>>
<<Hello, Maria;>>

Gotcha. A secondary cascade of datobjects unfolds in my glARs, a beautiful origami infosphere, everything Maria Isildor Renkos a.k.a Augstar, sector vice-administrator for the twelve hundred planets of the Orion arm and eighteenth wealthiest individual in the known universe, considers important enough to trust to her virtual memory.

Like most people, she trusts it with her entire life.

Commlinks, business plans, bank accounts, passwords, cooking recipes, childhood photos, secret trysts, holiday recordings, favorite ARnet episodes – a glittering mountain of information. Information a smart man can make use of.

<<executing loki'sBag v.2.21;>>
<<transferring...;>>

Casually glance around, stick a couple penetrator clips into my pocket. Hunters continue their gear shakedown.

<<backup complete;>>
<<executing odin'sEye v.1.00: 50% mem capacity: keywords finance, bank, gcred, transfer protocols;>>

Augstar moves the Atlas from side to side, spins up the projectile cannons with a whirling hum, checking the feed system, powers them off. Shoulder launchers pop out of their protective casings, payload tips visible as launch ports open and close, pop back down. Standard pre-combat checklist. The opaque memplas cockpit hides her physical body, my VI hides my digital intrusion.

<<anticipated runtime: ten hours;>>
<<appending VI jen'sFuture: Gate upload confirmed on completion;>>
<<9:59:59;>>

Done. As long as I survive the next nine hours and fifty nine minutes, and the Gate doesn't blow, my baby will finally have a cure, paid for by Augstar's unwitting generosity. Won't even matter if they pay me or not – it's a poor Agent who doesn't have contingencies.

Gotta survive though, and it looks like Monocle's thinking the same thing. Situation's gotten too far out of hand and they're bailing out; plan is to head to the main shuttle port, snag an Icarus, and then back to the Gate – call through a private ship from there. Hightail out before Government shows up, shoots us all into a sun. He patches through an enhanced combat VI, definitely not an off the shelf version. Too crisp, too fast to be anything other than top of the line milspec.

Combat cloud updates with new munitions, capabilities, roles. Rhinestones checks in at fast attack/scout, claims a moving speed of ninety-five kilometers per hour. Have my doubts, but that suit's like nothing I've seen before. Almost looks like biohacking. Some interesting biomonitor readouts coming over the cloud too, thetawaves registering way above human-standard. Don't even want to know how many drugs are flowing through his blood right now.

Wraparounds has a column of datobjects all to himself, long list of submunitions in the Hydra. Highex, penetrators, HV, cluster mines, everything a narcissistic sociopath could ever want... including tacnukes. Fuck. Cloud puts him at tactical engagement, frontlines. Makes sense with an assault suit.

Augstar's listed as heavy support, naturally. Not much else an Atlas is good for. Projectile cannons are filled with HV kinetics, shoulder launchers a mix of highex and flechette sprays. Good combo, Agency standard for unknown deployments when heavy resistance is suspected. Check the last datobject.

Interesting. Me and Monocle listed as tactical support, infops. We'll be coordinating the others, filling in where needed, generals watching the battlefield. Not sure I'm happy he thinks that highly of my combat skills. Better to be underestimated, ignored, anonymous. Wraparounds sends a query, wants to know why I'm higher in the chain of command. Monocle tells him to shut up, follow orders – time to move out.

Head out of the shuttle bay, leave the Vee behind – road is too packed with wrecks and bodies for it to make much progress. Gonna be almost a two click hike down the spaceport access road, buildings lining the sides. Good ambush terrain.

Rhinestones takes point, Augstar and her mech cover the rear, the rest of us in a loose triangle in the middle, constantly scanning and updating the combat cloud. Augstar deploys a cluster of overwatch drones from a small pod in the Atlas to improve coverage, they fan out above us like wasps.

Surrounding structures are cracked and shattered, slowly spreading flames giving off greasy black smoke. Hope none of the other guests had luggage like ours – most weapon systems are self-sealed but you never know.

Emerge onto the main thoroughfare, combat cloud chimes multiple threats inbound – two indistinct shapes fifty meters ahead and to the right, hiding in a half open shuttle bay; one more twenty meters to the left, looks like it's on a roof.

Wraparounds raises his gauntlets and triggers three seeker munitions. They whip off on bright rocket trails, and the triple crump of highex detonations echoes through the air. Flames and dust shoot into the sky as the thirty-meter-tall structures crash down into rubble.

More chimes, a baroque symphony of crystal death. Visual overlay shows oddly twisted red outlines weaving in and out of the buildings surrounding the wreckage-strewn passageway, closing on us from every direction, no two shapes the same. Target counter puts it at twenty-three hostiles. Noise must have attracted them.

Monocle fires off a Six Sixteen round to the left. Five outlines disappear, along with three more buildings, stone pulverized into billowing dust by multiple highex impacts. The smoke grows thicker, glARs kick up visual enhancement a notch to compensate. Rhinestones sprints into a warehouse on our right, blade bared, where five more flashing threats are gathering.

He disappears through an open door and they start winking out; one, two, three four five. Half a minute later, he emerges dripping green ichor and brown blood – none of it his.

No, no, NO! GlARs update – last shuttle initiating debarking procedures from the port, someone managed to bypass my override disable. Ping an alert to the cloud, time to pick up the pace.

A sudden surge of noise, cannon fire hammering from behind, Augstar pouring a torrent of kinetics into what looks like an oversized lizard twenty-meters-tall with the beak of a toucan, gouging huge craters and chunks of flesh from its scaly hide as it charges *through* a building at us with its mouth gaping wide.

She walks the Atlas backward, still hammering the lizard with fire, until she finally hits something vital and it collapses with a roar, meter-long teeth gnashing as it goes down. Blood pools out of its body and mingles with the hundreds of corpses already littering the street. One claw twitches, then lies still, vast bulk slowly deflating.

Shit, threat vector from above. Whirl and spin, glARs already presenting a target solution, finger squeezing the trigger as a two-meter flying *thing* with a mouthful of fangs descends towards my head. Shot takes it center mass and it crashes to the ground, jagged tail whipping deep grooves in the pavement while feathered wings thrash until the death throes cease.

Put a round in its shark-like head to be sure, glARs tag it SB-08. No time to look up the classification. Monocle fires off another Six Sixteen round, three more of the creatures circling us vaporize into mist, gutters continue their red march to the sea.

Submunitions from Wraparounds streak through the air again, another set of seekers. Four more outlines waver and vanish. Eight left, closing fast. A sudden blur and Rhinestones is flipping past us, sword impaling a chitinous wolf, and then whipping out to disembowel a horned frog the size of an aircar leaping down from above, six legs tensed to crush Monocle into paste.

Guts slither and splat onto the concrete, bulbous eyes clouding over while a thick tongue drips acid onto the ground, and then Rhinestones is dashing into another building, sword trailing like an extension of his arm.

Augstar's cannon unleashes its thunderous roar once more, and the last outline blinks and fades away to half a mangled corpse splayed across a broken moverbike, flesh and steel twisted and torn. Three pairs of eyes set into a broad and wrinkled face stare glassily down the street at building facades obliterated by four minutes of nonstop violence, cracked structural beams splintering out like rotted bone. My glARs pings another update on the shuttle – pulling away from the dock.

Breath comes in short tearing gasps as we finish sprinting the last half click to the port, passing more shattered ruins and a mangled bridge covered in corpses, but it's too late. The last Icarus is lifting out of the water, steam billowing under it in thick clouds as the plasma jets fire, but it's moving erratically, skewing side to side. Magnify, eight times zoom...

No fucking way. Cloud of flying creatures, looks like the one I shot earlier, are swarming around the vessel, whipping their tails into it, tearing knifelike gashes open all over the midstructure. They shouldn't be able to shred the memplas composite that easily, but nothing these monstrosities do makes sense anymore. Several seize hold of a larger panel with their claws and start worrying at it with those massive jaws, looks like they're going to rip it off—

There it goes. One dives at the opening, tumbles out half a second after getting inside and spirals down into the water, most of its head missing.

Couple armed folks on board at least. They won't last long though, four more fliers lining up to charge inside while the Icarus slowly continues lifting, Gehenna V looming large in the background like a bruised sunfruit. Wings tuck in tight to streamlined bodies, tails arching behind as they plummet toward the wounded shuttle.

And they're in.

Three are rebuffed immediately, falling back torn and shredded, but the fourth makes it, tail slithering like an eel as it wriggles inside. The Icarus suddenly tilts to one side, then manages to right itself, plasma plume glowing even brighter as acceleration increases, gaining even more height.

Movement.

A shape flies out of the ragged tear, twisting and tumbling. Activate glARs target lock, clean and enhance... A man has his arm locked around the creature's neck while he stabs it in the underbelly repeatedly, snapping fangs tearing at his shoulders, a jagged tail lodged through his chest – they plummet to the water below, blood trailing like raindrops.

<<warning;>>
<<Class Three submunition deployed;>>
<<warning;>>
Gate-damned maniac!
<<warning;>>
<<trajectory line overlay: three seconds to impact;>>
<<origination point: assault tacsuit designation "Wraparounds";>>
<<projected yield: two kilotons;>>

<<*warning;*>>

Turn away just in time to avoid permanent retina damage to my unshielded eye, bright actinic glow of nuclear fire momentarily changing late midday into high noon. Quickly spin back, mad whirl of kaleidoscope fragments smearing across the sky.

A cotton white mushroom cloud slowly ascending into the heavens.

The last Icarus trailing heavy plumes of smoke as it lurches brokenly toward the resort, a crippled bird with no wings.

The growlingly violent subsonic rumble of a tacnuke explosion roaring through, followed by the higher pitched scream of the Icarus passing overhead, plasma bloom sputtering and dying.

Metal screeching and tearing as the shuttle impacts on the volcano's southwestern flank, splintering trees into matchsticks, secondary explosions rattling off like firecrackers.

Silence.

SPACEPORT MILTON, GROUNDSIDE

Timestamp – 19.45.22LT:08.42.50OT:03.18.407AG

"We have to get these people into the shuttles, Lyle!" Candice can feel her voice cracking as she struggles to be heard over the constant din of panicked human beings.

Her connection to the global cloud is completely worthless at this point, and every attempt to ping Lyle results in a meaningless hash of gibberish feeding back into her own display. The physical reality isn't much different – scrambled crowds of resort guests scream and claw their way down the spaceport thoroughfare, fighting each other in a mad rush to escape the relentless assault of biohacked monstrosities.

Those at the edge of the crowd are picked off and dragged into buildings, agonizing screams inevitably cut short. Those in the middle fare just as poorly – a flock of two-meter-long creatures with feathered wings and bullet-shaped heads descend constantly to savage and rend unprotected flesh.

To fall is to die, trampled beneath a churning forest of legs, and Candice can feel unpleasantly mushy lumps underfoot as she and Lyle struggle toward the shuttle docks. The twenty minutes since Lyle pulled the Vee up to the turbulent chaos overwhelming the spaceport access road seems like twenty years ago.

"They ain't listening, boss!" Lyle grimaces in frustration as he tries to keep the area around them somewhat clear, brandishing a projectile thrower he secured from the Vee's storage locker. Some guests back away, eyes wide, but most don't even register the weapon in their panicked attempts to flee the onslaught of bioterrors. "It's a mob now, ain't nothing to do but get ourselves to a shuttle and try to fit as many onboard as possible."

"The last reliable update I got from the net said we only had two shuttles groundside. There's no way we're going to be able to fit everyone inside!"

"Guess we'll just have to make a couple trips then, boss." Lyle's grin is sardonic and he continues shoving a way through the crowd. "That update put one in Dock A, and the other in C; which one you want us to head for?"

"We'll go for C," Candice responds. "It's closer, and they're both bio-locked in case of emergency. With the net not working, we're probably the only people left alive who can get them open at this point. You help me get these people on board the shuttle at C, and then you'll have to head for A on your own – I hate to send you out alone, but you're more likely to make it through the crowds than I am."

"Don't like leavin' you alone either, but you're right – ain't no way you're fightin' through these maddened sheep."

Candice winces. "Cabrones they may be, Lyle, but we're responsible for getting them out of this deathtrap."

Lyle nearly stumbles as the crowd thins out momentarily, and seconds later he and Candice realize the reason for the temporary reprieve.

Barely ten meters ahead, the roadway temporarily narrows from a broad shop-lined avenue to a four lane access bridge, buildings on both sides replaced by churning water filled with debris.

Writhing across the pitted white concrete are several giant tentacles covered in suckers, their length easily curling the thirty meters to the other side of the roadway and back. A swell of water washes over the guardrails, and the rubbery bulk of what looks to be a gigantically oversized squid emerges from the turbulent murk and blankets its heaving mass across half the road. Its head and body tower at least sixteen meters above wildly grasping tentacles, and all Candice can think of is one word.

"Kraken," she whispers under her breath, subconsciously triggering the activation on her compact holdout, feeling the cool plastic grip slide into her palm.

Candice inhales deeply, and then settles into a firing stance, arms and knees slightly bent as she brackets the towering monstrosity leaning over the roadway in her glARs, the projectile thrower's integrated target beacon flashing a small red dot at the projected point of impact. Her finger tightens on the firing stud as she lets it settle on one of the four sets of tire sized eyes spaced equidistantly around the middle of the brown and orange mottled body.

The giant orbs, rotating independently up to this point, snap into focus as several people gather enough nerve to try and flee to the other side.

A small group of ten, bright red nu-silk body coverings marking them as high ranking members of the Court of Finance, sprint out from under the awning of a warehouse fronting the bridge. They barely make it two steps before a tentacle casually crushes one of them into the ground with enough force to crack the concrete, while another three are wrapped up in lightning quick tentacle strikes before being unceremoniously stuffed into the kraken's jagged beak.

The other six crimson garbed figures make it another two steps before they too are swept off the bridge by a lashing blow from one of the massive appendages draping the crossing. Misty vapor vents from five slits across the top of the creature's head as it slips back under the water, oily ripples marking its descent.

Candice fires several shots at the descending kraken, the harsh bark of her weapon bouncing off the nearby warehouse walls, but the projectiles spark and ricochet off its preternaturally hard skin. It finally disappears below the lake surface, and Candice stares, stunned, at the now empty roadway, the buzzing roar of the mob muffled and distant in her ears.

She can feel herself stumbling forward several steps, balance unsteady, before a hand grips her shoulder and pulls her to a halt.

"Candice. Candice!" Lyle's voice is hoarse and strained as he spins her around to face him, and for a long moment all they can do is stare through their glasses into each others eyes.

"What's happening to our world, Lyle?" Candice whispers.

"Shit. Looks like those people ain't gonna stay cooped up forever," Lyle warns. "When they get to us, get ready to run, and don't stop for anything. My gut tells me that monster ain't too far away."

Candice nods and grabs his hand, and then a surging tide of humanity envelops them. Frenzied faces in torn business suits, evening gowns, swimming outfits and casual daywear push and jostle as they start streaming across the empty stretch of road, many pawing frantically at glARs that no longer display a comforting filter between their eyes and reality.

Some stumble to a halt, vacantly staring at their surroundings, catatonia sapping any remaining will to survive, while others are almost frothing at the mouth in their desperate need to continue living another second longer.

The force of the stampeding herd knocks Candice and Lyle around like toy boats on a storm-wracked sea, and she can feel Lyle's grip tighten as they fight to stay upright and moving.

Her heart wrenches when she sees multiple people at the edge of the crowd get knocked into the water, pushed aside by the relentless press of flesh.

Some of the fallen try to climb back up, scrabbling at the concrete retaining wall, while others kick out and swim, aiming for the shuttle docks visible half a kilometer away.

Several of the younger, more athletic ones look like they might make it, until they abruptly start disappearing underneath the water, yanked down like fishing bobbers, their assailants unseen and unheard. A brief upwelling of bubbles marks their passing.

A hiss of water vapor fills the air, mist blowing across the roadway, and the kraken reemerges, rising up like an aquatic titan, tentacles rearing high into the air. An instant of shocked silence covers the crowd like a smothering blanket, and then pandemonium ensues as the tentacles descend.

Candice's hand is suddenly torn away from Lyle's as resort guests redouble their already panicked efforts to cross the open killing ground.

Rubbery limbs lined with cruelly barbed suckers begin their merciless harvest, plucking screaming bodies from the bounteous harvest flooding the road before depositing them into the gnashing beak of the kraken – young, old, rich, poor; the tentacles don't discriminate.

A handsome man in a tattered suit that Candice belatedly recognizes as the obnoxious augstar host from the dinner earlier is unceremoniously shoved headfirst into the kraken's maw, followed by an older couple draped in jewelry, and she hates herself for feeling glad that the beast didn't choose her.

People stumble and lurch like drunks as yet more tentacles start lashing the ground, crushing all those unfortunate enough to find themselves beneath the hideous weight into splintered ruin, driving giant cracks and fissures into the road itself that threaten to dissolve its structural integrity.

Jagged chunks of concrete tumble into the water as the kraken continues its relentless assault, and the support beams underlying the causeway glisten briefly in the dusky haze of late afternoon before they're obscured once more by the fleshy whips descending again and again, maiming and rending.

Gasping, sobbing, her short term memory a whirlwind torrent of confused images, Candice finally makes it to the other side, joining the slow trickle of people lucky enough to pass through the terrible gauntlet.

Behind her, the slaughter continues unabated, whipcrack impacts shattering the air like penetrator shots as the kraken pulverizes the road again and again.

Candice tries to gather her thoughts, and suddenly remembers Lyle being wrenched away from her. She looks wildly around for him, and almost sobs in relief when he staggers up to her a moment later, the left side of his face masked in blood beneath his glARs, a long gash creasing his temple. They clutch each other wordlessly before continuing into the dubious safety of the shuttle port itself, a gleaming steel and crystal edifice with piers radiating out in a semicircle into the lake.

The entrance to the port is a broad curving wall of memplas windows, inset with several large openings allowing access to the black and white tiled interior through automated sliding panels. A translucent sea foam green roof spirals above the structure like the shell of an enormous sea creature, creating a gauzy submarine atmosphere inside the main atrium.

Intricately etched bare steel columns coil like strands of seaweed to support the roof, the artwork adorning their sides simple hieroglyphs representative of the various activities at the resort. The terrifying sounds from outside turn muted and faint as the doors close behind Candice and Lyle, completing the underwater illusion.

Candice takes a moment to gulp some oxygen into her burning lungs, and surveys the interior. The main reception area is mostly empty, a few scattered bodies sprawled along benches and walls. She's uncertain if they're dead.

Looking past the burnished wooden ticketing counters down the docking pier archways, Candice sees throngs of people crowding the two piers that have shuttles still berthed at the end, though it looks like no one's been able to enter the actual ships yet. With a grunt, she forces herself to break into as much of a run as her body can handle, heading for the rightmost of the eight majestic arches. Lyle keeps pace, sharp catches in his breathing patterns the only sign of discomfort he's willing to let show.

The two pass beneath a sign that reads "Pier A" and emerge into a concourse roofed with dark wooden beams, supported by more twisting steel columns, a swarm of frightened people packed along its length. The spacious construction affords a beautiful view of the surrounding environment, but also serves to highlight just how dangerous and exposed anyone passing through is to the swarming packs of winged creatures circling out over the lake.

Three of the beasts make a lightning quick pass from one side of the concourse to the other, but seem unwilling to land and continue the carnage, high-pitched shrieks echoing from the vaulted ceiling the only evidence of their brief appearance.

The vast crowds of people sprawled out on the floor or slumped against the guardrails appear too shocked or weary to move any further, and a low susurration of fear rises at the creatures' brief flyover before descending back into the scattered cries and wails of individual agonies.

Candice and Lyle do their best to avoid stepping on anyone as they make their way down the concourse toward the end of the pier, where a packed wall of bodies churns in continuous motion, ebbing and swelling against what seems to be a cordon of armed guards at the side of the shuttle.

Lyle starts shoving a path through the mob by dint of sheer force, knocking people to the side with carefully placed elbows, displaying his projectile accelerator when anyone starts getting too belligerent, until they finally emerge at the front of the crowd. Five men and three women stand with fully automatic shredder pistols in a loose semicircle around the shuttle door, weapons pointed out at the surging mass, faces hard and cold.

At the door itself are three people, a young man and woman in once expensive finery, along with a bruised man in a ragged hotel uniform hunched over the biometric lock.

"Wendall!" Candice shouts, recognizing the crouched figure. "Wendall, it's us, Candice and Lyle!"

Wendall spins around from the door and then gasps as the richly dressed young man next to him clubs him in the lower back with a shock baton.

"Now, now, remember our deal, you get the door open and you get out of here alive," he sneers, as Wendall writhes on the ground, "and right now I'm not seeing that door open. Moira, be a dear and go see how those peons know our dear Wendall."

He gives Wendall a vicious kick and drags him back to the shuttle door.

The young woman next to him smiles unpleasantly and walks several meters closer to Lyle and Candice, staying comfortably behind the line of security personnel.

"So what's *your* story then?" she drawls, examining her hand. She tuts disapprovingly on seeing a chipped nail, pale eyes narrowing behind her red and gold glARs. Candice tries to establish a local cloud connection to send her hotel credentials but the woman denies the request almost as soon as Candice sends it. Frustrated, Candice opens her mouth.

"I'm Candice Sterling, hotel senior manager, and I need to get this shuttle running so we can start evacuating people to the spaceport! I don't know if you noticed, but it's a massacre out here with those *things* running loose! Please, you have to help us get everyone loaded up on the Icarus so we can get them to safety."

The woman tuts again. "Oh no, darling, I don't *have* to do anything, especially not for a peasant like you." She smiles mockingly, but no touch of mirth appears in her ice cold eyes. "You see, Henri and I are going to take this shuttle through the Gate to somewhere safe, and your plan of stranding us on the spaceport with all these commoners sounds *absolutely* dreadful."

She glances around. "And since we're the ones with the guns, I think you'd better scuttle on back to whatever hole you crawled out of, and be thankful your betters let you enjoy whatever miserable amount of time it is you have left."

She turns and walks back to where Wendall is still trying to get the door open, Henri kicking him every now and then when it looks like he might be slowing down.

Candice can feel the rage boiling through every vein in her body, and her hands are clenched and shaking. She draws in breath to scream at the callous young couple, but pauses on feeling Lyle's hand turning her around. He leans down towards her and puts his mouth next to her ear.

"Boss," he says in a low voice, "there's still another shuttle. I hate the fact these little turds are leaving people here to die as much as you do, but there ain't nothing to be done against eight armed guards. I could take out two, maybe three, you might get another three, but that still leaves too many unaccounted for, and I doubt they're shy about using those shredders. We've gotta write this one off and make do with what we have."

Candice takes a deep breath, and then nods, though the anger still pours through her. What Lyle says makes sense, and as much as she would like to drown the sociopathic Henri and Maggie with her bare hands, getting as many people to safety has to remain her primary goal.

A sudden shout draws both of their attention back to the shuttle. Wendall finally has the door open, and Moira darts inside, while Henri bends down next to Wendall and hoists him to his feet, whispering into his ear.

Wendall's face pales in horror as Henri drags his limp and unprotesting body over to the line of guards, and with a violent heave he throws Wendall out in a sprawled heap onto the concrete of the pier.

Candice and Lyle rush over to help Wendall as he disappears beneath the feet of a mob growing visibly angrier by the second, the frightened guests sensing that they won't be allowed on board. The security guards slowly retreat back into the shuttle in a tightening semicircle, clubbing away anyone who gets too close, shredders whining ominously as they cycle up to readiness.

The last guard ducks inside the hatch and it slides closed, unleashing a primal roar of rage from those outside close enough to see what transpired. Fists start hammering on the side of the ship in an angry staccato.

"Wendall!" Candice yells out.

Lyle finally manages to clear away enough of a space for Candice to help Wendall off of the floor, but his brief time under the trampling feet of the mob shows its toll on both face and body.

Wendall's face is cut and bloodied, one eye swollen nearly shut and his right foot is bent almost all the way backward, grotesquely flopping like a gaffed fish. Candice slips a shoulder underneath his right arm to lever him upright. Lyle takes the other side, quietly wincing as Wendall's weight settles on his cracked ribs.

"I'm, I'm so sorry, ma'am," Wendall sobs. "They saw my uniform badge and made me use your access codes, they said you were probably dead and at least this way I could save myself. I was so scared, and then they threatened to kill me if I didn't help... Oh Gate above, I'm sorry!"

"It's okay, Wendall, it's going to be okay." Candice tries to keep her voice soft and reassuring, but the stress hammers at her insides harder than ever. She pauses a moment to make sure she doesn't take it out on her injured assistant, focusing on keeping her breathing calm and steady.

"The important part is you're alive, and we can still lift off in the other shuttle. Let's try and get these people calmed down and make our way to—"

Wendall interrupts. "Ma'am, we have to get out of here now! That man told me they were going to start the secondary thrusters at the dock."

Lyle grunts. "Time to get moving then, 'less we want to see what the lobster goes through in the pot. Even the secondary thrusters need at least a half kilometer safe zone to keep from boiling people alive – right here next to the dock, casualties are gonna be total."

"Those fucking monsters." Candice spits the words out. "There's no reason not to use the maneuvering jets to get out onto the lake, they'll save ten seconds at most using the thrusters."

"Can't argue with you there, boss, but we better get moving. It's gonna be hard enough making our way back through this bunch carrying Wendall, and it usually only takes a couple minutes to get the power plant online on an Icarus. We need to get behind some shelter, pronto."

Candice nods, and the three of them start pushing through what's turning into an ugly riot. Hands continue to beat on the side of the shuttle, pounding their rage into the uncaring memplas panels, while chunks of concrete and debris rain down from above, those in the back throwing whatever they can get their hands on, not caring who it hits.

Multiple people fall flailing into the water, inexorably pushed over the edge of the pier by the press of bodies, adding to the cacophony.

Candice and Lyle try to shield themselves as best they can while keeping Wendall upright, but all three are bruised and battered before they finally emerge into the relative calm of the concourse and its carpeted floor of broken souls.

"Leave... me behind... just go..." Wendall's voice is faint, almost inaudible, the pain of his injuries overwhelming his senses. His head lolls back and forth as the three lurch forward towards the main port building, the roar of the mob eclipsed constantly by odd shrieks and bellows from the creatures rampaging outside. "Not... going to make... it far enough... away..."

"Stop that right now, you ass," Candice replies, grunting with each step. "I'll be Kufit's whore if I turn into one of those money-grubbing pluto shiteaters to try and save my own hide. We're getting off this rock, together, so shut up and hang on. Lyle, how much time do you think we have left?"

"Started a timer in my local cache when they shut the doors – I'd say we have about a minute left before they fire those thrusters off," Lyle says. "Port's right there, but it's gonna be tight."

Candice replies by lowering her head and picking up the pace, even though her entire body is screaming for rest. The broad archway into the main building looms up ahead of them, automatic memplas doors waiting to slide open at a sign of movement.

"Thirty seconds." Lyle's voice is strained, his free hand pressed tight against his side. The doors seem an eternity away.

"Fifteen seconds."

"Five seconds."

The doors hiss open as the three cross the final few meters of the concourse, and with a last ditch surge of energy they race through, Wendall's twisted foot bouncing behind like so much dead weight before they collapse on a waiting bench.

A thunderous roar starts up from outside until the doors slide shut and mute it. A heartbeat later, tidal waves of boiling water vapor wash up against the memplas like the breath of an angry dragon. The watery green light inside the main reception slowly dims until it feels like an isolated undersea grotto, surrounded by fog, the world outside soft and distant. Candice stares at the twisting clouds, and then shakes her head slowly.

"There's no way anyone on that dock lived through that, did they, Lyle?" she asks woodenly.

"Not a chance, boss. If it's any consolation, they died as pretty close to instantly as you can get. Probably never even knew what hit them."

"...Gate-DAMN those culo-licking chingadores! Self-loving Kufit fuckers!" Candice's voice breaks and cracks as she angrily stands up from the bench.

She storms over to the broad bank of viewing windows that comprise the entire south wall of the main building – normally there for guests to witness the glorious spectacle of shuttles taking off and landing, the awesome majesty of flight, expansive view now obscured by rolling clouds of mist generated by the sudden chemical interaction between superheated plasma and the cold clear water of Lake Basalt.

She presses her forehead into the cool memplas and stares into the roiling grey clouds, searching for any sort of answer to the casual mass murder she just witnessed.

Lyle comes up and stands beside her, wrapping an arm around her side, half supporting her, half supporting himself. "We still have a ways to go before this show's gonna be over, and something tells me it ain't getting any easier."

"How do you do it, Lyle?" Candice leans her head on his shoulder, still staring into the mist. "How do you keep going in the face of such awful things, such inhumanity?"

Lyle sighs, expression distant. "I've been part of those awful things, Candice, and there's no way to avoid it. You push it to the back of your mind, and try not to think about it, until it catches you unaware, late at night."

Lyle's voice trails off for a second before he continues, softer, sadder. "It eats at you, at your very core, makes you wonder how people can stand to live their lives that way, not caring at all for how they treat anyone else, not worrying about the destruction they cause. Some hide it away, pretend it doesn't affect them, grow to enjoy it. Others rail against it, try and fight, end up dead. Me, I saw what it was doing to me, and I stepped away from it once I had the opportunity, put it as far away as I possibly could. Looks like it found me anyway."

He stares at the mist in silence, ragged streamers thrashing in the wind, and sighs. "Sometimes, I think those that fought it and died were the ones with the right idea, only there were never enough of them to make a difference. Too many accepted it as 'the way things are,' or 'the price of safety,' but it seems to me that it'll never go away if no one takes a stand, if no one tries to protect those who can't protect themselves."

Lyle turns his head to look at Candice's profile, her black hair tousled and ragged, frayed strands jutting every which way. "You ask me how to endure the inhumanity? Find something human, something that can see beyond the shallow now, and protect it, no matter the cost. Find something worth loving that's not yourself," he says softly. "I ran away before, but it was the running that let me find what I needed, and I'll be damned if I let her give up now."

Several tears trickle down Candice's cheeks, and she slowly wipes them away. She hugs him tight, still looking out at the now dissolving tendrils of fog. "And you're right, we can't give up now," her eyes narrow, "especially not now."

Clearly visible through the now dissipated fog is the moving silhouette of an Icarus preparing to ascend, primary plasma thruster glowing white hot as it vaporizes the water behind the craft. The shuttle slowly starts lifting out of the water as it picks up speed across the lake, roiling cloudbanks of steam rippling out like shockwaves from the furious torch of energy flaring out of the thrusters set in its stern.

Candice and Lyle gasp simultaneously.

A writhing tentacle snaps out of the water and coils itself around the front half of the shuttle, quickly joined by a second and a third, their lengths drawn taut until with a sudden jerk they drag the now wildly oscillating ship beneath the surface of the water.

An incandescent bloom of light erupts into a bulging dome of water, and then into the characteristic cloud of a venting fusion chamber, mushroom stalk spearing into the sky.

Candice and Lyle's glARs tint completely black immediately, inbuilt light sensors automatically compensating for the brilliantly brief glare.

The memplas viewing windows rattle and shake in their frames as the pressure wave passes through the building a moment later, and an angry surge of water crashes halfway up the side of the ten-meter-tall panels before receding back down into the lake. The two look at each other, stunned.

"I guess that takes care of the kraken," is the only thing Candice can think to say, mind still reeling at the sheer impossibility of what just happened. Lyle shakes his head in bemused wonder and limps over to check on Wendall, who's moaning softly on the cushioned bench. He leans down to get a closer look and frowns.

"Shit, boss, we gotta get Wendall into that other shuttle, stabilize these injuries. He's in a bad way. I'm no medical specialist but I wouldn't be surprised if there's some internal bleeding going on."

The two of them hoist Wendall onto their shoulders once again, and pass through the cavernously empty port building until they reach a sign that reads "Pier C."

The automatic doors slide open as they enter a concourse identical to the one they fled through just moments earlier, but one with far fewer moaning people on the floor – it appears most of the wounded went instinctively to the closer Pier A.

Candice calls out to those most likely to be ambulatory, and soon a ragged entourage of around twenty people trail her and Lyle as they carry Wendall to the end of the pier, those in the group whole enough to move assisting those who can't.

The crowd of people earlier gathered at the end of the pier are nowhere to be seen, washed away by the water surge Candice surmises, only a few bedraggled souls hardy enough to cling to something lying in a daze on the dock.

She motions Lyle to take Wendall as she flips open a small access panel set into the side of the shuttle. With a quick series of key presses she enters an override code for the Icarus door lock – it beeps green and then slides open. Lyle carries Wendall inside as Candice turns to the disheveled group of guests clustered nearby and raises her voice.

"Please, listen to me, everyone. We're going to get you all inside, but we have to make sure the injured aren't harmed any further, so no pushing or shoving on the way in. The Icarus has plenty of room, and if we do this calmly we can do it quickly."

The group appears too stunned and weary to muster any sort of protest, and Candice starts directing the flow of people into the shuttle, triaging the most obviously injured closest to the small medical station in the back.

Nearly ten minutes pass on Candice's glasses before everyone is finally loaded onboard, and she makes a final sweep of the area – the only shapes left are the tangled arms of the dead. With one last mournful thought for those left behind, Candice jumps inside the Icarus and locks the three magnetic bolts sealing the door. As the metal thunks home, she makes her way to the control room in the front of the ship, where Lyle is running through the preflight checklist. She takes a seat next to him in the copilot's seat and syncs her glARs to the shuttle's cloud.

"Is Wendall doing okay?" Candice asks, concerned.

"Got him stabilized in the medstation, along with two other people that looked the worst off," Lyle responds. "That's all the room we have in there, though I did pass out tranqs and aidkits to the rest of the injured. About all we can do for them right now. Other than that, all systems show green, boss – we're ready to vamoose on out of here. Just say the word."

Candice gives a sharp nod of assent and watches Lyle power up the maneuvering jets, simple water propulsion devices that max out at fifty kilometers an hour.

He guides the Icarus out from the dock and faces the nose toward the middle of the lake, preparing for departure. Candice brings up a feed from the shuttle's exterior cameras in her glARs – several different views cycle through before she settles on one from the rear of the craft aimed at the receding shuttle port. Smoke rises from multiple buildings and the lack of movement is eerily disquieting.

"Entering departure zone, activating secondary thrusters." Lyle's voice is calm and professional, focused on the liftoff procedure. "Ten percent power. Twenty-five percent power. Fifty percent power."

Candice can see the port complex spreading out across her glasses as the ship rises into the air, odd streaks of movement in the outer warehouse sections, dust and smoke billowing up from collapsing buildings. She triggers the zoom function on the camera to get a better look, but suddenly the view lurches and wobbles, and several readouts start blinking red. Lyle's hands fly feverishly over the controls as he works to level the Icarus out.

"Shit, not good. That earlier explosion must've banged her up against the dock, thrown one of the thrusters out of line, and the preflight didn't catch it. The secondaries aren't gonna be able to take us up high enough. Have to bring her back down and go for a cold start with the main plasma bloom from the lake surface."

"Isn't that dangerous?" Candice asks.

"Incredibly so, boss," Lyle responds. "The main engines aren't designed for small shifts in power; they're there for the brute force getting out of a gravity well requires. Normally we'd fire them at two clicks up, plenty of room for error if something goes wrong. We fire 'em down here and hit a rough patch of water, or get a turbulent steam pocket, and that'll be all she wrote."

He frowns, a considering light in his eyes, before continuing. "And that's not even getting into what that acceleration is gonna do to the wounded if we punch it too hard – half the people back there aren't even strapped in to a harness, they're too badly hurt. Gonna have to take this one nice and easy, feather the controls."

Lyle sets the shuttle back down in the water before running a quick diagnostic on the main plasma engine. Candice flips through the cameras again, trying to find another viewpoint to check out the curious motion she saw earlier.

Multiple explosions flare up in the general area she was looking at before, but none of the sensors have the right angle to see exactly what's happening. The only concrete image they show is a circling flock of the same flying creatures that harassed their terrifying escape along the thoroughfare, wheeling and diving at something on the street below.

They have an eerie grace as they dive, multicolored feathered wings tucked tight against sleek, scaly bodies; powerful blunt-nosed heads opening to reveal row after row of serrated teeth; powerful hind legs and whiplike tail streaming behind. As she watches them arrow down, several of the creatures abruptly explode, bodies pulped and mangled, and the flock twists away from whatever it was that drew their attention, wings flapping rapidly. With a start, Candice realizes they're headed directly toward the shuttle.

"Lyle. I don't want to alarm you, but I think it's time we go. Like, right now, rapido, we need to go." Candice's voice is hurried as she transfers the sensor datobject to Lyle's glARs. He grimaces and shuts down the diagnostic.

"Well, everything I saw looks clean; guess there's no time like the present." The flying shapes grow larger, closing the distance to the shuttle at an alarming pace." Triggering main ignition sequence in three... two... one..."

A dull roar envelops the shuttle and Candice can feel her seat shake as the plasma bloom fires, the view from the rear sensors instantly enveloped in steam. Lyle slowly starts feeding more power into the bloom, and the Icarus responds by jolting forward, harshly at first, but gradually leveling off as it gains speed. Lyle permits himself a small grin.

"I don't want to jinx us, boss, but I think we're almost—"

His words are cut off by the violent sounds of rending memplas from the back of the shuttle, followed by the repeated crash of multiple *somethings* impacting the sides of the ship.

Candice and Lyle both look around wildly and start cycling through the sensors, hastily swiping from one datobject to the next, until they find a feed straight out of an aughorror.

The swarm of flying creatures, looking like nothing more than winged sharks circling around their prey, dive-bomb the Icarus, lashing at its sides with razor-sharp tails again and again. Several icons start blinking orange, and then red on the structural datobject linked in each of their glARs. A schematic of the shuttle pops up, displaying a bloody crimson gash in the back right quadrant, and Lyle swears.

"Gate-dammit, we just lost structural integrity! We gotta clear these things out and jury rig a patch, otherwise we're never leaving atmosphere!" He turns to Candice. "Keep us steady and level while I get this sorted; you see the altitude indicator here?" He expands a shared control panel of the ship and highlights the appropriate sections. Candice nods.

"Don't let it shift from where it's at," Lyle says. And don't change the power settings unless I tell you to – there's no telling what'll happen to the frame if we overstress it too quickly. If things get bad we'll have to take the chance, but I'm not running that risk just yet. Oh, and one other thing..."

Lyle cups his hand around Candice's head and kisses her deeply on the lips before forcing himself to pull away. They stare into each other's eyes.

"I love you, Candice."

"I love you too, Lyle."

Candice can feel her cheeks prickling with heat as Lyle levers himself out of the pilot's seat and unholsters his projectile launcher, but she forces herself to remain focused on the flight controls. He pauses at the entrance hatch for a brief second, expression implacable.

"Be back before you know it."

Then he's gone.

The hatch shuts behind him and Lyle immediately races to the back of the shuttle, ignoring the pain flaring up from his aching ribs. He passes several knots of people, those with minor enough injuries to retain consciousness, babbling and frightened by the sudden assault.

Lyle briefly assures them that everything will be fine as he hurries past, hoping as he says the words that they'll be true. A minute later he arrives at the rear passenger compartment, the last part of the ship before the door leading to the small medunit set in the lower aft section.

Chaos reigns.

A jagged, meter-long rent is visible in the side of the shuttle, dusky rays of sun glimmering through as the air whistles and howls past. Knifelike tails continue to plunge through the side of the ship like harpoons into a whale, their razor-sharp tips visible for the briefest of instants before whipping back out and disappearing, leaving behind further gashes of destruction.

A scrabbling sound manifests over the screaming wind as multiple claws fight their way into the main gap, raking and tearing at the hole to widen it, ragged talons scoring through metal and memplas with a thin screech until they're replaced by nightmarish bullet heads filled with oddly glistening teeth. The compactly powerful jaws fasten around the edges of the tear and *wrench*, until suddenly the entire side panel flies off with a grinding roar. The wind screams harder.

Lyle stabilizes his arm on a seat and takes aim at the now three-meter square opening, waiting for the inevitable assault. An instant later, a thrashing shape shoulders its way in, taloned claws gripping the sides of the hole, feathered wings silhouetted against the lurking mass of Gehenna V in the orange sky.

Two dead black eyes in a slick streamlined head swivel around until they focus on Lyle, who calmly shoots the creature directly in the face. Its head explodes into a mangled ruin, surprisingly bright red blood spraying the walls for a brief instant until it's sucked out of the opening by the force of the passing air.

Four more winged horrors appear at once, clawing at each other in their haste to get inside. Lyle pulls the trigger as fast as he can, hoping he's aiming for vital spots in the chaotic whirl of motion. He sees three of the creatures fall back out, heads and torsos shredded, but can't find the fourth—

Shocking, agonizing pain in his chest. Lyle looks down to see a tail glistening with blood protruding from his right pectoral, the sudden coughing spasms wracking his body detailing the damage to his lung.

The creature itself is visible in the left corner of the compartment, wings wrapped tightly around its body – must have snuck in underneath the others. It gnashes its jaws together as its dead black eyes stare malevolently at Lyle's face.

With a grinding tear of muscle, Lyle forces himself to switch the projectile launcher over to his left hand and squeezes off a round at the monster; a gaping hole appears in its left flank and it screeches in pain, blood spraying into the air.

Another screech pierces the din, and the wiry creature pushes off powerful back legs toward the opening in the side of the shuttle, wings shaking out for flight, survival instincts engaged.

Lyle's world suddenly spins as the tail impaling his chest pulls him closer to the hole, wind whipping past like a miniature tornado, the creature's slavering jaws emanating the rank stench of death. Its broad tongue rasps over glittering fangs.

The shark-like flier contracts its tail to jerk Lyle closer yet again, dragging him roughly over the shuttle floor, and the violent movement causes an onslaught of agony – helplessly he watches the projectile launcher fall from the suddenly nerveless fingers of his left hand. Grimacing in pain, he sends one last message through the shuttle's cloud.

<<Not gonna make it, baby. Get out of here. Find someplace safe to land and repair, and then leave this place. Never stop fighting. I love you.>>

<<Execute priority program bugOut v.1.0.0;>>

The glARs commands are quick and instinctual, even through the pain, right hand twitching inside his haptic glove – message sent in less than a second. Acceleration shivers the frame of the ship as it obeys Lyle's last command, the burst of movement whipping the intertwined forms out into empty air, and as they begin their plummeting freefall to the water below, Lyle finds one last surge of strength.

"You fucking demon!"

The knife whispers as it slides out of the forearm sheath.

"Stay the fuck away from her!"

Bullet head whipping frantically back and forth as the blade plunges into it over and over, one eye a bloody ruin, hind claws frantically tearing into his stomach.

"You stay the fu—"

Brilliant cleansing light.

No more words.

INTERLUDE

tiMEstamP ef.10.** <<SIGN--2^%AL CORR*#UPTE())*D>*(&*>

--hunger rage tear rend motion leap warm drip search—
<<infosource detected;>>
<<exe.comMatrix v.a.1.02;>>
<<initializing...;>>
<<electronic warfare suite online;>>
<<synchronize global cloud;>>
<<searching...;>>
<<searching...;>>
<<global cloud not found, execute diagnostic sweep;>>
--sound location inside RAGE barrier crush leap--
<<diagnostic complete;>>
<<total integrity 100%;>>
<<weapon systems 98% // est. cellular repair twenty seconds;>>
<<chromataphore charge 92% // est. full charge ten minutes;>>
<<repair subsystems 100%;>>
<<sensor systems 100%;>>
<<mitochondrial network 100%;>>
<<all systems nominal;>>
<<initiate local scan;>>
--tracks targets triggers TAMPERING RAGE--
<<proximity cloud located;>>
<<encryption triple alpha;>>
<<interrogative;>>
<<handshake: biomarker X, subset – prime;>>
<<access granted;>>
<<locating personal files;>>
--PERSONA EGO RAGE SHADOW ANIMUS--
<<updating local memory cache;>>
<<buffering...;>>

<<local memory cache synched;>>

--ANTITHESIS RESISTANCE WRATH RAGE--

<<Welcome back, Doctor;>>

--XANDER.

XANDER

Darkness.

I stand inside an underground lab, tables and walls slowly mutating and folding back in on themselves in the odd geometry of dreamscape, rock melting into steel melting into memplas melting into rock again. I am a precocious nineteen-year-old, newly arrived at my very own Government funded hacksite, and I'm eager to get to work. The past three years have been spent learning about the approved weapon systems, their operating parameters and roles, and I can already see several ways to improve them. My apprenticeship is concluded, and I have been given the reins of creation.

The soberly dressed man standing standing next to me senses my eagerness – a tiny quirk tightens the corner of his thin-lipped mouth, the closest to a smile I've ever seen him display. His face is harsh, severe, all angles and planes, much like his mind. A closely cropped layer of light brown hair covers the top of his head.

"Will this suffice for working conditions, Doctor Lillibridge?" His voice is dry, emotionless.

"Yes, Councilor Rocon, this will do just fine." The enthusiasm bubbles out of my dreamself. "Five functioning bioforges, a lab-integrated VI, and multiple containment chambers – yes, this will do just fine indeed."

The lab is paradise. The world above is a paradise as well, though one I have been informed I will rarely visit.

"Good." His tone is inflectionless. "Remember, you are to make whatever improvements to the biostructs you deem necessary to enhance their combat efficiency, but you will not test them on the surface. The risk is too great that someone will see what they are not supposed to see, and we cannot allow that to happen. Do you understand?"

I frown, but nod my head. Being unable to test new iterations in broader spaces will make it more difficult to judge their efficacy, and I tell him so.

"The creation conditions are excellent here, but my testing will be hampered without a full planetary surface to work with. I still don't understand why I'm not allowed to use one of the Shadow Worlds," I tell him.

The thin lines of his eyebrows draw down as he stares at me. "You will do as you are told, Doctor, and perhaps if you prove your worth you will be transferred to one of the Shadow Worlds." His voice turns cold. "But until you can fully apply yourself to the business of creation for the *sole* purpose of aiding humanity, you will do your work *here*." I wince, and he continues in an even colder voice.

"Yes, Doctor, I am well aware of your theories regarding eHydro, as well as your *pets*. That nonsense will cease immediately. I have brought you to this moon to further very specific areas of combat research, very traditional areas of combat research. You are ordered to apply your not inconsiderable mental faculties to those areas, and those areas alone."

Unblinking eyes regard me.

"Do we understand each other?"

"Of course, of course." I wave off his concerns. "I am fully committed to helping humanity win this war, Councilor, let me assure you of that. It's just that there's still so much about eHydro we don't understand, and if I can just get these splices to balance out—"

"Combat. Upgrades. *Only*." His voice could freeze helium. "Once you have shown you can be trusted to run a lab without utilizing it for your personal use, we will revisit the discussion of eHydro. You may have had some novel ideas, and perhaps you think they might even work, but the others assure me that eHydro integration with living beings is simply not possible." I open my mouth to protest, and he stares at me again, steel colored eyes boring into my very essence of being. "I'll ask one more time: Do we understand each other?"

I shuffle from foot to foot. "Yes," I mutter. "I understand."

"Excellent. You have a brilliant mind, but you need to apply it to what *we* need you to do. What humanity needs you to do. Never forget that, Doctor Lillibridge."

He slowly fades away into a grey shadow as his words echo through the shifting lab, bouncing and reverberating off the bewildering profusion of equipment sprouting from every surface. A desktop tunneling microscope repeats his last word in a rumbling bass. Doctor Doctor Doc-tor Doc... tor... Doc... Doc...

"Doc. Hey, Doc. You awake?"

The voice pierces through my skull like a memplas drill bit. I open my eyes and wince at the light stabbing down from overhead, light that gradually resolves into an emergency strip set into rough igneous rock, cables and pipes on the ceiling running alongside each other like metal arteries.

Guess we're still in the tunnel then. Figures. Lousy assistant can't even find a decent medchamber. I guess he did keep me from bleeding out, but his idea of a bandage is less than ideal. I rather liked that shirt.

"Yes, yes, I'm awake, must you be so loud? I swear, you sound like a Gate-damned harpy."

"See if I save your ass next time then. You owe me, Doc. Where the fuck are we supposed to go now?"

I groan at the aching pain in my side as I slowly lever myself into a sitting position. Sweat immediately bursts forth from my forehead – a bad sign. If my body starts shutting down now, there's no way we're going to make it back to the lab. I force myself to my feet, ignoring the pain, willing it away. The words come rasping out as I speak.

"We need to keep following this tunnel, it should open up just above the employee village. There's an access tube to the lab there that we use to bring cargo shipments down; one of the apartments. Once we get inside, we can make our way to Central Core and trigger the killswitch, try and bring things back under control."

He laughs, harshly, mockingly. "You really think we're going to be able to bring things back under control, Doc? There's an entire hotel full of dead tourists on the other side of this volcano, a lot of whom look to be fairly well connected in the plutocracy. You think no one's going to miss them?"

I start off down the corridor, hand pressed to my side. The pain is quite intense. "Don't worry about them, Government will cover it up. Landslide, helicopter crash, gas leak, bad fish, whatever the sheep need to hear to convince themselves that everything is business as usual. As long as we have the data on Prime, we've got nothing to worry about. It's too important for Government to risk losing."

I turn to look at him as I stumble along the corridor. He makes no move to help, content to walk alongside me, face scowling like he just ate a bitterfruit when he hears the mention of Prime again. He clearly doesn't understand the masterpiece Prime represents, a new leap forward for humanity, a leap Government will forgive any act to possess.

He's silent as we continue down the passageway, lights regularly passing overhead, one every fifty meters according to my glARs. At our current pace, we're projected to reach the exit in another fifteen to twenty minutes. My visual overlay shows us as two green dots underneath the northeast flank of the volcano, two ants slowly crawling our way to freedom, buried beneath millions of tons of rock. Good thing I'm not claustrophobic.

We continue in this fashion for what seems like forever, but what my glasses informs me is only eighteen minutes, until we finally reach the exit, a dirty grey metal door set into the rocky bones of the volcano, a portal out of our underworld.

The handle screeches loudly as my assistant turns it and slowly pushes the heavy mass into the cooling dusk air, dim shades of twilight covering the surrounding jungle in a mantle of blurred shapes and hidden depths. We step out onto a rocky ledge overlooking the employee village, a nested series of apartment buildings and arcologies rising out of the shadows below, and the glowing bulk of Gehenna V looms over us like the baleful eye of an angry giant, simultaneously surveilling and illuminating.

The reflected light from the gas giant is enough for us to make our way down the twisting dirt road leading to the village without turning an ankle, but it dies out less than a meter into the shadowed jungle flanking the road. I activate the lowlight function on my glARs to search for any biostructs luring in the gloom, but it fails to add any clarity to the scene – a confusing welter of twisting vines and tangled undergrowth fills my vision in a false green puzzle, and I flip my glasses back to normal enhancement.

We warily continue traversing the road, heads constantly scanning back and forth, fearfully searching for threats. A lurid red glow lights the sky behind us, back near the resort – something on fire, no doubt. It adds a bloody tinge to the nightscape.

Five harrowing minutes later, our half glimpsed nightmares in the jungle dusk fail to materialize as anything more substantial than subconscious fears, and we make it to the outskirts of the village without incident.

White memplas buildings rise out of the trees like giant molars bursting forth from lush green gums, tinted windows staring down at us like the vacant pupils of a many-eyed beast. The air is hushed, silent, the morgue-like atmosphere of an abandoned Fundie cathedral.

We approach the outpost of civilization bursting forth from the surrounding jungle like an outcropping of pale stone, and something nags at my subconscious. Something is out of place. Suddenly, it hits me, and I put a hand on my assistant's shoulder, pulling him into the vegetation lining the road before he can enter the urban environment.

"Wait," I hiss at him, motioning at the buildings. "It's not right."

He looks at me, perplexed. "What do you mean, 'not right?'"

"There are no people. We should've seen at least one person moving around out there by now, a looter or something, and there's absolutely no motion. There's no sound either, listen."

His ears perk up and I see understanding dawn on his face when he finally notes the complete absence of normal jungle activity. The raucous nighttime squealing of dwarf apes fails to pierce the evening air, and the quiet murmur of a city at work is gone, replaced by complete and utter silence.

"We need to wait here a moment and take a closer look," I whisper to him in a low tone. He nods fearfully.

I bring up the zoom function on my glARs and focus on the closest building, pushing aside one of the broad almond palm leaves covering our heads in order to get a better view. It's a hulking, eight-story habitation module almost sixty meters away, festooned with massive strands of ivy creeping up its sides like verdure fountain spray.

Shit.

Just as I feared, wispy tendrils of what looks like white moss drape across every opening, feathery beards obscuring doors and windows beneath a gauzy veil. Further examination reveals hundreds of cocooned shapes tucked into various archways and recessed areas, completely covered in the white substance, like the two-meter eggs of a giant hen.

167

"Gate-dammit." I punch the loamy jungle turf and wince as the motion tugs at my injured side. "Of all the fucking places to find Leechers."

"Leechers?"

I glance over at my assistant, dialing my glasses back to standard magnification as his befuddled face fills my vision, a porous moon. I push the lab notes datobject over to his glARs and give him a moment to review the specifications. A minute passes, then two.

"Doc? You gonna tell me about those things, or should I just file them under 'likely to kill and eat us' and leave it at that?"

Crap, that's right, he lost his glARs back in the lab.

"Yeah, SMP-04, "Leecher" for short, another one of the subspecies for standard grav environments. They were originally designed as an experimental ambush model, low profile, quick snatch and grabs. They're a heavily modified trapdoor spider variant, about the size of a large dog." I sniff. "Not very useful as they were, to be honest."

I set my glARs to external display and pull up the SMP datobject from my lab files. With a quick finger twitch, I put it on external display, a small panorama streaming from the right side of my glasses onto the ground. He leans down to get a closer look.

"You see that white stuff, how it shimmers slightly?" He nods. "That's *my* addition, only possible through the use of eHydro. It's like a spider's web, only it's been enhanced with eHydro to create a local cloud linking the Leechers in a combat net. When deployed, they head to an area that fits the programmed target profile, and then they start spinning out threads. Anything that breaks one triggers an immediate attack response from the closest linked creatures, and they inject the victim with an extremely potent hallucinogenic. Once the victim's been incapacitated, they get dragged back to an isolated area and cocooned up. That's when the real magic happens."

My assistant looks like he's going to be ill, his face going a pasty white. He slowly mutters, "Do I even want to know what happens when they've been 'cocooned?'"

"Well, that's a particularly ingenious biohack if I do say so myself," I respond, unable to hide the small note of pride in my voice. "You see, eHydro has a very interesting sympathetic response to materials it's spliced into – it's what makes stuff like memplas self-sustaining. In some way, the nature of the element gives it almost a type of 'memory' when gathered together in sufficient quantity, like each bit knows where every other bit is at all times, and where they should always be at when put into a stable configuration. Hence the name 'memory plastic.'"

A brief pause to scan for any movement – none. We haven't been noticed yet. I continue.

"What I've done is infuse all those strands with eHydro to create a biological combat cloud, much like what our glARs produce when linked to each other, with the eHydro acting as both data storage and collection. When a subject is cocooned, the silk starts to infiltrate the body wherever it senses high amounts of neurological activity, and then it transfers those signals to the biological cloud for upload to any combat elements in the area through their glARs. Effectively, once we figure out the frame of reference that that species uses for thought, we can find out anything they know once they've been cocooned. The lab databases are quite extensive at this point."

My assistant's jaw drops open. "So let me get this straight. You spliced eHydro into living matter, doing something widely regarded as totally impossible, and you used it to create mind-raping spiders?" He looks at me, aghast. "Seriously, what the fuck? What is wrong with you? You Gate-damned lunatic, you're worse than Kufit!"

I draw back slightly, affronted by his reaction to my brilliant hack.

"Need I remind you that we're in a war for our very *survival*? I do what I have to do to ensure humanity has a future. I've made the Leechers far more useful than they were before, and they'll save countless soldiers' lives with their intelligence gathering capabilities."

He shakes his head, presumably in disgust, but I ignore it. What I said was true, the Leechers *will* save lives, no matter what it takes for them to gather their information, and what cost the price of victory when utter annihilation is the only other option?

I continue on. "However they came to be here in the village, the fact remains that we must deal with them if we want to make it to the lab and get off this rock alive. It looks like the entire colony from the lab is up in the village – they're designed to stick together for support – but they're not naturally aggressive, so we should be able to proceed fairly openly. The only thing is, you'll have to be very careful when walking, and not just with your feet. Those threads get draped over *everything*, and all it takes is one careless elbow or wayward knee to call forth the hounds. Relatively speaking, of course, they're actually spiders."

"No shit, Doc, you've already highlighted that unpleasant fact multiple times. Dog-sized spiders. Real bang-up job you did there. Thanks."

I motion to move further into the jungle on a flanking path in order to approach from cover. We slowly start pushing our way through the undergrowth, and gradually the outer shell of buildings looms before us, the air eerily devoid of sound in the darkening gloom.

The only noises are what we bring with us – the rustling of synthsilk on leaves and branches, shallow breaths panting through the air like a tomb exhaling, the occasional scuff of a foot on a rock. Finally we emerge from the rich vegetation, a mausoleum masquerading as a city inviting us to enter. Gossamer white strands flutter in the breeze like angel hair.

Slowly, oh so slowly, we creep into a narrow alleyway between two warehouses, gently probing the air in front of us with questing hands, ducking beneath threads stretched between the walls and ground, carefully high stepping over barely seen tripwires. The sound of scuttling claws echoes faintly in the air, no doubt a Leecher responding to a broken strand somewhere. I can hear my assistant's breaths getting shorter, sharper, panicky.

"Relax," I whisper at him. "They only swarm around the immediate area of a break. As long as we're not too close, we'll be fine."

He stares back with overly wide eyes, whites clearly visible even in the darkened alley.

"What's 'too close'?"

"Oh, they tend to stay contained in a fifty-meter radius. If we do end up triggering a break, it's only a short run to escape."

He sighs slightly in relief. "Okay, that doesn't sound too bad then."

"Of course," I continue, "they've also been biohacked to spin those threads across any opening they find, so the key is making it fifty meters without causing another break." I purse my lips. "In the current trials, I think about 2 percent of subjects manage to evade their first break. None evaded a second."

His breathing quickens again into shallow pants. Perhaps that was the wrong thing to say. It would appear my assistant suffers from an irrational fear of arachnoids. Peculiar. I should probably calm him down before he hyperventilates.

"But..." I draw the word out, "none of those test subjects were human, nor were they aware of the Leechers' capabilities. We'll be perfectly fine."

His eyes frantically flit around the surrounding environs for several seconds before settling back down into something approaching normality, his breathing slightly less labored. He wipes a hand across his brow, and then meets my eyes again.

"Fine, fine, whatever, fine. Let's just get through this, and stop fucking talking about those fucking spiders. Fuck."

I nod, and we continue down the alley, moving at a glacial pace, avoiding countless strands of beautiful white death.

A long ten minutes later we reach the far end and peer out at what would normally be a bustling street, filled with moverbikes and people enjoying the nightlife of a bustling resort world, garishly decorated signs advertising pleasures in both real and Aug-space, along with all the sundry comforts of a self-contained employee town.

Instead, ghostly strands slowly swing back and forth in the air, glinting when they catch the light of Gehenna V, countless egg-like cocoons barely visible in doorways and recessed alcoves. The silence is deafening, and the normally well-lit streets lie numb beneath a mantle of darkness.

I take a quick glance down both sides of the street. Nothing moving. I slowly creep out and pad across the lightly pitted concrete, marked with moverbike lanes that flash bright yellow and red in my glARs – a neon highway with no one left riding but ghosts. I can hear my assistant slowly shuffling behind me past a decorative iron railing surrounding a cafe.

twing

The sound is faint, but unmistakable. I look back. He just snapped a thread. Gate-dammit.

"Move," I yell, turning and sprinting down the street. No time to worry about where it leads, I can set up new waypoints once we escape the immediate threat.

I put my head down and churn my legs as fast as possible, ignoring the sudden fiery burst of pain in my side. Luckily, the middle of the street seems clear of threads – a minor blessing. Need to alter the thread distribution pattern when I get back to the lab, though, bump up the selection criteria from ten meters to a twenty-meter maximum.

I reach an intersection and take a hard left, narrowly dodging a thread spun down from a light pole. Should be safe here, we're far enough away from the trigger zone that the Leechers will leave us alone...

Where is he? A sudden scream from behind answers the question almost as soon as I ask it.

Shit.

Shit, shit, shit.

I take a few more steps down the street, and another cry rings out, fainter this time. I can hear a slight scuffling noise from back around the corner. My feet want to keep moving, but I make them stop. I have to consider this rationally.

He's been useful before, no doubt about that, and he's also conversant with several areas of the lab – a plus if my glARs goes down. On the flip side, this requires me to risk my life to save him... Is he worth it?

A brief twinge of pain from my side and I grimace. I owe him a debt, an unpaid life of my own. He could have left me for dead in that volcano, no one the wiser, and there's no way I'm letting him claim the moral high ground, not with his constant whining about my methods.

I have to rescue him. I take a quick look around.

There. Looks like a construction crew was repairing a water main and dropped their tools when the madness started. I grab a shovel, the thick heft of its grip comforting in my hands, and head back into the intersection toward my assistant.

I round the corner as the screams start trailing off into whimpers, carrying through the still night air. My assistant is sprawled face down in the street, a Leecher perched atop him, pinning him to the ground with its meter-long body and long, jointed legs. I slowly approach, shovel cocked back over my shoulder in a two-handed sportball grip, grainy wood digging into my palms.

I draw closer to the oversized arachnid, and it gradually retracts a set of dripping fangs into a neutral position beneath its bulbous head. Eight glossy black eyes stare in my direction, unblinking, and then it skitters off him in a sudden burst of movement, heading directly toward me, flowing over the ground like dark mercury.

A flashing vision of pointed legs and extended fangs arrowing through the air and I'm swinging the shovel as hard as I can, screaming in pure reflex. The shock of impact sends shivers down my arms, the meaty thunk of high density durasteel impacting flesh quickly replaced by the sounds of the shovel clanging as it falls from my numbed fingers onto the street.

It sounds like a train is rushing past me, thunderous roar echoing in my ears. My whole body seems to be shaking and trembling, adrenaline surge twitching my nerve fibers like overtuned guitar strings.

Just as quickly as they arrived, the primal instincts disappear, adrenaline retreating back into its glandular home, extracting its price along the way.

My legs shake like a newborn copig, threatening to collapse in a rubbery puddle, and I almost fall over. The narrow tunnel I'm looking through slowly fades away and I become aware of my surroundings again – the Leecher lies twitching at my feet, crushed thorax leaking viscous ichor in a rapidly growing puddle, its fangs slowly retracting and extending in the midst of spastic death throes.

I shiver once, involuntarily, and then quickly step around it and hurry over to my assistant, lying motionless in the middle of the road. I kneel down next to him – his shirt is torn and ragged where the creature latched on. Two puncture marks slowly ooze a trickle of blood from his right scapula. I roll him over, and he stares at me with wildly rolling eyes that have become almost entirely pupils.

"Hey, c'mon, we gotta go," I say in a low voice, shaking him back and forth. "There's going to be more of them along very quickly. They also have a trigger to swarm if a node drops out of the cloud. We need to vacate the premises posthaste."

He giggles. "The itsy bitsy spiiiiiiideeeeeer, crawled out the nightmare spooooouuuut..."

Crap. The poppy venom's already kicked in. He's higher than a gliderkite at this point, which is *not* going to make this any easier. I lever an arm underneath one of his shoulders and we struggle to our feet – I have to pull him almost all of the way up. The entire time he coos and laughs at invisible visions, gabbling nonsense in a singsong voice. I can only hope the trip doesn't turn bad, or else we're totally screwed.

I manage to get him moving down the street and we round the corner, the click-clicking of Leecher claws rapidly growing louder behind us. He starts trying to conduct an orchestra in time to the noise, and it's all I can do to keep him from falling over as we stumble down the road.

"Pretty noises, girls and boyses, the monster's on the looooooose..."

"Shut up!" I hiss fiercely at him, and his head narrowly misses breaking another strand. "Concentrate on walking."

"Walk the talk but balk at the light, the gene genie genius stalks tonight..."

His voice trails off and he starts weeping. I curse and roughly pull him away from a cluster of strands spraying out from a cafe umbrella.

Cocooned shapes are visible through the windows, clumped together, white flowers with bulging petals. My glARs counts fifty-three and I quickly banish the information – not pertinent to our current predicament.

"So beautiful, so beautiful, so cold and so dutiful... Gate dammed demons! Gates gates traits, we shift and meddle and peddle our wares and wear what we should beware but never stop to think..."

His rambling is now beyond the realm of annoying. I grit my teeth and press on, side burning, carefully guiding him under and around hair-thin summoners of death, our odd dance weaving its way across the city like a drunken reveler, circling and looping around webbed archways and trapped alleys. Only three more blocks to the lab entrance.

"Not alone, not alone, the galaxy's not our home, and who can say from whence they roam..."

Hab complexes rising around us, ghostly strands fluttering from empty balconies. Two more blocks.

"Silent, empty, and who cares to look?" He laughs hysterically. "Gaze upon our works, ye mighty, and rejoice, for is this not what we desire? The perfect stasis of our own oblivion? Oh, if only we had bothered to care..."

One more block. My glARs outlines a doorway at the end of the street, set into the side of a modest ten-story hab – the address of the cargo tube. We skirt several abandoned moverbikes lying wrecked in the middle of the street, threads angling off them to benches and light poles, until finally we come to a halt in front of the opening, my assistant swaying back and forth next to me.

I sigh.

Of course the entrance is covered in a tight web of threads. Of course. I query my glARs for building schematics but nothing comes back. The entire global net is down, a crazed maelstrom of static and jagged data spikes.

There's supposed to be a larger garage access to the tube around here, but every single alley we've passed has been covered in an almost impenetrable wall of shimmering death. We're even less likely to get through those cramped quarters alive than if we take our chances with the interior of the house. Looks like we'll have to do this the hard way.

I turn to my assistant.

"Whatever part of you is still lucid in there needs to listen up, and listen carefully. The lab entrance is in apartment 2G in there, but to get to it we have to break through these threads. Naturally that's going to trigger an immediate response, so we're going to have to make a mad dash to get there before the Leechers get us first. Now, I have no idea what's inside, so whatever you do, don't stop moving until we're in the lift."

His eyes twitch back and forth, and he nods jerkily. I doubt he comprehended half of what I said, but there's no other option.

"Okay. Hold my hand, don't stop moving, and get to apartment 2G. Ready?"

He giggles and drools. Fan-fucking-tastic. I take a deep breath.

"Go!"

I sprint at the doorway, dropping a shoulder to barrel through the threads, my assistant right behind me. The strands part easily with their distinctive *twing*, and we're swallowed up by the stygian darkness of the building.

We run through the dark and I desperately swing my head back and forth, glARs pumped to max lowlight enhancement, barely able to pierce two meters of the engulfing blackness.

The halls are lined with hundreds upon hundreds of cocoons, aberrant growths sprouting like a ghastly fungus, webbed strands stretching everywhere. My assistant's hand clamps my own like an industrial vise, near the point of breaking bone, entirely dependent on me to guide him. I wonder if he thinks he's in some sort of dream right now.

I sprint past several apartment doors, assistant in tow, the numbers flashing as we pass – 1A, 1B, 1C... shit. We need to find the stairs, go up a level. The walls come alive with the stiletto clack of claws, a hideous counterpoint to the constant *twing* of snapping threads.

A stairway icon with an arrow pointing to the left appears briefly on the wall in front of me, partly hidden behind two large cocoons sandwiching a smaller one. Arms pumping, legs churning, we barrel through the eggs, careening off unpleasantly squishy objects.

A small hand clutching a doll protrudes from the half-finished cocoon as we race past it toward the next glARs icon – I refuse to acknowledge the thin strands wrapping and merging into its skin. Not pertinent. Mad laughter echoes behind me as we run – my assistant hallucinating once again.

"Behold the fruits of our labor, Doc," he screams as a shadowy figure suddenly leaps out of the dark, scrabbling claws seeking purchase but narrowly missing. It vanishes behind us. "Behold our beautiful children, grown fat and rich on our glorious work! Oh, what a brave new world we've created!"

Our shoes thunder up the flight of stairs that emerges in front of us like a stampeding herd of nu-buffalo, twisted black shapes crawling over the walls as we race past, gently waving their legs in the air like a forest of spiked thorns. I vault over a cocoon lying across the top of the landing, crushing a smaller one hidden behind it as I land. Fluids leak out beneath my boots and I briefly stumble. Not pertinent. I quickly push myself back upright with my free hand, and then we're off again down the nightmare hallways of the hab complex.

I feel the hot breathing of my assistant on the back of my head, a gentle breeze waving through my hair, his hand still squeezing the blood out of my fingers. "Can you hear our fate approaching?" he bellows, overcome again with that mad laughter. "Can you sense the blade dropping toward your neck? Snicker snack!"

I risk a quick glimpse behind and immediately wish I hadn't. A boiling flood of Leechers are flowing after us along the floor, the walls, the ceiling, crawling over each other in their haste to sink glistening fangs into our exposed flesh. I face forward and pour on an extra burst of speed, momentarily outdistancing my assistant and the cresting wave behind him.

2E, 2F... 2G! I slap my hand on the bioscanner and the door swings open, light spilling out into the hallway in a blinding torrent, the inside mercifully clear of webs and oversized spiders. Looks like the security protocols held. I jump inside, and seconds later my assistant lurches through, eyes wide and frothing at the mouth.

He crashes to the floor and I quickly move to slam the door, secure the room. Just before it's about to close, several insectile legs insert themselves in the gap between door and frame, and it halts, unable to fully latch shut.

"Shit!" I scream, and drop my shoulder into the door, pressing all my weight against it to keep it from flying open. I can feel the weight of the Leechers on the other side, wedging their legs in to provide better leverage. "Get over here!"

My assistant lumbers to his feet and joins me at the door, face slack and eyes vacant.

"Hold the door shut while I open the tube," I yell at him. He nods dumbly and leans against it. I can see the gap widening inexorably as I turn away, centimeter by horrible centimeter. I hope he doesn't realize what's waiting on the other side; judging from his earlier reaction to news of the Leechers, in his current hallucinatory state it might set off a full-blown catatonic shutdown.

I dash through the lightly furnished living room, past a standard kitchen module into the bathroom, and slap my hand against the wall right beside the shower unit. A panel rotates and a keypad slides out, pure physical interaction to prevent any glARs detection. Breathing heavily, I quickly enter my thirty-two digit alphanumeric code and press my thumb against the bioscanner.

"Come on, come on, come on," I mutter harshly, willing the machine to validate my identity faster. Finally, it beeps once, and the back of the shower slides away to reveal a bright transport lift, three-meters-square, big enough to carry any but the largest materials the lab occasionally needs from outside sources. I sprint back out to the living room.

My assistant is still leaning against the door, but it's clear he's losing. The gap has widened far enough that several Leechers are visible on the far side, fangs extended, claws waving like a field of hideously barbed blooms. The color slowly drains away from his face in direct proportion to the number of claws thrusting into the room, making it an interesting study in contrasts. I rush over to one of the couches and push it near the door.

"Get ready to run," I pant, breathless. "I'm going to slide this into place and then we *sprint* to the bathroom. No stopping, just jump into the tube as soon as you get in."

Two more deep breaths, and I slide the couch in place.

"Go go go go go!"

My assistant wastes no time, crashing past me and through the doorway into the bathroom. I straighten up from the couch and follow him in a dead run. Almost instantly I hear the couch splinter, the door shoving it across the floor, and the clicking of claws fills the apartment. I dash through the kitchen, into the bathroom, and with a surprised scream I leap through the rapidly closing lift door, barely clearing it before it hisses shut. I turn toward my assistant, who sits against the wall underneath the control panel with an idiotic grin on his corpse white face.

"What the *fuck*? You almost trapped me out there! I would have been killed!"

He looks at me and smiles even wider. "Look, Doc!" He grins proudly. "I pressed the button! Mommy always said I could press the button! Ice cream for everyone!"

His eyes glaze and he slumps over, passed out, his body finally wilting under the strain of the hallucinogen and our frenetic flight. I sigh, and collapse against the opposite wall, one hand pressed to my side in a futile attempt to staunch the agonizing pain. The lift lurches into motion, and I stare up at the glowstrips lining the featureless metal ceiling.

"Gate save me from fools and lab assistants."

We continue our descent back into the lab.

ROB

Tired. So Gate-damned tired.

Aftermath of the battle lies all around us while we withdraw from the spaceport, bodies littering the ground like so many twisted dolls, human and abomination alike, identical in their immobility. Ashes rain from heavy clouds above, dirty tears of a dying world falling like wet snow.

Following Augstar and Monocle past blown out windows coldly grinning down on us from blasted warehouses, flames banked low in the ruins, guttering shadows dancing in the night. Rhinestones takes point, dragging his sword carelessly on the ground behind him. A trail of sparks follows him like lost puppies. Wraparounds sulks at the rear – no one's really interested in talking with him after that stunt at the spaceport.

Monocle ripped him three new assholes and confiscated his other tacnukes, asked him how we're supposed to get off the planet now that he blew up the last shuttle.

Spoiled brat didn't have an answer, couldn't think past the bloodlust of the moment – typical. His silent moping is tangible over the cloud.

Reach the far end of the road, emerge onto the highway leading back up the beach toward the resort. Scan the area for transport, but nothing's available, all the Vees so much tangled wreckage. Gonna have to walk it to the worker's village. Not a short trip. Set a glARs waypoint and ping the others.

Check the projected route overlaid in my right lens. Interesting.

Looks like we're gonna head right past the shuttle wreckage. Global sats still feeding solid data to my glARs, the worm keeping everyone else locked out. Three angry red eyes wink up at the sat feed, one smaller than the rest: spaceport, resort, shuttle. Zoom in on the smallest

179

conflagration – the burning pieces of an Icarus trailing away from a secondary road into the jungle. Highway overlay puts the wreckage right on top of the main access branch to the worker village.

Not much talking happening while we walk, gravity of the situation starting to sink in to their narcissistic little heads. All the toys in the world won't save them if they can't get off planet before Government arrives to cover up the mess.

Only one shuttle left now, buried deep in those lab files I scooped earlier, sitting underneath the crust of the moon in an illegal hacksite. Last chance to escape this nightmare.

Hunters don't know about the backup plan yet. Felt like letting Wraparounds sweat for a bit, realize just how stupid firing that tacnuke was. Doubt he'll learn his lesson, not the way he looks at the world.

Can't even comprehend there might be consequences to his actions, might be alternatives other than his impulsive whims. Not like that shuttle was going to breach atmosphere anyway, not with all those holes shredding its sides. Could've tracked it, waited for it to land, taken it for ourselves. Now it's so much useless junk.

Told them we needed to head to the village, but didn't tell them why.

Need all the edges I can get, and information's always been power.

Continue down the deserted highway, trudging through the green-lit darkness of a glARs enhanced night, air stilled of normal nocturnal sounds. Look back to see Wraparounds flinch at the sudden thunder burst punctuation of a fuel cell rupturing as the raging spaceport fires continue to spread. The measured tread of Augstar's Atlas provides our marching beat, pistons and servos clashing in syncopated harmony. Combat cloud updates the threat analysis every second – nothing.

Just us.

Make our way past the resort junction along the smaller turnoff, glARs indicator leading us like a will o' wisp. Volcano looms up to the right, placid darkness of the lake to our left, jungle all around. Central resort tower rises out of the smoke and flames up on the volcano flank, a black obelisk wreathed in flickering green flames, vision modifiers compensating automatically in the dim light.

Zoom in briefly to see shattered window panes and broken structural elements running halfway up the side of the jutting spire, ripped apart by who knows what, tattered girders lying exposed like splintered bone. Zoom back out and refocus on the road – alert pings a proximity warning, shuttle wreckage nearby.

Scattered pieces of unidentifiable debris appear in the underbrush and along the highway, some smoldering, most dark and mangled, breadcrumbs leading us around a gentle curve in the road. Icarus left a trail as it came down – not surprising. Surprising part is it holding together this long in the first place. Tacnukes generally don't leave much intact – pilot must have punched the fusion bloom to get out of the initial explosion.

Finish rounding the curve, crushed concrete furrow gouging a path into the jungle like a penetrator round carving through flesh, trees pushed aside from the force of the crash into splintered ruin.

Rhinestones halts at the edge of gaping tunnel carved out by the shuttle's violent descent, staring inscrutably into the gloom with that blank face, blade twitching at his side like a cat's tail. Monocle and I join him.

Brief, hurried discussion over the cloud while Augstar and Wraparounds keep watch, natural desire for information warring with the urge to escape. Curiosity wins out – even now they can't believe they'll ever get caught. Stupid. We fan out into the jungle, following the trail of destruction, picking our way over debris; Augstar's Atlas grinds obstacles underfoot rather than go around.

Spread out through the jungle as we walk, distinct silhouettes disappearing into the darkness one by one until I'm walking alone through a graveyard of weeping sap trees, pale flesh glistening in the night. Wonder how I got here. Wonder if I'll leave. Timer ticks down to eight hours, *jen'sFuture* stirring in its shell.

Change of scenery, glasses flashing a quick alert. Green lines frame a boxy shape tilted against the trees in a small clearing in front of me, belly buried in an impact trench, nose slightly pointed at the sky. Looks like the central fuselage of an Icarus. Quick scan of the area doesn't reveal any environmental hazards, seems the engines and fuel cells got ripped off on the way through the underbrush. Lucky. Icarus fusion plants go big when they go, heavy element reactions unleashed in one last spasm.

Swing around the side for a closer look – not so lucky. Half the outer skin's been stripped completely off, some from the tacnuke, most from the crash. Memplas is tough, but there's not nearly enough on an Icarus to stand up to a crash like that. Might be enough on a dreadnaught – memplas becomes exponentially stronger the more there is. Also becomes exponentially heavier, some weird trick with mass the techies haven't figured out yet.

Peek inside, scenes from a charnel house opening up before my eyes. Corpses lie scattered like rag dolls, several flash fried, others merely severed and mangled from being slammed around like rag dolls. Wrinkle my nose at a familiar stench. Smells rotting, corrupt, unnatural. Smells like wealth. Smells like death. Pull back outside and make my way up to the front section, walking alongside the crippled flank of a grounded bird.

Step over more fallen branches, their broad leaves black wedges in the dim light reflecting down from the gas giant overhead, half my vision shadowed and unclear, the other half bright green and covered with datobjects.

Used to the dichotomy, but it never truly feels natural, especially not at night – mind trapped between two realities. Cockpit looks intact, no major structural integrity loss, memplas nose cone scratched and battered but slowly self-repairing. Thicker material at the front, designed to take the brunt of reentry into an atmosphere. Remarkable stuff, memplas. Pulped vegetation covers the hemispherical viewport, collected detritus of multiple impacts. Scrape some off to look inside.

Shock. I drop to a knee, hard.

Feels like someone just hit me in the gut, world turning foggy, nonexistent wind roaring through my ears. Shake my head like a punch-drunk fighter, try and regain some balance.

Slowly get back up and look inside again. Scene hasn't changed.

My baby, my Jennifer, is sprawled limp in the pilot's chair, head lolling to one side, no trace of *basilis terminus* marring her face, her right leg whole and attached. It's bent at an awkward angle, but it's there, she's there, my girl is healthy again.

...

Except it's not her. It can't be her. She's in the medical facility back on Kepler III, fighting for her life, fighting for another day of 'life', burning nerve damage constantly assaulting her psyche, killing parts of her off. She never complains, never quits, but I can see the pain in her eyes, the soul-crushing fatigue of an unending torment of agony, day in, day out.

Deep breath. Shake my head again, clear the last of the cobwebs. Look back in and see Jennifer...

No, the woman in the chair twitch briefly before falling still again, safety restraints holding her upright.

Shit. She's still alive. Gotta get her out of there.

Sprint back around to the side of the shuttle, squeeze in through one of the numerous tears marring the ship, sprint past ruined bodies and sparking cables, clear a way to the cockpit door. Frame is crumpled and bent, but anything breaks if you apply enough force in the right spot. A few footsteps later I'm crouching next to the chair, examining vitals.

Still breathing, good. Pulse low and thready, not good. No obvious injuries to face or upper body, restraints may have caused some minor internal bruising but shouldn't be anything serious. Lower right leg's going to be a problem, pants fabric shouldn't be tenting up like that near the shin. Pull up the Agency triage datobject in my glARs, it confirms a compound fracture. Gonna need to set that.

Glance around the cockpit, take stock of available resources. Standard loadout of an Icarus includes several first aid kits, one of which should be... there. Hit the access panel to swing a thin case out from the wall, take a look inside, hoping the maintenance teams kept it stocked. Cold shock of relief – everything's there. Quick scan, glasses highlight the necessary items for wrapping and splinting a break – sterilizing agents, painkillers, gauze, synthsilk bandages, several telescoping rods that snap out into a brace. Grab them all and head back over to the seat. She hasn't moved.

Cut open the cloth surrounding the break, peel it back, white bone peeking out from a dark red landscape. Breath catches when I see it. Done plenty of field-op procedures, but this one feels different. Personal.

Disinfect, clean, grip and set. She lets out a small moan. Gauze, bandage, splint and bandage again, glARs providing a checklist if needed. It's not needed. Probably qualify as a medic at this point from all the fieldwork I've had to do out on assignment. Chasing down biohackers is rarely a clean business – seen too many friends disappear over the years.

Finish fastening the last wrap, still no reaction from the crumpled form. Bend over and gently start cleaning the cuts on her face, wiping away the blood and grime. Reminds me of caring for Jennifer as a baby, sitting with her during sick nights, blotting the fever sweat from her brow. Then later sick nights, helpless against the growing grey corruption stealing across her features, unable to make the world better for her, unable to fix things, only thing I could offer a damp cloth and a father's hand.

Never got to spend enough time with her, always too busy taking care of everyone else's nightmares, the bitterest of ironies. Missed her first steps, Mute-King of Tringon saw to that.

Couldn't make her first day of school, no one else qualified to deal with a three-planet outbreak of Black Ebola the Shining Brotherhood decided to unleash. Ditto for graduation, had to shut down a rogue splicer who thought it would be great fun to rewire people's eyeballs into their waste orifices through an influenza vector.

Birthdays in absentia, sportball games unattended, synthcello recitals gone unheard. Always busy working for Government, always busy saving the galaxy, same old story day in and day out. She never complained, always had a smile for the too few occasions I was able to get home, but that's no life for a child. No life for a father.

Saw all the memories on glARs, of course, recorded by my ex-wife, and then later by friends and neighbors, but it wasn't the same. I wasn't there. And when she needed me most, when the Dragon Cult unleashed a strain of *basilis terminus* on Scipio III, I wasn't there again. Could only try and pick up the broken pieces afterward.

Dragon Cult won't ever bother anyone again, made sure of that, but Jennifer's still in that hospital, still waiting to be saved, somehow still believing in her dad.

In me.

Unlatch the restraints, gather the limp woman into my arms, head back down the charnel house corridor and out into the jungle night. Lay her down softly on the ground for a moment, stare up at the stars, alone in the hot darkness of a ruined world.

Can't save my Jennifer, at least not yet. Need to make sure that data transfer goes through.

But I can save this Jennifer. For once, I can be there.

SHUTTLE WRECKAGE

Timestamp – 20.41.46LT:09.39.14OT:03.18.407AG

Candice groans, and groggily opens her eyes. The dark air around her is rich with the thick scent of loam and crushed earth, but underneath it lies the tang of ozone and smoky char of burnt vegetation. Her face is pressed against the dank soil of jungle undergrowth, and she slowly becomes aware of an insistent throbbing from her right leg. She briefly enjoys the sensation of lying down and doing absolutely nothing before her mind suddenly clicks back into focus.

"Lyle!"

The outburst is accompanied by a brief scrabbling of limbs. Candice tries to spring to her feet, and then falls back gasping at the sudden pain flaring up her leg. She collapses to the ground, a breathless sob escaping her throat. Suddenly a hand is supporting her, gently rolling her over to a sitting position.

"Easy, ma'am, easy, you've suffered quite a shock. It's a miracle you survived that crash with nothing worse than a broken leg."

Hearing the word 'ma'am' momentarily fills Candice with hope, but then she looks up into the worried face of a middle-aged man dressed in dark acticamo fatigues, his thinning hair drooping lankily around his head, creases emanating out from tired grey eyes, and her heart falls.

The man is not Lyle. He wears a pair of standard bureaucratic glARs, boxy black frames surrounding slightly tinted lenses, though they're curiously out of place perched atop the combat gear covering the rest of his body. He looks extraordinarily average, and she can't recall ever seeing him before in her life.

"Who are you? Where am I?" Her voice is panicky and shrill.

The man winces. "Please, please, calm down. My name's Rob, and we need to get you out of here. Your Icarus crashed close to the resort

185

– we're on the southwest side of the volcano right now." He briefly looks around, and turns back to Candice, his eyes gentle. "It's not safe for you here."

"Well no shit, genius." Candice can feel herself hiding her fear in bitter sarcasm. "There's Gate-damned abominations running around eating everyone, some sort of armed lunatic blew up my shuttle, and now I'm talking to a man whose outfit screams 'Government.' You think it might, maybe, just possibly, be 'not safe?'"

Rob winces again.

"And how are we supposed to get out of here," Candice continues. "That twisted pile of metal sitting over there was the last shuttle on this planet, so unless you can pull some sort of fusion drive out of your pocket, we're stuck here until WHAT THE FUCK IS THAT!?"

Rob sighs and turns around to see Rhinestones emerging from the trees, sword still dragging along the ground behind him, crimson veins outlining the hyper-stylized muscles of his suit.

His faceless mask shifts with Rorschach shadows in the flickering light of multiple blazes, and it's clearly obvious where Candice's outburst came from. He looks the epitome of biohacked terror in a nightmare-filled dreamscape, unfathomable to those not used to dealing with the fringe elements of the galaxy. Scattered fires from the shuttle crash give the clearing a twisted appearance, immaterial phantasms dancing from tree to broken tree. A message pops up on the combat cloud.

<<Who's this then?>>

Rob subvocalizes into the throat mic wrapped around his neck. <<Survivor of the shuttle crash. Taking her with us.>>

A new stream enters the cloud as Wraparounds walks into the clearing, shouldering aside a small tree. Candice's eyes go wider still, whites clearly visible even in the darkness.

<<REALly?1? Dunt thnk sheEs gonnA kep up. bettr Ditch her>>

<<No. She's under my protection, and I'm not leaving her behind.>>

<<hahAHAHAHa old man u dont hav ne 'protection" excpt wut we giv u., shes to slow an not imprtnt>>

Wraparounds casually points a finger at an uncomprehending Candice and fires off a micromunition from his Hydra. The small explosive flechette enters her chest with a sodden thump and flings her body back against the bulk of the shuttle. Candice slams into the torn metal almost halfway up before crumpling into a ragdoll heap, blood quickly pooling underneath her lifeless form.

<<nuff time wsted LEss go>>

Rob stares at the mangled shape of what was once a living human being for several seconds, face immobile, and then turns to face Wraparounds. He casually walks toward him, slowly closing the ten-meter distance separating the two.

"You may not realize it," Rob says out loud, continuing his stroll, "but in the Agency they teach us a lot about weapon and armor systems. In fact, we have an almost encyclopedic knowledge on just about everything ever constructed." His tone is bored, commonplace.

<<wut teh fuq do i care OLD man,. stop yammmering wit OLDspeek an mov, we gotta bail this shthole>>

"I thought you might find it interesting," Rob continues in the same lecturing voice, coming to a stop directly in front of Wraparounds, the bulky assault suit towering over Rob's stocky frame, "that the Daison-Eno mk.V tacsuit, assault designation 'Marauder,' compatible with a wide variety of complementary weapon systems, including the Daison-Eno munitions deliverance system 'Hydra,' is vulnerable to a standard penetrator shot *if* that shot is delivered precisely to the middle of the T-juncture in the accompanying helmet system from a distance of no more than one meter."

As the words leave his mouth, Rob calmly triggers the glARs quick-release command on his underarm holster. The gun appears in his hand, as if by magic, and he fires a penetrator round directly into the middle of Wraparound's face.

A small hole accompanies the sudden bark of sound and the rest of the visor turns a gory shade of arterial red as the hyper-dense tungsten round ricochets countless times along the inside of the armored helmet and down the rest of the suit, pulping flesh and bone alike. A small trickle of blood leaks out of the hole, and the corpse of Wraparounds topples over to the ground like a felled tree, sending tremors through the dirt as it hammers into the soil.

"Just figured you might find the knowledge useful," Rob says softly, staring down at the armored tomb. He flicks the holdout back into his sleeve and looks back up into the point of Rhinestones' sword, Monocle and Augstar flanking to either side, weapons leveled. Rob looks at them, expression flat.

"He was a loose cannon, he killed someone I told him not to, and if you ever want to get out of here in something other than a one-way trip into the nearest sun, I'm the only one who can show you where the last shuttle is on this entire moon. We're headed to a secondary entrance in the worker village, and from there to the lab." Rob pauses, coldly meeting the eyes lurking beneath a wide-brimmed hat, a faceless mask, an opaque canopy, taking their measure. He continues.

"You can kill me, of course, but unless you want to try searching a three thousand square kilometer facility with no cloud support, no passkeys to get in, and the certain knowledge that Government ships will drop through the Gate immediately after I die and my dataworm dissipates, allowing a flood of information to pass through to *many* no doubt interested parties on the other side, then you'll lower those weapons and we'll continue on our way."

Rhinestones' sword stays steady as a rock, tip centimeters from Rob's nose, featureless head still covered in shifting veils of darkness – intent inscrutable. Rob stares unblinkingly at Monocle's hat-shaded face, his grey eyes tired and hard behind thick black frames, final contingency glARs commands poised to trigger at a thought or the cessation of such thought.

In the corner of his vision the countdown to *Jen'sFuture* ticks down – slightly over six hours remaining.

Monocle stares right back at Rob for several tense seconds, the anticipation of violence heavy in the air. He suddenly barks a sharp laugh, and Rhinestones' blade returns to his side in an unseen blur of motion, tip trailing in the dirt once more. Monocle holsters his Six Sixteen and walks over to Rob.

"Son, you've got some big brass ones on ya, and I can appreciate that. You're going to fit right in." He claps a hand on Rob's shoulder and turns him to face the road. "Now whatcha say we head on down to that lab and get ourselves outta here?" He winks at Rob and leans in closer, but his eyes stay hard. "I never much cared for Franco anyway, bit of a self-involved turd if you want my honest opinion. Always going on about how popular and important he was, like that gave him power."

Monocle smiles, and inclines his head at the corpse. "I think both you and I know what true power is, and how it's used, and I can respect that. Tell ya what – I'm always looking for qualified people to help me out in my many business endeavors, especially those conversant with the language of power. I think you could be a mighty fine addition to the team."

Rob nods, but notes that the gleaming eyes beneath a broad-brimmed hat never lose their cold, cold stare, even as his voice prattles on about how useful Rob could be, even as his hand casually tosses another mini-thermal on top of Wraparounds' armored tomb, even as his face goes through the muscle contortions a less-observant person would consider a smile.

Rob nods, and knows there's no way one of them is making it off the planet as long as the other still lives, a shadowy duel for supremacy finally brought into the open, that age-old grinding wheel labeled survival of the fittest. The Agency taught him many lessons, and how to identify a calculated betrayal was not one of the harder ones.

Rob nods, and steps through the underbrush back toward the road, pinging a new glARs waypoint to the cloud, leading the remaining three hunters to the secondary lab entrance hidden within the workers village, leading them all to an inevitable confrontation he realizes he's beginning to look forward to – a chance to balance the scales against those who think that money and influence will forever grant them immunity from the consequences of their actions. A chance to once more illustrate the difference between a thinking man's definition of power and a sociopath's.

A chance to make another difference in the fight he's been waging his entire life, a cause momentarily lost, but fanned once more into life by the casual brutality of idle murder.

One final reckoning. One final redemption.

The sounds of their passing fade away and the lights disappear into the distance, Candice's body slowly cooling in the still night air. Insects gather to feast on the unexpected bounty as darkness claims the clearing once more.

XANDER

Timestamp – 20.57.37LT:09.55.05OT:03.18.407AG

A juddering thump rattles through my bones, and the lift slides to a halt. The ride was slow, boring, and my assistant's pernicious snoring instigated thoughts of justifiable homicide multiple times on the way down. Somehow, I refrained.

Barely.

I glance over at him in irritation as he grunts and twitches his foot, looking for all the world like a sleeping dog dreaming of chasing flycats, completely oblivious to the outside world. The Leecher venom continues its hallucinogenic voyage through his veins, and he lets loose another ear-rattling snore.

The thunderous sound nearly drowns out the sound of the lift doors sliding open and I cautiously peer out, wincing yet again at the stabbing pain coursing through my side as I gain my feet. Nothing immediately rushes in to disembowel us as my head clears the edge of the doors – a pleasant change of pace. I take a moment to survey the room, relying primarily on whatever vision enhancement my glARs can provide.

The lab datobjects that would normally provide me full-spectrum remote sensor coverage of the entire facility are staticky and jagged in my display, their information corrupted by whatever malicious code currently lurks within the main arrays.

The room is actually remarkably clean compared to the one from which we left the lab earlier, a good sign that Prime, or any of the other species, probably aren't nearby. All the lights are functioning properly, revealing row upon row of stacked identical white plastic transit containers, each carefully labeled with a small transmitter chip that displays the contents to those with the proper glARs clearance.

A winding series of metal tracks covers the ceiling like an upside down series of model railroads, a lone gripping clamp hanging motionless the only evidence of the integrated lab VI.

Normally the clamps would be busy with the everyday mundanity of lab maintenance – lifting supplies in and out, delivering food to various holding pens, shuttling bioblocks to the assembly chambers, clearing waste or failed experiments to the lava tubes – but with the main arrays down the entire system is still and lifeless, a shell without a ghost.

I pull my head back inside and walk over to my comatose assistant, drool puddling beneath his slack lips. Hmmm.

"Heurfff! Wargleblargle grngle snrrrow oW OW OW OW!"

I stop kicking him. Looks like he's awake now, his head wildly swinging around as his brain tries futilely to reboot itself. I'm not going to hold my breath that *that* goes off without any glitches, and I'm proven right when he tries to stand up and succeeds in ramming his forehead directly into the side of the lift's metal wall, leaving a small scuff mark to join the many others already covering the cargo lift. He lets out a muffled groan and slides back down to the floor.

"Oh no you don't," I say in a grimly cheerful voice, reaching down to grab his grimy shirt. "It's time to rise and shine. We've got work to do!" I haul him to his feet, abetted by an occasional kick. A small voice in my head wonders if I'm being slightly vindictive, and then I remember his snoring.

One last kick and he's on his feet, groggily swaying back and forth, eyes bloodshot and roiling. Great. There's no way he's going to be functional until the venom clears his system, and since we don't have twelve hours to wait for that to happen, I'm going to have to figure out some way to clear it out instead. I motion for him to follow me out the lift doors and into the cavernous storage room.

We walk down an aisle between the supply containers, a brief summary of the contents flashing in my glARs and overlaying itself on top of the individual crates, my internal credentials parsing the RFID chip encrypted transmissions. *Primary amino acids, oxygen based, 3kg; Heavy organics, Jovian, 8kg; Protein chains, varied, 4kg; Metals and submetals, crystalline, 25kg;* the manifests scrolling past like so many floating pages of a book.

I pause as a thought occurs, and place my hand on several of the crates, overriding the local bioscanner security – as head of the lab I have complete access to all materials, including those normally handled solely by the VI.

I direct my assistant to grab several specific smaller opaque containers from inside each of the larger crates I opened until he's loaded up with a veritable mountain of boxes, looking like he just finished a particularly excessive day of shopping for shoes. Walking toward the doorway set into the far wall, he mutters unintelligibly under his breath – I don't bother trying to figure out what he's saying.

Our footsteps echo in the quiet serenity of the supply room, clattering off the immaculately spotless tile, until we come to a halt in front of a gleaming metal door. I place my hand on the bioscanner set into the wall on my right.

Nothing happens. I shake my head. Of course nothing happens, the VI is down, and the security system is programmed to default to containment if the VI ever goes down, a failsafe I never planned on using.

The crates are designed to be remotely accessed and have their own individual security systems, but the lab itself relies on the panoptic eye of the semi-sentient program in charge of running things.

I tap in my local override code on the small keypad set below the bioscanner, and the door slides open halfway before grinding to a halt, the whine of its servomotors sounding like a particularly angry gnat as the metal slab tries futilely to complete its sole designed function. Flickering shadows appear on the floor in front of the partially open area.

Fantastic.

I cautiously repeat my head around the doorframe scouting technique from earlier, and the hallway beyond does not inspire confidence. Long rents slash across the smooth rock walls, and in multiple places, piles of rubble indicate where parts of the ceiling has collapsed.

Half the light strips are shattered and broken, the other half intermittently flickering on and off as the local power circuits try to reroute around dead areas.

Nothing moves in the entire forty-meter stretch leading to the T-junction at the end of the hall, where, incongruously, a painting still hangs on the wall, recessed light illuminating it perfectly in a tiny island of order.

Nervously, I slide the rest of my body around the door and start creeping down the hall, my assistant close behind. A sudden gnashing of gears makes us jump, but it's just the servomotors in the door finally burning out, unable to slide the door past the ruined portion of the wall in which it's set. We continue our tense advance, one heart-pounding step at a time, until we come to a halt at the end of the hall and the lone pool of light.

On the wall hangs an oil painting of early generation skhips scattering out from a blue and green planet. A small plaque reads 'Diaspora.' Two facility signs appear in my glARs, triggered by RFID chips in the wall. They overlay the painting's frame to each side, like phantom ships that managed to escape their two-dimensional prison.

One reads *Central Core*, and the arrow points to the left. The other reads *Maintenance/Specimen Chambers*, with a corresponding arrow to the right. I turn to the left and hiss in disappointment. Obviously it wouldn't be that easy.

A giant rockfall blocks the entire corridor before us, ceiling utterly collapsed, leaving no other choice but to circle the long way around. All areas of the lab interconnect with each other, even if it's only through emergency maintenance ducts, but some connections are a much longer walk than others. Going through the specimen chambers is definitely one of the longer ones.

I sigh, and lead my assistant down the right passageway, which stretches off interminably into the distance. The lights continue flickering as we make our way past doors staggered along the length of the hallway, alternating sides every five meters.

Each door subtly brightens in my glARs as we near, identifier triggers overlaying their dull grey exterior. *HVAC Primary Monitor Station, Power Substation Gamma, Bathroom, Plumbing Utility Access Delta, Secondary Server Array (8), Bioforge Theta...*

I pause before the ghostly letters spelling out *Bioforge Theta*, and then punch in my security code to override the door. It slides open, revealing a small room with an infpanel, several plastic desks with a chair at each one, and two hatches set in the wall, pristine and untainted by the chaos of the hallway outside.

I let loose a pent up breath of relief, and quickly motion my assistant inside. He stumbles in, nearly spilling his cargo of boxes, and I hiss at him to set them down as I relock the door, which he does, if rather ungracefully. He then collapses into one of the chairs and starts twitching, a light string of drool gathering at the corner of his mouth.

I ignore him and cross the room to the infpanel, taking a seat at the desk directly in front of it, already activating the local cloud protocol on my glARs. I establish contact with the infpanel and disconnect it from the central servers – corrupted as they are, they'll be of no use to me here.

I reboot it in standalone mode, connected solely to my glARs and the unseen bioforge hidden behind several layers of rock, its presence betrayed only by the two hatches in the wall.

After the infpanel finishes restarting, I pull up the design function for the bioforge and quickly start loading boxes from the floor into the rightmost hatch. As the forge ingests each one, a new list of ingredients appears on the design menu, color coded for primary functions and compatibilities, options branching off each one based on the limited basic designs housed within the bioforge itself. Multiple trips to the hatch later, I have enough Terran specific molecules and bioblocks to finally create a cure for my assistant. I grab a pair of hapgloves from the desk and slide them on.

My first step is to toggle into the custom creation option and start weaving strands together – I'm going to design several different DNA sections to slightly alter the genes in his cells, which will create a protein antibody that only recognizes the toxin, and then a slight upgrade to his kidney and liver cells to filter out the captured molecules without undue harm.

That will be followed up with an epigenetic tweak to recode his genome back to its previous form to prevent unintended tumor growth, and finally a virus carrier to transport the whole package into his bloodstream, along with a high density liquid nutrition supplement with appropriate RNA interference to fuel quick expression of the antidote.

My fingers twitch in the gloves, crafting disparate parts into one unified whole. On the display, the colored strands writhe around each other in a rainbow explosion, and then collapse into a delicate chain of gently pulsing links – viable genetic expression. I confirm creation.

Five minutes later, the leftmost hatch pops open with a ding, and I reach in to retrieve a small ampoule filled with a slightly cloudy liquid. I grab an injector from one of the desk drawers and slot in the antidote; it slides home with a satisfying thunk. Placing my finger on the injection trigger, I walk over to my assistant, who is now slumped over the desk, head cradled on top of his arms, comatose and snoring once again.

"This might feel... odd," I say to his unconscious form. Grinning, I place the rounded nose of the injector on his neck above his carotid artery and pull the trigger.

With a soft hiss, the needle penetrates skin, the cloudy solution slithering into his bloodstream, infiltrating his body in under a second. I pop the ampoule out, walk over and place it in the rightmost hatch for reclamation, and then take a seat and prop my feet on the desk.

This could prove to be mildly entertaining.

For the first few seconds, he continues snoring, and then he shoots bolt upright in his chair, a sudden patina of sweat covering his skin, arms locked rigidly out in front of him.

The sweating intensifies, and then he starts screaming as the heat residue from cells working far beyond what they're normally accustomed to registers in his shocked brain. His body starts shaking uncontrollably.

Hmm. It *probably* won't burn him alive from the inside out. I was careful in how quickly I allowed the genes to express, and the supplement shouldn't be enough to trigger runaway cell growth. Never any guarantees in science, though.

He continues screaming for several more seconds, and then abruptly his face goes white and he falls off the chair and pisses himself.

That would be the kidney and liver alterations, right on time. Maybe I should've propped him over the toilet first. At least his bladder didn't explode – that's never fun to clean up after.

"And how are we feeling after our brain on drugs?" I ask him sardonically, feet still propped on the table. He's curled in the fetal position and moaning.

"You... are... such... an asshole..." He groans, his voice trembling. "Gonna hit you... soon as I... can move..."

I laugh. "Consider that payback for making me piss myself the last time we were in the lab. Come on, let's go get you cleaned up."

A short while later, having taken care of the necessary biological functions and scrounging some clean clothes from a utility closet, we're huddled together back in the bioforge room, planning the next course of action.

We're each decked out in a blue one-piece techsuit, pockets covering most of the available surface areas. I also took the opportunity to rewrap my side with a bandage improvised from some synthsilk shirts, and spliced together some rudimentary antibiotics in the forge to keep infection from setting in.

"So how are we supposed to get to Central Core with the ceiling collapsed," my assistant asks, gobbling down a candy bar. Seems one of the other assistants kept an emergency supply of snacks in the utility closet, and I hadn't realized how hungry I was until I saw chocolaty nougat staring me in the face. We may be an interstellar species unlocking the secrets of the genetic universe, but some things are timeless.

"Brphhllrmm grmphrr," I reply, and then hastily finish chewing and swallowing. "Let's try that again – 'specimen chamber.' Well, 'chambers,' to be precise."

He looks apprehensive. "So these 'specimen chambers,' they're totally not where psychotically vicious genehacked monstrosities hang out when they're not busy eating everyone in sight, right?" His voice is mournful.

"Got it in one," I reply, reaching for another candy bar. "Whenever this lab creates what could be a viable species, I have to ensure that it functions in the appropriate environment and under appropriate stimuli. Otherwise," I tear open the wrapper, "well, what's the point in making them?" Another delicious mouthful of refined sugar and carbohydrates.

"The chambers are also used for testing purposes as relates to combat viability – there's no use splicing together an organism that functions in the lower atmosphere of a gas giant if it won't do exactly what you want it to do when alien leviathans start attacking."

Another apprehensive stare. "So that means... what, exactly? What are we going to run into down there?" He pauses for a moment. "And why do we have to go through another deathtrap? Haven't we been through enough of those already?"

I shrug. "It's the only other way to Central Core. There's a lift that travels the length of the specimen chambers, and at the far end it connects to the main reclamation facility in charge of recycling all the elements that keep the facility running. There's a series of maintenance tubes that run through the chambers, so we can flush any of them if we need to replace the environmental conditions, and those maintenance tubes also connect the reclamation plant to Central Core for redundant energy and material flow throughout the facility."

Another candy bar goes down the hatch.

"Mmmm. As for what we'll run into, I honestly have no idea. If that lunatic opened all the containment gates, it could be anything, though the larger terrestrial creatures should be physically constrained to their chambers. There's quite a bit of memplas keeping them cooped up, since they can be quite, ah, ferocious at times."

He looks ill. I cock my head to the side, thinking. "The water based creatures would've escaped up into the lake, but the exotics most likely died when their atmospheres lost pressure and shunted into the reclamation plant. Some of them are very resilient, however, and could possibly be alive. They'd be rather upset at the change in their living conditions though."

He holds up a hand. "So, let me get this straight here. What you're saying, is that we're basically sitting ducks on that lift, going through a series of opened cages whose inhabitants want nothing better than to tear us limb from limb, and said inhabitants, who will be filled with a murderous rage, might still be hanging out, looking for a snack?"

I nod. "Essentially – yes. Hopefully all the smaller ones made their way to the surface, like the Leechers."

He shudders. "Please, enough with the giant spiders. I think I'd be okay if I never had to think about them for the rest of my life."

I finish one last candy bar, and then stand, sighing contentedly, pain back down to tolerable levels. "Well, if we do get eaten, at least we were afforded the opportunity to eat first. Let's go take a tour of the shadow lab."

We walk out of the bioforge room and back into the flickering corridor; I take the lead and head away from the junction toward the specimen chambers. My assistant trails several steps behind, a glum look on his face whenever I glance back. Several times we freeze at the sound of unfamiliar noises, but each one turns out to be a false alarm – sparks hissing from a broken light strip, a glass beaker kicked underfoot, a rockfall in the distance. Finally, we arrive at a nondescript door that projects *Specimen Chambers – Access Alpha* into my glARs. I override the security lock and peek inside.

The interior of the room is cavernous, maybe twenty-meters-tall, and dimly lit, most of the light strips overhead smashed and shattered. A layer of thin fog covers the ceiling, wisps gently roiling from unseen air currents.

In front of us is a large open lift platform surrounded by guard rails, a small control podium set slightly off-center the only feature on the monotonous slab of the lift. To our left, a track stretches off into a massive tunnel almost one hundred meters in diameter. The titanic passage is bored through the rocky crust of the moon, its far end lost in the darkness, and a much thicker layer of cloudy mist occludes the upper third of its tremendous height.

I scan the area more closely with my glasses and catch the distinctive sheen of threads woven across the double doorway to our right; I'm pretty sure that leads to the larger cargo lift on the surface I couldn't locate earlier. Going that way is definitely out – I decide not to mention the Leecher threads to my assistant. No point in ruining a fresh pair of pants.

The chamber appears clear of any creatures, so I gingerly step inside, trying to watch every direction at once. Nothing leaps, pounces, or spits acid at me, and I hop over the guard rail surrounding the lift to examine the control podium – all systems appear nominal. I beckon my assistant over.

He hurries out from behind the door and scrambles onto the lift, thankfully not noticing the webbing covering the other exit from the cavern. I establish a local connection to the podium, bringing up the emergency override, and once again bypass the security protocols.

"Looks like we still have power, though there's some alarming structural damage messages here," I whisper to him. "I'm going to try and start it up." He nods silently, crouched down next to me, eyes scanning in all directions. I trigger the initiation procedure for the lift.

Several loud clunks echo through the chamber, and then the platform starts slowly moving down the track toward the tunnel, gradually picking up speed until it's moving at a brisk walking pace. We make our way into the tunnel, lift squealing along a rough patch on the guiding rail, and something shrieks in the fog and goes flapping off into the darkness with the heavy beat of leathery wings. I flinch and cower lower, trying to make myself invisible against the floor of the lift.

I notice my assistant doing the same.

Fortunately, whatever it was must have been a surveillance species since it doesn't circle back around to attack us. After a few tense minutes we both stand back up, and I can hear a soft inhalation of surprise from my assistant as he fully takes in our surroundings.

The walls on either side of us are composed of translucent fifty-meter panels of memplas, reaching all the way to the roof of the tunnel, and extending down its length as far as I can see. Within each panel sits a five-meter, multi-door access lock – large enough to admit combat drones and supplies to test the abilities of those contained inside.

Behind the clear barriers lies a wide variety of environments: lush jungles, rolling savannas, baking deserts, misted swamps, ice locked tundras, and others with twisted, alien geometries that bend the eye in disturbing angles, all maintained by a vast series of energy lamps, terraforming drones, and pressure manipulators.

Every access lock we pass is open, scattered tracks of the former inhabitants leading out into the tunnel, dirt and leaves and spattered puddles mixing together in a thin slurry. Several shapes lie motionless near some of the entrances, blood pooling and mixing with the rest of the debris, species turning on each other in the mad rush for freedom.

Survival of the fittest.

"Are these..." his voice catches and he licks his lips. "Are these all things you've created? All bioweapons?"

"Not all," I reply in a soft murmur. "These are the small to midsized species, the ones normally deployed in multiple groups for recon or asymmetrical warfare. The big ones are further down."

"The big ones? What do you mean, 'the big ones?'"

I pause, shaping my thoughts. "Well, in most cases, the small and midsized species are plenty strong enough to clean out a colonizable world, but occasionally we need something that can take just as much punishment as it can dish out." I look over at him. "And we're talking about a lot of punishment here, especially on rebellion worlds. HV kinetics, tacnukes, energy displacers, all the weapon systems we've come up with over the years. The first thing rebels do, those who study history, is seize the local Government garrison and familiarize themselves with the weapon systems. Then they start using them."

"Hold on a second, rebellions?" He sounds confused.

"Yes, yes, rebellions. Sometimes people forget that Government is the one keeping them safe, and they try to take matters into their own hands. When you're stuck on a planet and you're fighting an interstellar polity, it only ends one way. Government loads up the Peacekeepers and Gates them in to restore order. The historical records don't really cover it that much, but the information's there if you care to read between the lines."

We pass another containment chamber, wisps of dirty fog seeping out and blocking any visibility further than four meters inside, even to my glARs. I really hope the species housed there escaped elsewhere. We do *not* want to run into Beguilers in an enclosed area. The lift slowly crawls by, the fog swirling and coiling as it passes, strange shapes briefly forming and then dissolving back into harmless vapor. I continue speaking.

"If a rebellion proves itself skilled and determined enough, and the Peacekeepers can't get the job done, Government sends in the big guns. Remember, we're talking about habitable planets here, so kinetic pulverization is not the preferred outcome – they'd prefer to keep the real estate values up." I wave my hands expansively. "Instead, the Peacekeepers pull out of the system, and a new ship enters, one filled with what we like to call Titans. Massive organisms, some of the finest creations of biohacking ever made," I pause, "apart from my work with eHydro, of course – designed to shock and awe any foolish enough to stand in their way, and utterly destroy those who would still fight against their lawful Government."

"So these things are selective then," he asks, face pale once more. "They don't just indiscriminately rampage across a planet?"

I nod. "If the rebels cease their misguided attempts at splintering the human race, then they have nothing to worry about. The planet can quickly be brought back into the fold and happily integrated back into Hegemony."

"And how many times has that actually happened?" His voice is intense, pressing. I look away.

"Well, ahh, they don't actually consult with me on actual deployments, I just made sure the splices lined up correctly and the organisms performed to the required specifications. Back while I was still on the combat program, naturally," I add bitterly.

He snorts. "You can lie to yourself all you want, Doc, but you know just as well as I do that if they're using your 'big guns,' then there's no way anyone's making it out of there alive. All it would take is one recording of your 'children' in action, and Government would splinter apart like so much dead wood. You're just as much responsible for killing all those planets as whoever actually gave the order."

I flush and turn back to him. "Don't get all high and mighty with me! Or have you forgotten that you're in the middle of a top secret, highly illegal biohacking facility that *you* also happen to work at?"

His face turns beet red, and he clenches his fists. "That's a Kufit-damn lie and you know it! I came here to help the human race, to develop cures and enhancements, to make people's lives better. Not to help build an army of abominations that kill entire planets. Me and the other techs, we were here to do something good. If I'd had any idea what you were really up to I would've shot you into the sun myself!" He almost spits out the last sentence.

"Well, guess what," I yell at him, voice cracking in rage. "I *am* here to help people, or did you completely miss the part where I told you *aliens are wiping out the human race*? How long do you think we'd hold together if we let entire sectors splinter off and form their own governments? What in the entire history of our species makes you think we wouldn't immediately start squabbling over resources and power? And all the while, *they* would keep wiping out planets, keep driving us further and further back, until eventually we wouldn't have anywhere else to run and we would be *extinct*! Dead! Gone forever!"

We're standing nose to nose again, just like in the amphitheater, centimeters from each other, eyes angrily glaring. "I will gladly wipe out any number of rebellions on any number of planets if it meant humanity would endure." My voice is cold, low. He responds in a tone that could freeze vacuum.

"You're not saving humanity, Doc. You're killing it. There's a reason those people are rebelling, and it's because of scum like you. Scum who want to control what to think, how to feel. Scum who don't realize that creating your own life is the very *essence* of humanity!" He draws in a deep breath before continuing.

"People like you, like Government, you just don't get it. You either don't think about the consequences of what you do, or you simply don't care, and all your petty rules and restrictions do is cause more and more to rise up against you. I thought I could help people with my splicing, but I was wrong." He spits to one side. "Selfish pricks like you will always be there to corrupt it."

"I'm not corrupti—!" My mouth slams shut as the lift dips precariously and then crashes into the floor in a tortured shriek of metal, sending both of us smashing into the control console. A cloud of dust rises into the air, gradually coming to rest on top of us as well as the now slanted surface of the lift, capsized like a hydroyacht running atop a reef. I look around, dazed.

"Well this is another fine mess you've gotten us into," I hear my assistant mutter, rubbing the top of his head gingerly. I notice my left elbow is throbbing from where it hit the console, though I appear to have escaped any serious injury. I lever myself to my feet unsteadily, braced against the downward slope of the lift surface; next to me my assistant does the same.

Ahead of us, the reason for our abrupt halt becomes abundantly clear – a twenty-meter section of track lies ripped and torn to pieces, presumably by one of the species as it escaped. The still sparking segments would have been a dead giveaway if that fool hadn't been distracting me with his bleeding-heart whimpering – as it is now, we'll have to make our way on foot the rest of the way to Central Core. I trigger the lowlight enhancement on my glARs to get a better look down the tunnel.

Hmmm, some sort of rockfall appears to have taken place here as well, though as I scan further, the texture on the rock looks very strange, mottled almost...

I feel my heart suddenly pounding hard enough to almost break through my ribcage. Wildly I look around for an escape – the lift crashed on top of the entranceway of the chamber to my right, no help there.

I glance left, and even through my terror I'm momentarily stunned. The entire fifty meters of memplas is shattered and melted, self-regeneration mechanisms overwhelmed by the sheer scope of destruction. Without hesitation, I careen down the canted surface of the lift and run across the rocky tunnel floor over to the broken memplas wall. I can hear a startled oath behind me, and then footsteps in pursuit. He catches up to me as I'm clambering over a mound of memplas into the darkened chamber that expands impossibly high overhead, glow panels twinkling like stars above us, almost as if we were on the surface of the moon, a forest barely visible off in the distance.

"What the shit, Doc," he gasps, breathless. "Why did you take off like that?"

"Quiet!" I shush him urgently. "We need to get into the maintenance tunnels, there should be an access hatch nearby. Look for a metal hatch set into a rock or a tree."

He doesn't move, and clasps his arms across his chest. "No. I'm tired of running all over the place and you not telling me anything until it's already bit me, or clawed me, or tried to suck my brains out or whatever. I want to know what we're doing this time."

I grimace – of all the times for him to grow a spine. "Very well, very well, I'll explain as we look, stick close by." I gesture vaguely at the trees as we move further into the twilight chamber, an almost idyllic pasture of lush grass interspersed with scattered rock outcroppings, though random large patches appear to have been burned and scorched by an intensely hot flame.

"You see those trees over there?" He nods. "Well, the creature that lives in this chamber normally resides in those trees. Do you know how I know it's not currently residing in those trees?"

I see his face fall, and he says slowly, "It's in the tunnel ahead of us, isn't it?"

"Bravo, we'll make a real thinker of you yet." I clap my hands lightly, mockingly. "Therefore, we need to get as far away from here as possible before it notices we've intruded on its territory." I look behind us, still clear for now. I turn back. "And it's *very* territorial. One could almost say murderously so."

"But what is it? What's got you so scared? You haven't acted like this around any of the other creatures." His voice is low, penetrating.

"It broke out of a three-meter-thick wall of memplas, isn't that reason enough?" Gate-dammit, I'm whining. I hate whining.

"What *is* it, Doc?"

"Hrmmm, how to put this... It's, well, it's the reconstituted DNA of *allosaurus fragilis* combined with the double wing structure of *anisoptera libellula*, and then some assorted odds and ends from various megafauna classes along with some Gate-fuel meta materials woven in..." I pause slightly for a second, and in a small voice finish with, "...oh and it also breathes fire."

He stumbles to a halt, eyes spreading wide. His mouth works soundlessly for a moment, putting the pieces together, then finally gets the words out.

"Are you trying to tell me you made, and let's be real clear here, an honest to Gate, real life *dragon*?!"

I give a quick nod.

"But what on Terra would Government want with a dragon, of all things? There's no way they'd ever keep that a secret!"

"I didn't make it solely for Government." He stares at me, uncomprehending. I stare right back.

"I know at this point you probably think I'm some sort of deranged psychopath, killing people off for the sheer pleasure of it, but I meant what I said earlier. I *am* helping people. Unfortunately, that means I have to do a lot of things I never pictured myself doing, especially when it comes to biohacking." I snort bitterly. "I'm not going to lie, if it's a choice between making what Government wants, and atomizing inside a sun, I would prefer to live. But," and I can't help but let the excitement creep into my voice, "every so often I get to make something for *me*. Something wondrous, something no one has ever seen before, something children can point and stare at and be amazed by."

I let out a soft sigh. "Something beautiful."

He gazes at me for a long moment, and then shakes his head back and forth as if to clear it. "So why are we running from it, then?"

I feel my cheeks heat up. "Umm, the territoriality thing, and the breathing of fire, and the two-meter talons and fangs... I still have some bugs to work out. Suffice it to say, us standing around here talking is a bad idea, especially if it wakes up. It always wakes up cranky."

"Cranky, huh? Gate save us from scientists and fools. Let's get out of here then, I'd hate to end up a dragon's breakfast after we've come so far." He idly kicks a small rock into the grass in front of us, producing a slight clang.

We look at each other, and then sprint forward, eyes feverishly scanning the ground. I shout in triumph as my glARs outline a circular hatch set into an outcropping of rock protruding from the soil, and in answer, a deafening roar reverberates from the tunnel. We both flinch, and I quickly enter the security override, jamming at the keys frantically in my haste. Seconds later, we're clambering down an access ladder as fast as our arms and legs can move, the hatch sealing shut with a solid finality, a shadow briefly flashing above it before it closes.

ROB

Timestamp – 21.02.13LT:09.59.41OT:03.18.407AG

Another echoing roar of explosions from a fracturing Six Sixteen shell; another wave of scuttling black death destroyed. Huddled inside the cargo lift, willing it to get to the bottom faster, hideously twisted creatures raining body parts from above as Monocle and Augstar pour torrents of fire back up the shaft. Rhinestones dispatches any that get through with quick, economical thrusts of his sword, edge still impossibly keen after all the fighting.

The lab datobject calls them SMPs, Leechers, been chasing us constantly since we entered the village. Tried to warn the other three about breaking the strands, but a ten-meter Atlas doesn't fit anyone's definition of subtle. Busy fending them off the entire way down – Monocle's bandolier is more than half empty and Augstar's ammo reserves are running low for the main guns. Skittering of their claws almost drowns out the weapon discharges at times.

More explosions, more projectiles, more ichor splattering down on our heads – a grisly shower of foul phlegm. Pick off a spider approaching Rhinestones from behind with a penetrator round, he dashes to the side and cleaves one in half as it descends at my head. No time to think of wrong or right, who's protecting who, only survival. The severed halves pass to either side of me and soddenly impact the growing pile of twitching parts on the floor.

Lift slams to a halt at the bottom of the shaft, almost knocks me over; place a steadying hand on the leg of Augstar's Atlas, feel the tremors as she fires off another fusillade from the cannons. Empty casings tinkle as they scatter near my feet, floor of the lift nearly covered in rolling cylinders, delicate brass chimes drowning beneath a rising tide of dark blood. The insane onslaught of giant spiders continues without pause.

Push off the Atlas' leg and sprint over to the huge cargo door, pull up the emergency security override code on my glasses with a quick finger twitch, hatch hisses open as I pound in the code, gloved fingers stabbing keys in staccato bursts. Next room looks to be a secondary storage center, dark as a midnight tomb, filled with crates and who knows what else.

Ping Rhinestones to clear it, he's better equipped for it than anyone, and Monocle and Augstar are the only things keeping us from being overrun. He dashes through, lightning quick, red veins glowing bright, sword tip sparking on the floor. The sounds of carnage erupt as he passes through the doorframe.

Give him a three second lead and then follow him through, Augstar and Monocle still trying to clear the shaft. Room beyond is filled with more chitin-spiked horrors, attempting to swarm Rhinestones, ghostly green in the glARs enhancement. They're not succeeding – his sword spins around in a blur of motion, dancing through corpses that don't yet know they're dead, effortlessly slicing grotesquely warped creatures into quivering chunks. I pick off several that are creeping my way, single penetrator shots to the head, ping Monocle to join us.

He glides through the door, still firing Six Sixteen rounds into the cargo shaft, weapon belching flame with each shot. Spry for an old man, moves like a ballet dancer, feet delicately skipping over scattered corpses like they're not even there. Moves like a Black Colony operative.

He pops in a quick reload, hands blurring with each shell he slides home, and then fires a round at Rhinestones before immediately spinning around and firing the rest back at the shaft. The micromunitions split apart right before they reach the red veined suit and a rolling tide of explosions echoes through the room – Rhinestones tangos in time with their thunderous beat, a strobe-lit psychopath, clearing out the few SMPs to escape the tearing concussions. More explosions echo from the lift tube. I ping Augstar.

Her Atlas slowly grinds through the door, bent at the waist, lurching backward, shoulder-mounted launchers spewing a continuous cloud of flechettes through the opening, vaporizing the boiling black tide on the other side into a fine mist. She continues to back several steps away, and then switches over to two highex rounds, my glARs displaying an alert.

Dive behind some crates for cover as the room is briefly lit by a searing noontime flash of light, sound overwhelming my ears in a deafening roar. Stand back up to see a twisted pile of rubble where the cargo doors used to be, effectively sealing off the tube. No more bugs getting in, but we're not getting out that way either. Doesn't matter.

Shuttle's the only option left.

The sound of silence rings in my ears. Finally take a breath, adrenaline crash turning my legs into quivering jelly. All I can do not to fall over. Been in some intense Agency field ops before, but *never* anything like that. Definitely going to have night terrors for a couple weeks, assuming we make it out.

Assuming *I* make it out.

Slide a new magazine into my penetrator, last one left. Better make it count.

GlARs waypoint sits over the southeast door, a gentle arrow leading the way out of the charnel house. Walk over to the door, trigger another override, watch it slide open. Web of threads cat's cradles the opening, motion Rhinestones to take point once again. He brushes them aside with a casual wave, cascading snaps parting the web into gauzy strands that briefly fill the air, then he darts into the next room.

We follow him in, quickly setting a perimeter, combat cloud updating constantly. Tense moment while we wait for another mad rush, but nothing happens. Must have cleared out all the ones close enough to respond. Glance around the room, glARs filling in unseen details from the lab schematics, ghost green wireframe melding with lowlight vision.

Standing on what looks like a receiving area, massive tunnel stretching out directly in front of us, heavy clouds concealing the ceiling.

Atmosphere must have escaped from somewhere. Should be a lift leading into the tunnel, but it's missing, empty docking bay a gaping socket in the expansive emptiness of the rough hewn rock floor. Single door to the east, schematics label it *Maintenance Access A/Central Core*.

Door isn't big enough for the Atlas to fit through, doubt Augstar is willing to leave it behind. Going to have to head through the tunnel, circle around to Central Core the back way – shuttle tunnel is only accessible from there.

Have to find a way to get rid of these three before then. Know they're planning on spacing me as soon as we get the shuttle out of here. Can see it in Monocle's eyes, way he's constantly watching my movements, sizing up my abilities. Can see he knows I'm doing the same thing right back, two wolves warily circling each other, fangs gleaming behind drawn back lips. Other two are oblivious – to them this is a game gone bad, and they're only worried about getting out before it gets worse.

For us, predators used to the peculiar half vision of shadow ops, it's the comforting routine of death.

Ping the fog shrouded tunnel in the combat cloud, link to the Central Core schematics and —

Something leaps out of the lift bay, the air *shimmering* like heat waves off hot sand. Barely sensed blur in the darkness, glARs struggling to track it, threat vectors going crazy in the cloud. The shape descends toward Rhinestones and he rolls out of the way, faster than thought, sword whistling in a brief parry. Coruscating blue sparks fountain into the air from the glancing contact between his blade and whatever attacked him.

A *scream* echoes through the chamber, sound I've never heard before – something ripped from the deepest recesses of humanity's shared primal hindbrain. The monster in the night, lurking beyond the campfire.

Another flash of movement, more blue sparks spraying across the blackness, Rhinestones' sword weaving a flickering net against the eye-wrenching blur of his assailant. Another *scream* pierces the air.

Suddenly, something appears, a hulking three-meter mass of rippling muscle and jagged spines. It drops to all fours, tail lashing chunks of rock out of the ground behind it in scything arcs. Monocle immediately fires a Six Sixteen round at it – roiling orange fire blankets the platform.

Dust fills the air, and then parts, the creature bursting through in an eye-tearing flash of motion. Claws rip at Monocle, who narrowly falls back out of the way, talons whispering past his face, and he watches the gaping rents in the monster's flesh knit back together as it moves.

The momentum of its charge takes it past Augstar, and it almost casually reaches up and severs the Atlas' right arm. The cannon crashes to the floor and fills the cavern with a dirge-like clang, like the tolling of a cracked funeral bell. GlARs finally matches a hit from the lab datobject, buried deep within a hidden archive. Information scrolls past, feel my eyes widen in growing shock.

<<designation: Prime;>>

<<threatClass: double omegaPlus(unknown);>>

<<estimated loadout: biointegrated combat cloud, eHydro regeneration structure, meta-material desynched skeletal musculature, enhanced chromatophore stealth system, multiple – >>

I cut the summary and sprint for the eastern door. Agency taught us to recognize an unwinnable fight, when to retreat – this definitely qualifies. Penetrator isn't going to do shit against something that shrugs off Six Sixteen rounds, and this is a perfect chance to bolt for the shuttle. No one notices my escape, too busy trying to stay alive.

Reach the door, punch in the security override yet again, wait for the system to acknowledge. Look back, sounds of Augstar firing off multiple HV rounds from the remaining Atlas cannon thundercracking the air – Prime shrugs the kinetics off like so many hailstones and charges at her, snaking across the ground on all fours. Its claws dig into the floor like hot knives into butter, and rock chips splinter out like shrapnel.

Rhinestones tries to intercept with a leaping strike, Prime's tail flicking the sword aside as blue sparks cascade yet again, but the shift in momentum is enough to disrupt the creature's furious rush. It sinuously weaves past the Atlas, scoring deep grooves into the side of the machine's left leg with a raking pass of talons, and leaps back down into the lift bay. Monocle fires another Six Sixteen round and more explosions fill the chamber, a mix of highex and monofil erupting out of the lift bay and shattering the ceiling into a dirty rain of jagged gravel spraying out in all directions.

The door finally opens and I rush through, pausing only to trigger the security lock behind me. Muffled weapons discharges filter through the two-meter-thick memplas reinforced steel, and dust drifts down from the polished rock ceiling overhead. A flashing glARs waypoint leads me up the corridor, booted feet pounding the floor as I run.

Come to a T-junction and curse – waypoint leads me right into a pile of fallen rock blocking the hallway. Hastily check for an alternate route, fingers twitching the lab schematics in a dizzying whirl until an option presents itself. Spin one hundred and eighty degrees and sprint back through the intersection once more, lone island of light illuminating a painting on the wall to my left. No time to look – mission just turned into a race to the shuttle.

Three doors blur past my right side before the waypoint flashes a green arrow, door identifier reads *HVAC Primary Monitor Station*. Slam another security override and burst through, quick scan revealing multiple banks of heavy machinery and memplas duct openings.

Waypoint flashes above an opening set into the northern wall, looks tall enough to run inside of. Won't be comfortable though, only one and a half meters high, gonna be bent over the whole time. Least I won't have to worry about being swept away if the automatic reclamation system triggers from all the firepower going off in that tunnel.

Tear the grate off and crawl in, straightening up into a crouching run after several steps. The roof slopes gently upward, gradually clearing room overhead.

Ten meters in and the duct goes vertical, climbing notches set into the memplas-like miniature reliquaries. Must be here for physical scans in case anything ever goes wrong. Good old Government redundancy.

Scramble up the shaft, arms and legs churning like pistons. Seventy-two seconds pass fighting my way higher, then belly over the top, back into a crouching run. Duct looks brighter up ahead, thirty meters or so, odd flashes bursting through.

Look down as I pass into the oddly flashing area and almost stumble. Main HVAC corridor runs right above the tunnel, and I can faintly see the battle still raging down below through the clear memplas floor, highex going off like fireworks and burning away the mist in patches, figures darting in and out of the swirling grey.

Like watching gods struggle amongst the clouds.

A running fight dances through the tunnel – Prime harrying the hunters' every step, leaping in for savage strikes from the walls and ceiling, ignoring gravity like it's not even there, absorbing every bit of punishment they can dish out and dashing back in for more.

Glowing red furrows crosshatch Rhinestones' suit, and Augstar's Atlas limps with an awkward hitch, one of the servomotors gone, but she's still pouring munitions at Prime as fast as the mech will fire, Rhinestones interposing his blade whenever it gets too close, Monocle distracting with the Six Sixteen every time the creature is on the verge of breaking through their triangular formation.

Quick ping in my glasses from the digiworm, still monitoring the lab VI, keeping it locked down. Tunnel sensors are spiking, constant alerts threatening to overwhelm the system and trigger a flush – billions of liters of water cycling through from the lake, clearing out all the chambers and returning their basic compounds to the reclamation plant. Water probably shouldn't reach the HVAC ducts.

Not a big fan of *probably*.

Put my head down and run faster, ignoring the scream of overtaxed muscles, drawing on every ounce of Agency training beaten into me over the years. Need to make it to Central Core. Need that shuttle. Don't care what kind of monsters try to get in the way, nothing's stopping me from making it back to my girl.

Hold on, Jennifer. Daddy's on his way.

LAB *GENESIS*

Timestamp – 21.26.04LT:10.23.32OT:03.18.407AG

Three figures dash down a cavernous tunnel, shadowed end expanding toward infinity, and the steady drip from a memplas-edged sword silently chases their heels. Some of the fluid is clear, cold, alien, expelled from the innards of a creature none of them has ever seen before.

It steams as it hits the rocky floor, and seems to move under its own power. The rest of the fluid, the majority, is incandescent red, welling out of a hundred cuts and gashes on an experimental biotech suit, rivulets coursing down a wavering arm and pooling off the monofil tip of a living weapon, one that dumbly repairs its perfect razor exterior after each beading drop, shedding jagged atoms like bloody dandruff.

Rhinestones triggers another three cc's of *stim* and feels the fatigue receding, banished from his mind by the complex cocktail of chemicals coursing through his veins. His arm steadies, just in time to parry another whiplash series of strikes from the tireless nightmare harrying their every step, constantly seeking their flesh with its impossibly sharp talons and serpentine tail.

Prime.

He considers it grimly ironic that the hunters have become the hunted, fleeing for their lives from a creature they willingly loosed, thinking themselves invincible with their glamorous tech and unlimited funds.

There's always something stronger, he muses, whipping his sword through the complex katas of *kenjutsu*, turning aside those blows that would be immediately fatal, suffering weakening strikes as the price for another minute or two of life. He is intimately linked with his suit, the old biotech prototype an extension of himself, pharmocopic compounds filtering through his blood and powering the eHydro infused armor.

213

The newer versions Black Colony uses have more bells and whistles, but this is the first suit he designed, five short years ago, the one that served as a base for all the others that came after, and he wears it like a second skin – biohacked musculature granting him preternatural speed and strength, the abilities of a demigod.

Abilities that come with a price, however, for each drop of blood the suit spills is a drop of blood no longer flowing in his veins. His heart jumps raggedly until he pushes two cc's of *calm* into his system, riding the turbulent edge of overdose like the world's largest wave, somehow balancing right on that chaotic edge.

He designed many of the compounds himself, his life a product of twenty years intense schooling under the most demanding biohackers and chemists his father could procure, along with engineers and physicists who taught him the fundamentals that led to the biosuit, preparing him to take over the family business once he came of age and could contribute to the corporation – no wastrel sons in the house of Eno; the pursuit of profit and excellence above all. Memplas and Government made the family company rich, but it is a poor CEO who does not diversify, and biohack-derived chemistry application looks to be an area Government is *very* interested in, especially now that the suits are in production.

Thoughts of the past vanish beneath another flashing exchange, lightning quick claws raking and rending, another percentage point dip in the biosuit's integrity, internal sensors flashing a warning yellow on the integrated glARs display covering the inside of the featureless helmet.

Memplas muscle fiber is tough, resilient, but even it has limits – limits Rhinestones is all too fearful he's reached. He triggers two cc's of *adreno* and the fear dissipates, subsumed beneath a neurochemical rush, the surge of energy flooding his entire being like caged lightning.

With a thunderous shout he goes on the offensive, raining a series of punishing blows on the *oni*, the demon. It briefly falls back under the assault, writhing beneath the flurry of strikes, massive gashes opening on its forearms and upper body.

A sudden *scream* and it retreats, scuttling up the one of the clear memplas sheets lining the tunnel, perched halfway up like some sort of malignant tumor, a swollen black tick clinging to its host. He triggers the ocular zoom function in the suit and can see the wounds already closing up over pulsing internal organs, the creature regenerating at an astonishing rate of speed, entropy reversing in a wholly unnatural way.

He is envious.

The biosuit has self-repair functions, but compared to the speed with which the *oni* heals itself, he might as well be wearing dumbtech metal armor from pre-Diasporan Terra. The suit labors to seal the many cuts marking his body, but he knows it's a losing battle, the best efforts of the Daison-Eno labs is nothing compared to the graceful lethality of the killing machine currently besieging the group, entropy somehow harnessed and reversed at the molecular level.

Rhinestones watches the last gaping wound on the *oni* quiver shut and realizes it's only a matter of time before the wicked claws land a final blow, the impossible sharpness of their edges tearing through him one last time, his life spilling out in an unknown tunnel deep within the crust of a backwater moon.

He knows this, feels it in his bones, yet refuses to accept it; that everything he's planned for his entire life, all his hopes and dreams, can be so suddenly snuffed out, so quickly extinguished.

He refuses to accept he no longer has control, because it simply does not occur to him that that could be an option.

The creature *screams* again, tense muscles quivering, and fires multiple spines from its body at eye-blurring speed. He parries three, the force of their passing jarring the sword in his grip, but a fourth impales itself into his upper thigh, needle point piercing muscle and bone alike, and he grunts in pain.

Warning icons cascade down his display and the biomonitor blinks frantically, a checklist of destruction to the shell that houses his spirit, but he triggers another three cc's of *calm* and ignores them all, letting the suit compensate for the loss of control in his leg. A timer counts down ominously at the corner of his vision – the spine carried some sort of neurotoxin that isn't immediately fatal due to the suit's defenses, but his lifespan is now measured in minutes.

He ignores that too.

The creature suddenly drops back down to the cavern floor, rock splintering and cracking under its weight. Dust billows up from the impact, and slowly it stands up on its hind legs, twice the height of a man – humanoid, and yet so very inhuman, eyes gleaming in the stygian gloom. It casually bats aside two highex rounds fired from the

Atlas; explosions ripple the memplas behind it into fractured sheets that immediately begin to self repair. A razor-edged tail lashes the ground with whipcrack snares; once, twice, thrice. Teeth glisten in a Cheshire Cat grin.

Rhinestones stares into those cold, dark eyes and feels them boring back into his soul, piercing the blank facelessness of his suit's mask.

There's an intelligence within them, a hunger, the devouring emptiness of an event horizon, and he proffers his blade in quick salute to that perfectly honed void.

Very few can say they've danced with Death itself.

Both figures subtly tense, the air crystallizing around them, and then chaos erupts like the heart of a supernova.

Rhinestones dashes forward and triggers every remaining store of *adreno*, *zerk*, and *chrono*, blade trailing behind him in the low sweep position. The drugs hit his bloodstream and time immediately slows to a crawl, amplified by the suit – he can see all potential outcomes before they even happen, the ultimate chess game, the ultimate high, a wave of potentialities awaiting only his action to collapse down into reality, yet all paths lead to the same destination.

He shuts down the beeping biomonitor with a frozen synapse thought – its mechanical warnings immaterial to the final outcome. He knows the auguries of his fate, the chemicals' oracular vision – all that matters is the now.

The *oni* sprints toward him on all fours, gouging deep scores in the ground, and it moves molasses syrupy slow – the bounding lope of a predator closing for the kill. He can count the individual shards of rock it kicks up as each scimitar talon grinds through the floor, muscles expanding and contracting in a beautiful symmetry of motion. It pulls itself upright just before they clash, powerful blows sweeping in at his head, and he wants to weep with joy at the sheer perfection in front of him.

Reflexes take over, a lifetime of study. He becomes one with the blade.

Crane Kisses the Lake, a set of talons passing less than a hair's width overhead, the blade carving a deep furrow in the *oni*'s side, other talons raking down his back in delightful agony.

Reed In Monsoon, twisting underneath the flashing backhand, spine grinding in his femur while more spines clatter to the ground, severed as the blade flashes skyward along the *oni's* back, razor tail curling and punching through his left bicep.

Mountain Sleeps Lightly, the blade smashing down like an avalanche, detached chitinous forearm flopping on the ground before he's flying back from an organ pulping kick, abdomen torn and gushing, viscera sliding loose.

Phoenix Rises, uncoiling like a spring, soaring toward inevitability, the blade whipping into skin, flesh, bone, deeper and deeper, forcing its way to the core, claws punching into his chest and squee—

Augstar and Monocle continue to race down the tunnel, deeper into the darkness. Behind them, the grisly scene draws to its final conclusion. Rhinestones' sword lies buried deep within the creature's torso, bisecting it almost to the midline, steaming blood gushing onto the cavern floor.

Rhinestones himself is held aloft by a clawed hand thrust directly into his chest, and his arms and legs briefly spasm as Prime clenches its talons around the mangled remains of his heart, squeezing it into so much useless muscle fiber and tissue. Another echoing *scream* rips through the tunnel and Prime flings the lifeless corpse away – the body crashes violently into one of the memplas wall panels and slides to the floor, a broken and ungainly husk robbed of its vitality.

Augstar continues watching the feed from one of the Atlas' rear sensors, internal VI compensating for the lurching gait of the badly damaged machine, and she shudders violently inside the mech's cockpit as the creature does something impossibly unreal.

The hulking figure – fluid leaking from the sword still impaled in its chest, half its back spines missing – reaches down and picks up its own severed forelimb, contemplating the clawed appendage before ramming it back on top of the neatly amputated stump of its left arm.

It then wraps its right hand around the join and holds the limb in place for several seconds, muscles bulging and twisting, before curling and uncurling the talons on its left hand, combat functionality fully restored.

Augstar can hear whimpering, and with a start, realizes it's coming from her own mouth, a sound she never thought she'd make. Sector administrators, especially those from one of the Hundred Government Families, make others whimper, their whims literally law for thousands of planets and the billions of people upon them.

Augstar's hands have wielded the power of life and death for close to twenty-two years now, ever since her initial appointment as a planetary governor at the edge of nineteen, and she thought she knew every secret Government kept – a lifetime of bureaucratic maneuvering revealing the skeletons in all the closets, even those tucked away in the Council of Five.

With a start, she realizes she doesn't, and whimpers again.

She angrily forces herself back under control and commands the mech to redline the servomotors, but they're already maxed out, warning diagnostics steadily accumulating along the bottom of her HUD. A glance over at the offensive system tab reveals three canisters of flechettes, five highex missiles, and twelve hundred penetrator rounds left, but they might as well be wet wads of tissue for all the effect they've had on the creature already.

It appears there are some things in the galaxy that even an Atlas class mechanized combat platform cannot deal with. She licks her lips nervously, trembling finger hovering over the AM self-destruct, Rhinestones' grisly death fresh in her mind, but even now the will to live is too strong.

The fervent desire, the completely illogical belief, even in the face of overwhelming evidence, that somehow a miracle will occur.

She pulls her finger back and quickly programs an attack profile for the remaining highex missiles, a staggered launch designed to impact precisely around the creature in a cage of destructive force, perhaps disabling it long enough for her to escape this waking nightmare and return to the world she knows, the world she owns. A world free of permanent consequences for her actions.

A flash of motion in her rear visual feed reveals the sinuous lope of a jagged form on all fours, tail twisting to counterbalance, rapidly closing the distance from behind. She swivels both shoulder launchers to a reverse launch angle and fires off the last of the missiles. They descend in a twisting pentagram around the monster, contrails weaving through the air.

The familiar thunder of detonation rolls through the tunnel yet again, cataclysmic gouts of flame and rock fountaining up into the air, the shockwave of superheated air briefly whipping past in a maelstrom of sensor static. Ahead of her, Monocle briefly stumbles as the gust front hurricanes past him, but his pace doesn't falter and he continues to slowly outpace the deteriorating Atlas. Suddenly, the servomotors seize up in the mech's right leg and it grinds to a halt, the air curiously silent. Nothing moves behind her.

She screams at Monocle but he doesn't look back, rapidly disappearing into the distance, arms and legs churning in that metronomic gait.

<<You bastard! How dare you leave me!>>

<<Sorry sweetie.>> A ghostly electronic chuckle. <<Try and keep it busy for a while, if you don't mind. Got a shuttle to catch, a life to live, and I don't plan to- >>

The cloud cuts out, all parties disconnected, and she sees a massive roar of explosions illuminate the tunnel in front of her, multiple Six Sixteen rounds set to maximum dispersal, a literal wall of fire cascading out like some fantastic light sculpture.

A deep rumbling briefly echoes through the cavern, the sound like that of water rushing down a giant pipe, and an underground wind roars past again, writhing banks of fog ripping past in tattered shreds, drawn in by the vacuum created by the inferno. Her sensors hash and craze with digital ghosts, temperature readouts spiking briefly, and then steadily dropping lower and lower.

The mini-cyclone dies down a minute later and her sensors clear up just in time to see a myth swooping down at her from above.

"Oh you have *got* to be shi—"

Rob curses as he continues his desperate pace through the HVAC system set above the tunnel. His glARs just pinged an emergency alert – sensor traffic finally overwhelmed the digiworm, automatic flush is on the way, a portion of the lake even now diverting down into the underground complex.

He glances through the clear memplas floor of the tube, and then stares, eyes caught by the scene playing out beneath his boots. The unfolding chaos is oddly surreal, even from the jaded perspective of an Agency operative.

Darting through the clouds below, shimmering wings flashing with oddly glinting specks of light, a massive reptilian form swoops and dives at the ten-meter-tall Atlas stranded on the tunnel floor. Billowing waves of flame issue from its mouth, and it twists and plunges, rolling to avoid the brief bursts of penetrator fire rattling forth from the mech's remaining arm cannon. It shoots past the Atlas in a rush of air before climbing back up to the top of the tunnel, mist curling behind in a vortex wake.

Rob sees it briefly pass beneath him, no more than five meters away, scaled dorsal ridges tapering back to a lightly armored tail, limbs tucked tight against its body while delicate wings vibrate constantly. His breath catches momentarily at the sheer grace of the creature – something that so patently shouldn't exist, yet does, flitting through the air in defiance of all commonly held theories of physics.

Several heavy penetrator rounds punch through the tube behind him and the trance is broken, shards of memplas spalling out from the exit vectors, narrowly missing his left side. Rob swears briefly and continues on, sprinting as fast as his crouched over stance will allow.

Down below, the fight rages on, the dragon unwilling to get too close to the chattering arm cannon. It eels through the air around the Atlas, raining continuous sheets of flame onto the crippled mech. The hardened armor withstands the furnace blast heat for the moment, though sections are beginning to melt and deform.

Suddenly, the barking cough of multiple flechette canisters discharging at once rattles through the cavern, thousands of tungsten shards splitting the air like a giant shotgun blast from the Atlas' shoulder mounts.

Hundreds of the tumbling pieces of metal tear through the dragon's delicate wing membranes, and it plummets to the floor in a ragged spiral, bellowing in pain as it falls. Unnoticed by all, a jagged figure races on all fours toward the mech from behind, closing distance at an alarming pace, a chill wind curling in its wake. The temperature continues to drop, accompanied by a distant roar at the very edge of audibility.

The dragon hits the ground and its massive bulk rolls awkwardly, coming up to rest against the lift rail in the middle of the tunnel in a tangle of legs and shredded wings. Scrabbling furiously with curved claws, it levers itself to its feet, and shakes its scaly head briefly before blasting a fireball at the roof in rage and turning to advance on the mech in a low run. The Atlas' arm cannon spits out a chattering burst of penetrators that whistle past the sinuously weaving body, gouging massive craters in the memplas walls, but then the cannon falls silent, barrel spinning impotently, a dry clicking issuing forth from the empty ammunition bin. Inside the cockpit, Augstar shrieks in frustration as she watches the massive serpent draw closer and closer.

The dragon completes its charge, smashing a shoulder into the Atlas and sending it sprawling to the ground. It leaps on top of the mechanical construct to pin it, and then pours a torrent of flame directly into the memplas faceplate, a terrified face briefly visible before the incandescent torch burns clear through and splashes out from the rocks beneath the mech. The dragon swipes the immobile machinery several time before stretching its head to the ceiling and bellowing a triumphant roar.

An answering *scream* announces the arrival of Prime, and it leaps at the beast perched atop the broken mech, talons extended hungrily. The two tumble onto the floor, a furious welter of rending fangs and tearing claws, blood spraying out in huge sheets. Seconds later, Prime dashes back, several chunks missing from its already scarred and gouged right side, two talons broken from its left foot, steaming ichor spattering the rocks as it moves.

The dragon shrieks and blasts flame at the scuttling figure, but misses, depth perception irrevocably altered from a gouged out eye, half its skull sheared down to the bone. It limps in a defensive circle, right forelimb badly bent and twisted, long rents in its breastplate shedding thick red blood – Goliath warily eyeing David while the two prepare for another exchange. The chill wind continues to whistle past, subsonic roar growing louder and louder.

With a deafening shriek, the dragon suddenly coils in on itself like a snake and rears up to spew more fire, but Prime darts in, thrusting razor-sharp claws deep within the dragon's side, aiming for the softer underbelly scales. With a rippling twist, Prime tears a massive hole open and starts ripping out chunks of flesh, driving in to the vital organs its combat sensors tell it lie deep within. The dragon vomits a thick stream of blood, and then collapses on its side and dies, remaining eye glazing over in a cloudy film. Prime continues its butcher's work for several minutes longer, finally emerging from the corpse dripping blood and bits of flesh, fangs snarling in triumph.

The roar filling the tunnel now sounds like a tornado, wind whipping the dust into blinding sheets. It teeters on the edge of a physical force, a battering ram of invisible atoms driving all before it with a deafening howl.

Prime tilts its head back to the ceiling and *screams* again, tendons and muscle visible in places beneath hideously shredded chromatophore skin trying futilely to repair overwhelming local damage, and then a tidal wave of water hits the battlefield like a cresting tsunami, sweeping everything to the darkened end of the tunnel.

Deep within the facility, the automatic reclamation systems continue cycling up to full power, vast filtration pumps readying to receive the incoming influx of materials.

XANDER

"Almost... there..." I gasp for air, my voice harsh and grating, throat raw. The maintenance tube feels like it's been going on forever, the dream of a never-ending hallway whose door gets further and further away the longer you run. The waypoint indicator on my glARs shows only a kilometer left, but I'm beginning to think it's lying to me, trapping us forever in the stifling dark, buried beneath tons and tons of rock with no escape, an eternity under—

A ringing slap hammers stars before my eyes, and I'm suddenly face to face with my assistant, his face tense in the dim red lighting filling the tube.

"Doc! C'mon, snap out of it!"

"Gate-dammit, ow! Why did you hit me?" I rub a hand along my aching jaw – one of my teeth definitely feels loose – and glare at him. Is he starting to crack under the strain?

He suddenly looks worried. "Doc, you've been mumbling and staring at the ground. You haven't moved a step. I thought you were just tired, but then you wouldn't respond when I started calling your name. I've been trying to get through to you for over three minutes!"

Shit. He's not the one cracking under the strain. I contemplate my body acting outside of my conscious decision and an ice-cold shiver runs down my spine. That loss of self, however temporary...

"Don't worry about it," I say roughly, pushing past him to start down the tube once again.

"Are you sure you're—"

"I said don't worry about it! One foot in front of the other, until we get to Central Core. We can sort things out there once we bring this lab back under control."

We resume our stumbling jog and I fall silent, saving my breath for the all-important task of feeding oxygen to aching muscles. My glARs ticks the meters down, slowly, relentlessly.

500 meters.

400 meters.

300 meters.

A cool wind caresses my face, lifting some of the sweat away. It feels gentle, soothing, the refreshing breeze of a perfect day at the beach, surf softly rumbling as the breakers roll in...

Gate-dammit.

"RUN!" My voice cracks, and I frantically try to squeeze more motion out of lead filled limbs, my body screaming its protest from every overtaxed cell. The stumbling jog turns into a flailing run, breath coming hot and heavy. The breeze intensifies around us.

250 meters.

The rumble grows louder, gentle rollers turning into crashing foam cresting the seawalls.

200 meters.

A cold hurricane gale whips at my face, drawing stinging tears from my eyes.

150 meters.

The freight train roar of a tidal wave fills the tube, crashing all around us, deafening, stunning in its intensity. Mist droplets float in the air, the delicate forerunners of a massive host.

100 meters.

A massive giant punches me from behind, his fist cold and dire. Vision spinning all around, water engulfing my limbs, sound suddenly deadened, helter-skelter tumbling crashing smashing glancing lungs straining chest heaving—

0 meters.

I burst into the gaping emptiness of a reclamation chamber and a sudden rush of oxygen floods my lungs, stomach floating in that particular disorientation of freefall. I plummet toward the massive cistern below, giant plumes of ejecta drifting all around me like liquid wings.

Sudden impa—

...

Blackness recedes, water all around, back in the depths. Lungs screaming once again. Kick desperately, following the bubbles streaming up from my noise and the glARs orientation arrow. Vision closing in, spots dancing in my retinas, fighting with every ounce of willpower not to succumb to the involuntary reflex of inhalation.

Surface! Shuddering gulps of air rack my body, fill tormented alveoli, the sweetest thing I've ever tasted.

"Doc!"

The voice is faint, distant.

"Xander!"

The familiar collection of syllables penetrates my foggy brain and I thrash my arms to stay afloat. I look around, sodden heaviness of my clothing threatening to drag me back down below. Through the haze of mist suffusing the area, almost fifty meters away, I see my assistant perched on a walkway overlooking the churning surface of the reclamation pool, a ladder leading out of the water next to him. I start kicking toward him, but instead of growing closer, the ladder recedes, the current pulling me backward.

"Doc, you gotta kick harder! You have to *move*!" His voice is frantic, concern underlying every shouted word. I try to make my unwilling body obey, but it won't listen, muscles overtaxed and spent. I take a quick glance over my shoulder and—

Shit. Wish I hadn't done that. Rising up from the water like a giant windmill laid on its face is one of the first reclamation stations, pulling me closer with every revolution of its rapidly churning metal arms. It's designed to skim off the larger chunks of matter that still need to be rendered down into component parts, split them off to the next stage of reclamation while the majority of the water and smaller particulates get filtered elsewhere.

Unfortunately, I appear to be one of those larger chunks, and the station wasn't constructed with gentleness in mind. The metal arms beat the water like some horrendously oversized whisk, and despite all my kicking and flailing, I'm being drawn in as remorselessly as a fish on a hook, the powerful currents overwhelming my merely human capabilities. The mechanical whine of the turbine fills my ears, and I take one last breath before curling into a ball, hoping against hope to make it throu—

PAIN tumbling impact pain PAIN clenching drowning scre—

I regain consciousness and immediately vomit, a thin stream of water and blood pouring out of my mouth, causing me to curl up and convulse in the fetal position, an agonizing sense of dislocation and *wrongness* emanating from my already injured side. My glARs somehow survived the underwater pummeling, and the biomonitor readouts they're displaying have some alarming graphics attached to several locations on my abdomen – various internal organs crushed and malfunctioning. My assistant kneels over me, water dripping from his hair and clothes onto the hard metal walkway on which I lie, right hand wiping his mouth.

"Shit, Doc, you don't look so hot," he mutters. I vomit again, another stream of dark blood.

"Grggrgkk."

"Had to give you mouth to mouth after I finally managed to pull you out, you were down there for a while.

"Blgrchchagghh."

"Guess that machine got you pretty good, huh?"

With a sheer effort of will I force my body to stop convulsing, though the pain consumes almost my entire being.

"I'm dying... you idiot," I croak through clenched teeth. "Liver's... gone... spleen's not... looking that great... either... lots of bleeding... maybe an hour left..."

His face pales. "Shit, we gotta get you to a medical center then." He looks around. "We have any of those down in this part of the lab?"

"Central Core... first," I hiss, motioning him to help me up. "We have to... shut Prime... and the others... down..." He levers me up to a standing position and I scream in agony at the motion, hot spikes of pain hammering my midsection. He supports my arm over his shoulders, and I gasp, "...after that... I'll fix myself... bioforge..."

My voice trails off, the pain too much to bear, white hot agony radiating through every nerve fiber. My world narrows down to placing one foot in front of the other, arm clasped to my side as if that will somehow make the hurting stop. I weakly nod my head in the appropriate direction when we intersect various other walkways, trusting to my glARs to lead us to Central Core, the green waypoint icon wavering in front of me like a desert mirage.

Step.

Step.

Step.

A brief pause, assistant opening a locker and removing something from within, too tired to care what it is.

Step.

Step.

Step.

A door opening, shutting behind us, clanking sounds of the reclamation cavern stilling away into a hushed silence.

Step.

Step.

Step.

A biometric scanner in front of my face, alphanumeric keypad underneath. I stare at it dumbly.

"Doc, you gotta override the security," my assistant whispers at my side.

Woodenly punch in the appropriate key code, again trusting my glasses to remember my memories properly, watch the door slide open, a large room filled with high density server clusters stretching out before us. The clusters huddle together like black obelisks, monuments to near infinite realms of data, featureless surfaces hiding the complexity within. A thin memplas cage surrounds each dark grouping, material protection against the elements.

Step.

Step.

Step.

Central Core rises before me, a starkly naked monitor set into the wall, several chairs tucked underneath the desk below it. I collapse into the middle chair, hot blood leaking down my side, and implement a connection to the local cloud.

<<Interrogative;>>

<<handshake: biomarker X, primary;>>

<<access granted;>>

<<Welcome back, Doctor;>>

<<*initialize system restore: backdate one Standard day – implement VI reboot option Gamma;*>>

<<*initializing...;*>>

A door opens in the distance, a sudden intake of breath, and I hear the sound of rushing feet, gradually growing louder. I slowly turn my head and see a man with grey eyes set behind a pair of boxy black glARs dashing through the clusters at me.

For some reason he looks familiar.

ROB

Sprint down another corridor, frantically chasing a glowing green waypoint ghost. Top-down map schematic shows me almost to Central Core, only one more security override to go, a quick dash from the HVAC substation through a couple hallways. Digiworm's busy keeping the lab VI quiescent, struggling against a sleeping giant that's slowly awakening. It's not gonna hold much longer. *Jen'sFuture* continues its countdown in the corner of my glARs, less than an hour left.

Gotta get to that shuttle, get out before I lose control.

Barrel around a corner, feet briefly slipping on the gleaming white tiled floor, right myself with a quick hand slap on the floor. Last security door coming up fast, visible at the end of the hallway. Rooms flash past on either side, no time to look at what they might contain. Punch in another override – thirty-two digit alphanumeric code burned into my brain at this point. Door hisses open.

Tech center spreads out in front of me, server clusters bursting out of the floor like dirty fungal growths. Can only imagine the corruption hiding inside their nondescript exteriors. Quick scan the room and —

Kufit-fucker!

No wonder the digiworm's losing control, that Gate-damn biohacker is rebooting the system! How the fuck did he make it back here?

No time for questions, need to shut him down. Hard. Sprint through the server clusters, see him slowly turn around, one hand clutched to his side.

GlARs enhance, blood dripping down to the floor, probability of lethal wound eighty-four point three percent. Wasn't trained to take chances, penetrator drops down into my hand, spin past the last memplas cage. Finger on the trigger, a neuron twitch away from turning his head into pink mist.

Voice from my right stops me dead in my tracks, an unwelcome surprise. Find myself falling victim to the biggest rookie mistake Agency warns against.

Never get target locked. Always check *all* your surroundings first.

Quick glance over, projectile launcher filling my vision, face behind it haggard and drawn, eyes filled with determined intensity, a shock of brown hair gleaming wetly under the soft white light of the ceiling glowstrips. Quick datobject query indicates he's one of five assistant techs at the lab, primary focus on genetic manipulation to combat disease vectors, human and non-human alike. Only been at the lab for a year, no traces of involvement with the lab director and his genespliced horrors running around outside.

Doesn't matter one iota. Need to protect humanity from all of his kind, the destruction they produce.

His finger clenches on the trigger, forearm muscles tensing, blue techsuit rolled up past his elbows – he's got the drop on me, no question. Could still take out the director, have a clear shot at his head, but I'm not feeling particularly suicidal, especially with the countdown timer to *Jen'sFuture* ticking down.

Slowly lower my penetrator to the floor, raise my hands in the air, ask him what he wants to do next. He seems nervous, unsure, unused to holding someone under duress.

Might be able to turn that to my advantage later.

A brief exchange with the biohacker at the terminal, and the assistant beckons me over to one of the chairs, forces me to sit, though he's smart enough not to put me right next to his boss. Director's face is grey, ashen. GlARs updates probability of lethal wound to ninety-four point three percent.

A small consolation.

Director starts talking to me, voice low and breathy, wants me to reverse the digiworm. Seems like the lab VI can't reboot up to full functionality while the worm's still in the system.

What can I say? I do good work. Agency taught me well.

He also promises to let me go after they regain control, let me take the shuttle, get a head start before Government arrives and sanitizes the area. Seems to think this is a minor setback for his lab, his work, a brief glitch in the system.

I laugh in his face, tell him what I think of his *work*. Tell him that biohackers, genesplicers, every single Gate-damn human-betraying one of them should be fired into the closest star, purified with the cleansing light of a sun. They killed Old Terra, they killed my family, they almost killed my daughter, and I'll be Gate-damned if I let them kill anything else under my watch.

He doesn't respond, stares at me, eyes vacant – he's not much longer for this world, maybe an hour left, tops. Doubt he heard a word I said. Seen plenty of dying men, and he definitely fits the description. More blood drips onto the floor, a steady stream of crimson jewels.

Sudden presence from behind, projectile launcher pointed at me once again. Brown hair tells me to get rid of the digiworm, cede control of the lab, let them engage a 'killswitch' and bring things back under control, keep more people from dying. Gives a self-righteous speech on saving the innocent, protecting those who can't protect themselves. I laugh at him too.

His body trembles, mouth pursed tight, projectile launcher unwaveringly pointed at my head.

Is this where it ends? So close to redemption, yet never crossing that finish line? *Jen'sFuture* continues its slow countdown – twenty-seven minutes left.

He doesn't pull the trigger. Instead, he says something shocking. Mind struggles to comprehend.

He offers to turn the director and lab over to the Agency after they shut the creatures down, testify about what he's seen, what he's heard, name those who recruited him. Name those in Government who helped conceal this abomination. Doesn't matter if it takes him down too, says he thought he was here to help people, make their lives better.

His voice shakes with rage.

Take a look at him, size him up.

He's not bluffing.

Director doesn't respond, lost in his private agony. Don't think he realizes the quality of his compatriot, the steel hidden within, doesn't understand the unbreakable will of a man unwilling to sacrifice his beliefs for money or power. He's too busy thinking about his own goals, his own desires, thinking about how he can continue pursuing his own twisted dreams, even on the verge of death.

I stare at the narrowed eyes behind the gaping mouth of a projectile launcher and feel shame. Once upon a time, I thought I was that man, doing the right thing because it was the right thing to do. Helping people.

Today's events tell a different story. *I* let those creatures loose on an unsuspecting world. Needed the money for Jennifer, but there's no getting around that one simple fact. Resort may have been full of Government leeches and plutocrat parasites who deserved to be torn apart, but the people of that city didn't deserve to die. Hotel staff didn't deserve to die.

That manager didn't deserve to die.

Picture her crumpled body lying back in the jungle, so similar to my baby, and the hollow twisting in my gut is so intense it hurts. *I* put her there, cut her life short, sacrificed one Jennifer to save another.

The realization hits hard.

How am I any better than the monsters I've spent my life hunting?

Turn back around to the console, trigger the digiworm's self-destruct code. The baleful red tide of forbidden zones rolls across the visual server representation in my glARs like a smothering blanket, coruscating interdiction nodes sparkling one last time and then gone. Lab VI starts pulling itself back together, reintegrating processes, bootstrapping back to the limited self-awareness it calls thought, getting ready to once again resume command and finally wake from this nightmare dream.

Watch the arrays slowly come online, most flickering with malfunction reports from collateral damage caused by the worm. Tell the assistant we're gonna have to fix those, bring the VI back to full integration. Also tell him to keep his boss alive – want as much information from that freak show as I can get. See how deep this rabbit hole goes.

Hijack the director's security clearance from his glARs – he doesn't even notice, too busy dying – and the zones turn the cool blue of admin level clearance. Start splicing code, patching digital wounds.

There's work to be done.

CENTRAL CORE
Timestamp – 21.59.30LT:10.56.58OT:03.18.407AG

The sterile crispness of the server room carries the unmistakable coppery tang of fresh blood, a growing pool spreading beneath the chair of a slumped man in a torn blue maintenance suit, the steady dripping from his side metronomic in its regularity. One hand drapes across the stained side of his suit, the other dangles to the floor, limply twitching back and forth. He lies unmoving against the edge of a desk, his gold embossed glARs tinted almost opaque, concealing pale blue eyes locked behind closed eyelids. He might almost be considered a corpse except for the very faint tremble in his chest, a shallow breath every few seconds.

On the other side of the desk, several meters away, Rob continues inputting commands into the main array of Central Core, working to repair enough of the damage from his worm to restart the VI. Multiple windows filled with scrolling code cover the infpanel set into the wall, and the view inside his glARs is just as chaotic – numbers and symbols flashing past and twisting into new configurations almost quicker than thought.

His hands move swiftly on the projected keyboard, as well as twitching commands through his hapgloves directly. Standing several meters behind him is Xander's assistant, projectile launcher clasped loosely in one hand, barrel aimed vaguely in Rob's direction. He stares at Xander thoughtfully, and opens his mouth to speak.

"You know he's probably going to die, right?" He looks over at Rob.

"Would prefer that he didn't." Rob's reply is terse, attention focused solely on repairing the VI. "Need to know what he knows. *Who* he knows."

The assistant grunts. "We can probably stabilize him if we get him to one of the bioforges. There's plenty of base materials in the lab he can access to repair most of the damage. As much as it pains me to praise that lunatic, he's probably the best biohacker I've ever seen. Might even be on Kufit's level." He shudders. "Not that that's necessarily a good thing."

Rob turns slightly to look behind, fingers relentlessly churning out new code. The assistant tenses, weapon raising slightly at the movement, and Rob laughs mirthlessly.

"Relax, I'm not going to try anything. Just wanted to ask a question."

"And that is...?" The assistant's voice is wary.

"Why haven't you shot the both of us and made your way to the shuttle? Just wipe your hands of this mess and bail out? Surely you must have considered it?"

"I... that is... well..." He stammers, empty hand gesturing as if searching for the right words. "I guess it never occurred to me. I'm not like *him*." An angry glance at Xander. "I don't sacrifice people so I can get what I want. I told you before, I came here to make people's lives better. I'm not a murderer."

Rob shakes his head sadly. "No. No, you're not. You're an idealist, and this universe is no place for an idealist to live." He turns back to the infpanel, code still scrolling across it feverishly. Several array clusters gradually shift from the dark red of corruption to a light teal functionality, but the vast majority are still damaged from the worm.

Rob continues working.

Xander suddenly twitches and moans, still grabbing his side, and levers himself slightly more upright in his chair.

"I see the good doctor Frankenstein is still with us," Rob mutters, hands never slowing their graceful dance on the keyboard.

"...wuzzah... name's... Xander... not Frank..." Xander replies woozily. "Research notes... where's my notes... killswitch..."

Rob snorts. "I'm working on it, but why don't you go right ahead and grab those. I'm sure they'll come in handy later. There's going to be a lot of very interested people who are going to want to see everything you've recorded in this lab."

Xander stares blankly for a moment, and then slowly brings up a projected keyboard, haptic gloves momentarily forgotten. He raggedly taps in several commands with a blood-spattered hand, and a download prompt appears on the main screen, in addition to the one inside his glasses. He confirms the prompt and a progress bar starts gradually filling, terabytes of information compressing themselves into nested shells huddled within each other.

They ride an electron stream through the air into the external memory of his glARs unit, a complete record of everything he's ever done at the lab, the most precious jewels in his collection. Xander slumps back down against the desk while the data transfers, mind elsewhere once more. Rob piggybacks the feed and creates an extra copy in his own glARs before turning back to his work with the server clusters.

The room falls silent for several minutes. "So why did you come work here in the first place," Rob eventually asks the man standing behind him.

"I told you, to help people," comes the response. The man's voice is strained, exhausted.

"But biohacking only leads to pain and suffering, I can tell you that for a fact." Rob's voice remains calm, professional. He finishes repairing another cluster and moves on to the next one. "Every time someone thinks they're going to help others with biohacking, it always starts with good intentions." He sighs. "And then it always ends with twisted abominations, unwilling test subjects, millions dead from plagues and mutations and virusbombs."

"But that's exactly what I want to fix!" The words come out with an intense fervor. "There are so many things we could cure with biohacking – illnesses, genetic mutations, cancers... aging itself. The problem is, people are worried about biohacked vectors that do what you're talking about, the hacks that slip into our bodies and change who we are, the hacks that redefine *us*."

He pauses for breath. "The project I've been working on, the work I've been doing, is to create a hack that establishes the body's baseline genetic state, *and then prevents that from changing*. Think of it as making your immune system impenetrable, able to ward off all outside changes that would lead to a breakdown in function. A perfect defense, and not just for humanity either. We could apply it to our crops, our animals, lower our destructive impact on the world around us."

His eyes shine, alight with an incandescent inner vision. "Once people don't have to worry about a rogue hack infecting them, then we can start working on making humanity better. Augmented muscle and skeletal structures, more efficient internal organs, increased cognitive capabilities, specific environmental adaptations... the possibilities are endless! We can finally take control of evolution and make it serve us instead of the other way around."

Rob is silent for a moment, mulling over the impassioned words. He's heard them before in a thousand different ways, always to justify some horrible course of action, the inevitable excuse making all biohackers fall back on when finally confronted with their sins. He clears his throat.

"So who would control this hack, then? Who's in charge of making sure it gets out to everyone?"

The man looks nonplussed. "Why, Government of course. That's their job."

Rob snorts in laughter, unable to contain himself. "Right. The same Government that has you developing this hack in a lab that's also being used to create things *he...*" he nods his head at the slumped Xander, "...dreams up. Don't be naive. They'll dole your work out to the top functionaries and lackeys, anyone rich enough to afford it, and let the rest of humanity starve in the gutter, just like they always do. In fact, it wouldn't surprise me if they planned to alter your work a bit, design in a backdoor that Government could use to disable or control people, all for the sake of 'security' of course." He laughs again, bitterly. "And that's not even mentioning the further divide your biohack will create between the haves and the have-nots. Only now it won't be an economic disparity, it'll be the length of life itself. You really think Government is going to just give that to the masses?"

Rob closes another window, only three clusters left. He continues talking. "Listen to me, kid. Government doesn't care about doing the right thing. Get that through your head right now. Some of the people I've taken down over my years with the Agency, well, let's just say that sending their backers into a sun would've been much more satisfying, and a much better use of my time." His voice turns sour. "Unfortunately, the Agency works *for* Government, and those at the top have a wide variety of resources at their disposal."

He looks back again. "Incidentally, that's the only reason I haven't taken that gun and shot the both of you." Rob chuckles. "What, you think you're safe standing three meters away? Kid, I've been working for the Agency for over thirty years. If I wanted that gun I would have had it already." His face turns grim. "No, what I want is your testimony. That, and your boss's records, are finally going to force Government to face some consequences that have been a long time coming." He finishes repairing another cluster; two windows of code remain on the infpanel. Both Xander and Rob's glARs give a small chime as the records finish downloading. Xander groggily raises his head again.

"Consequences... hah... the real consequences... are what happens... when we lose sight... of... the big picture..." He coughs weakly. "You shut this lab... down... and humanity... has no chance..."

Rob glares at him. "You biohackers, always with the Gate-damn excuses. 'My work is so important.' 'Humanity is doomed without my genius.' Pfah!" He spits angrily at the ground.

"Is... Jasper... the VI... rebooted enough... to recover deep memory?" Xander's voice is thin, reedy.

Rob nods uncertainly. "Yeah, the memory architecture is fully restored, working to link up the last of the VI functionality to access your 'killswitch.' Be a little bit longer yet for full access, but you should be able to call out anything saved in there."

"Jasper... display datobject... JC201:FL... segments three... through eight..."

The majority of the infpanel turns into a standard sensor feed, crystalline clarity like looking through a freshly cleaned window. A timestamp in the upper left corner of the feed indicates a date three months ago, identifying location censored out, the image paused on the scene of what looks like a desert at nighttime, three small moons floating above the horizon in a rough triangle, a dimly lit structure visible in the foreground. Xander waves a hand weakly.

"...initiate..."

The scene jumps into motion, the view shifting as whatever the sensor was mounted on turns to look over to its right. Two figures in bioarmor suits that look eerily familiar to Rob are lying on top of a sand dune, faceless masks focused on the structure below. He tries to place what they remind him of, when he sees the shape of a sword strapped to each of their backs and silently curses. Rhinestones' suit was bulky, massive, crude. These are sleek and terrifying, slight bulges dotting the arms and legs, no telltale red veins to give them away.

The view swivels back to the building.

A sudden flash of light splits the night, and what looks like a teardrop of shining metal plummets out of the sky. It craters into the ground with a massive smash, sand immediately billowing up around it. The sensor feed switches to thermographic, the thick red blob of the intensely hot object sitting motionless as the sand gradually settles back down. The feed switches back to enhanced lighting.

The world seems to explode.

The metal teardrop splits apart into hundreds of vaguely humanoid shapes flowing toward the structure, blasts of what look like pure plasma rippling forth from their upper appendages. Missile contrails streak out from the structure in return, the heavy crump of highex detonations filling the air, huge explosions roiling into the atmosphere, along with the distinctive crack of HV rounds. Several of the metal figures stumble as they take a direct hit, the metal deforming under the blows, but it rapidly reshapes itself back into its original form and they continue advancing. With a shuddering roar, an entire corner of the structure collapses, torn apart by the relentless plasma bursts. More figures flow off the dwindling teardrop.

The feed zooms in on the destruction. Blurry human troops in tacsuits can be seen firing frantically at the advancing swarm, a constant barrage of penetrators, highex, and an occasional Six Sixteen round, shrieking in silent agony as plasma incinerates their bodies, even the near misses proving fatal from the passing of super-heated air. The sensor quickly scans over as one of the metallic figures goes down, victim of countless heavy penetrator rounds, the successive impacts splintering into the same spot and creating a small crack. A brief fountain of glowing purple gas spurts out of its midsection as it falls.

The remaining figures pause briefly, an ominous subsonic rumbling echoing out even above the explosion of highex, and then they redouble their assault on the structure, pouring nonstop streams of plasma into its rapidly disintegrating walls. With a shattering roar, the entire building collapses in on itself, structural supports utterly destroyed, melted away by the power of small suns. The metallic figures draw back and form a semicircle around the burning ruins, nearly one hundred meters away, and a synchronized sheet of plasma crashes into the wreckage like a wave of pure energy, creating a dazzling noon time brilliance. When the blinding glare disappears, only a blackened crater remains, sand fused and glassy around it.

Rob draws in a breath, realizes he's been holding it the entire time. "What the—"

"...wait... more... to come..." Xander's ragged voice cuts him off.

The figures move to head back to the diminished teardrop, and the ground erupts under their feet, a swarm of insectoid shapes swarming over the right side of the group, carpeting the sand. Rob shudders as he remembers his encounter with the roaches in the jungle earlier, the death of the Professor.

Chaos ensues as the alien figures react to the ambush, plasma flashing the scuttling roaches into smoking husks, but more of the aliens are on the ground, still and lifeless. The roaches continue their leaping attacks, moving together like an unstoppable wolf pack, overwhelming individuals with strikes from all sides, the sheer volume of their numbers breaking the cohesion of the alien unit into a series of frantic individual battles.

Another whisper of movement and the skies are suddenly alive with winged serpents, swooping down on the swirling melee from above, savaging burnished limbs with powerful jaws and whipping tails. More gleaming shapes fall to the ground, bits and pieces torn off by the dive-bombing fliers, and intermittent blasts of plasma spray out from the remaining figures, their greatly diminished numbers now huddled into a defensive cordon, desperately trying to fend off the coordinated attacks from ground and air.

Lightning flashes through the night and four more teardrops slam into the ground, metallic shapes flowing off and into the battle, multiple plasma salvos crackling through the air with blinding intensity. The view shifts away from the battle and focuses on the back of the two bioarmored figures, following behind them as they bound away from the combat at an incredible rate of speed, plasma coruscating through the night sky, and then the feed stops, figures frozen in midstride.

"What... How..." Rob can feel himself at a loss for words and frowns. His job is to know the information everyone else doesn't, and now he's on unfamiliar turf.

Xander gives a death's head smile, face grey and sallow. "The Agency... doesn't know... quite as much... as it thinks..." He winces in pain. "We're... at war... and you have... no idea... how terrible they are..." Another rattling cough. "I do... what I must... no other choice..."

A deep silence fills the room, Rob trying to process the sudden information overload, Xander's assistant quietly keeping watch through the shock of witnessing actual visual evidence of the aliens, Xander himself struggling to stay conscious. A soft chime announces another cluster coming back online. One window remains open on the infpanel, lines of code scrolling relentlessly past.

"But, but why keep this a secret?" Rob's voice is stunned. "If we're at war, we need to mobilize everything we have. What about the Peacekeepers? The Black Colony regiments?"

"Who... do you think... was in those suits..." Xander asks grimly. "Look at... how quickly... you were ready... to kill me... just a few minutes ago... for biohacking..." He pauses for breath. "If Government... revealed that we were... at war with aliens... *and* splicing an entire army? It would be... anarchy... especially... if people... found out... about Prime..."

"'Prime'? What do you mean, 'Prime'? Are you talking about —"

The screech of tearing metal rips through the room, two sets of claws punching through the infpanel screen. It vomits a fountain of sparks and dies, the claws wrenching it back and forth in its frame. They finally break the screen loose from its moorings and fling it from the wall, the blurring panel barely missing Rob's head as it flies past. The gaping hole where the screen once sat reveals a twisting mass of cables strung from numerous metal supports running along the top of a dark and narrow maintenance serviceway.

A hulking, jagged figure starts crawling out, chromatophore skin swirling in riotous patterns, deep gashes covering its entire body. Steaming clear fluid oozes from the wounds, and it drags a snapping mass of braided cable caught along its splintered back spines.

Prime sees Xander and *screams*, grasping talons reaching for his head.

The sudden bark of the projectile launcher echoes in the room, once, twice, thrice. Prime's head snaps back each time, and it *screams* again as it thrashes at the wall, severing some of the cables now stretched away from the empty screen frame and tangled on its body. Several coils fall free, dangling like hissing serpents, the ozone tang of live current standing hairs on end.

Rob leaps up from his seat and grabs one of the crackling power cables, sparks arcing from the end, and jams it into Prime's mangled side. Electricity courses through the beast's body and it shrieks in pure rage, arcing current visibly flashing between its fangs. The sizzle of melting flesh fills the air, and with a sudden twist, it backhands Rob with a massive blow, sending him flying back into the memplas cage of a server cluster. He hits with a sickening thud and crumples to the ground, head lolling limply, eyes closed.

Xander staggers out of his chair and almost falls over, his assistant quickly dashing forward to support him, projectile launcher clattering to the ground in his haste to keep Xander from toppling. Prime continues convulsing, trapped halfway out of the rough stone wall, fangs snapping furiously as it tries to disentangle from the electrocuting wires, claws gouging huge chunks of rock as they flail in scything arcs.

Xander motions his assistant toward a nearby door marked *Bioforge Delta/Shuttle Bay* on his glARs, and they hobble toward it, a trail of blood spattering the ground behind them. Xander leans on his assistant's shoulder for support, one foot dragging limply behind. They pass through the door and it hisses shut behind them.

Prime finally disentangles itself from the confines of the crawlspace and crashes down to the floor, pausing for a moment before slowly levering itself upright with one muscular arm. It limps toward Rob with a hitching gait, breath ragged, curling and uncurling its talons like a fighter cracking his knuckles before a bout, and its eyes dance with a furious rage.

The olfactory sensors set around its neck register the DNA trace of Xander's blood, and Prime turns toward the door set into the wall near the control station. With one last piercing *scream*, it limps over to the door and smashes it relentlessly with jackhammer blows, tearing the steel off in great sheets and splintering the memplas core before ripping the entire door out of the frame and flinging it aside. Prime stalks through the opening, tail lashing the air, and it disappears down the hall after Xander.

Rob remains limp, motionless, sprawled against the server like a broken doll. The room falls silent once again.

241

XANDER

Timestamp – 22.08.07LT:11.05.35OT:03.18.407AG

The floor pitches and sways under my feet like a storm-racked sea, legs shuffling drunkenly, someone's hand supporting me along yet another Gate-damned corridor. A pox on all hallways! It feels like I've spent my whole life running along this bounded path, walls closing around me, every door the illusion of freedom, but in the end, it's just another portal to another linear cage.

Run forward and live, fall back and die, the binary choice, zeros and ones forever fighting.

So unlike the complexity of splicing! An overwhelming plethora of expressions, entwinings, mutations, multitudinous branches of possibility, paths spiraling off in an infinite fractal progression. The beautiful potentialities spin like dancers, and they whisper my name as they twirl...

"...xander..."

"...Xander..."

"Xander!"

A shock of cold reality snapping through my brain and I'm back in the corridor, sick waves of pain pulsing from my ruined side. My assistant desperately tries to pull me along – I try to help as best I can but my feet drag at the end of my legs like eighty kilogram weights. A *scream* echoes through the air behind us.

"Gate-dammit, Doc," he sobs, muscles straining to keep us moving, "you've got to help me out or we're dead. Dead! That thing's after us again..." He gulps for air in huge gasping breaths. I try to get my bearings.

The rock walls surrounding us are smooth, polished, soothing landscape murals splashed across them in vivid primary colors, an attempt to bring the open space of the moon's surface to a place far beneath its crust. The gentle white lighting of the glowstrips brings out the almost frenetic cheerfulness of the drawings, like something found in the terminal ward of a pediatric hospital. It's amazing what the mind focuses on sometimes, I muse, and then muse upon my musing...

I feel that my mind may not be functioning quite properly at the moment. But then, how would I know? Does the insane man know he's insane, or does he view himself as the one island of sanity in a sea of chaotic confusion? Do we ever truly know the rationality of our own actions, our own desires?

The steady beeping of my glARs interrupts my thoughts, ominous biomonitor warnings crowding the screen. Blood pressure and heart rate are at critically low levels, estimated blood loss almost two liters, brain waves dipping and spiking alarmingly, several organs already grey and gone. The *scream* rips along the walls again – definitely getting closer.

Banish the biomonitor warnings, pull up the lab schematics. We're almost to the shuttle bay, one last curving hallway with several rooms along its length, but we'll never make it, not with Prime tracking us down, not with my failing body. At this rate, even if we did make it, I'd be dead before we cleared atmosphere. Need a trauma ward, not an Icarus emergency medkit. We stumble on regardless, my vision spinning, glARs displays dancing over the walls like luminescent fireflies, the wireframe grid of my personal Eden shifting and wavering under the merciless stare of its god. So many names, so many classifications, so many temptations.

Another jolt of reality, the spiking pain from my side becoming impossibly more intense. Almost go down, knees buckling, that hand steadying me once again. The schematic wavers in front of me, cavorting will o' wisp laughing at our material existence. I snarl at it, and my attention catches on one of the room names. *Bioforge Delta*. Feels like that should ring some sort of bell. Feels like it should mean something, trigger a memory of a time when the world made sense. Thoughts are sluggish, colliding against each other in the hot darkness behind my eyes. So tired. A *scream* jolts me awake.

Crystal moment of lucidity, the last surge of adrenaline from cells that don't know they're dead.

"Next door... we have to... go inside..."

"What?! No, Doc, we have to get to the shuttle. Forget the killswitch, we have to LEAVE! That Prime thing, it is literally right behind us!"

I twist my head, the effort almost causing me to black out. He's not joking. Limping down the corridor after us, staggering against the walls, banshee *scream* wailing forth is my creation. My shadow. It's getting closer. I turn away.

"Listen... to me!" I put as much energy into my voice as I have left. It's not much. "Get us... to that room... or we're both dead..."

He swears a blue streak of invective, but thank the Gates above, he listens. We lurch to a halt in front of the door, *Bioforge Delta*, and I clear the bioscanner, VI restored enough for the security system to function once more. Door hisses open, we almost fall through, door hisses shut.

He swears once more when he sees the door behind us is the only way out, but I motion for him to lay me down on the table near the two bioforge hatches set against the back wall. He hustles me over and helps lower my body to the unforgiving surface, and then turns back to the room's exit. A massive force slams into the door from outside, metal denting in under the impact of the blow, a horrifying display of raw power. My assistant jumps a little, and then slumps down to the floor against one of the grey paneled walls, eyes shut tight.

"Well, that's it then." He laughs bitterly, mockingly. "So close to actually escaping this nightmare, and I'm right back where I started, trapped in a room and waiting to die. Thanks a bunch, Doc." He puts his hands over his face and buries his head between his knees.

I ignore him and open a connection to the cloud, not much time left.

The door shudders again, dust trickling down from the ceiling glowstrips, gently sparkling as it falls.

<<Interrogative;>>

<<handshake: biomarker X, primary;>>

<<access granted;>>

<<Welcome back, Xander;>>

<<Jasper, initiate PrimeTemplate v.beta.1;>>

<<PrimeTemplate v.beta.1 functioning;>>

DNA dances before my eyes.

<<execute subsequent changes, save as Prime v.beta.12;>>

My fingers dance in the hapgloves, subconsciously crafting the insight that seems to have occurred so long ago.

<<changes saved;>>

<<initiate biohack Prime v.beta.12;>>

*<<warning, Xander, Prime v.beta.12 requires appropriate genetic template,
and has not been permutation verified;>>*

<<Jasper, initiate biohack Prime v.beta.12;>>

<<Prime v.beta.12 confirmed;>>

<<initializing...;>>

<<Prime v.beta.12 executing;>>

My hands fall limp in exhaustion. It's done.

One of the large panels set into the wall next to my assistant swings open, a padded medunit sliding out, multiple transfusion lines extending from the revealed lab transport system visible behind the now open space. The clamps release their grip, and the IVs coil and fall across the restraint system on the bed like brightly venomous snakes, life-giving poison waiting to fill my blood. The door shakes again, another dent jutting out, the ear-piercing squeal of tearing metal singing through the room.

My assistant leaps to his feet, a look of utter confusion on his face. He stares over at me.

"...help me... onto the bed... and hook me up... to those transfusers... any vein works... hurry..."

He nods dumbly and levers me upright, then carries me over to the medunit, grunting with the effort. He deftly slides the transfusion needles into my veins, one after the next, until a multicolored forest of tubes sprout from my body, leading back into the shadowed hole of the transport system.

"I don't know what you think this is going to accomplish, Doc, but whatever it is, I hope it was worth sentencing us to death." His voice drops back down into the despairing tones of the terminally condemned. "I doubt it will be though..."

I laugh, or cough, or choke. It's getting hard to tell at this point.

"...remember... when we talked... about Prime... being my only child...? Weaving... my DNA... into the template...?"

He nods uncertainly. The door tolls sonorously to the sound of raging punches.

"...I wasn't... quite... truthful... with you... nor with... the lab records..." The first transfusion slowly drips into my body, and I feel my muscles tense, precursor strands prepping the way for what is to come.

My mind clears momentarily, nerve blockers kicking in, and I cough liquidly.

"...Prime... is actually... *me*..."

He whistles, air sucking in between clenched teeth. A *scream* from outside.

"...I cloned... myself... used it as... a template... designed the hack... to augment... a normal human... regardless of genome..." The second IV spreads its tailored payload like a fiery network of freezing acid, my body twitching under the strain, minimized as it is beneath the nerve blockers. Without them, the pain would have driven me under by now.

I continue.

"...not quite... universal yet... couple more tests... would've had it... hack needed... to be useful... on easily obtained material..."

Dazzling pinbursts of light flash behind my eyes, consciousness finally shutting down. I refuse to acknowledge it, refuse to give in to the demands of material *I* control. Reach up and grip his arm with the dying fervor of a zealot.

"...take... my glARs... get the formula... to Government... tell them... synthesis... not... opposition..."

The third IV tries to drag me down into blackness, the welcoming sleep of oblivion. I let go of his sleeve, my hand falling slack, last iota of strength fading away. He removes my glARs, slides them into one of his pockets, then pulls off my hapgloves. I feel my eyes drifting shut, hot wisps of steam rising from my body, and I gasp with the pain.

"...remember... I do what... I have to... because... *I MUST*..."

A *scream* accompanies me down into the voi —

ROB

Oooof.

Gate-damn, that *really* hurt.

Eyes shudder open, feels like a Vee ran me over. Quick internal glARs scan, survey the damage.

Couple broken ribs, bruised sacrum, mild internal bleeding – twitch my hands and feet – no spinal damage though. Some good news at least.

More important question. Why am I still alive? 'Prime' didn't seem the forgiving sort.

Access the VI, last array finally back online. Ask for the sensor feeds for the past thirty minutes, scan through—

Ouch. Looks even worse from this perspective. Lucky to be alive. Real lucky. Watch the aftermath, both biohackers heading through the door, monster chasing them, tearing through metal and memplas like it's not even there.

That explains the mangled chunk of architecture lying next to me. Decide to sit here a while longer, survey the situation first.

Speed through the next ten minutes, nothing happens, was out for a while. Halt the feed. Query the system for the director's current location.

New feed pops up, small room near the shuttle bay, director on a table, tangle of tubing leading into his body, heat shimmering all around him.

Kufit only knows what he's doing to himself. Assistant huddles in a corner, staring at the door, trying to squeeze his body through the wall. Switch to hallway feed.

No wonder he's trying to turn invisible. Monster's beating on the door, and it's not happy. Gonna get through eventually, most likely sooner rather than later.

Should probably do something about that. He *is* my star witness after all.

Bring up the VI again, request killswitch option.

...nothing.

Fine. We'll do this the hard way.

Send a couple sniffer programs into the system, focus on the lesser used clusters. They sprint through the code, coursing like hounds, tracking clues.

Couple false positives, filter them out, refine the search. Keep an eye on the hallway feed, monster's taken off another layer of door.

Need to hurry.

Jackpot.

Director spliced a biotrigger inside every one of his abominations, nice little hidden cluster of cells, hit 'em with the right pulse of radio frequencies and they trigger a catastrophic cell failure across the entire organism. Ends up a puddle of goo.

Elegant.

Clever, too, hid the activation sequence in the lab's remote memory, VI never even knew it was there. Explains why my sniffers missed it the first time, during the initial infiltration. Hit the activation, punch in the security codes I just scooped.

Shit.

Activation protocol requires a biometric handshake, second layer of authentication. Monster's almost through the door, no time to root the system and get around it. Look around the room, gotta be something useful here.

Bingo. Plenty of biometric material splattered all over the floor. Just gotta go get it.

Slowly push myself to a kneeling position, right ankle feels a little funny. Take a step toward the wreckage of the main terminal—

Leg crumples under me, fall to the floor like I've been shot—

Penetrator cracks through the space my head was filling a millisecond earlier, burying itself in the memplas cage of a server cluster further down the room.

Shit shit shit.

Crawl for cover back behind the cluster, cycle the VI feed to cover the room, figure out who tried to kill me.

...room shows empty. Doesn't make sense. Unless—

Twist and dive toward another cluster, ankle throbbing in pain, a second penetrator smashing into the cage where I was just sitting. Memplas cracks and spiderwebs but doesn't break, slow repairs already filling in the gaps. Scramble to put memplas between me and the threat.

Monocle. That sneaky fuck.

Activate countermeasure program, erase my location from the VI feed, start scanning for code discrepancies. Now that I'm looking, I can *feel* him, drifting through the cloud like a ghost, digisig visible only by the negative space it leaves.

Quickly slam a block on the internal defense protocols, don't want him taking control of those. Watch the datobject disappear entirely as he slices it out of the cloud, cutting transmissions to that part of the VI entirely. Brief digital grapple as we both try to backtrace and infiltrate each other's glARs, countermeasures resolving lightning quick, but it appears we both know the importance of hardened systems and our respective operating systems remain secure.

Only two people on this planet with the training to cover their tracks like that, code me to a stalemate, get into an Omega class VI system – and I'm one of them.

Thought that stupid dragon got him in the tunnel. Should've known he wouldn't go down that easy.

His voice rings out in the room, taunting. Wants me to be afraid, wonder how he could survive a dragon, a flood, a bioengineered killing machine.

Wants me off balance, lets me know he's coming after my family after he slowly tears me apart, the unspeakable things he'll do to Jennifer, heal her just to hurt her over and over until she begs for death.

Almost respond, body twitching, rage misting my eyes, but manage to tamp the anger down – classic psy-ops. He's trying to push me into something rash, stupid. Already know how he survived, that he's perfectly capable of following through on his threats.

Black Colony takes the functional psychopaths, humanity's most brilliantly flawed monsters, and then polishes them until they gleam, dark, and twisted, and full of spiky madness.

Can't reason with a rabid dog. Can only put it down.

Penetrator shot slams into the side of the memplas, barely missing my arm – time to move again. Belly crawl to another cluster, squirm around the side, stare at the wall. Not a good location, rapidly running out of cover. Fortunately, it looks like he lost the Six Sixteen, otherwise I'd already be dead. Unfortunately, it's more than counterbalanced by the fact he has a penetrator, and I don't. Flash to the hall sensor, monster's clawing its way through, couple more minutes at the most. Tough break, assistant, looks like you're on your own. Good luck.

Gonna need a lot more luck of my own.

Options, options, gotta be a way out of this.

Search through the room resources – he's already disabled the fire-suppression system, can't choke him out with targeted foam. Internal defenses already sliced out, VI rail network doesn't extend into Central Core, glowstrips the non-explosive type.

Not much available on the digital front. Switch to the physical.

Stick my head out, quick scan around the corner of the cluster, trusting my left eye to see true. Option. Assistant left his weapon by the desk when the monster burst through, can see it poking out beneath the broken splinters of the ruined console. Duck back behind the cluster, no shot this time. Another quick glance, head popping out of a different spot, looking for movement.

Sudden flash draws my attention – right eye sees a figure walking down the middle of the room, penetrator sweeping side to side, the remorseless hunter stalking his prey.

Left eye sees nothing. Ignore the trap.

He's not the only who likes to keep one eye on reality.

Gives me an idea though, take cover one last time to get it ready, quick and dirty codesplice.

Go with a broad-spectrum AV dispersal, lab VI set to create multiple copies of my movements on any glARs in the cloud, redisperse every half second, full simulated combat suite.

Deep breath. Squeeze my right eye tightly shut.

Execute program *Dragon'sTeeth*, roll out of cover, invisible selves splitting off like funhouse mirrors sowing dazzling distractions, plant on good leg and leap, penetrator shot cracks the air, sudden crushing pressure in lower leg, sliding across ruined tiles, hand clenching polyresin grip, estimated threat vector triangulating off previous shot, roll and squeeze trigger once twice answering thunder slamming back, finish roll penetrator clattering from nerveless hand, take cover —

Bastard. He's better than me.

I sigh and slump back against the cage, slowly open my right eye, check to see how bad it is. Blood slowly pulsing out of my stomach, left leg a ruined mess, right arm almost useless, biomonitor flashing countless warnings. Fingers still work on the minute sensors in my hapgloves, but there's no way I'm shooting anything now. Quick review of my feed shows a spray of blood flying up from an empty patch of the room, might have glanced him, but there's no denying he won the battle.

Hopefully I hit something important, put him down for a bit, give me a chance to finish uploading *Jen'sFuture*.

Mocking voice fills the air, bouncing off the walls like ricocheting flechette rounds, dashing that hope. He's still alive, still armed, still looking for his kill. He knows he won the battle.

Not gonna let him win the war.

Countdown to *Jen'sFuture* ticks down, a soft chime, eight minutes left. One contingency plan left, one last option I never wanted to use. Agency training goes deep, every situation accounted for, even the ones labeled 'worst case.'

Trigger the self-destruct on my worm in the Gate, watch as a massive flood of panicked glARs accounts and help requests fly out of the node, twenty-four hours of madness finding its way out into the universe. Slip my report to the Agency into the backdoor channels, stream providing cover. Report's carefully edited, of course, wouldn't do to let them get distracted by some of my earlier actions. They're gonna need to focus on Government, focus on the scum who've been lying to everyone this whole time. It's about time people learned the truth.

Slow sound of footsteps approaching. Sigh again.

Sorry, baby. Looks like daddy's not gonna make it home after all.

EDEN, GEHENNA GATE

Timestamp – 22.12.13LT:11.10.41OT:03.18.407AG

A tiny emerald orb floats sedately in the vacuum, its backdrop the planet-sized weather systems churning across the face of a burnt-umber gas giant, delicately lit by the reflected photons of a distant star. Tiny sparkles of light wink into being with metronomic regularity alongside the moon, the peculiar violet hue of Transit permeating incandescent fireflies. The Gate sheds the energy from their arrival across the vastness of space, and the vacuum greedily drinks it in.

On the flag bridge of the *Riodu* class dreadnaught *Partycrasher*, a man wearing the gold-flecked insignia of a Peacekeeper sector commander scowls into the glARs display of his assault helmet, ramrod stiff in the harness strapping him into his combat pod. A thick layer of shock gel fills the cocoon, a memplas chrysalis waiting for the right moment to birth its unmoving larva, keeping it safe for now from the relentless press of gravity during a ten-G thruster burn.

He scans the rest of the bridge through the transparent clearness of the gel, ensuring that all pods are locked down and potential hazards stowed in their respective compartments. Even a pen becomes a sword in zero gravity, he thinks grimly, remembering the gruesome aftermath of a maneuvering exercise in which a young trooper forgot to secure his personal effects.

His right hand twitches along the leg of his matte grey tacsuit, fingers subtly dancing in the ornately filigreed gloves, and the implanted haptic sensors relay his commands through the fleet cloud as fast as thought. He highlights one of the five bridge officer feeds open on his screen and broadcasts on a direct transmission, tracheal patch converting the subvocalized whispers into normal speech.

"Any word yet on what we're facing, Chen," he asks the feed tagged Sensor Ops.

"Nothing yet, sir," the man on the other end of the feed responds, pushing over the threat vector analysis. The space around them is clear, empty for light minutes, gravitic sensors and lidar revealing the occasional stray atom of interstellar dust. "Gotta be honest though, it would help if I knew what we were looking for."

The first man grunts. "Orders from Government were to haul ass through the Gate with every Fleet ship within three jumps physically able to move, set up a cordon around the moon and Gate, and then await further instructions." He grunts again, unhappily. "I know just about as much as you do, Chen, and I don't like it. We're to ignore all transmissions from anyone except Government ships, and under no circumstances are we to scan the moon itself."

Chen's eyes widen slightly. "But that's a violation of basic operating protocols, Aidan. What if there's something down there, a threat? We're sitting ducks up here."

"These orders come from levels of Government it would be unwise to ignore, my friend," Aidan replies, "and don't forget the 'sir' on an open feed." He chuckles lightly. "It would be a Gate-damn shame if I had to space my oldest friend for insubordination."

"Yes... sir." Chen grins. "I'll let you know if we get anything; right now it's just Fleet elements Transiting through." He pauses. "Hold on a minute, that's not one of ours..." The blaring siren of General Quarters echos through Aidan's earbuds and the interior of the ship, his glARs feed flashing red at the edges. Figures stiffen and prepare for combat, munition platforms cycling up to readiness, gunnery officers linking with their individual VIs and pushing refined firing solutions into the cloud.

Aidan feels a slight pressure through the shock gel as *Partycrasher* lurches onto a new course, fusion thrusters flaring under hastily enacted evasion protocols, the memplas super-structure of the ship flexing slightly under the stress of the turn.

While the ship continues unsheathing her fangs, a new channel appears on Aidan's display, the only image an intertwined 'B' and 'C' on a field of frozen static. A heavily modulated voice crackles in Aidan's earbuds, the distortion making it impossible to tell whether male or female.

"Tell your ships to hold their fire, Commander, unless they want to find themselves on the wrong side of an AM torpedo."

"Identify yourself," Aidan snaps. "How did you gain access to this cloud?" In his glARs, surrounding the anomalous feed, five different engagement options present themselves, arrayed from best to worst case based on the estimated strength of the intruder and the current velocities of Aidan's own ships.

A complex stream of alphanumeric digits flashes over from the interloper, a Fleet registry code, but one unlike any Aidan has ever seen before. The *Partycrasher's* VI pings a verification chime on his glARs – ship identified as the *Gungnir*, a *Ghost* class dreadnaught, commanding officer RESTRICTED. The General Quarters alarm ceases, overridden by the newcomer's credentials. More updates flow through Aidan's glARs, a reordering of the Fleet command structure. The graphic shifts into a new form, a fuzzed static square now occupying the topmost hierarchy complete with Fleet-wide override protocols, Aidan's normal command structure beneath it. The voice continues.

"Who we are is unimportant. What *is* important is that your combat elements quarantine that moon and keep anything from escaping through the Gate." The voice pauses momentarily. "Let me be clear here, Commander. You are to capture any sort of vessel that attempts to leave that moon, and if capture is not possible, you are to terminate it *immediately*. You will not scan its interior, you will not respond to any communications from it, and if you do capture something, under no circumstances whatsoever are you to do anything other than keep it isolated in a containment field no closer than one kilometer to your hull until we have a chance to retrieve it. Is that understood?"

Aidan can feel his teeth clenching, and he forces himself to respond emotionlessly to the grating voice. "Understood, sir. My elements are at your disposal. Should we anticipate any sort of weapon dispersal from the moon itself?"

"Don't worry about the moon, Commander. That's what we're here for. You just maintain your quarantine. *Gungnir* out."

Aidan feels the tension headache of an overly stressed jaw crowding his senses, and he takes several deep breaths before highlighting the feeds of his bridge officers. "Ladies and gentlemen, here's the situation. We have no idea what's going on down below us..."

The jungle night is alive with the unfamiliar sounds of creatures fighting, screaming their dominance to the balefully glaring gas giant eye above. In the absence of an overriding directive, what primal instincts remain in their twisted bodies surge to the forefront of biohacked brains, driving them to seek the thrill of the chase, the warm rush of blood spilling from prey, the feel of life slipping away. The overwhelming urge to control is all that drives them now.

Fires rage throughout the gutted structure of the resort, a blazing beacon drawing countless shapes like moths to a flame. Flying, crawling, slinking, they approach the towering inferno and fall upon one another, a never-ending tide of fang and fur and chitin, dancing their sacrifice before the primordial altar.

A charging slab of pure muscle and jutting bone tramples its way over the gnashing fangs of a tentacled lynx stalking toward a broken water feature, eviscerating it with a sweep of jagged horns. It falls in turn to a cast of falcons swooping down from a fifteenth story window, firelight gleaming off their razor quill feathers and cruelly barbed beaks.

An ambulatory urchin with the legs of a millipede snatches one of the fliers out of the air with the whip-crack lash of its prehensile tongue, and then takes down several others in pinpoint spine volleys before scuttling off into the ruins of a moverbike, coiling its body around the central frame. The creature lets out a steam-kettle hiss seconds before a massively scaled foot crushes it into paste, the house-sized lizard the foot belongs to tearing a path through the glittering remains of the resort entryway, golden columns cracked and scattered like the broken stalks of wheat after a tornado.

A blood-dimmed tide is loose, anarchy sweeping forth, beasts slouching from shadow to shade while the corpses of thousands litter the ground in twisted forms of repose. Out in the lake, the water churns to a boil from the raging battles taking place beneath the surface, huge shapes momentarily broaching from chthonian depths. Writhing tentacles whip into the air and violently wrap around the pendulously floating shapelessness of an amorphous airborne jellyfish, flagella trailing through the chopping waves. The massive sac vomits a fountain of bilious acid from multiple sphincters, and the tentacles retreat back below the water in search of easier prey. The shapeless horror drifts on, spreading a noxious trail of poisonous compounds as it goes. Gnarled shapes float to the surface in its swirling wake.

Over in the city, the ghastly silence of a holocaust cloaks the night air with a stifling weight. The biological subsuming of clean-edged architecture into curving egg sacs continues apace, buildings swaddled in ever increasing strands of white filament, dark figures scuttling over every surface.

They click and preen, scraping gruesome appendages over glossy black shells, gleaning information from each new addition to the gestalt. One of the eight-legged forms stares out across the gently swaying jungle treetops, coldly incomprehensible eyes dissecting the verdant panorama in a spectrum of wavelengths. Down below, the streets lie empty, stark, motionless but for the voiceless screams of countless memories flitting among delicate threads.

Overhead, the stars scatter and shift in the firmament like wandering deities, forming incomprehensible constellations as they cavort around one another. Seven of the stars twinkle and grow larger, sparks descending from on high like the pinpoint tips of wrathful celestial swords. The atmosphere screams as the glowing comets plunge to the darkened moon below, an apocalyptic clarion call heralding their passage.

Whipcrack sonic booms roll out over the jungle in staggered pulses like a juggernaut's footsteps, HV kinetic tungsten rods flashing through the night sky in glowing lines of meteoric fire. The ground rocks in mini-quakes as the projectiles impact, vegetation instantly mulched and vaporized, the ground cratered and smoking from the intense energy transference. Dirty mushroom clouds rise into the air in a ragged circle, and an angular shape barrels through the debris, plasma thrusters screaming like banshees, melting a clear path through the crowded air.

Bare seconds before the plasma would begin to backsplash against the steaming earth, the thrusters cut off and a *Ferret* class assault shuttle slams into the churned devastation, bioarmored troops disgorging from its flanks while the craft shudders to a crunching halt. Six of the leanly muscled silhouettes dash next to a lone splintered tree thrusting up into the sky like a monument, somehow still standing after the destructive barrage, and one of them crouches over near its trunk. A brief electronic exchange, and a door slides open, bark sliding away to reveal a passageway down. The troops slip inside like phantoms, the only indication of their passing a brief disturbance in the slowly falling clouds of dust.

Behind them, the red hot hull of the shuttle pings as it cools, metal settling back into less stressful configurations, the craft itself squat and lurking in the ruined moonscape. Around it, the jungle stirs.

XANDER

Ti*3tamP fa.*1.0* <<__$!GN^@^L *##*ORR*-8-P`?><E**.,ED*==()*>

I'm in the lab once more, standing in my office. All around the walls shake and waver, delicate sand castles holding back an unseen tide. The dreamscape snaps into place, and Councilor Rocon appears in front of me, eyes tight and angry, a lifeless mannequin.

It is fifteen years ago.

Time jumps into motion, and his mouth moves, words falling out with the dull weight of memory.

"I'm taking you off the weapons project."

"What?" My voice is shocked, disbelieving. I did not see it coming then, and it still hurts to see it now.

"You've wasted too much time on fruitless experimentation with eHydro, something I specifically told you not to pursue. The weapons project needs members who are committed to ideas that work, not advancing their own pet theories." He pauses, glaring. "I brought you here, gave you control of this lab, because the other scientists said you were a genius. Something special." He sniffs. "Instead, I get a petulant child who fails to grasp the opportunity he has been afforded, one who wastes his time on a dead-end path that others have assured me will not pan out."

I scowl. "The work I've done on eHydro is setting the stage for breakthroughs that will win this war for us. I fail to see how it is my responsibility that your 'scientists,'" my voice turns mocking, "cannot comprehend my calculations. Perhaps if they opened their minds up to new possibilities, instead of blindly following the tracks others have already made, we wouldn't be losing."

Two bright spots of color appear on his thin cheeks, the angriest I've ever seen him. "You are *done* with the weapons project," he hisses, "and if you want to continue your existence outside of the interior of a star, you will do *nothing* except work on upgrading our crop yields. Consider yourself lucky I have no one to replace you with."

I fume, hands at my sides. "You don't understand. My experimentation with eHydro, I wouldn't be doing it if there wasn't something *there!* I'm only a year away, maybe two at the most, from integrating it into a biological form, and the math is solid. This will provide results – all I need is a little more time."

His voice turns cold. "I have given you time, more time than you deserved. I have watched you waste resources on a hopeless pipedream, against my express orders – seduced by your own intelligence into believing you cannot possibly be wrong. I have been waging a war for humanity against a foe I cannot stop, and I no longer have the patience to cater to your ridiculous *whims.* You will *not* bother me with this eHydro nonsense any longer, IS THAT UNDERSTOOD?"

My mind screams at me to respond, continue pressing my case, but I force my mouth shut, lips clamped tightly together. Councilor Rocon stares at me for a full minute, colorless steel eyes burning into my face. Finally, he nods. "Good. You may yet be salvageable. We all contribute, Doctor Lillibridge, and if you cannot contribute, then you are of no use to me. I have an entire galactic sector to take care of, and perhaps if you work hard enough – for long enough – on the crop yields, I may find a place for you in the weapons project once more. Until then, I am cutting your resource allocation to one quarter of what it was before – crop design is much less intensive than weapon systems. You will not see me again until I deem you reformed enough to help humanity in our fight."

My hands clench even harder, fingernails drawing blood from my palms. I can feel the hot liquid well and bead up, trickling down the outside of my fists. I glare silently into his frozen eyes, and a single drop falls, slowly tumbling under gravity's inexorable force. It hits the floor, and everything disappears in an eyeblink instant.

<<exe.cloudSys v.4.2.09;>>

<<main array detected;>>

<<intializing...;>>

I float through the whispering darkness, a disembodied voice echoing around me. The words take shape in slowly writhing worms of *nothingness* crawling across the black, eating their way into my mind.

Their touch is cold, alien.

<<connection complete;>>
<<exe.bootstrap v.1.4.5p;>>
<<buffering...;>>
<<initializing...;>>
<<bootstrap initialized;>>
<<configuring...;>>

Complex geometric shapes spring into existence behind the wormtrails, spreading portals opening a view into the architecture of a non-Euclidean universe. Five hundred and twenty degree circles intertwine with six-sided squares, their points curling together into a self-enclosed hemisphere. My mind screams at the impossible mandalas gradually replacing the darkness in all directions.

<<exe.fullScan v.3.2.48;>>
<<initializing...;>>
<<protein markers detected;>>
<<sufficient biomass detected;>>
<<exe.primeShift v.a.1.02;>>
<<initializing...;>>

Taste the soothing icefire of electromagnetic pulses coursing across raspy tongue, intermingled with spicy bursts of ultrasonic pings. Infraviolet waves thrum, caress limbs, photons dancing quantum patterns across muscles quivering in anticipation. The mandalas bulge and swell, barbed faces staring at/through/around each other. Infinity consumes their eyes in a never-ending spiral. Their mouths open, and I hear gravity.

<<primeShift 48%;>>
<<exe.combatSuite v.12.2.09;>>
<<buffering...;>>
<<initializing...;>>

Running dashing scuttling pacing loping sprinting rushing spurting flowing falling rippling streaming teeming thronging swarming tearing tattering shredding clawing slashing splitting dripping... A deathly eternity of muscle memory. There is only kill and be killed. No quarter. The all-consuming visages nod approvingly, towering over everything, voidworms sinuously twisting across the few remaining scraps of blackness.

<<primeShift 72%;>>
<<exe.gateSplice v.a.1.02;>>

<<sufficient eHydro detected;>>
<<initializing...;>>

The universe opens. Countless lives trail behind me, a cracked sliver of a vast whole, but the perspective is not right, angels skewing into shadows as the attention of a hopelessly vast **MIND encompasses my thoughts and I** *feel the last bits slipping away* —

<<primeShift 93%;>>
<<exe.idSynthesis v.a.1.01;>>
<<warning;>>
<<biofeed integrity compromised;>>
<<idSynthesis v.a.1.01 disrupted;;>>
<<primeShift 98%;>>
<<warning;>>
<<unable to reinitialize;>>
<<warning;>>

I open **our eyes.**

Prime is standing in front of me, clawed hand **holding us up** by my neck, puckered chunks missing all along its scarred and gashed forearm **and we will flense it to the bone with our talons**, but first I have to break free from the stranglehold. I twitch **our razor lined articulated tail and drive it into the exposed side** of Prime – it stumbles back and bellows furiously, still dragging me by the neck. I whip my fist around to break its grip, **kicking our foot into its face and** Prime staggers from the unexpected assault. I kick it again and it goes flying across the room, crashing into the shattered and warped doorframe, its ponderous bulk crushing the ruined remains of the hatch. It drops to the floor and *screams.*

We fall to all fours and *scream,* **lashing the Branderson Executive Suite mk. five medical unit** behind me into a cloud of foam padding and metal splinters **with our tail.** I scan the room, **our senses drinking in the abundant sources of energy pouring** from the sparking glowpanels set into the ceiling, their **plastic polymer casings cracked and leaking** electricity from Prime's rampage through the door, deep grooves scoring the rock above. I notice my assistant/**prey//secondary** cowering in a corner, his eyes bulging nearly out of their sockets. **We**

prepare to strike/offer my hand to help him up and he sprints for the exit, **heartbeat racing at one hundred and thirty-five beats per minute, lungs operating at ninety-five percent maximum efficiency** and he dives over the slowly rising form of Prime to the hallway outside. He disappears from view and **we sense footsteps receding** into the distance. The opening is abruptly filled with the cracked and bleeding figure of Prime struggling back to its feet.

    <<*warning;*>>

My brother/daughter/self stares at me with furiously glowing eyes and **crouches in an attack vector**, talons digging into the polished volcanic floor of the lab room, and suddenly **we leap, our fangs baring to rend and tear.** I swing my fists at the closest thing I have to **prey//primary, estimated combat efficiency – sixty-eight point two percent.**

Clear blood flies through the air as **we collide in a glorious flurry of flashing hate, our claws shredding** through Prime's torso and legs while it drives multiple strikes **into our lower abdomen**, seeking to **impair our optimal internal functionality, combat subroutine theta.** I aim for the already wounded parts of Prime so I can incapacitate it and escape after my **prey//secondary** to the shuttle. **We roll out** into the hallway in a twisting ball of **narrowly dodged eviscerations** and straining muscles, slamming **each other into walls while our razor tails** parry like fencers, splintered shards of rock spraying out from each **lightning quick strike dodge attack defense.** Red emergency lights start to flash and whirl overhead.

    <<*warning;*>>

    <<*Omega protocols accessed;*>>

    <<*warning;*>>

We continue our struggle **for dominance, kill or be killed**, down the somehow too small corridor. Our shadows surge and dance across the walls in the crimson gloom. **Cut the hindlimb tendon, claw descending at our head, rocking back dodge, falling to all fours and dash forward, raking talons** across Prime's legs again and then spinning back through the air from **a vicious kick that splinters multiple protective scales** guarding my stomach. Prime follows up its momentary advantage with a flurry of gashing blows, forcing **us to scuttle back, damage sensors singing.** Jagged claws rip across **our forelimbs and dorsal spines. We wait for our sister/son/self to** overextend, **combat efficiency** significantly lessened by the wounds already marking its body, **and then we piercing grip** its stumbling frame and **fling our shadow**/creation into an opening, its limbs flailing as it careens into the cavern beyond.

Screaming, **we** lunge after it. I enter the cave, **and our sensors reveal** an Icarus shuttle sitting in a supporting gantry of steel struts reinforced with memplas, **their resonance ringing through** my ears, its clear nose facing down a **seven hundred and eighty-one point six-meter** tunnel to my right, thrusters barely visible in the tunnel opening to **our three hundred and twenty degrees from magnetic north.** The walls glisten with the sheen of **igneous rock, probability of collapse zero point zero one percent,** under the strobing red lights covering the **one hundred and eighty-two point seven-meter** hemisphere's bumpy ceiling. I see **our** assistant/**prey//secondary** climbing the gantry staircase, arms and legs pumping furiously, making his way toward the shuttle bridge **twenty-four point six-meters above the ground and we must** get to the shuttle and help **squeeze the last drop of blood from his twitching corpse** before he escapes. I run at the scaffolding.

<<*warning;*>>

<<*Omega protocols accessed;*>>

<<*warning;*>>

Prime leaps on **us from behind, dislocating our** right arm with a savage jerk, the bone grinding as it **shifts inside our massive frame, tearing thirteen muscle fibers and three ligaments along** its passage.

Prime drives a **spiked claw**/hand deep within my exposed **lower carapace**, shredding several **nonessential combat** organs. I try and twist away from the blow, sensing the **massive degradation to combat efficiency** if the invading claws are allowed to continue **savaging our backup toxin filter and secondary heart**. I *scream* **and trigger a volley of chitin spines** into Prime's face and upper chest. It *screams* and falls back, scrabbling to remove **our acid injecting barbs** from its flesh. I grip my **spiked forelimb and wrench our** shoulder back into place.

Prime finishes clearing the spines from its body, **combat efficacy reduced by negligible levels due to designed immunity**, and I can feel **our repair mechanisms** knit my body back together. **We assess our prey//primary**. Clear fluid from countless wounds drips and steams as it hits the ground, *self* **contained within** the blood reacting to **separation from the** *Self*, and I'm grimly pleased to see Prime favoring

263

its right side, too much biomass lost from previous wounds to **recover the entirety of** *Self*. **We scan our internals and** note a drop of only two percent efficiency, **our** *self* **drawing from the linkage to** *Self* to rapidly close the cuts and gashes covering my body. I tense and prepare for **our killing rush**.

The sudden **registering of sonic/thermal/gravitic** activity in the open mouth of the **thirty-two point six-meter-high** cavern reveals six hulking figures wearing **Daison-Eno mk. II biopharmacopic augmented battle suits** sprinting into the room from the lab entrance, **Daison-Eno mk. VI combi-projectile launchers** already chattering short bursts of **morphine derivative sedative darts into our flesh, and we laugh**. The compounds are immediately neutralized by the enhanced tox-filters **circulating through our** blood – **combat efficacy loss negligible**.

The **Black Colony fast reconnaissance team, projected combat efficacy threat level beta** immediately spreads out into a **swarm formation, primary objective overwhelm and capture**, four of the suits advancing **toward us, one flanker to each side, threat vectors swirling through our sensors**.

Our lips draw back from my teeth and I burst into motion, driving **our limbs into the floor in blurring strides**. I advance on the **prey//tertiary. We effortlessly cleave one's head from its shoulders** with a quick pass, **razor talons licking out and through its** biosuit like monowire through an overripe pumpkin. **Our tail impales another** in the chest, **carving through bone and heart in a beautiful shower of vitality**.

Blood sprays from the gaping wound and **we retract our tail and smash our** fist up and through the third figure's **underprotected belly, grabbing its spine and ripping it back out through its own midsection in a shower of viscera**.

<<*warning;*>>

<<*Omega protocols initializing;*>>

<<*warning;*>>

Hypervelocity kinetic penetrators rip through our body in a violent cascade, combat efficiency down one point two percent, and we *scream*. Turning, we fling the spine at a fourth prey//biosuit still spitting munitions into us, and explode into a charge. The grisly vertebrae clatter off its face and it flinches, and then we arrive in a welter of fangs and claws, breaking both of its elbow joints in jolting pops. It drops the Daison-Eno mk. III combi-projectile launcher, and we rip its legs off in a convulsive heave, kicking the falling torso into a wall. It mewls piteously for four point two nine seconds before expiring.

The cavern flashes with an actinic glare and a massive blow impacts my right leg. I tumble through the air and crash to the ground, **our right hindlimb sheared halfway up** the thigh. **Our sensors report a twenty-seven point three percent drop in combat efficiency.** I snarl and scramble onto **our three remaining limbs, tail** instantly compensating for the change in balance. Standing next to my severed leg is one of the two remaining **prey//tertiary**, priming another **Daison-Eno limited-engagement antimatter aerodynamic projectile** in his hand. **We trigger a shuddering burst of spines** and he slumps over, impaled through **both eyes, throat, and all major arteries**, the disc clinking gently as it falls to the floor. The cavern flashes again, **our** *self* **vaporized by the shuddering annihilation** of matter and antimatter, and I *scream*.

Our sensors register kinetic motion from the shuttle gantry, and **we sense the last** biosuit bounding up the open frame switchback staircase, pursuing **our prey//secondary**.

I **flow forward on quicksilver claws, limited to eighty-three percent of max speed from the** loss of my leg. The **prey//tertiary fires seventeen Daison-Eno titanium alloy projectiles** at the sprinting figure of my assistant, sudden holes punching through the walkway at **two thousand eight hundred meters per second**. He dives for cover behind several crates stacked on the bridge connecting to the shuttle, **their contents clear to our millimeter wave sensor band, threat level//negligent. We dig our talons into the metal girders** and start scaling the scaffold.

More shots ring out, the biosuit continuing **its hasty advance, unaware of our scuttling climb**. The constant barrage pins **our prey** in place, **standard Black Colony operating procedure when advancing on an entrenched foe without support elements. Estimated survival time of prey//secondary – six point five seconds. We must hurry.**

My **claws** pull **us** from beam to beam, **our** *self* **draining from our tattered stump while** I continue climbing skyward. Finally/**one point six seconds later**, I reach the railing surrounding the top level and **we** leap through the air with a savage uncoiling of muscles in our remaining hindlimb at the biosuited figure taking aim at my cowering/**cowering** assistant/**prey//secondary, its digit point zero nine seconds away from closing the circuit** on the projectile launcher's firing panel. **Our forelimbs slam together** like the violent thunderclap of *SELF*, and the suited head **bursts apart**, body collapsing into a masterless marionette's sprawl. My assistant turns and runs toward the shuttle hatch – **we spin and lunge after the prey//secondary, closing the gap by twenty meters per second, estimated intercept in three point six four seconds.**

<<warning;>>
<<Omega protocols initializing;>>
<<warning;>>

Impact from the side, **our prey//primary tackling and flaying** my left side. We tumble across the top of the gantry in a whirlwind melee. I bite Prime's arm with **our fangs, tearing gobbets of *self* free**; its tail repeatedly punches through my **upper secondary ventricle, redundant systems triggering, combat efficiency lowered a further six point seven percent.** I twist and roll, swiping my **talons across the previously damaged lower abdomen**, drawing forth a gushing **spray of** hissing clear fluid. We stagger toward the railing, **talons rending and splitting extremities, *self* sheeting** across the crosshatched metal floor in spurting waves. **Our sensors detect the shuttle hatch opening, and then closing, two point eight seconds later,** and suddenly we're falling over the railing, plummeting to the rocky floor below, **plunging our razor tail into he/she/their spine while talons splinter our bones and we clamp fangs deep within pulsing arteries.** A serrated coil wraps around **our throat.**

<<warning;>>
<<Omega Protocols initialized;>>
<<warning;>>

I/**we** hit/**smash** into/**onto** harsh/**unforgiving** ground/**rock** my/**our** body/**body** bouncing like a rag doll. We stare into my sibcreliationg's eyes, **watching** the spark of *self* flicker and **die. A thundering** roar **drowns** our **perceptions,** the shuttle engines fire, **and the searing** light **of** a **plasma** sun **washes** over us.

I scream.

ROB

Pain makes me want to scream, but can't. Gotta buy more time, make him think he hasn't broken me yet, hold out until *Jen'sFuture* finally spreads its wings and flies. Can't let the cat grow tired of toying with his captive mouse, else the paw comes down.

One hundred and eighty seconds left.

Monocle's combat knife digs its way deeper into my mangled shoulder, probing the damage, and another burst of agony tenses my neck. Acid rolls through my brain, monofil edge scraping across a nerve cluster, feet drumming on the floor helplessly. He chuckles and pulls the knife out, twirling it in front of my face with his good hand. Blood slowly drips down the blade. Asks me if I like the look.

Hundred and seventy.

His left eye is a jellied mess, vicious gash running from forehead to chin, bone showing through in places. He laughs and laughs, dried blood covering his face flaking down like dandruff. Auburn hair's been burnt down to stubble, skin peeling and blistered across his scalp, ear a tattered mess. His remaining eye glints crazily behind the monocle's clear lens, madness dancing gleefully deep within the pinpoint pupil.

Tell him he should fire his barber.

He cackles and digs the knife into my shoulder again, recreating the damage my penetrator did to him. He severs a tendon and my fingers go slack and numb, more blood welling out of the wound. Feel my teeth grinding, surprised they haven't cracked yet. Take advantage of his intense concentration to weave a phantom net around his glARs feed, shunt it into a duplicate shell of the main system. Don't want him realizing what's going on in the background.

Hundred and fifty.

One last shearing cut and he leans back on his haunches, surveying his twisted work, knife dangling in a loose grip. He frowns briefly, and

I fear he's noticed my deception, but then he flips the knife in his hand and smashes the solid brass pommel into the open wound in my shoulder, shattering the bone.

Try not to vomit from the pain. Barely succeed.

He laughs again, calls it perfect.

Hundred and forty.

My head lolls over to the side, see the dark stain spreading across my tacsuit from the trauma, ragged hole in my shoulder a pulped mass of flesh, white flecks of bone scattered within. It's almost a mirror image of the same stain spreading across his upper chest, our only difference the hastily wrapped field bandage covering the hole my penetrator punched through his tacsuit. His left arm hangs limp at his side, fingers lifeless, and he stares at my twitching body, blade spinning absentmindedly in his functioning hand.

The cold insanity of a sociopath watches me through an unblinking eye, and then he starts in on the bloody mess of my ruined leg, knife flicking through cartilage and ligaments like a surgeon's scalpel. He whispers as he works, a litany of atrocities he's planning for my baby, my Jennifer.

Hundred and fifteen.

Ride the wave of misery and tune him out as best I can, focusing on what's important. Pull up my connection to the lab VI, hiding the finger twitches of the haptic sensors in my right glove as spasms while he continues disassembling my joint. Isolate a certain set of emergency commands for Central Core and disable them with a quick splice.

Wouldn't do to give him any clues too early. Trigger another set of commands, triple authenticate acceptance orders required, override with the director's codes, use a bit of his blood smeared across my glARs from when I rolled for the projectile launcher earlier. VI accepts and initializes, warnings blazing in my vision.

Hundred.

Sudden burst of searing agony and a black tunnel clamps down, sight quickly returning with a sick clarity. He holds up my kneecap, tucks it into a pocket. Wants to keep it for a souvenir, says he's going to keep it on his mantle, right next to my daughter's skull.

Says he wants the matching pair though.

He bends over my other leg and sinks the blade in again.

Eighty.

Drop deep within myself, find my core, isolate and ignore the messages my cells insist on sending me. Pull up a picture of my baby instead, focus on her smiling face, her beautiful hair, the laughing joy of a toddler's first steps, the coltish awkwardness of a first date, the grinning poise of a young woman's first trip off planet, hiking pack filled almost to bursting.

Think of better times.

Sixty.

Fresh jolt of exquisite pain blasting through my system, and he raises my blood soaked patella in front of my face, forcing me to look at it, his hand a deep crimson. He laughs at my expression and places it in his pocket with the other one, then inserts the tip of his knife into the hole in my abdomen, peeling away layers of fat and muscle in long strips.

Forty.

View starts to waver and blur, greying at the edges, biomonitors chiming ominously. Force myself to endure, take the pain, let it flow through me like an impossibly vast ocean of lava melting my very essence. Focus on the brightness of *Jen'sFuture*, a complex series of triggers calling in every favor I've ever been owed, wiping her from Government's databases, setting up shell accounts for the ridiculous amounts of wealth that will soon transfer from the late Augstar's vast coffers, creating cover identities and false trails so no one will ever know who my baby was, not unless she wants them to, free to live her life.

Thirty.

He's created a twisting gash bisecting almost my entire midsection, hot wetness flowing down my waist. He sheaths the knife, and then reaches inside of me, hand gripping a loop of intestine. With a grunt, he starts wrenching slippery coils out of my body, letting them slide wetly to the ground between my legs. I struggle not to pass out, and cough a thick spray of blood into the air, chest heaving and spasming.

Twenty.

A soft glARs alert brings my attention away from the incandescent fire ripping me apart. Looks like the lab shuttle is making an emergency takeoff, engines going hot in the exit tunnel. Quick rewind on the feed, see the assistant scamper inside. Silently grin through the pain, blood dripping down my mouth – wish him luck. He wasn't a bad sort, for a biohacker. Better hurry, though, gonna be close.

Ten.

Defiling hand rips out the last of my intestines, flings them away like some gruesome snake trailing through the air.

Five.

Progress bar laboriously creeps along, barest sliver of nothingness separating dreams from reality.

Three.

His hand dives back inside, pushing its way past my kidneys, crushing my liver in a flare of sensation. The pain is all consuming. I am trapped in a race that will not end.

One.

An eternity of time passes before my mind, all the memories I ever wanted, all the dreams I never lived, all the hopes and failures of a life I can only call my own. The digit lies frozen in my eye, a sadistic face filling the room behind it, mouth locked in an expression of snarling hate. His hand reaches for the life-giving organ pounding in my chest. I look at him and can only feel a disgusted contempt, especially for those who have the power to live well and choose otherwise, thinking only of their solitary lust for control. Such an ugly waste. Scum.

Zero.

A shuddering sigh escapes my cracked and bloody lips, the pain momentarily forgotten at the sight of a simple blinking number. The finish line approaches.

Zero.

Watch the last piece of the datobject upload to the Gate cloud, slot itself into the VI, a shimmering jewel of hope, my final farewell to my baby. The VI spreads its wings and vanishes in an electron sparkle. Gonna make sure you have a chance, I promise her, voice quiet in my head. Gonna finally make a difference for you. Daddy loves you.

Zero.

"Hey," I whisper, his hand digging up into my ribcage. He pauses and stares at me uncomprehendingly, face inches away from mine, eye fully consumed by madness as his fingers caress my twitching heart.

"See you in the sun."

Execute *Shiva'sFire*.

GEHENNA SYSTEM

Timestamp – 22.17.01LT:11.14.29OT:03.18.407AG

A stream of electrons races down fiber optic cabling, faster than the speed of thought that triggered it into motion. It pauses almost imperceptibly at a routing station, dashing through a maze of logic gates, and emerges slightly altered, accompanied by four identical siblings, each of them bearing a message, their bodies configured into mobile keys. They burst back into the cable tunnels, galloping heralds streaming through the conductive lattice weaving the laboratory together, intertwining and separating as they move toward their respective destinations.

One by one, the siblings split off, darting down appropriate junctions on their own missions, until only the original remains in a rapidly narrowing channel. It continues its solitary journey through kilometer after kilometer of the moon's crust, a bright spark of information surrounded by the frozen stasis of energy trapped in stable orbits, solidified magma barely moving through the long eons. Eventually, the messenger reaches its goal, an unremarkable metal sphere roughly five meters in diameter set deep within the basaltic earth. Nearby lava continues its silent climb to the surface, irresistibly forced out by the churning atomic engine in the moon's core.

Five electron keys glide into waiting locks, settling into place like birds roosting, simultaneously perching into identical configurations. A brief series of events unfolds. Logic gates test the recently arrived configuration, confirm the results, and send out messengers of their own. Sensors acknowledge receipt, activate higher order functions, and complete the missing link of a winding circuit chain. Relays shift and click into new positions, the thrumming hum of energy coursing through their spiraling helix veins allowed to waver and dissipate.

The magnetic containment field preventing two hundred kilograms of antimatter from interacting with the surrounding environment

271

winks out of existence in five Class A Daison-Eno capital ship warheads spaced along the subducting fault line of Mount Zali'ah.

Sixty-four dreadnaughts rotate into position, orbiting the moon in a loose shell twelve hundred kilometers above the surface. They settle in to a standard Fleet blockade formation, thrusters flaring briefly with final course corrections. The two kilometer long cylinders look like thin cigars, dark grey memplas covering their entire length, studded sporadically with round weapon deployment portholes, aerodynamic properties nonexistent. They are born and die in vacuum, the harsh cosmic radiation their constant companion, gravity's pull a deadly embrace. The ships warily watch the space surrounding the moon through multiple sensor eyes, probing for targets.

A sixty-fifth ship, larger and sleeker than the others, looking more like a tapered wedge covered in asymmetrical protrusions, continues to hold station almost six hundred kilometers directly above Mount Zali'ah, kissing the edge of the moon's atmosphere. Its seven giant fusion thrusters burn constantly, fighting the force irresistibly dragging it to the surface below.

A steady stream of shuttles pour out of its four ventral bays, darting into orbital insertion patterns. Accompanying the shuttles are salvos of kinetic projectiles floating out of the many rounded weapon ports dotting the dreadnaught's sides, drifting away from the hull of the ship. Once the hyperdense rods reach a safe distance, one-shot chemical engines fire, and they rain down through the atmosphere like streaking meteors, ionized lightning bolts crackling in their wake. They hit the dark surface of the moon in miniature pinpricks of light, appearing like distant stars in the night to those watching from above. Monitors dutifully record the destruction.

Suddenly, night turns into day, and the sensor eyes scream in unison, delicate components withering under the blinding glare erupting from the moon, distant twinkles engulfed by the heart of a star revealed up close. Jagged incandescent cracks split their way across the night-shrouded face, shining through water and earth alike, spreading over thousands of kilometers, a massive rift that violently shatters into five inconceivably huge domes of glowing rock and plasma expanding out into space, tearing away great chunks of the moon's skin as they boil forth.

A timeless instant of frozen surprise, almost as if the entire universe is waiting to see what will happen next, and then the verdant orb begins to tremble and quiver like an enraged beast. The eye-searing jigsaw disappears, replaced by a sullen red glow that rapidly brightens to orange, and then a yellow verging on pure white, almost competing with the previous violation of crustal integrity.

Mount Zali'ah explodes.

A molten geyser of liquified rock nearly five kilometers in width vomits into the air at over three thousand meters per second; the titanic forces driving the moon's interior through the sudden breach. At the same time, a tidal wave of lava spills out along the shattered fault line in both directions, a smothering vanguard of superheated gas that gradually spreads over the seismically shifting surface, flashfiring everything in its path, entombing the once lush jungle under hissing rock.

Weather systems swirl and fray in the cyclonic bursts of air pressure, clouds forming where millions of kilograms of lava make contact with the moon's many oceans, instantly converting water into steam. Hurricanes and tornados start their howling march through the night sky.

The wedge-shaped ship slowly spins on its axis, thrusters firing desperately, shuttles frantically trying to abandon their insertions and reattach themselves to their parent craft. The dreadnaught is almost perpendicular to the violence exploding from below, plasma trail radiating white hot from acceleration, when the debris cloud finishes its journey out of the gravity well.

The heavier chunks of ejecta are already solidifying and falling back to the moon, unable to reach escape velocity, but the lighter elements continue their journey into space. Thousands of superheated rock shards punch through the dreadnaught's memplas hull, a furious shotgun blast shredding flesh and metal alike.

The projectiles rip their way into the ship, the sheer force of the concussive strikes overwhelming the structural integrity of the normally impervious hull. Internal atmosphere gouts out in hissing blasts, and the wedge tumbles and rolls back toward the raging planetoid, three of its seven thrusters maimed and destroyed, plasma venting from the engine compartments in glowing plumes, containment fields overwhelmed by the violent impacts.

The crippled dreadnaught trails smoke and flames as it hits the upper mesosphere, kinetic collisions expanding into a more forgiving medium, pieces ripped away by the growing resistance of air molecules. It plummets toward the fiery landscape of the wounded world and screams as it dies, wind whistling through countless structural breeches and jagged tears. Glowing sparks of falling stone rain down with it, a meteoric shower of blazing tears caught in gravity's inexorable clutch.

A small shape rises through the cataclysmic spray of debris on a pillar of blue flame, clawing its way up from the surface like a falcon dodging lightning bolts, thrusters howling at maximum thrust.

The broadsword profile of an Icarus dances and rolls, spiraling around the disintegrating dreadnaught, weaving in and out of the tumbling wreckage, memplas nose scarred and pitted by multiple microfractures slowly knitting back together, wing panels dented and torn – a moth doing its best to avoid the candle.

The shuttle climbs higher and higher, seeking the sanctuary of vacuum, punching its way through impact after glancing impact. The frame shakes and rattles like an out of control meteorite, engines pouring their fusion hearts into the thinning sky, and the Icarus screams its ascent, piercing the thinning bands of wispy atoms barricading it from space, thrusters flickering and sputtering as the systems collapse and shut down one by one.

With a final gasp, the Icarus bursts through the exosphere, tumbling and twisting in the chill blackness of space, small puffs of air escaping from its tattered wings. The moon burns beneath it, massive lightning bolts crackling along the swirling storm systems that cover the entire upper hemisphere – the glowing heart of a planet laid bare in a gashing scar that stretches from pole to equator. An invisible band of ultraviolet lidar scans the hull of the silently drifting shuttle, probing with photon-light fingertips.

"Sir, I think we have something here."

Aidan minimizes the maneuvering reports streaming in from the other ships moving to avoid the debris ejected from the eruption.

He highlights Chen's feed in his helmet and grunts, parsing the datobject.

The sensor officer highlights a recent lidar scan of an object that broke orbit, moving in a clearly artificial pattern. The scan reveals a shape battered and broken, but one undeniably that of an Icarus.

"Hmmm... sure it's not one of ours?"

"Not a hundred percent, but near close enough that I'd be comfortable putting money on it, sir." Chen's voice is slightly confused. "It's broadcasting a legitimate Fleet signal, but it's not one the VI's seen before. According to *Partycrasher*'s database, that code hasn't been ID'ed anywhere in over ten years."

"And we're sure it's not one of our dearly departed 'friends?'" Aidan grimaces internally at the biting sarcasm in his voice. A sector commander can't afford to show unprofessionalism.

"Totally, sir," Chen responds, not commenting on Aidan's momentary lapse. "They've been using a very specific frequency the entire time and they haven't deviated once from that channel. Tried to listen in, but I couldn't break the encryption before everything started getting all explodey."

"Gate-dammit, you idiot, are you trying to get us killed?" Aidan scowls. "It's fairly obvious that's a Government black ops ship of some sort, and you're trying to hack their communications?"

"Well... they're dead now, what's the big deal? It's not like they caught me doing it." Aidan looks at Chen's not particularly remorseful face and his scowl deepens.

"I swear, one of these days I'm gong to space you, you unrepentant scoundrel... And don't forget to say 'sir' on open channels!"

"You betcha, sir," Chen grins. "Anyway, that shuttle for sure isn't ours, and it definitely isn't a mysterious Government covert organization's, so my vote is that we go take a look at it."

Aidan sighs. "This is a military ship, Chen, you don't get to vote. I make decisions, and then you're supposed to carry them out. Not the other way around."

"Of course, sir, you're absolutely right, sir, decide away, sir." Chen keeps smiling. "However, we're the only ship that has an intercept on that shuttle without going through those debris vectors, so my vote is for checking it out."

Aidan closes his eyes and sighs again. "Some days, Chen... very well. Hopefully there's something onboard that explains why a moon just cracked open like an egg." He opens a channel to the ship captain.

"Lizbeth, Chen thinks he has something. Lay in a course for the following coordinates. Oh, and Chen, notify Gate Control of our status."

"Aye aye, sir."

Aidan watches the two ships match velocity through an outside feed, the deep grey body of the *Partycrasher* pulling alongside the drifting shuttle like a whale nosing up to a minnow, capturing and stabilizing it in a directed magnetic containment field.

More sensors probe at the crippled ship for several minutes before gradually pulling it into an open bay set into the dreadnaught's aft third. *Partycrasher* reverses her course and plots a controlled fusion burn to rejoin the rest of her sisters, the shuttle bay doors slowly closing around their prize.

"So, do we have any idea what's inside there?" Aidan pulls up scan after scan of the Icarus, every conceivable sensor available prodding at the crippled shuttle lying motionless and restrained inside the quarantined bay.

"There's a person in a shock gel pod, he's alive, and he's been blathering something about aliens," Chen replies in an offhand tone, cycling through his instruments. "He's probably crazy; the world *did* just blow up around him." Chen purses his lips thoughtfully. "I'd probably be going crazy."

"I just... I don't... Gate-dammit, Chen, we weren't supposed to contact anything from the surface, remember?" Aidan shoots him a withering glare over the feed.

Chen lifts an eyebrow, the glARs equivalent of a shrug. "They're dead, remember? Besides, I was curious."

"Remind me to tell you an Old Terra saying about curiosity sometime," Aidan says. "Very well, send what we have over to Gate

Control. I'm sure there's someone much higher up than me that gets to deal with this mess. And don't forget to say sir!"

"Yes sir, sending sir..." Chen trails off, dark eyes narrowed in focus. "Now *that's* an odd reading..."

A sickly purple pinpoint glows in the deep space between the smoldering moon and the gas giant it orbits. The zero-point crack increases in luminosity until it seems like a new sun is being born, the mind-wrenching phosphorescence tainting the grey ships surrounding the scorched jungle world with a pale violet, sympathetic flecks flashing deep within their protective memplas shells. Just when it seems like the light must consume the entire system, it blinks out, revealing an alien vessel almost a thousand kilometers long, delicately twisted shape subtly curving in on itself. Iridescent highlights shimmer across a quicksilver hull, and the purple refulgence somehow reverses motion back into its warped form.

The last of the purple glow disappears, and the massive construct *contracts* into a spiked ellipsoid a quarter of its previous size, swept back spines bristling along its entire length. Plasma flares out in vast arcing bolts, racing up the spines and then discharging across the void.

Dreadnaughts vanish by twos and threes, erased from existence.

"Prepare another wave of AM flashers, intersperse high yield warheads in attack profile delta, staggered launch. All ships initiate evasive pattern echo, local VI optimization." Aidan's voice is calm even as the universe reels around him, impossibilities given concrete shape. Battle updates stream through his display, ships and crews lost, munitions expended, and he grunts from the sudden mass of a giant sitting on his chest. The *Partycrasher* slowly rolls away from an incoming plasma blast, fusion engines engaging full thrust in a massive bloom of energy.

Crushing amounts of G-forces ripple through the ship, shock gel absorbing the brunt of the deadly weight.

The *Partycrasher* barely edges out of the flashing red impact zone before the plasma bolt arrives, multiple impact warnings blaring through the ship cloud. The bolt itself misses the ship, but the residual energies from its passing burn out half the front port quadrant sensors. Chen swears and alters the tactical display's input to compensate for the sudden gap in coverage. Another three dreadnaughts disappear from the tactical sidebar.

"Sir! Incoming message from Gate Control!" Chen's voice is sharp, eyes flicking over multiple glARs feeds, coordinating the display with the best possible composite he can compile from his degraded sensors.

"Put it through. Lizbeth, get us in position to provide supporting fire to *Zalcis* and *Archanich*."

"Yes, sir." The husky voice sounds strained, the blonde woman in the feed juggling projected impact zones, debris clouds, and relative velocities streaming into her glARs from the ship VI while she tries to keep the *Partycrasher* alive. Another surge of acceleration slams through the vessel, and Aidan grunts again, the shock gel cushioning some, but not all, of the blow. He triggers the audio feed labeled 'Gate Control.'

"Is this Commander Aidan Vladimir?" The voice is shrill, harried.

"Speaking."

"Commander, you are under immediate orders to proceed back to the Gate and Transit through pursuant to Government regulation 3425, paragraph four, Subsection F, under authorization of galactic sector governor Councilor Rocon Tringe."

"I'm not leaving my people out here!" Aidan snaps back, watching four more dreadnaught icons blink and vanish. The flanks of his formation are crumbling, the massive intruder methodically wiping ship after ship from its place in line. He snarls and sends a quick series of commands for the outermost ships to focus on evasion. The orders speed out, but another two ships writhe and die, helpless before the onslaught, and he curses.

"We need backup immediately! We're under attack from, from, from *something*!"

"Commander, I'm afraid you don't have a choice." The voice is suddenly weary, broken. "The Councilor has invoked Subsection F. Your ship is carrying vital information critical to the survival of the human race, and your VI has already been overridden under his direct orders.

This is now officially a Case Delta."

A deluge of surprised shouts and error messages fills the inside of Aidan's helmet, and then vanishes – everyone in the ship locked out of the combat cloud, their feeds cut. Before the tactical map disappears, it shows the ship shifting to a least-time course to intersect the Gate, a violent crash stop at the end risking fifteen point eight percent degradation to the ship's engines. The voice continues in Aidan's earbud, the only other noises now the straining frame of the hull moaning under max acceleration.

"I'm sorry about this, Commander. Everything in this system is now expendable to the goal of your ship Transiting through that Gate." A shuddering breath. "The other ships' VIs have been overridden as well – their only objective is to cover your escape, by any means possible. As soon as you're through, the Gate will blow behind you, pursuant to Government regulation 2671, paragraph eight, Subsection A. After that, you're not my problem anymore."

"I don't understand," Aidan whispers in a shocked tone. "I don't understand."

"We must protect humanity, Commander. Gate bless."

The feed cuts out, and the ship moans again.

The actinic flashes of plasma burst across the void of space, and crews die where they pass, melting and running like candles in a furnace. The ships fire their weapons up until the last second, vessels swarming toward the quicksilver behemoth like minnows attacking a shark, an all out assault with no thought of retreat. Missiles detonate their payloads, gamma rays sleeting out in the crushing annihilation of matter and antimatter, and rippling boils of light erupt across the massive frame of the impossible craft.

One of the long metal spikes deforms and droops under the relentless explosions, and then snaps off of the alien ship in a crystallized spray of twitching droplets. The broken shard spins away through space, iridescent sheen fading from its surface in a slow leeching of color until it's the dead grey of burnt ash. Bursts of energy immolate more dreadnaughts in a furious barrage, and then the *ship* twists and *contracts* itself into another configuration, this time a spinning disc almost five hundred kilometers across. More missiles race toward it.

The *Partycrasher* flips end over end, preparing to crash translate through the Gehenna Gate, thrusters firing a massive burst of deceleration to slow to an acceptable Transit velocity. The grey cylinder barrels toward the concentric rings of the Gate structure, fusion torch flaring before it, hull shrieking through the silence of vacuum from the stress. System malfunctions and warnings flow through the uncaring VI, and the decel burn continues.

A drawer breaks free in the lowest level of *Partycrasher* and three crewmembers are instantly pulped when it smashes through their combat pods at greater than thirty-Gs, liquified remains dribbling out with the shock gel. Luckily, the bulkhead holds against the impact, thick memplas spiderwebbing from the drawer pressed against it, keeping the sudden projectile from piercing through the rest of the ship. The VI annotates the incident in the ship log, and pours more thrust into the fusion bloom – casualty rate within acceptable parameters.

Against the backdrop of the swirling gas giant, the metallic disc spins faster and faster, creating a blurring sense of motion that cannot possibly be real. Suddenly, its shimmering center unfolds like a blooming flower's petals and an opening appears, a vast window. Space warps in the revealed area, and with a grim burst of sick purple light, the madly gyrating ring opens a Gate fully three hundred and fifty kilometers in diameter.

On the other side is the impossible radiance of an event horizon.

Starlight shifts and warps in the incredible surge of gravity bursting out of the Gate, photons dragged down in redshifted smears, a purple resplendence limning the rotating halo like a mad god's aura.

Atmosphere streams off of the ruined moon in a massive funnel, spiraling its way through space toward the wildly twisting ring. The gaping maw sucks in dreadnaughts like ants circling into a drain, their frames splintering apart under the terrible force, and they join the rapid flow of material pouring through the cosmic rift. Ahead of the *Partycrasher*, the Gehenna Gate twists and shakes like a tree in a gale, concentric rings barely holding their own miniscule tear in space and time open.

Partycrasher's hull shrieks and two engines fall offline as the barest edge of the gravitic lens brushes across its frenzied Transition out of the Gehenna system. The last thing the ship's VI records as it slams through the dissolving portal is the giant revolving structure sweeping its baleful glare across the remaining ships around the planet, consigning their atoms to crushing oblivion, snatching vast chunks of the garden world and stretching them apart like taffy while the hideous beam rips the moon to ragged shreds.

The dreadnaught barely clears the Gate on the other side before the concentric rings collapse with an awful finality, rocking the wounded ship with waves of almost mundane energy that the memplas easily repels. The remnants of the explosion fade behind it in a sullen red circle, like the feeble glow of a dying sun.

Partycrasher slowly lines up its next jump, one of many remaining, and limps its way back home, crew trapped within.

EPILOGUE (CENSORED)

Timestamp – CENSORED

A thin man in ascetically sparse robes stares at the image frozen on the infpanel in front of him, his eyes distant. Reflected off his wire-framed glARs is the last sensor record of the *Partycrasher*, taken while fleeing the Gehenna system – an entire planet deformed and shattered, pulled apart like an angry child with an insect.

"But why haven't they used it before..." he murmurs to himself, one finger tapping restlessly on the top of the darkly stained wooden desk.

He sighs, and returns the infpanel to its neutral display, the translucent screen displaying the slowly rotating insignia of the Security Council, two eyes staring at each other across a point-down sword piercing a golden Terra. A small brass plaque next to the screen is the only other adornment on top of the horseshoe shaped desk. "Councilor Rocon Tringe" is etched in a looping cursive across the plaque's surface.

He pushes his chair away from the desk and stands up, gazing at the brown-haired man manacled to a medunit on the middle of the red carpet covering the center of the room. With another sigh, he circles around the side of the desk and moves to stand next to a medunit.

Wire-frame glasses look down into angry brown eyes.

"And what am I supposed to do with you..." he muses, hands lightly gripping the side of the medunit. "It turns out the good doctor was right after all, and you're the only person who made it off that moon alive."

He leans down. "You're the only person who talked to him, near the end. The only one who can give us insights into his work, into the direction he was taking his eHydro research. The only one who witnessed... Prime."

Brown eyes flash with fury as the prisoner struggles against his restraints. "You son of a bitch. Xander was biohacking abominations, and I want no part of it. You have his glARs, recreate your own Gate-damned research!" He impotently rattles his chains again, hands clenched into fists, and then spits at the man, saliva tracing a line across one angular cheekbone.

Councilor Rocon reaches up to wipe his face, and his expression never changes from icy disinterest. "Watch yourself, Dr. Gauss. You have value to me, but that value only extends so far. I am in charge of biohacking affairs for the Council of Five, which, by extension, means I am in charge of biohacking affairs for the entirety of the human race, and *I will do whatever it takes to win this war*."

He turns away from the medunit and slowly paces across the lush carpet, gaze slipping past the priceless artifacts and works of art lining the walls of the chamber. The thin synthsilk of his robe gently whispers with each measured tread.

"I must confess, I never expected Dr. Lillibridge to succeed in his work. I was assured by countless 'experts' that eHydro synthesis with biological forms remained a pure impossiblity, a theoretical pipedream."

He pauses in midstride. "Apparently, I was wrong. *They* were wrong." He resumes pacing. "You witnessed the power of his creations, what happened when Dr. Lillibridge enabled the 'Prime' protocol on himself, Dr. Gauss. For some reason, he didn't immediately rip you to shreds, and I want to know why."

He gently clasps his hands together and returns to the side of the bed, looking down on the figure of Xander's once assistant. "If Dr. Lillibridge's creation can do even a tenth of the things he seemed to think it capable of, then we might finally have a chance. I doubted him before. I will not make the same mistake again. The information you have is important, Dr. Gauss, important to our entire species, and I will make any sacrifice if it ensures the survival of humanity."

The manacled figure laughs bitterly. "You sound just like him, like Xander, willing to sacrifice everyone else if it meant your twisted goals were that much closer to completion." Gauss' eyes flash hot with anger.

"'Humanity' is a noble word, 'Councilor,' but what price the universe if it costs us all our souls? What you're doing, what Xander did, is the very essence of 'inhumanity,' treating people like objects instead of human beings.

"I saw what that transformation did." He shudders, memories pressing to the surface. "I saw what Xander turned into. I know you'll get the information out of me eventually, I'm not stupid, but I will *never* willingly cooperate with someone who views us as pawns to be moved around the chessboard, as meat to be thrown into the grinder." His eyes close tight, shoulders slumping. "Do what you must, 'Councilor,' but you've already lost. Even if you win this war, you'll have killed what makes us human."

Councilor Rocon walks back to his desk and takes his seat once again, hands steeping underneath his chin. "Very well. That is your choice to make, however imprudent it may be, but I *will* find out what you know. One way or another." He triggers a datobject in his glARs, and two armed troopers in unmarked acticamo step through the large wooden double doors at the end of the room.

"Take Carlos here to the deep cells."

The troopers salute crisply, one hand clasped in front of their heart, and advance to the middle of the room. They each grab hold of one side of the medunit and maneuver it out, wheels sinking deep within the plush carpet, leaving furrowed tracks behind. Xander's assistant lies woodenly in the frame, unmoving the entire time, the limp resistance of non-cooperation the only thing he has left.

Councilor Rocon watches the trio depart through the heavily engraved doorway and opens a drawer in his desk. He reaches in and pulls out a heavily battered pair of glARs, gold logo set into the side of sleek black frames, and slowly rotates them in his hands.

Steel eyes contemplate the wealth of knowledge trapped within, the summation of a genius's life, and a cold smile briefly curls the corner of his thin lips.

"Oh yes, Carlos Gauss. I *will* have that information..."

Eyelids languidly open, revealing a pair of startling green irises in a lightly tanned and freckled face, black wisps of hair falling across delicate cheekbones. Pupils dart from side to side, confused, and the woman in the medunit quickly sits upright, trying to orient herself in a dark and unfamiliar room. She kicks the blankets off and drops to the floor in a crouch. Her knees wobble and shake, and she almost falls to the cool tile floor.

With a quick grab, her slender hand snatches the side of the bed, and she levers herself upright, taking in her surroundings in the dim light permeating the air. The thick folds of blackout curtains cover an entire wall, hanging down from an automated rail set into the four-meter-high ceiling, two plump recliners facing each other in front of them.

A small table with several shadowy objects on it sits equidistantly between the chairs. The medunit, a top of the line model she's surprised to note, sits in the middle of the broad rectangular area, a wide variety of diagnostic machines surrounding it like retainers at court. Stylishly opaque memplas doors space the other three walls, and the one opposite the curtains swings open, light spilling forth.

"Who's there," she cries, startled.

A thin man in a one piece hospital suit and clear glasses walks in.

"Ma'am, I'm under very specific instructions that you should put on the glARs on that table before talking to anyone here. There's also a robe hanging on the back of the door should you wish to clothe yourself." He brings the glowpanels in the ceiling up to half strength, bathing the room in a soft white glow, and then closes the door as he exits. The woman blushes and stumbles over to the memplas door panel, grabbing the robe and wrapping it around her suddenly chilled body.

She turns and walks over to the table, but halts halfway there, frozen by the sudden flare of realization. Slowly, she reaches down and touches her right leg, running her hands over her thigh, touching her knee, bending over to feel her calf and foot.

Her lower lip quivers, and then she straightens back up and haltingly walks the rest of the way to the chairs, collapsing into the leftmost one. She picks up a set of glARs, childish pink frames covered in pastel flowers, and slides them over her eyes.

"Hey, baby. It's daddy. Sorry I couldn't be there, but it looks like I finally found a way to get you cured..."

Tears fall from beneath the glasses, like glittering diamonds onto the cold floor below, and a ghost tells her he loves her.

She drops her head into her hands, shoulders hunched in racking spasms, and her flawless skin glows in the muted light.

END OF BOOK ONE

Special Thanks
Iain Banks, Michael Crichton, Terry Pratchett, L.E. Modesitt, Jr.,
Mike Futter, our test readers, and all of the people on social media for
being so excited about this book

The adventure continues...

PRIME

SPLICE

PROLOGUE

Timestamp – 22.13.24LT:12.48.03OT:05.17.412AG

A crystal glass glows crimson, dark liquid reflecting the dim light of muted glowpanels. Slender fingers hold the delicate container in a loose grip, idly swirling the contents in a brief vortex, small drops beading over the side to run uncaringly onto the richly woven rug below. Intense green eyes stare inscrutably into the twisting depths, and fine black hair frames the flawlessly tanned skin of a young woman's face. She raises her free hand to her right cheek, plain golden rings adorning each finger, and touches the smooth skin there in a gesture that's almost automatic. The gentle warmth of living flesh surprises her, as it always does.

With a sigh, she reaches down for a pair of pink glARs covered in pastel flowers. The cheap plastic frames contrast sharply with the opulent stonework of the gilt-edged table in front of her chair, and the cool chill of the marble brushes her trailing fingertips like a ghost's caress. Off in the distance, thunder rumbles through the dark air.

The woman briefly lifts the glasses up and stares into their unseeing lenses, her reflection peering back as if through a mirror darkly, before putting them back onto the black-flecked marble. With a quick twitch of a finger, she initializes a datobject command from her haptic rings, reestablishing their linkage with the glARs. The wall comes alive with light and sound, a thin flicker of photons streaming out of the right corner of the pink frames. She muses tiredly on the amount of money required to obtain something so simple looking as the plain golden bands, the cost of subtle power, and a familiar voice washes over her. It's a voice she hasn't heard in the flesh for five years.

"...so that's what it boils down to, honey. I don't think I'm making it back. Not anymore. I've done all I can, finally got you a cure, and I'm going to miss you so much."

The voice from the wall pauses for breath, a harsh tinge of pain underlying the words. "I've included everything I know from this whole messed up situation, all the data my glARs recorded, along with the lab files I scooped."

Ragged anger, the feed twisting back and forth like someone shaking their head. "Government lied to us, baby. They lied to us all. What you do with the information is up to you, and I'll love you no matter what, but now you have the resources to make those bastards pay."

Another pause, thunder rattling the curtained floor to ceiling windows. "Don't make the same mistakes I did. Live your life, baby, live it as intensely as you can. There's always something worth fighting for. I love you, Jennifer." A last rattling breath, and the feed cuts off, the viewpoint frozen on the blurred image of a battered man in acticamo rounding the corner of a memplas server cluster cage, the left half of his face a ruined mess. A cracked military-style monocle covers the bloody socket of his left eye.

Jennifer raises the glass to her lips and takes a small sip, her gaze staring blankly past the image on the wall. The crystal stills, small bubbles popping on the surface of the fluid while it settles into gently sloshing waves. Moisture wells at the corner of her eyes, but does not fall into tears. She flicks a finger and triggers another datobject, erasing the grim scene faster than an eyeblink, and replaces it with other times, other memories.

The projected viewpoint cycles through several images – a younger version of herself hiking with several friends, their vivacious laughter echoing off the rocky walls of the canyon while they climb; a birthday cake with seven candles, a smiling stocky man with thinning grey hair sitting across the table, telling her to make a wish; her old body thrashing and moaning in a hospital bed, the right side of her face scaly and dead, right leg missing at mid-thigh.

She pauses the feed on the last one, and stands up from the cushioning embrace of the chair, her hand unconsciously going to her cheek once more, black nusilk nightgown flowing soundlessly down like dreams falling.

Jennifer looks around the cavernous shadowed room, her eyes narrowing. Rare hardwoods cover the edges of the vaulted ceiling, a prince's ransom in molding, and priceless works of art hang from the walls, paintings and light displays ranging from pre-Diaspora old-Terran grandmasters to the latest functional abstracts from Nephilia II. Their subtly twisting edges draw the eye in vertiginous spirals. The rug at her feet, a monochromatic orbsilk hunting scene, is spattered with flecks of red from the vintage wine – bloody raindrops falling on the hunters' heads.

She walks across the rug to one of the opaque windows stretching from floor to ceiling, wineglass shifting to her other hand. Her fingers tighten on the crystal, knuckles white under the force of her grip, and the rings on her hand shift across the glass with a grating scrape.

Thunder rumbles from outside again, closer, like the war drums of an advancing army. Another finger twitch of the haptic rings and the window turns transparent. Beyond the crystal clear memplas, an apocalyptic storm advances across a pale salmon sky.

Towering clouds pile up on each other over the gritty silicon mesas of Belisa III, one of the binary red dwarf suns barely visible over the stupendous storm front, its white dwarf sibling already concealed. Great sheets of acidic rain advance toward the memplas window, gradually darkening the sky with their torrential flood, and harsh blue lightning flares constantly. The thunder is almost continuous, great steel drums booming an uptempo rhythm, and then the gust front hits the manor with a physical force, driving a tsunami of crystal particulates over the surrounding curtain wall.

Jennifer doesn't flinch as the initial shockwave of fine sand and water strikes the window in a slithering rush, scouring and pitting the memplas in jagged streaks. She's seen these dreadstorms for the past five years. The mansion is already beginning to heal itself from the assault. Covering an entire estate in memplas is expensive, she thinks, but money is the one thing that will never be a problem again.

She frowns sadly. The titanic fortune of a dead woman, vaporized beneath the fiery breath of something out of myth and legend, now hers to plunder at will – one last parting gift from her father.

Her eyes tighten. Like all gifts, this one came with a price. The memories of a moon shredded and torn like taffy, molten core ripped asunder by a powerful weapon – a Gate-linked black hole devouring the planet containing the last recorded location of her father, her *dad*. The system Gate transmitted up until the very end, both to Government and *fusion*, the custom VI her father created to funnel her a new life. She's reviewed the final seconds of data until they're engraved in her mind.

One ship made it through, crash Transitioning at the upper limits of Gate bleed-off – a mere thirty kilometers per hour faster, and the ship would have smeared itself across two systems in briefly spectacular showers of quark-gluon interactions. A Government Peacekeeper ship – the *Partycrasher*.

Contents unknown.

She almost winces remembering the resources it cost to buy that name. In her previous life, she would have considered it an impossible sum. In her new life, it's merely a rounding error, currency that might not have ever even existed.

Just like the *Partycrasher* and her crew. Despite every gcred she's thrown at the problem, the ship refuses to resurface after those last few seconds in the Gehenna system. Every inquiry, every private investigator, every crawling data spider leads to that same blank wall – a clueless shrug and a vacant face, current whereabouts difficult to find, secrets buried deeper than even the most confidential Government security access levels. Every back door channel a failure.

Every channel but one.

"Hey, Jenna." *fusion*, her Virtual Intelligence, pings the house speakers. "Got an incoming feed. Sounds like what we've been waiting for."

"I'll take it in here, *fusion*, thanks."

The VI's voice turns hesitant. "Jenna... are you sure about this? You know I'll support you no matter what, but once we go down this path... I just want to make sure you don't regret it later."

Jennifer takes another sip of wine, and then turns from the window back to the chair. She leans down to a dark-varnished side table and removes a stylish pair of translucent glARs, composed almost entirely of memplas, and gently twirls them before her eyes.

"Thank you, *fusion*, but I'm sure. I need to know what happened to dad. I need to know what's happening, what Government is really doing, the stuff we haven't been able to find out on our own." Jennifer takes a deep breath, and settles the glasses over her face.

"I need to know about... Resistance. Put it through, *fusion*."

Jennifer drains the last of her wine and places the glass back on the table, next to an almost empty bottle. A feed opens across the right side of her vision, a window to another place. The digital avatar of a pleasantly smiling, nondescript woman with a jade hairclip in her brown and blond hair stands in front of a plain white wall. She opens her mouth.

"Good evening, ma'am. I'm happy to tell you that you're the lucky winner of our recent contest promotion, and you've won an all expenses paid trip to the greatest party location in the galaxy, Vegas Five. I'll just need you to send some personal information first, so we can begin booking you a courier ship."

"I'm sorry, you must have the wrong commcode. Luck is what you make it, and I don't enter contests." Jennifer's response is calm, but she can feel her heart racing inside her chest. The code words match perfectly with the info she found in her private glARs mail account several days ago, which means Resistance has information on the *Partycrasher*, and is willing to set up a meeting.

"Our mistake, ma'am. We'll make sure to remove you from the system. Have an interesting day."

The feed flicks out, and a gently pulsing datobject appears in its place.

<<I checked it, it's clean. One ticket on a tramp freighter, the *Sun Dancer*, leaving in six hours.>> *fusion*'s words scroll down the inside of her glARs. <<This is it, Jenna. Point of no return. 'Here be dragons,' and all that.>>

Trafficking with Resistance, that semi-nebulous group dedicated to ending Government's monolithic control, is a quick way to disappear forever, but Jennifer can't bring herself to care. There's a ship out there filled with people who can tell her more about her father, someone who knows where he's at. Even now she knows there's no way he would ever die, and she'd crack Terra itself to track them down.

<<Confirm the ticket, and let's start packing. It's time, *fusion*.>>

Jennifer gestures the feed closed, and stands up from the chair, bumping the marble table. The wine bottle teeters and falls, crimson fluid sloshing over the side. Ignoring the mess, she strides from the room, hapgloved fingers busy issuing commands to her AI assistant.

The doors close behind her and the room falls into a heavy silence, punctuated only by thunderous rumblings from the clouds above. Brief flashes of lightning illuminate a steady drip onto the plushly woven face of a man on horseback, staining him darker and darker with every strobing splash.

Childish pink glasses stare vacantly at the chaos raging outside, alone in the room once more.

About the Authors

Chris Kluwe was a punter in the National Football League. He played college football at UCLA. A musician, gamer, and radio host, he lives with his wife and children in California. He is the author of *Beautifully Unique Sparkleponies.*

Andrew Reiner is the executive editor of Game Informer Magazine. A musician, gamer, and video show host, he lives with his wife and daughter in Minnesota. *Prime* is his first book. He hates punters.

40325213R00167

Made in the USA
San Bernardino, CA
16 October 2016